Letters of Catherine Benincasa

St. Catherine of Siena

Contents

LETTERS OF CATHERINE BENINCASA

by

St. Catherine of Siena

SAINT CATHERINE OF SIENA AS SEEN IN HER LETTERS

TABLE OF PERSONS ADDRESSED

LETTERS OF CATHERINE BENINCASA

ST. CATHERINE OF SIENA AS SEEN IN HER LETTERS

I

The letters of Catherine Benincasa, commonly known as St. Catherine of Siena, have become an Italian classic; yet perhaps the first thing in them to strike a reader is their unliterary character. He only will value them who cares to overhear the impetuous outpourings of the heart and mind of an unlettered daughter of the people, who was also, as it happened, a genius and a saint. Dante, Petrarch, Boccaccio, the other great writers of the Trecento, are all in one way or another intent on choice expression; Catherine is intent solely on driving home what she has to say. Her letters were talked rather than written. She learned to write only three years before her death, and even after this time was in the habit of dictating her correspondence, sometimes two or three letters at a time, to the noble youths who served her as secretaries.

The modern listener to this eager talk may perhaps at first feel wearied. Suffocated by words, repelled by frequent crudity and confusion of metaphor, he may even be inclined to call the thought childish and the tone overwrought. But let him persevere. Let him read these letters as chapters in an autobiography, noting purpose and circumstance, and reading between the lines, as he may easily do, the experience of the writer. Before long the very accents of a living woman will reach his ears. He will hear her voice, now eagerly pleading with friend or wrong-doer, now brooding tender as a mother-bird over some fledgling soul, now broken with sobs as she mourns over the sins of Church and world, and again chanting high prophecy of restoration and renewal, or telling in awestruck undertone sacred mysteries of the interior life. Dante's Angel of Purity welcomes wayfarers upon the Pilgrim Mount "in voce assai piu che la nostra, viva." The saintly voice, like the angelic, is more living than our own. These letters are charged with a vitality so intense that across the centuries it draws us into the author's presence.

Imagination is inclined to see the canonized saints as a row of solemn figures, standing in dull monotony of worshipful gesture, like Virgins and Confessors in an early mosaic. Yet, as a matter of fact, people who have been canonized were to their contemporaries the most striking personalities among men and women striving for righteousness. They were all, to be sure, very good; but goodness, despite a curious prejudice to the contrary, admits more variety in type than wickedness, and produces more interesting characters. Catherine Benincasa was probably the most remarkable woman of the fourteenth century, and her letters are the precious personal record of her inner as of her outer life. With all their transparent simplicity and mediaeval quaintness, with all the occasional plebeian crudity of their phrasing, they reveal a nature at once so many- sided and so exalted that the sensitive reader can but echo the judgment of her countrymen, who see in the dyer's daughter of Siena one of the most significant authors of a great age.

II

As is the case with many great letter-writers, though not with all, Catherine reveals herself largely through her relations with others. Some of her letters, indeed, are elaborate religious or political treatises, and seem at first sight to have little personal colouring; yet even these yield their full content of spiritual beauty and wisdom only when one knows the circumstances that called them forth and the persons to whom they were addressed. A mere glance at the index to her correspondence shows how widely she was in touch with her time. She was a woman of personal charm and of sympathies passionately wide, and she gathered around her friends and disciples from every social group in Italy, not to speak of many connections formed with people in other lands. She wrote to prisoners and outcasts; to great nobles and plain business men; to physicians, lawyers, soldiers of fortune; to kings and queens and cardinals and popes; to recluses pursuing the Beatific Vision, and to men and women of the world plunged in the lusts of the flesh and governed by the pride of life. The society of the fourteenth century passes in review as we turn the pages.

Catherine wrote to all these people in the same simple spirit. With one and all she was at home, for all were to her, by no merely formal phrase, "dearest brothers and sisters in Christ Jesus." One knows not whether to be more struck by the outspoken fearlessness of the woman or by her great adaptability. She could handle with plain directness the crudest sins of her age; she could also treat with subtle insight the most elusive phases of spiritual experience. No greater distance can be imagined than that which separates the young Dominican with her eyes full of visions from a man like Sir John Hawkwood, reckless free-lance, selling his sword with light-hearted zeal to the highest bidder, and battening on the disorder of the times. Catherine writes to him with gentlest assumption of fellowship, seizes on his natural passions and tastes, and seeks to sanctify the military life of his affections. With her sister nuns the method changes. She gives free play to her delicate fancy, drawing her metaphors from the beauty of nature, from tender, homely things, from the gentle arts and instincts of womanhood. Does she speak to Pope Gregory, the timid? Her words are a trumpet-call. To the harsh Urban, his successor? With finest tact she urges self-restraint and a policy of moderation. Temperaments of every type are to be met in her pages--a sensitive poet, troubled by "confusion of thought" deepening into melancholia; a harum-scarum boy, in whose sunny joyousness she discerns the germ of supernatural grace; vehement sinners, fearful saints, religious recluses deceived by self- righteousness, and men of affairs devoutly faithful to sober duty. Catherine enters into every consciousness. As a rule we associate with very pure and spiritual women, even if not cloistered, a certain deficient sense of reality. We cherish them, and shield them from harsh contact with the world, lest the fine flower of their delicacy be withered. But no one seems to have felt in this way about Catherine. Her "love for souls" was no cold electric illumination such as we sometimes feel the phrase to imply, but a warm understanding tenderness for actual men and women. It would be hard to exaggerate her knowledge of the world and of human hearts.

Yet sometimes Catherine appears to us austere and exacting; unsparing in condemnation, and unrelenting in her demands on those she loves. Many of her letters are in a strain of exhortation that rises into rebuke. The impression at first is unpleasant. We are tempted to feel this unfailing candour captious; to resent the note of authority, equally clear whether she write to Pope or Cardinal; to suspect Catherine, in a word, of assuming that very judicial attitude which she constantly deprecates as unbecoming to us poor mortals. And perhaps the very frequency of her plea for tolerance and forbearance suggests a conscious weakness. Like most brilliant and ardent people, she was probably by nature of a critical and impatient disposition; she was, moreover, a plebeian. At times, when she is quite sure that men are on the side of the devil, she allows her instinctive frankness full scope; it must be allowed that the result is astounding. Yet even as we catch our breath we realise that her remarks were probably justified. It is hard for us moderns to remember how crudely hideous were the sins which she faced. In these days, when we are all reduced to one apparent level of moral respectability, and great saintliness and dramatic guilt are alike seldom conspicuous, we forget the violent contrasts of the middle ages. Pure "Religious," striving after the exalted perfection enjoined by the Counsels, moved habitually among moral atrocities, and bold vigour of speech was a practical duty. Catherine handled without evasion the grossest evils of her time, and the spell which she exercised by simple force of direct dealing was nothing less than extraordinary.

It is easy to see why Catherine's plain speaking was not resented. She rarely begins with rebuke. The note of humility is first struck; she is always "servant and slave of the servants of Jesus Christ." Thence she frequently passes into fervent meditation on some special theme: the exceeding wonder of the Divine Love, the duty of prayer, the nature of obedience. We are lifted above the world into a region of heavenly light and sweetness, when suddenly--a blow from the shoulder!--a startling sense of return to earth. From the contemplation of the beauty of holiness, Catherine has swiftly turned us to face the opposing sin. "Thou art the man!" A few trenchant sentences, charged with pain, and the soul which has been raised to celestial places awakes to see in itself the contradiction of all that is so lovely. Into the region of darkness Catherine goes with it. It is not "thou" but "we" who have sinned. She holds that sinful heart so near her own that the beatings are confounded; her words now and again express a shuddering personal remorse for sins of which she could have had no personal knowledge. Her sense of unity with her fellow-men lies deeper than any theory of brotherhood; she feels herself in sober truth guilty of the sins of her brothers: her experience illustrates the profound truth that only purity can know perfect penitence.

Catherine is then saved from any touch of Pharisaism by her remarkable identification of herself with the person to whom she writes. But to understand her attitude we must go further. For she never pauses in reprobation of evil. Full of conviction that the soul needs only to recognise its sin to hate and escape it for ever, she passes swiftly on to impassioned appeal. Her words breathe a confidence in men that never fails even when she is writing to the most hardened. She succeeded to a rare degree in the difficult conciliation of uncompromising hatred toward sin with unstrained fellowship with the sinner, and invincible trust in his responsiveness to the appeal of virtue. When we consider the times in which she lived, this large and touching trustfulness becomes to our eyes a victory of faith. That it was no mere instinct, but an attitude resolutely adopted and maintained, is evident from her frequent discussions of charity and tolerance, some of which will be found in these selections. She constantly urges her disciples to put the highest possible construction on their neighbours' actions; nor is any phase of her teaching more constantly repeated than the beautiful application of the text: "In My Father's House are many mansions," to enjoin recognition of the varieties in temperament and character and practice which may coexist in the House of God.

Catherine had learned a hard lesson. She saw in human beings not their achievements, but their possibilities. Therefore she quickened repentance by a positive method, not by morbid analysis of evil, not by lurid pictures of the consequences of sin, but by filling the soul with glowing visions of that holiness which to see is to long for. She never despaired of quickening in even the most degraded that flame of "holy desire" which is the earnest of true holiness to be. We find her impatient of mint and cummin, of over-anxious self-scrutiny. "Strive that your holy desires increase," she writes to a correspondent; "and let all these other things alone." "I, Catherine--write to you--with desire": so open all her letters. Holy Desire! It is not only the watchword of her teaching: it is also the true key to her personality.

III

We have dwelt on Catherine, the friend and guide of souls; but it is Catherine the mystic, Catherine the friend of God, before whom the ages bend in reverence. The final value of her letters lies in their revelation, not of her dealings with other souls, but of God's dealings with her own.

But in presence of the record of these deep experiences, silence is better than words: is, indeed, for most of us the only possible attitude. The letters that follow must speak for themselves. The clarity of mind which Catherine always preserved, even in moments of highest exaltation, and her loving eagerness to share her most sacred experiences with those dear to her, have given her a power of expression that has produced pages of unsurpassed interest and value, alike for the psychologist and for the believer. Moreover--and this we well may note--her letters enable us to apprehend with singularly happy intimacy, the natural character and disposition of her whom these high things befell. In the very cadence of their impetuous phrasing, in their swift dramatic changes, in their marvellous blending of sweetness and virility, they show us the woman. Some of them, especially those to her family and friends, are of almost childlike simplicity and homely charm; others, among the most famous of their kind, deal with mystical, or if we choose so to put it, with supernatural experience: in all alike, we feel a heart akin to our own, though larger and more tender.

The central fact in Catherine's nature was her rapt and absolute perception of the Love of God, as the supreme reality in the universe. This Love, as manifested in creation, in redemption, and in the sacrament of the Altar, is the theme of her constant meditations. One little phrase, charged with a lyric poignancy, sings itself again and again, enlightening her more sober prose: "For nails would not have held God-and-Man fast to the Cross, had love not held Him there." Her conceptions are positive, not negative, and joyous adoration is the substance of her faith.

But the letters show us that this faith was not won nor kept without sharp struggle. We have in them no presentation of a calm spirit, established on tranquil heights of unchanging vision, above our "mortal moral strife." Catherine is, as we can see, a woman of many moods--very sensitive, very loving. She shows a touching dependence on those she loves, and an inveterate habit of idealising them, which leads to frequent disillusion. She is extremely eager and intense about little things as well as great; hers is a truly feminine seriousness over the detail of living. She is keenly and humanly interested in life on this earth, differing in this respect from some canonized persons who seem always to be enduring it *faute de mieux*. And, as happens to all sensitive people who refuse to seclude themselves in dreams, life went hard with her. Hers was a frail and suffering body, and a tossed and troubled spirit; wounded in the house of her friends, beset by problem, shaken with doubt and fear by the spectacle presented to her by the world and the Church of Christ. The letters tell us how these, her sorrows and temptations, were not separated from the life of faith, but a true portion of it: how she carried them into the Divine Presence, and what high reassurance awaited her there. Ordinary mortals are inclined to think that supernatural experience removes the saints to a perplexing distance. In Catherine's case, however, we become aware as we study the record that it brings her nearer us. For these experiences, far from being independent of her outer life, are in closest relation with it; even the highest and most mysterious, even those in which the symbolism seems most remote from the modern mind, can be translated by the psychologist without difficulty into modern terms. They spring from the problems of her active life; they bring her renewed strength and wisdom for her practical duties. An age, which like our own places peculiar emphasis and value on the type of sanctity which promptly expresses itself through the deed, should feel for Catherine Benincasa an especial honour. She is one of the purest of Contemplatives; she knows, what we to-day too often forget, that the task is impossible without the vision. But it follows directly upon the vision, and this great mediaeval mystic is one of the most efficient characters of her age.

IV

Catherine's soaring imagination lifted her above the circle of purely personal interests, and made her a force of which history is cognisant in the public affairs of her day. She is one of a very small number of women who have exerted the influence of a statesman by virtue, not of feminine attractions, but of conviction and intellectual power. It is impossible to understand her letters without some recognition of the public drama of the time.

Two great ideals of unity--one Roman, one Christian in origin--had possessed the middle ages. In the strength of them the wandering barbaric hordes had been reduced to order, and Western Europe had been trained into some perception of human fellowship. Of these two unifying forces, the imperialistic ideal was moribund in Catherine's time: not even a Dante, born fifty years after his true date, could have held to it. Remained the ideal of the Church universal, and to this last hope of a peaceful commonwealth that should include all humanity, the idealists clung in desperation.

But alas for the faith of idealists when fact gives theory the lie! What at this time was the unity of mankind in the Church but a formal hypothesis? The keystone of her all-embracing arch was the Papacy. But the Pope no longer sat heir of the Caesars in the seat of the Apostles; for seventy years he had been a practical dependant of the French king, living in pleasant Provence. Neither the scorn of Dante, nor the eloquence of Petrarch, nor the warnings of holy men, had prevailed on the popes to return to Italy, and make an end of the crying scandal which was the evident contradiction of the Christian dream. Meantime, the city of the Caesars lay waste and wild; the clergy was corrupt almost past belief; the dreaded Turk was gathering his forces, a menace to Christendom itself. The times were indeed evil, and the "servants of God," of whom then, as now, there were no inconsiderable number, withdrew for the most part into spiritual or literal seclusion, and in the quietude of cloister or forest cell busied themselves with the concerns of their own souls.

Not so Catherine Benincasa. She had known that temptation and conquered it. After her reception as a Dominican Tertiary, she had possessed the extraordinary resolution to live for three years the recluse life, not in the guarded peace of a convent, but in her own room at home, in the noisy and overcrowded house where a goodly number of her twenty-four brothers and sisters were apparently still living. And these had been years of inestimable preciousness; but they came to an end at the command of God, speaking through the constraining impulse of her love for men. From the mystical retirement in which she had long lived alone with her Beloved, she emerged into the world. And the remarkable fact is that in no respect did she blench from the situation as she found it. She "faced life steadily and faced it whole." A Europe ravaged by dissensions lay before her; a Church which gave the lie to its lofty theories, no less by the hateful worldliness of its prelates than by its indifferent abandonment of the Seat of Peter. Above this sorry spectacle the mind of Catherine soared straight into an upper region, where only the greatest minds of the day were her comrades. Her fellow-citizens were unable to entertain the idea even of civic peace within the limits of their own town; but patriotic devotion to all Italy fired her great heart. More than this--her instinct for solidarity forced her to dwell in the thought of a world-embracing brotherhood. Her hopes were centred, not like Dante's in the Emperor the heir of the Caesars, but in the Pope the heir of Christ. Despite the corruption from which she recoiled with horror, despite the Babylonian captivity at Avignon, she saw in the Catholic Church that image of a pure universal fellowship which the noblest Catholics of all ages have cherished. To the service of the Church, therefore, her life was dedicated; it was to her the Holy House of Reconciliation, wherein all nations should dwell in unity; and only by submission to its authority could the woes of Italy be healed.

Catherine's letters on public affairs--historical documents of recognised importance--give us her practical programme. It was formed in the light of that faith which she always describes as "the eye of the mind." She was called during her brief years of political activity to meet three chief issues: the absence of the Pope from Italy; the rebellion of the Tuscan cities, headed by Florence, against his authority; and at a later time the great Schism, which broke forth under Urban VI. During her last five years she was absorbed in ecclesiastical affairs. In certain of her immediate aims she succeeded, in others she failed. It would be hard to say whether her success or her failure involved the greater tragedy. For behind all these aims was a larger ideal that was not to be realised--the dream, entertained as passionately by Catherine Benincasa as by Savonarola or by Luther, of thorough Church-reform. Catherine at Avignon, pleading this great cause in the frivolous culture and dainty pomp of the place; Catherine at Rome, defending to her last breath the legal rights of a Pope whom she could hardly have honoured, and whose claims she saw defended by extremely doubtful means--is a figure as pathetic as heroic. Few sorrows are keener than to work with all one's energies to attain a visible end for the sake of a spiritual result, and, attaining that end, to find the result as far as ever. This sorrow was Catherine's. The external successes which she won--considerable enough to secure her a place in history-- availed nothing to forward the greater aim for which she worked. Gregory XI., under her magnetic inspiration, gathered strength, indeed, to make a personal sacrifice and to return to Rome, but he was of no calibre to attempt radical reform, and his residence in Italy did nothing to right the crying abuses that were breaking Christian hearts. His successor, on the other hand, did really initiate the reform of the clergy, but so drastic and unwise were his methods that the result was terrible and disconcerting--the development of a situation of which only the Catholic idealist could discern the full irony; no less than Schism, the rending of the Seamless Robe of Christ.

With failing hopes and increasing experience of the complexity of human struggle, Catherine clung to her aim until the end. There was no touch of pusillanimity in her heroic spirit. As with deep respect we follow the Letters of the last two years, and note their unflagging alertness and vigour, their steady tone of devotion and self-control, we realise that to tragedy her spirit was dedicate. Her energy of mind was constantly on the increase. Still, it is true, she wrote to disciples near and far long, tender letters of spiritual counsel--analyses of the religious life tranquilly penetrating as those of an earlier time. But her political correspondence grew in bulk. It is tense, nervous, virile. It breathes a vibrating passion, a solemn force, that are the index of a breaking heart. Not for one moment did Catherine relax her energies. From 1376, when she went to Avignon, she led, with one or two brief intermissions only, the life of a busy woman of affairs. But within this outer life of strenuous and, as a rule, thwarted activities, another life went on--a life in which failure could not be, since through failure is wrought redemption.

From the days of her stigmatization, which occurred in 1375 at Pisa, Catherine had been convinced that in some special sense she was to share in the Passion of Christ, and offer herself a sacrifice for the sins of Holy Church. Now this conception deepened till it became all-absorbing. In full consciousness of failing vital powers, in expectation of her approaching death, she offered her sufferings of mind and body as an expiation for the sins around her. By word of mouth and by letters of heartbroken intensity she summoned all dear to her to join in this holy offering. Catherine's faith is alien to these latter days. Yet the psychical unity of the race is becoming matter not only of emotional intuition, but established scientific fact: and no modern sociologist, no psychologist who realizes how unknown in origin and how intimate in interpenetration are the forces that control our destiny, can afford to scoff at her. She had longed inexpressibly for outward martyrdom. This was not for her, yet none the less really did she lay down her life on the Altar of Sacrifice. The evils of the time, and above all of the Church, had generated a sense of unbearable sin in her pure spirit; her constant instinct to identify herself with the guilt of others found in this final offering an august climax and fulfilment.

During the last months of her life--months of excruciating physical sufferings, vividly described for us by her contemporaries--the woman's rectitude and wisdom, her swift tender sympathies, were still, as ever, at the disposal of all who sought them. With unswerving energy she still laboured for the cause of truth. When we consider the conditions, spiritual and physical, of those last months, we read with amazement the able, clearly conceived, practical letters which she was despatching to the many European potentates whom she was endeavouring to hold true to the cause of Urban. But her spirit in the meantime dwelt in the region of the Eternal, where the dolorous struggle of the times appeared, indeed, but appeared in its essential significance as seen by angelic intelligences. The awe-struck letters to Fra Raimondo, her Confessor, with which this selection closes, are an accurate transcript of her inner experience. They constitute, surely, a precious heritage of the Church for which her life was given. Catherine Benincasa died heartbroken; yet in the depths of her consciousness was joy, for God had revealed to her that His Bride the Church, "which brings life to men," "holds in herself such life that no man can kill her." "Sweetest My daughter, thou seest how she has soiled her face with impurity and self-love, and grown puffed up by the pride and avarice of those who feed at her bosom. But take thy tears and sweats, drawing them from the fountain of My divine charity, and cleanse her face. For I promise thee that her beauty shall not be restored to her by the sword, nor by cruelty nor war, but by peace, and by humble continual prayer, tears, and sweats poured forth from the grieving desires of My servants. So thy desire shall be fulfilled in long abiding, and My Providence shall in no wise fail."

V

Psychologically, as in point of time, St. Catherine stands between St. Francis and St. Teresa. Her writings are of the middle ages, not of the renascence, but they express the twilight of the mediaeval day. They reveal the struggles and the spiritual achievement of a woman who lived in the last age of an undivided Christendom, and whose whole life was absorbed in the special problems of her time. These problems, however, are in the deepest sense perpetual, and her attitude toward them is suggestive still.

It has been claimed that Catherine, a century and a half later, would have been a Protestant. Such hypotheses are always futile to discuss; but the view hardly commends itself to the careful student of her writings. It is suggested, naturally enough, by her denunciations of the corruptions of the Church, denunciations as sweeping and penetrating as were ever uttered by Luther; by her amazingly sharp and outspoken criticism of the popes; and by her constant plea for reform. The pungency of all these elements in her writings is felt by the most casual reader. But it must never be forgotten that honest and vigorous criticism of the Church Visible is, in the mind of the Catholic philosopher, entirely consistent with loyalty to the sacerdotal theory. There is a noble idealism that breaks in fine impatience with tradition, and audaciously seeks new symbols wherein to suggest for a season the eternal and imageless truth. But perhaps yet nobler in the sight of God--surely more conformed to His methods in nature and history--is that other idealism which patiently bows to the yoke of the actual, and endures the agony of keeping true at once to the heavenly vision and to the imperfect earthly form. Iconoclastic zeal against outworn or corrupt institutions fires our facile enthusiasm. Let us recognize also the spiritual passion that suffers unflinchingly the disparity between the sign and the thing signified, and devotes its energies, not to discarding, but to restoring and purifying that sign. Such passion was Catherine's. The most distinctive trait in the woman's character was her power to cling to an ideal verity with unfaltering faithfulness, even when the whole aspect of life and society around her seemed to give that verity the lie. To imagine her without faith in the visible Church and the God-given authority of the Vicar of Christ is to imagine another woman. Catherine of Siena's place in the history of minds is with Savonarola, not with Luther.

Catherine confronted a humanity at enmity with itself, a Church conformed to the image of this world. Her external policy proved helpless to right these evils. The return of the Popes from Avignon resulted neither in the pacification of Christendom nor in the reform of the Church. The Great Schism, of which she saw the beginning, undermined the idea of Christian unity till the thought of the Saint of Siena was in natural sequence followed by the thought of Luther. Outwardly her life was spent in labouring for a hopeless cause, discredited by the subsequent movement of history. But the material tragedy was a spiritual triumph, not only through the victory of faith in her own soul, but through the value of the witness which she bore. Neither of the great conceptions of unity which possessed the middle ages was identical with the modern democratic conception; yet both, and in particular that of the Church, pointed in this direction. That ideal of world-embracing brotherhood to which men have been slowly awakening throughout the Christian centuries was the dominant ideal of Catherine's mind. She hoped for the attainment of such a brotherhood through the instrument of an organized Christendom, reduced to peace and unity under one God-appointed Head. History, as some of us think, has rejected the noble dream. We seem to see that the undying hope of the human spirit--a society shaped by justice and love--is never likely to be gained along the lines of the centralization of ecclesiastical power. But if our idea of the means has changed, the same end still shines before us. The vision of human fellowship in the Name of Christ, for which Catherine lived and died, remains the one hope for the healing of the nations.

CHIEF EVENTS IN THE LIFE OF SAINT CATHERINE

1347. On March 25th, Catherine, and a twin-sister who dies at once, are born in the Strada dell' Oca, near the fountain of Fontebranda, Siena. She is the youngest of the twenty-five children of Jacopo Benincasa, a dyer, and Lapa, his wife.

1353-4. As a child, Catherine is peculiarly joyous and charming. When six years old she beholds the vision of Christ, arrayed in priestly robes, above the Church of St. Dominic. She is inspired by a longing to imitate the life of the Fathers of the desert, and begins to practise many penances. At the age of seven she makes the vow of virginity. She is drawn to the Order of St. Dominic by the zeal of its founder for the salvation of souls.

1359-1363. Her ascetic practices meet with sharp opposition at home. She is urged to array herself beautifully and to marry, is denied a private chamber, and forced to perform the menial work of the household, etc. In time, however, her perseverance wins the consent of her father and family to her desires.

1363-1364. She is vested with the black and white habit of Saint Dominic, becoming one of the Mantellate, or Dominican tertiaries, devout women who lived under religious rule in their own homes.

1364-1367. She leads in her own room at home the life of a religious recluse, speaking only to her Confessor. She is absorbed in mystical experiences and religious meditation. During this time she learns to read. The period closes with her espousals to Christ, on the last day of Carnival, 1367.

1367-1370. In obedience to the commands of God, and impelled by her love of men, she returns gradually to family and social life. From this time dates her special devotion to the Blessed Sacrament. She joyfully devotes herself to household labours, and to a life of ministration to the sick and needy. In 1368 her father dies, and the Revolution puts an end to the prosperity of the Benincasa family, which is now broken up. Catherine seems to have retained to the end the care of Monna Lapa. In 1370 she dies mystically and returns to life, having received the command to go abroad into the world to save souls.

1370-1374. Her reputation and influence increase. A group of disciples gathers around her. Her correspondence gradually becomes extensive, and she becomes known as a peacemaker. At the same time, her ecstasies and unusual mode of life excite criticism and suspicion. In May, 1374, she visits Florence, perhaps summoned thither to answer charges made against her by certain in the Order. She returns to Siena to minister to the plague-stricken. She meets at this time Fra Raimondo of Capua, her Confessor and biographer. Her gradual induction into public affairs is accompanied by growing sorrow over the corruptions of the Church.

1375. At the invitation of Pietro Gambacorta, Catherine visits Pisa. Her object is to prevent Pisa and Lucca from joining the League of Tuscan cities against the Pope. She meets the Ambassador from the Queen of Cyprus, and zealously under-takes to further the cause of a Crusade. On April 1st she receives the Stigmata in the Church of Santa Cristina; but the marks, at her request, remain invisible. She prophesies the Great Schism. A brief visit to Lucca.

1376. Catherine receives Stefano Maconi as a disciple, and at his instance reconciles the feud between the Maconi and the Tolomei. She attempts by correspondence to reconcile Pope Gregory XI. and the Florentines. On April 1st the Divine Commission to bear the olive to both disputants is given her in a vision. In May, at the request of the Florentines, she goes to Florence. Sent as their representative to Avignon, she reaches that city on June 18th. Gregory entrusts her with the negotiations for peace. The Florentine ambassadors, however, delay their coming, and when they come refuse to ratify her powers. Thwarted in this direction, she devotes all her efforts to persuading the Pope to return to Rome, and triumphing over all obstacles, succeeds. She leaves for home on September 13th, but is retained for a month in Genoa, at the house of Madonna Orietta Scotta. After a short visit at Pisa, she reaches Siena in December or January.

1377. Catherine converts the castle of Belcaro, conveyed to her by its owner, into a monastery. She visits the Salimbeni in their feudal castle at Rocca D'Orcia, for the purpose of healing their family feuds. While here she learns miraculously to write. She also visits Sant' Antimo and Montepulciano.

1378. Gregory, in failing health, perhaps regretting his return, becomes alienated from Catherine. He sends her, however, to Florence, where she stays in a house built for her by Niccolo Soderini, at the foot of the hill of St. George. She succeeds in causing the Interdict to be respected, but almost loses her life in a popular tumult, and keenly regrets not having won the crown of martyrdom. After the death of Gregory, and the establishment of the longed-for peace by Pope Urban, Catherine returns to Siena, where she devotes herself to composing her "Dialogue." After the outbreak of the Schism, Urban, whom she had known at Avignon, summons her to Rome. She reluctantly obeys, and takes up her abode in that city on November 28th, accompanied by a large group of disciples, her "Famiglia," who live together, subsisting on alms. From this time Catherine devotes her whole powers to the cause of Urban. She is his trusted adviser, and seeks earnestly to curb his impatient temper on the one hand, and to keep the sovereigns of Europe faithful to him on the other. She writes on his behalf to the Kings of France and Hungary, to Queen Giovanna of Naples, to the magistrates of Italian cities, to the Italian cardinals who have joined the Schism, and to others. Fra Raimondo, despatched to France, to her grief and exaltation, evades his mission through timidity, to her bitter disappointment, but does not return to Rome till after her death. Catherine's health, always fragile, gives way under her unremitting labours and her great sorrows.

1380. Catherine succeeds in quieting the revolt of the Romans against Urban. She dedicates herself as a sacrificial victim, in expiation of the sins of the Church and of the Roman people. In vision at St. Peter's, on Sexagesima Sunday, the burden of the Ship of the Church descends upon her shoulders. Her physical sufferings increase, and on April 30th she dies, in the presence of her disciples.

BRIEF TABLE OF CONTEMPORARY PUBLIC EVENTS

1368-1369. Political Revolution in Siena. The compromise government of the Riformatori is established. The Emperor Charles V. is summoned to the city by the party worsted in the Revolution, joined by certain nobles. He arrives in January, '69, but is forced to withdraw by a popular rising. The nobles are excluded from the chief power and ravaged by feuds among themselves.

1372. Gregory XI. declares war against Bernabo Visconti of Milan, and takes into his pay the English free-lance, Sir John Hawkwood. Peter d'Estaing, appointed Legate of Bologna, makes truce with Bernabo. The latter, however, continues secretly to incite Tuscany to rebel against the Pope, inflaming the indignation of the Tuscans at the arbitrary policy of the Papal Legates, and in particular of the Nuncio, Gerard du Puy, who is supporting the claims of those turbulent nobles, the Salimbeni in Siena. Catherine is in correspondence with both d'Estaing and Du Puy. On April 22nd, Gregory, in full consistory, announces his intention of returning to Rome.

1373. Italy is devastated by petty strife: "It seems as if a planet reigned at this time which produced in the world the following effects: That the Brothers of St. Austin killed their Provincial at Sant' Antonio with a knife; and in Siena was much fighting. At Assisi the Brothers Minor fought, and killed fourteen with a knife. And those of the Rose fought, and drove six away. Also, those of Certosa had great dissensions, and their General came and changed them all about. So all Religious everywhere seemed to have strife and dissension among themselves. And every Religious of whatever rule was oppressed and insulted by the world. So with brothers according to the flesh--cousins, wives, relatives, and neighbours. It seems that there were divisions all over the whole world. In Siena, loyalty was neither proposed nor observed, gentlemen did not show it among themselves nor outside, nor did the Nine among themselves or with outside persons, nor did the Twelve. The people did not agree with their own leader, nor exactly with any one else. Thus all the world was a place of shadows."-- *Chronicle of Neri di Donato*.

A Crusade publicly proclaimed by the Pope.

1374. Plague and famine lay Tuscany waste. William of Noellet, the Papal Legate, refuses to allow corn to be imported into Tuscany from the Papal States. Hawkwood, probably at his instigation, ravages the country, and even threatens the city of Florence. Florence, enraged, rebels against the Pope, and appoints from the ranks of the Ghibellines a new body of Magistrates, known as the Eight of War. Meantime, Cione de' Salimbeni is raiding the country around Siena. The roads through the Maremma are insecure for peaceable folk, and the peasants are driven to take refuge in the plague-stricken town.

1375. Eighty Italian cities join a League, headed by Florence, against the Pope, with the watchword, "Fling off the foreign yoke."

1376. Gregory despatches ambassadors to the Eight of War, who scorn his proposals. Florence incites Bologna to revolt, and the Legate flees. The Papal Nuncio is flayed alive in the streets of Florence. The city is placed under an Interdict. Envoys are despatched to Avignon, who set forth eloquently, but to no avail, the grievances of the city. War is declared against Florence by the Pope, and Count Robert of Geneva, with an army of free-lances, is sent into Italy. Count Robert, laying waste the territory of Bologna, summons Hawkwood to his aid, and perpetrates the hideous massacre of Cesena. Catherine, sent to Avignon, fails to procure peace. Gregory, swayed by her representations, returns to Italy, and reaches Rome, after a difficult journey, on January 17th, 1377.

1378. Gregory, exhausted and disappointed by the continued discords in Italy, dies in March. The Archbishop of Bari, known as Urban VI., is appointed his successor. In July, peace is made with Florence, and the Interdict upon the city is raised. The harsh measures of Urban in dealing with the clergy arouse violent antagonism. In June, the Cardinals begin to circulate rumours challenging the validity of the election, and on September 20th they formally announce that the election was invalid, having been forced on them by fear, and appoint as Pope the Cardinal Robert of Geneva, who takes the name of Clement VII.

1379-1380. The Great Schism divides Europe. England remains faithful to Urban: France and Naples, after wavering, declare for Clement. War rages between the two Popes. The schismatic forces gain possession of the Castle of Saint Angelo at Rome, but are driven out by the forces of Urban, who in gratitude marches barefoot in solemn procession from Santa Maria in Trastevere, to St. Peter's. The city, however, later revolts against Urban, but is reconciled to him, partly through the efforts of Catherine. Queen Giovanna of Naples, having conspired against Urban's life, is excommunicated.

LETTERS
TO MONNA ALESSA DEI SARACINI

The young widow of noble family to whom this letter was written was the most cherished among Catherine's women friends. She seems, as often happens with the chosen companion of a fervent and powerful nature, to have been a person simple, lovable, and quietly wise. Having after her husband's death assumed the habit of St. Dominic, she distributed her possessions to the poor by Catherine's advice, but she evidently retained her home in Siena. This became a constant refuge for the saint from the overcrowded Benincasa household, and the scene of more than one charming episode in her life as told by the legend. For the Mantellate, or tertiaries of St. Dominic, were not cloistered, nor did they take the monastic vows; they simply lived in their own homes a life of special devotion.

To Alessa, Catherine left on her deathbed the care of her spiritual family. This intimate little letter dates from an early period in their friendship. In its homely, practical wisdom, as in the gentle loftiness of its tone, it shows the watchful and loving care with which Catherine entered into the details of the daily life of those whom she sought to lead with her in the way of salvation. The tests she proposes are as penetrating to-day as they were then.

In the Name of Jesus Christ crucified and of sweet Mary:

Dearest daughter in Christ sweet Jesus: I Catherine, thy poor unworthy mother, want thee to attain that perfection for which God has chosen thee. It seems to me that one wishing so to attain should walk with and not without moderation. And yet every work of ours ought to be done both without and with moderation: it befits us to love God without moderation, putting to that love neither limit nor measure nor rule, but loving Him immeasurably. And if thou wish to reach the perfection of love, it befits thee to set thy life in order. Let thy first rule be to flee the conversation of every human being, in so far as it is simply conversation, except as deeds of charity may demand; but to love people very much, and talk with few of them. And know how to talk in moderation even with those whom thou lovest with spiritual love; reflect that if thou didst not do this, thou wouldst place a limit before perceiving it to that limitless love which thou oughtest to bear to God, by placing the finite creature between you: for the love which thou shouldst place in God thou wouldst place in the creature, loving it without moderation; and this would hinder thy perfection. Therefore thou shouldst love it spiritually, in a disciplined way.

Be a vase, which thou fillest at the source and at the source dost drink from. Although thou hadst drawn thy love from God, who is the Source of living water, didst thou not drink it continually in Him thy vase would remain empty. And this shall be the sign to thee that thou dost not drink wholly in God: when thou sufferest from that which thou lovest, either by some talk thou didst hold, or because thou wast deprived of some consolation thou wast used to receiving, or for some other accidental cause. If thou sufferest, then, from this or anything else except wrong against God, it is a clear sign to thee that this love is still imperfect, and drawn far from the Source. What way is there, then, to make the imperfect perfect? This way: to correct and chastise the movements of thy heart with true self-knowledge, and with hatred and distaste for thy imperfection, that thou art such a peasant as to give to the creature that love which ought to be given wholly to God, loving the creature without moderation, and God moderately. For love toward God should be without measure, and that for the creature should be measured by that for God, and not by the measure of one's own consolations, either spiritual or temporal. So do, then, that thou lovest everything in God, and correct every inordinate affection.

Make two homes for thyself, my daughter. One actual home in thy cell, that thou go not running about into many places, unless for necessity, or for obedience to the prioress, or for charity's sake; and another spiritual home, which thou art to carry with thee always--the cell of true self- knowledge, where thou shalt find within thyself knowledge of the goodness of God. These are two cells in one, and when abiding in the one it behoves thee to abide in the other, for otherwise the soul would fall into either confusion or presumption. For didst thou rest in knowledge of thyself, confusion of mind would fall on thee; and didst thou abide in the knowledge of God alone, thou wouldst fall into presumption. The two, then, must be built together and made one same thing; if thou dost this, thou wilt attain perfection. For from self-knowledge thou wilt gain hatred of thine own fleshliness, and through hate thou wilt become a judge, and sit upon the seat of thy conscience, and pass judgment; and thou wilt not let a fault go without giving sentence on it.

From such knowledge flows the stream of humility; which never seizes on mere report, nor takes offence at anything, but bears every insult, every loss of consolation, and every sorrow, from whatever direction they may come, patiently, with joy. Shames appear glory, and great persecutions refreshment; and it rejoices in all, seeing itself punished for that perverse law of self-will in its members which for ever rebels against God; and it sees itself conformed with Christ Jesus crucified, the way and the doctrine of truth.

In the knowledge of God thou shalt find the fire of divine charity. Where shalt thou rejoice? Upon the Cross, with the Spotless Lamb, seeking His honour and the salvation of souls, through continual, humble prayer. Now herein is all our perfection. There are many other things also, but this is the chief, from which we receive so much light that we cannot err in the lesser works that follow.

Rejoice, my daughter, to conform thee to the shame of Christ. And watch over the impulse of the tongue, that the tongue may not always respond to the impulse of the heart; but digest what is in thy heart, with hatred and distaste for thyself. Do thou be the least of the least, subject in humility and patience to every creature through God; not making excuses, but saying: the fault is mine. Thus are vices conquered in thy soul and in the soul of him to whom thou shouldest so speak: through the virtue of humility. Order thy time: the night to vigil, when thou hast paid the debt of sleep to thy body; and the morning in church with sweet prayer; do not spend it in chatting until the appointed hour. Let nothing except necessity, or obedience, or charity, as I said, draw thee away from this or anything else. After the hour of eating, recollect thyself a little, and then do something with thy hands, as thou mayest need. At the hour of vespers, do thou go and keep quiet; and as much as the Holy Spirit enjoins on thee, that do. Then go back and take care of thy old mother without negligence, and provide what she needs; be thine this burden. More when I return. So do that thou mayest fulfil my desire. I say no more. Remain in the holy and sweet grace of God. Sweet Jesus, Jesus Love.

TO BENINCASA HER BROTHER WHEN HE WAS IN FLORENCE

One questions whether Catherine's brother would have relished the admonitions of his saintly sister, had he known what we learn through her biographer: that, feeling the temporal prosperity of her family to be a snare to them, she had earnestly prayed that they might fall into poverty. The petition was promptly granted: worldly losses, and the departure of two of the brothers for Florence, followed upon the Sienese Revolution of 1368. Apparently, family misunderstandings accompanied these readjustments. In the first of the present letters Catherine takes her elder brother to task for neglect of his mother, Monna Lapa. We do not know the effect of her remarks, but we do know that in the large family of twenty-four, no one except Catherine herself--first recluse, and later busy woman of affairs as she was--seems to have carried the responsibility for the mother's welfare. The mother lived for the most part with her great daughter, except when public interests took Catherine away from home--occasions to which poor Monna Lapa was never reconciled.

In the second of these notes, Catherine comforts her brother very sweetly, probably for the loss of his wealth. But if we may judge from the nature of the reflections addressed to him, the spiritual instruction by which Benincasa was capable of profiting was extremely elementary in character.

In the Name of Jesus Christ crucified and of sweet Mary:

Dearest brother in Christ Jesus: I Catherine, a useless servant, comfort and bless thee and invite thee to a sweet and most holy patience, for without patience we could not please God. So I beg you, in order that you may receive the fruit of your tribulations, that you assume the armour of patience. And should it seem very hard to you to endure your many troubles, bear in memory three things, that you may endure more patiently. First, I want you to think of the shortness of your time, for on one day you are not certain of the morrow. We may truly say that we do not feel past trouble, nor that which is to come, but only the moment of time at which we are. Surely, then, we ought to endure patiently, since the time is so short. The second thing is, for you to consider the fruit which follows our troubles. For St. Paul says there is no comparison between our troubles and the fruit and reward of supernal glory. The third is, for you to consider the loss which results to those who endure in wrath and impatience; for loss follows this here, and eternal punishment to the soul.

Therefore I beg you, dearest brother, to endure in all patience. And I would not have it escape your mind that you should correct you of your ingratitude, and your ignoring of the duty you owe your mother, to which you are held by the commandment of God. I have seen your ingratitude multiply so that you have not even paid her the due of help that you owe: to be sure, I have an excuse for you in this, because you could not; but if you had been able, I do not know that you would have done it, since you have left her in scarcity even of words. Oh, ingratitude! Have you not considered the sorrow of her labour, nor the milk that she drew from her breast, nor the many troubles that she has had, over you and all the others? And should you say to me that she has had no compassion on us, I say that it is not so; for she has had so much on you and the other that it costs her dear. But suppose it were true--you are under obligation to her, not she to you. She did not take her flesh from you, but gave you hers. I beg you to correct this fault and others, and to pardon my ignorance. For did I not love your soul, I would not say to you what I do. Remember your confession, you and all your family. I say no more to you. Remain in the holy and sweet grace of God. Sweet Jesus, Jesus Love.

In the Name of Jesus Christ crucified and of sweet Mary:

Dearest and most beloved brother in Christ Jesus: I Catherine, servant and slave of the servants of Jesus Christ, comfort you in the Precious Blood of the Son of God: with desire to see you wholly in accord with the Will of God, and transformed thereby; knowing that this is a sweet and holy yoke which makes all bitterness turn into sweetness. Every great burden becomes light beneath this most holy yoke of the sweet will of God, without which thou couldst not please God, but wouldst know a foretaste of Hell. Comfort you, comfort you, dearest brother, and do not faint beneath this chastisement of God; but trust that when human help fails, divine help is near. God will provide for you. Reflect that Job lost his possessions and his sons and his health: his wife remained to him for a perpetual scourge; and then, when God had tested his patience, He restored everything to him double, and at the end eternal life. Patient Job never was perturbed, but would say, always exercising the virtue of holy patience, "God gave them to me, God has taken them from me; the Name of God be blessed." So I want you to do, dearest brother: be a lover of virtue, with holy patience, often using confession, which will as often help you to endure your afflictions. And I tell you, God will show His benignity and mercy, and will reward you for every affliction which you shall have borne for His love. Remain in the holy and sweet grace of God. Sweet Jesus, Jesus Love.

TO THE VENERABLE RELIGIOUS, BROTHER ANTONIO OF NIZZA, OF THE ORDER OF THE HERMIT BROTHERS OF SAINT AUGUSTINE AT THE WOOD OF THE LAKE

It is in her letters to persons leading the dedicated life that one can most clearly study Catherine's own inner experience. When warning and consoling them, she is speaking to herself. This obscure girl had a way of writing to the great of this earth--and indeed to the very Fathers of Christendom--with the straight-forward simplicity of a teacher instructing childish minds in the evident rudiments of virtue. Often the sanctified common sense of her letters to dignitaries is the most noticeable thing about them. But when she turns to a holy hermit, the tone changes. The commonplaces of the moral life are assumed or left behind; she speaks to a soul that has presumably already brought its will into accord with the divine will in regard to all outward happenings, and she takes calmly for granted that this is a light and little thing. We proceed to the analysis of temptations more subtle and more alluring. Catherine has few superiors among religious thinkers in the power to trace self-will to its remotest lairs, in the deeper reaches of personality. In letters to such correspondents as Frate Antonio she often gives us, as here, precious records of her intercourse with her Lord.

In the Name of Jesus Christ crucified and of sweet Mary:

To you, most beloved and dearest father and brother in Christ Jesus: I Catherine, servant and slave of the servants of Jesus Christ, write and commend me in the Precious Blood of the Son of God, with desire to see you kindled and inflamed in the furnace of divine charity and your own self- will--the will that robs us of all life--consumed therein. Let us open our eyes, dearest brother, for we have two wills--one of the senses, which seeks the things of sense, and the other the self-will of the spirit, which, under aspect and colour of virtue, holds firm to its own way. And this is clear when it wants to choose places and seasons and consolations to suit itself, and says: "Thus I wish in order to possess God more fully." This is a great cheat, and an illusion of the devil; for not being able to deceive the servants of God through their first will--since the servants of God have already mortified it so far as the things of sense go--the devil catches their second will on the sly with things of the spirit. So many a time the soul receives consolation, and then later feels itself deprived thereof by God; and another experience will harrow it, which will give less consolation and more fruit. Then the soul, which is inspired by what gives sweetness, suffers when deprived of it, and feels annoyance. And why annoyance? Because it does not want to be deprived; for it says, "I seem to love God more in this way than in that. From the one I feel that I bear some fruit, and from the other I perceive no fruit at all, except pain and ofttimes many conflicts; and so I seem to wrong God." Son and brother in Christ Jesus, I say that this soul is deceived by its self-will. For it would not be deprived of sweetness; with this bait the devil catches it. Frequently men lose time in longing for time to suit themselves, for they do not employ what they have otherwise than in suffering and gloominess.

Once our sweet Saviour said to a very dear daughter of His, "Dost thou know how those people act who want to fulfil My will in consolation and in sweetness and joy? When they are deprived of these things, they wish to depart from My will, thinking to do well and to avoid offence; but false sensuality lurks in them, and to escape pains it falls into offence without perceiving it. But if the soul were wise and had the light of My will within, it would look to the fruit and not to the sweetness. What is the fruit of the soul? Hatred of itself and love of Me. This hate and love are the issue of self-knowledge; then the soul knows its faulty self to be nothing, and it sees in itself My goodness, which keeps its will good; and it sees what a person I have made it, in order that it may serve Me in greater perfection, and judges that I have made it for the best, and for its own greatest good. Such a man as this, dearest daughter, does not wish for time to suit himself, because he has learned humility; knowing his infirmity, he does not trust in his own wish, but is faithful to Me. He clothes him in My highest and eternal will, because he sees that I neither give nor take away, save for your sanctification; and he sees that love alone impels Me to give you sweetness and to take it from you. For this cause he cannot grieve over any consolation that might be taken from him within or without, by demon or fellow-creature--because he sees that, were this not for his good, I should not permit it.

Therefore this man rejoices because he has light within and without, and is so illumined that when the devil approaches his mind with shadows to confuse him, saying, 'This is for thy sins,' he replies like a person who shrinks not from suffering, saying, 'Thanks be to my Creator, who has remembered me in the time of shadows, punishing me by pain in finite time. Great is this love, which will not punish me in the infinite future.' Oh, what tranquillity of mind has this soul, because it has freed itself from the self-will which brings storm! But not thus does he whose self-will is lively within, seeking things after his own way! For he seems to think that he knows what he needs better than I. Many a time he says, 'It seems to me that I am wronging God in this: free me from wrong, and let what He wills be done.' This is a sign that you are freed from wrong, when you see in yourself goodwill not to want to wrong God, and displeasure with sin; thence ought you to take hope. Although all external activities and inward consolations should fail, let goodwill to please God ever remain firm. Upon this rock is founded grace. If thou sayest, I do not seem to have it, I say that this is false, for if thou hadst it not, thou wouldst not fear to wrong God. But it is the devil who makes things look so, in order that the soul may fall into confusion and disordered sadness, and hold firm its self- will, by wanting consolations, times and seasons in its own way. Do not believe him, dearest daughter, but let your soul be always ready to endure sufferings in howsoever God may inflict them. Otherwise you would do like a man who stands on the threshold with a light in his hand, who reaches his hand out and casts light outside, and within it is dark. Such is a man who is already united in outward things with the will of God, despising the world; but within, his spiritual self-will is living still, veiled in the colour of virtue." Thus spoke God to that servant of His spoken of above.

Therefore I said that I wished and desired that your will should be absorbed and transformed in Him, while we hold ourselves always ready to bear pains and toils howsoever God chooses to send them to us. So we shall be freed from darkness and abide in light. Amen. Praised be Jesus Christ crucified and sweet Mary.

TO MONNA AGNESE WHO WAS THE WIFE
OF MESSER ORSO MALAVOLTI

Catherine is well aware that the world can be as true a school of holiness as the forest cell. She writes to the noble lady, Monna Agnese Malavolti, in much the same strain as to Frate Antonio. The danger of spiritual self-will forms indeed one of those recurring themes which pervade her letters like the motifs of Wagnerian music--ever the same, yet woven into ever- new harmonies.

But the general subject of this letter is the "Santissima Pazienza," which is still frequently invoked by the common folk of Siena: and Catherine's analysis searches deep. Patience could hardly have been one of the virtues most native to the woman's valiant spirit, and one feels in her keen and solemn meditations that she had herself known the bitter and corroding power of the sin "that burns and does not consume," and that "makes the soul unendurable to itself." It is with convincing fervour and fulness that she presents impatience as the permanent condition of the lost. The little discussion of impatience in human relations, and of the "proud humility" resorted to by a soul ravaged by a sense of neglect, has also a very personal note. But it is still more clear in the letter that Catherine's had become the disciplined nature which can "endure a restless mind with more reverence than a tranquil one," if such be the will of God, and which has entered deeply into the joy that awaits the meek.

Monna Agnese must have stood in special need of these touching exhortations: she was a woman sorrowfully tried. Her son had been beheaded in 1372, in punishment for heinous sin; and now her only daughter had died. "For the which thing," writes Catherine, with one of her own inimitable phrases, "I am deeply content, with a holy compassion."

In the Name of Jesus Christ crucified and of sweet Mary:

Dearest daughter in Christ sweet Jesus: I Catherine, servant and slave of the servants of Jesus Christ, write to you in His Precious Blood, with the desire to see you established in true patience, since I consider that without patience we cannot please God. For just as impatience gives much pleasure to the devil and to one's own lower nature, and revels in nothing but anger when it misses what the lower nature wants, so it is very displeasing to God. It is because anger and impatience are the very pith and sap of pride that they please the devil so much. Impatience loses the fruit of its labour, deprives the soul of God; it begins by knowing a foretaste of hell, and later it brings men to eternal damnation: for in hell the evil perverted will burns with anger, hate and impatience. It burns and does not consume, but is evermore renewed--that is, it never grows less, and therefore I say, it does not consume. It has indeed parched and consumed grace in the souls of the lost, but as I said it has not consumed their being, and so their punishment lasts eternally. The saints say that the damned ask for death and cannot have it, because the soul never dies. It dies to be sure to grace, by mortal sin; but it does not die to existence. There is no sin nor wrong that gives a man such a foretaste of hell in this life as anger and impatience. It is hated by God, it holds its neighbour in aversion, and has neither knowledge nor desire to bear and forbear with its faults. And whatever is said or done to it, it at once empoisons, and its impulses blow about like a leaf in the wind. It becomes unendurable to itself, for perverted will is always gnawing at it, and it craves what it cannot have; it is discordant with the will of God and with the rational part of its own soul. And all this comes from the tree of Pride, from which oozes out the sap of anger and impatience. The man becomes an incarnate demon, and it is much worse to fight with these visible demons than with the invisible. Surely, then, every reasonable being ought to flee this sin.

But note, that there are two sources of impatience. There is a common kind of impatience, felt by ordinary men in the world, which befalls them on account of the inordinate love they have for themselves and for temporal things, which they love apart from God; so that to have them they do not mind losing their soul, and putting it into the hands of the devils. This is beyond help, unless a man recognizes himself, how he has wronged God, and cuts down that tree of Pride with the sword of true humility, which produces charity in the soul. For there is a tree of Love, whose pith is patience and goodwill toward one's neighbour. For, just as impatience shows more clearly than any other sin that the soul is deprived of God-- because it is at once evident that since the pith is there, the tree of Pride must be there--so patience shows better and more perfectly than any other virtue, that God is in the soul by grace. Patience, I say, deep within the tree of Love, that for love of its Creator disdains the world, and loves insults whencesoever they come.

I was saying that anger and impatience were of two kinds, one general and one special. We have spoken of the common kind. Now I talk of the more particular, of the impatience of those who have already despised the world, and who wish to be servants of Christ crucified in their own way; that is, in so far as they shall find joy and consolation in Him. This is because spiritual self-will is not dead in them: therefore they imperiously demand from God that He should give them consolations and tribulations in their own way, and not in His; and so they become impatient, when they get the contrary of what their spiritual self-will wants. This is a little offshoot from Pride, sprouting from real Pride, as a tree sends out a little tree by its side, which looks separated from it, but nevertheless it gets the substance from which it springs from the same tree. So is self-will in the soul which chooses to serve God in its own way; and when that way fails it suffers, and its suffering makes it impatient, and it is unendurable to itself, and takes no pleasure in serving God or its neighbour. Nay, if any one came to it for comfort or help it would give him nothing but reproaches, and would not know how to be tolerant to his need. All this results from the sensitive spiritual self-will that grows from the tree of Pride which was cut down, but not uprooted. It is cut down when the soul uplifts its desire above the world, and fastens it on God, but has fastened there imperfectly; the root of Pride was left, and therefore it sent up an offshoot by its side, and shows itself in spiritual things. So, if it misses consolations from God, and its mind stays dry and sterile, it at once becomes disturbed and depressed, and, under colour of virtue--because it thinks itself deprived of God--it begins to complain, and lays down the law to God. But were it truly humble and had true hate and knowledge of itself, it would deem itself unworthy of the visitation of God to its soul, and worthy of the pain that it suffers, in being deprived, not of God's grace in the soul, but of its consolations. It suffers, then, because it has to work in its chains; yes, spiritual self-will suffers under the delusion that it is wronging God, while the trouble is really with its own lower nature.

Therefore the humble soul, which has freely uprooted with eager love the root of Pride, has annulled its own will, seeking ever the honour of God and the salvation of souls. It does not mind sufferings, but endures a restless mind with more reverence than a quiet one; having a holy respectful knowledge that God gives and grants this to it for its good, that it may rise from imperfection to perfection. That is the way to make it attain perfection, for it recognizes better thereby its own defects and the grace of God, which it finds within, in the goodwill that God has given it to hate its mortal sin. Also, by meditating on its defects and faults, old and new, it has conceived hatred for itself, and love for the Highest Eternal Will of God. Therefore it bears these things with reverence, and is content to endure inwardly and outwardly, in whatever way God grants it. Provided that it can be filled and clothed with the sweetness of the will of God, it rejoices in everything; and the more it sees itself deprived of the thing it loves, whether the consolations of God, as I said, or of its fellows, the more gladsome it grows. For many a time it happens that the soul loves spiritually; but if it does not find the consolation or satisfaction from the beloved that it would like, or if it suspects that more love or satisfaction is given to another than to itself, it falls into suffering, into depression of mind, into criticism of its neighbour and false judgment, passing judgment on the mind and intention of the servants of God, and especially on those from whom it suffers. Thence it becomes impatient, and thinks what it should not think, and says with its tongue what it should not say. In such suffering as this, it likes to resort to a proud humility, which has the aspect of humility, but is really an offshoot of Pride, springing up beside it-- saying to itself: "I will not pay these people any more attention, or trouble myself any more about them. I will keep entirely to myself; I do not wish to hurt either myself or them." And it abases itself with a perverted scorn. Now it ought to perceive that this is scorn, by the impulse to judge that it feels in its heart, and by the complaints of its tongue. It ought not then to do so; for in this fashion it will never get rid of the root of Pride, nor cut off the little son at the side, which hinders the soul from attaining the perfection at which it has aimed. But it ought to kneel at the table of the Most Holy Cross, to receive the food of the honour of God and the salvation of souls, with a free heart, with holy hatred of itself, with passionate desire: seeking to gain virtue by suffering and sweat, and not by private consolations either from God or its fellows; following the footsteps and the teaching of Christ Crucified, saying to itself with sharp rebuke: "Thou shouldst not, my soul, thou that art a member, travel by another road than thy Head. An unfit thing it is that limbs should remain delicate beneath a thorn-crowned Head." If such habits became fixed, through one's own frailty, or the wiles of the devil, or the many impulses that shake the heart like winds, then the soul ought to ascend the seat of its conscience, and reason with itself, and let nothing pass without punishment and chastisement, hatred and distaste for itself. So the root shall be pulled up, and by displeasure against itself the soul will drive out displeasure against its neighbour, grieving more over the unregulated instincts of its own heart and thoughts than over the suffering it could receive from its fellows, or any insult or annoyance they could inflict on it.

This is the sweet and holy fashion observed by those who are wholly inspired of Christ; for in this wise they have uprooted perverted pride, and that marrow of impatience of which we said above that it was very pleasing to the devil, because it is the beginning and occasion of every sin; and on the contrary that as it is very pleasing to the devil, so it is very displeasing to God. Pride displeases Him and humility pleases Him. So greatly did the virtue of humility please Him in Mary that He was constrained to give her the Word His Only-Begotten Son and she was the sweet mother who gave Him to us. Know well, that until Mary showed by her spoken words her humility and pure will, when she said: "Ecce Ancilla Domini, be it done unto me according to Thy word"--the Son of God was not incarnate in her; but when she had said this, she conceived within herself that sweet and Spotless Lamb--the Sweet Primal Truth showing thereby how excellent is this little virtue, and how much the soul receives that offers and presents its will in humility to its Creator. So then--in the time of labours and persecutions, of insults and injuries inflicted by one's neighbour, of mental conflicts and deprivation of spiritual consolations, by the Creator or the creature, (by the Creator in His gentleness, when He withdraws the feeling of the mind, so that it does not seem as if God were in the soul, so many are its pains and conflicts--and by fellow-creatures, in conversation or amusement, or when the soul thinks that it loves more than it is loved)--in all these things, I say that the soul perfected by humility says: "My Lord, behold Thy handmaid: be it done unto me according to Thy word, and not according to what I want with my senses." So it sheds the fragrance of patience, around the Creator and its fellow-creature and itself. It has peace and quiet in its mind, and it has found peace in warfare, because it has driven far from it its self-will founded in pride, and has conceived divine grace in its soul. And it bears in its mind's breast Christ crucified, and rejoices in the Wounds of Christ crucified, and seeks to know naught but Christ crucified; and its bed is the Cross of Christ crucified. There it annuls its own will, and becomes humble and obedient.

For there is no obedience without humility, nor humility without charity. This is shown by the Word, for in obedience to His Father and in humility, He ran to the shameful death of the Cross, nailing and binding Him with the nails and bands of charity, and enduring in such patience that no cry of complaint was heard from Him. For nails were not enough to hold God- and-Man nailed and fastened on the Cross had Love not held Him there. This I say that the soul feels; therefore it will not joy otherwise than with Christ crucified. For could it attain to virtue and escape Hell and have eternal life, without sufferings, and have in the world consolations spiritual and temporal, it would not wish them; but it desires rather to suffer, enduring even unto death, than to have eternal life in any other way: only let it conform itself with Christ crucified, and clothe it with His shames and pains. It has found the table of the Spotless Lamb.

Oh, glorious virtue! Who would not give himself to death a thousand times, and endure any suffering through desire to win thee? Thou art a queen, who dost possess the entire world; thou dost inhabit the enduring life; for while the soul that is arrayed in thee is yet mortal, thou makest it abide by force of love with those who are immortal. Since, then, this virtue is so excellent and pleasing to God and useful to us and saving to our neighbour, arise, dearest daughter, from the sleep of negligence and ignorance, casting to earth the weakness and frailty of thy heart, that it feel no suffering nor impatience over anything that God permits to us, so that we may not fall either into the common kind of impatience, or into the special kind, as we were saying before, but serve our sweet Saviour manfully, with liberty of heart and true perfect patience. If we do otherwise, we shall lose grace by the first sort of impatience, and by the second we shall hinder our state of perfection; and you would not attain that to which God has called you.

It seems that God is calling you to great perfection. And I perceive it by this, that He takes away from you every tie that might hinder it in you. For as I have heard, it seems that He has called to Himself your daughter, who was your last tie with the outer world. For which thing I am deeply content, with a holy compassion, that God should have set you free, and taken her from her labours. Now then, I want that you should wholly destroy your own will, that it may cling to nothing but Christ crucified. In this way you will fulfil His will and my desire. Therefore, not knowing any other way in which you could fulfil it, I said to you that I desired to see you established in true and holy patience, because without this we cannot reach our sweet goal. I say no more. Remain in the holy and sweet grace of God. Sweet Jesus, Jesus Love.

TO SISTER EUGENIA, HER NIECE AT THE CONVENT OF SAINT AGNES OF MONTEPULCIANO

Two nieces, daughters of Bartolo Benincasa, were nuns in the Convent of Montepulciano. To one of them the following letter is addressed. One can read between the lines a lively solicitude. Never cloistered herself, Catherine had a close intimacy with cloisters, and knew their best and worst. She held in hearty and loyal respect the opportunities which they offered for leading an exalted life; to this Convent of St. Agnes she was peculiarly attached. At the same time, she was well aware, as other letters beside the present show, that even the best of cloisters afforded at this time scant shelter to young girls from emotional temptation, gross or fine. Her warnings to her niece have the authoritative tone of anxiety. Let us hope that Eugenia took them to heart; and that, leading the disciplined life of Catherine's desire, she became not unworthy to receive and apprehend in its full beauty the penetrating meditation on Prayer which forms the second part of the letter. The thoughts of this meditation, like many others in Catherine's letters, will be found amplified in her Dialogue--a colloquy between God and her soul, composed and dictated in trance during the year 1378. The following quotation illustrates an interesting passage of the letter:--

"In this way, vocal prayer can be useful to the soul and do Me pleasure, and from imperfect vocal prayer it can advance by persevering practice to perfect mental prayer. But if it aims simply to complete its number (of paternosters), or if it gave up mental prayer for the sake of vocal, it would never arrive at perfection. Sometimes, when a soul has made a resolution to say a certain number of prayers, I may visit its mind, now in one way, now in another: at one time with the light of self-knowledge and contrition over its lightness, at another, with the largesse of My charity; at another, by putting before its mind, in diverse manner as may please Me, and as that soul may have craved, the Presence of My Truth. And the soul will be so ignorant that it will turn from My Visitation, in order to complete its number, from a conscientious scruple against giving up what it began. It ought not to do thus, for this would be a wile of the devil. But at once, when it feels its mind ready for My Visitation, in any way, as I said, it should abandon the vocal prayer. Then, when the mental has passed, if there is time it can resume the other, which it had planned to say. But if there is not time it must not care nor be troubled or bewildered."

In the Name of Jesus Christ crucified and of sweet Mary:

Dearest daughter in Christ sweet Jesus: I Catherine, servant and slave of the servants of Jesus Christ, write to thee in His precious Blood, with desire to see thee taste the food of angels, since thou art made for no other end; and that thou might-est taste it, God bought thee with the Blood of His Only-Begotten Son. But reflect, dearest daughter, that this food is not taken upon earth, but on high, and therefore the Son of God chose to be lifted up upon the wood of the Most Holy Cross, in order that we might receive this food upon this table on high. But thou wilt say to me: What is this food of angels? I reply to thee: it is the desire of God, which draws to itself the desire that is in the depths of the soul, and they make one thing together.

This is a food which while we are pilgrims in this life, draws to itself the fragrance of true and sincere virtues, which are prepared by the fire of divine charity, and received upon the table of the cross. That is, virtue is won by pain and weariness, casting down one's own fleshly nature;--the kingdom of one's soul which is called Heaven (*cielo*) because it hides (*cela*) God within it by patience, is seized with force and violence. This is the food that makes the soul angelic, and therefore it is called the food of angels; and also because the soul, separated from the body, tastes God in His essential Being. He satisfies the soul in such wise that she longs for no other thing nor can desire aught but what may help her more perfectly to keep and increase this food, so that she holds in hate what is contrary to it. Therefore, like a prudent person, she looks with the light of most holy faith, which is in the eye of the mind, and beholds what is harmful and what is useful to her. And as she has seen, so she loves and condemns--holding, I say, her own fleshly nature and all the vices which proceed from it, bound beneath the feet of her affections. She flees all causes that may incline her to vice or hinder her perfection. So she annuls her self-will, which is the cause of all evil, and subjects it to the yoke of holy obedience, not only to the Order and its chief, but to every least creature through God. She flees all glory and human indulgence, and glories only in the shames and sorrows of Christ crucified: insults, outrage, ridicule, injuries, are milk to her; she joys in them, to be conformed with the Bridegroom, Christ crucified. She renounces conversation with fellow-beings, because she sees that they often intervene between us and our Creator, and she flees to the actual and to the mental cell.

To this I summon thee and the others: and I command thee, dearest daughter mine, that thou abide for ever in the cell of self-knowledge, where we find the angelic food of the eager desire of God toward us; and in the actual cell, with vigil and humble faithful continual prayer, divesting thy heart and mind of every creature, and clothing them with Christ crucified. Otherwise thou wouldst eat upon the earth, and there I have already said to thee, one should not eat. Reflect that thy Bridegroom, Christ sweet Jesus, wishes naught between thee and Him, and is very jealous. So as soon as He saw that thou didst love any thing apart from Him, He would go from thee, and thou wouldst be made worthy to eat the food of beasts. And wouldst thou not truly be a beast, and food for beasts, didst thou leave the Creator for the creature, and infinite good for finite and transitory things that pass like the winds, light for darkness, life for death, Him who clothes thee in the sun of justice with the clasp of obedience, and pearls of living faith, firm hope, and perfect charity, for him who robs thee of them? And wouldst thou not be foolish indeed to depart from Him who gives thee perfect purity--so that the closer thou dost cling to Him, the more the flower of thy virginity is refined--for those who many a time and oft shed a stench of impurity, defiling mind and body? God avert them from thee by His infinite mercy!

And in order that no such thing may ever happen to thee, be on thy guard: let not thy misfortune be such as to enter into any private conversation, with monk or layman. For if I were to know or hear it, even if I were much farther away than I am, I would give thee such a discipline that it would stay in thy memory all thy whole life; never mind who may be by. Beware neither to give nor receive, except in case of need, helping every one in common within and without. Be steadfast and mature in thyself. Serve the sisters tenderly, with all vigilance, especially those whom thou seest in need. When guests pass by and ask for thee at the gratings, abide in thy peace and do not go--but let them say to the prioress what they wanted to say to thee, unless she commands thee to go on thy obedience. Then, hold thy head bowed, and be as savage as a hedgehog. Keep in thy mind the manners which that glorious virgin Saint Agnes made her daughters observe. Go to confession and tell thy need; and when thou hast received thy penance, run. Beware, moreover, that thy confessors be not from the men who have brought thee up. And do not wonder because I talk so; for many a time thou mayest have heard me say, and it is the truth, that the talk of so-called pious men and women, full of depraved expressions, ruins the souls and the habits and practices of Religious. Beware that thou bind thy heart to none but Christ crucified; for the hour would come when thou wouldst wish to set it free and couldst not, which would be very hard for thee. I say that the soul which has tasted of the food of angels has seen in the light that this and the other things we were speaking of are an obstacle between itself and its food, and therefore flees them with the greatest zeal. I say that it loves and seeks what may increase and preserve it. And because it has seen that this food is better enjoyed by means of prayer offered in self-knowledge, therefore it exercises itself therein continually by all the ways in which it can hold closer to God.

Prayer is of three sorts. The one is perpetual: it is the holy perpetual desire, which prays in the sight of God, whatever thou art doing; for this desire directs all thy works, spiritual and corporal, to His honour, and therefore it is called perpetual. Of this it seems that Saint Paul the glorious was talking when he said: Pray without ceasing. The other kind is vocal prayer, when the offices or other prayers are said aloud. This is ordained to reach the third--that is, mental prayer: your soul reaches this when it uses vocal prayer in prudence and humility, so that while the tongue speaks the heart is not far from God. But one must exert one's self to hold and establish one's heart in the force of divine charity. And whenever one felt one's mind to be visited by God, so that it was drawn to think of its Creator in any wise, it ought to abandon vocal prayer, and to fix its mind with the force of love upon that wherein it sees God visit it; then, if it has time, when this has ceased, it ought to take up the vocal prayer again, in order that the mind may always stay full and not empty. And although many conflicts of diverse kinds should abound in prayer, and darkness of mind with much confusion, the devil making the soul feel that her prayer was not pleasing to God--nevertheless, she ought not to give up on account of those conflicts and shadows, but to abide firm in fortitude and long perseverance, considering that the devil so does to draw her away from prayer the mother, and God permits it to test the fortitude and constancy of that soul. Also, in order that by those conflicts and shadows she may know herself not to be, and in the goodwill which she feels preserved within her may know the goodness of God, Who is Giver and Preserver of good and holy wills: such wills as are not vouchsafed to all who want them.

By this means she attains to the third and last--mental prayer, in which she receives the reward for the labours she underwent in her imperfect vocal prayer. Then she tastes the milk of faithful prayer. She rises above herself--that is, above the gross impulses of the senses--and with angelic mind unites herself with God by force of love, and sees and knows with the light of thought, and clothes herself with truth. She is made the sister of angels; she abides with her Bridegroom on the table of crucified desire, rejoicing to seek the honour of God and the salvation of souls; since well she sees that for this the Eternal Bridegroom ran to the shameful death of the Cross, and thus fulfilled obedience to the Father, and our salvation. This prayer is surely a mother, who conceives virtues by the love of God, and brings them forth in the love of the neighbour. Where dost thou show love, faith, and hope, and humility? In prayer. For thou wouldst never take pains to seek the thing which thou didst not love; but he who loves would ever be one with what he loves--that is, God. By means of prayer thou askest of Him thy necessity; for knowing thyself--the knowledge on which true prayer is founded--thou seest thyself to have great need. Thou feelest thyself surrounded by thine enemies--by the world with its insults and its recalling of vain pleasures, by the devil with his many temptations, by the flesh with its great rebellion and struggle against the spirit. And thou seest that in thyself thou art not; not being, thou canst not help thyself; and therefore thou dost hasten in faith to Him who is, who can and will help thee in thine every need, and thou dost hopefully ask and await His aid. Thus ought prayer to be made, if thou wishest to have that which thou awaitest. Never shall any just thing be denied thee which thou askest in this wise from the Divine Goodness; but if thou dost in other wise, little fruit shalt thou receive. Where shalt thou feel grief in thy conscience? In prayer. Where shalt thou divest thee of the self-love which makes thee impatient in the time of insults and of other pains, and shalt clothe thee in the divine love which shall make thee patient, and shalt glory in the Cross of Christ crucified? In prayer. Where shalt thou breathe the perfume of virginity and the hunger for martyrdom, holding thee ready to give thy life for the honour of God and the salvation of souls?

In this sweet mother, prayer. This will make thee an observer of thy Rule: it will seal in thy heart and mind three solemn vows which thou didst make at thy profession, leaving there the imprint of the desire to observe them until death. This releases thee from conversation with fellow-creatures, and gives thee converse with thy Creator; it fills the vessel of thy heart with the Blood of the Humble Lamb, and crowns it with flame, because with flame of love that Blood was shed.

The soul receives and tastes this mother Prayer more or less perfectly, according as it nourishes itself with the food of angels--that is, with holy and true desire for God, raising itself on high, as I said, to receive it upon the table of the most sweet Cross. Therefore I said to thee that I desired to see thee nourished with angelic food, because I see not that in otherwise thou couldst be a true bride of Christ crucified, consecrated to Him in holy religion. So do that I may see thee a jewel precious in the sight of God. And do not go about wasting thy time. Bathe and drown thee in the sweet Blood of thy Bridegroom. I say no more. Remain in the holy and sweet grace of God. Sweet Jesus, Jesus Love.

TO NANNA, DAUGHTER OF BENINCASA A LITTLE MAID, HER NIECE, IN FLORENCE

This tender and playful little letter, with its childlike simplicity of fancy and gentle authority of tone, encourages us to believe that Catherine appreciated the full advantages of being an aunt. We have other indications that the many spiritual ties which held her as she grew older never weakened the bond of any natural affection. Indeed, Catherine re- created each natural bond, when possible, as a spiritual bond, an achievement none too common. Doubtless, many children grew up around her in the large Benincasa household. We know that at the time of the plague, in 1374, Lapa was bringing up eleven grandchildren in her own house. Of these, eight fell victims to the pestilence, and we have a glimpse of Catherine burying them with her own hands, and saying as she laid them to rest one by one, "This one, at least, I shall not lose." Of the little Nanna to whom this letter was written we know nothing, except that she was the child of the elder brother, who, as we have already seen, had moved to Florence.

In the Name of Jesus Christ crucified and of sweet Mary:

Dearest daughter in Christ sweet Jesus: I Catherine, servant and slave of the servants of Jesus Christ, write to thee in His precious Blood, with desire to see thee a real bride of Christ crucified, running away from everything which might hinder thee from possessing this sweet and glorious Bridegroom. But thou couldst not do this if thou wert not among those wise virgins consecrated to Christ who had lamps with oil in them, and light was within. See, then, if thou wishest to be a bride of Christ, thou must have lamp, and oil, and light. Dost thou know what this means, daughter mine? By the lamp is meant our heart, because a heart ought to be made like a lamp. Thou seest that a lamp is wide above and narrow below, and so the heart is made, to signify that we ought always to keep it wide above, through holy thoughts and holy imaginations and continual prayer; always holding in memory the blessings of God, and chiefly the blessing of the Blood by which we are bought. For Blessed Christ, my daughter, did not buy us with gold or silver or pearls or other precious stones; nay, He bought us with His precious Blood. So one wants never to forget so great a blessing, but always to hold it before one's eyes, in holy and sweet gratitude, seeing how immeasurably God loves us: who did not shrink from giving His only begotten Son to the opprobrious death of the Cross, to give us the life of grace.

I said that a lamp is narrow below, and so is our heart: to signify that the heart ought to be narrow toward these earthly things--that is, it must not desire nor love them extravagantly, nor hunger for more than God wills to give us; but ever thank Him, seeing how sweetly He provides for us so that we never lack anything.

Now in this way, our heart will really be a lamp. But reflect, daughter mine, that this would not be enough were there no oil within. By oil is meant that sweet little virtue, profound humility: for it is fitting that the bride of Christ be humble and gentle and patient; and she will be as humble as she is patient, and as patient as she is humble. But we cannot attain this virtue of humility except by true knowledge of ourselves, knowing our misery and frailty, and that we by ourselves can do no good deed, nor escape any conflict or pain; for if we have a bodily infirmity, or a pain or conflict in our minds, we cannot escape it or remove it--for if we could we should escape from it swiftly. So it is quite true that we in ourselves are nothing other than infamy, misery, stench, frailty, and sins; wherefore, we ought always to abide low and humble. But to abide wholly in such knowledge of one's self would not be good, because the soul would fall into weariness and confusion; and from confusion it would fall into despair: so the devil would like nothing better than to make us fall into confusion, to drive us afterward to despair. We ought, then, to abide in the knowledge of the goodness of God in Himself, perceiving that He has created us in His image and likeness, and re-created us in grace by the Blood of His only-begotten Son, the sweet incarnate Lord; and reflecting how continually the goodness of God works in us. But see, that to abide entirely in this knowledge of God would not be good, because the soul would fall into presumption and pride. So it befits us to have one mixed with the other--that is, to abide in the holy knowledge of the goodness of God, and also in the knowledge of ourselves: and so we shall be humble, patient, and gentle, and in this way we shall have oil in our lamp.

Now, then, we must have light--otherwise it would not be enough. This light has to be the light of most holy faith. But the saints say that faith without works is dead, so our faith might be neither living nor holy, but dead. Therefore we need to exert ourselves virtuously all the time, and leave our childishness and vanities, and not behave any longer like worldly girls, but like faithful brides consecrated to Christ crucified; in this way we shall have a lamp, and oil, and light.

The Gospel says that these wise virgins were five. So I tell thee that there must be five in each of us--otherwise we shall not enter the wedding feast of eternal life.

By these five it is meant that we must subject and mortify our five bodily senses, in such wise that we may never offend with them, taking through them or some of them unregulated pleasure or delight. In this way we shall be five, when we have subdued our five senses.

But think that that sweet Bridegroom Christ is more jealous of His brides than I could tell thee! Therefore if He should see that thou didst love anyone more than Him, He would be angry with thee at once. And if thou didst not correct thyself, the door would not be open to thee, to the wedding feast which Christ the Lamb without spot holds for all His faithful: but we should be driven away like bad women, as those five foolish virgins were, who, glorying only and vainly in the integrity and virginity of their body, lost the virginity of their soul, through the corruption of the five senses, because they did not carry the oil of humility with them, so that their lamps went out. Therefore it was said to them: "Go hence to buy oil." By this oil is meant in this place the flatteries and praises of men; since all the flatterers and praisers of the world sell this oil. As if it were said to them: "You have not wanted to buy eternal life with your virginity and your good works; no, you have wanted to buy the praises of men, and to have the praises of men you have wrought. Go now and buy praises, for you will not enter here." Therefore, daughter mine, beware of the praises of men; and do not want praise for any work that thou mayest do, for the door of eternal life would not be open to thee later. So, reflecting that this was the best way, I said that I desired to see thee a real bride of Christ crucified; and so I beg and command thee that thou try hard to be. I say no more to thee. Remain in the holy and sweet grace of God. Sweet Jesus, Jesus Love.

LETTERS ON THE CONSECRATED LIFE

Catherine is known in history as one of the great ascetics of the Church; these letters show her intimate attitude toward the mortification of the flesh. She was a woman called of God and her natural powers, constantly to assume the dangerous duty of convincing men of their sin; these letters give us her conception of the safeguards needed in the performance of that duty.

Both letters were written to Religious. Father William Flete was an Englishman, who, passing through Italy in his youth, became fascinated with the land, and spent the rest of his life in a hermit's cell in the Forest of Lecceto. The annals of the time throw some entertaining side- lights on his figure. Famous for his austerities and for the sanctity of his life, he was also a very impatient and somewhat intolerant person, given to carping criticism of his brother hermits. Catherine, in writing to him, analyses mercilessly the dangers of the ascetic life; one feels that not much self-righteousness could be left in a man after reading her trenchant phrases. Soon, however, she lifts him with her to the ardent contemplation of the perfect life; it is in words of singular beauty that she describes the attitude of generous loving-kindness, uncritical, humble and glad, with which the true servant of God considers all sorts and conditions of men: "Such a man rejoices in every type that he sees, saying: Thanks be to Thee, Eternal Father, that Thou hast many mansions in Thy house.... He rejoices more in the differences among men than he would in seeing them all walk in the same way; for so he sees more manifest the greatness of the goodness of God. He gets from everything the fragrance of roses."

In the letter to Sister Daniella, Catherine develops these ideas further. Of this "great servant of God" nothing is known except what Catherine's letters to her show. Something may be inferred from the fact that she is one of the few people to whom the greater woman writes as to a spititual equal. She repeats to Daniella the letter to Father William--such warnings, indeed, being needed by all persons leading the consecrated life--and then goes on, in the remainder of the letter as here given, to discuss those farther reaches of perfection in which charity has done its perfect work. Two things she wishes herself and Daniella to observe: the first is abstinence from critical thoughts. Let us not "judge the minds of our fellow-creatures, which are for God alone to judge." It is the key to her own method in her great cure of souls which she here gives us: "When it seems that God shows us the faults of others, keep on the safer side-- for it may be that thy judgment is false. On thy lips let silence abide. And any vice which thou mayest ascribe to others, do thou ascribe at once to them and to thyself, in true humility. If that vice really exists in a person, he will correct himself better, seeing himself so gently understood, and will say of his own accord the thing which thou wouldst have said to him."--The other point which Catherine urges on Daniella is the secondary importance of that life of mortification to which she firmly believes that they have both been called. "Good is penance and maceration of the body; but do not present these to me as a rule for every one. If either for ourselves or others, we made penance our foundation ... we should be ignorant, and should fall into a critical attitude, and become weary and very bitter: for we should strive to give a finished work to God, Who is Infinite Love, and demands from us only infinite desire." Surely, in this last thought Catherine has attained in a flash to sublime spiritual insight.

The Saints knew all about telepathy long before Societies of Psychical Research grew eager over the matter. It might surprise some modern psychologists to read the tranquil passage in which Catherine, assuming as a matter of course that any servant of God engaged in intercessory prayer has a mystical and direct knowledge of the condition of those she prays for, proceeds to warn Daniella as intelligently as any modern could do, though in different terms, as to the limitations within which this kind of knowledge can be trusted.

The little note with which this group closes is not written to a great recluse, but to a tailor's wife. With the simple, Catherine showed herself simple; but Monna Agnese is to lead the consecrated life no less than Sister Daniella. Catherine's plain directions to the one about her daily living evince the same mental clarity and sobriety as her exhortations to the other, and discriminate in much the same way between the excitement of religious practices and true consecration.

TO BROTHER WILLIAM OF ENGLAND OF THE
HERMIT BROTHERS OF ST. AUGUSTINE

In the Name of Jesus Christ crucified and of sweet Mary: Dearest son in Christ sweet Jesus: I Catherine, servant and slave of the servants of Jesus Christ, write to you in His precious Blood, with desire to see you in true light. For without light we shall not be able to walk in the way of truth, but shall walk in shadows. Two lights are necessary. First, we must be illumined to know the transitory things of the world, which all pass like the wind. But these are not rightly known if we do not know our own frailty, how inclined it is, from the perverse law which is bound up with our members, to rebel against its Creator. This light is necessary to every rational creature, in whatever state it may be, if it wishes to have divine grace, and to share in the blessing of the Blood of the Spotless Lamb. This is the common light, that everybody in general ought to have, for whoever has it not is in a state of condemnation. This is the reason; that, not having light, he is not in a state of grace; for one who does not know the evil of wrong, nor who is cause of it, cannot avoid it nor hate the cause. So he who does not know good, and virtue the cause of good, cannot love nor desire that good.

The soul must not stay content because it has arrived at gaining the general light; nay, it ought to go on with all zeal to the perfect light. For since men are at first imperfect rather than perfect, they should advance in light to perfection. Two kinds of perfect people walk in this perfect light. There are some who give themselves to castigating their body perfectly, doing very great harsh penance; and that the flesh may not rebel against the reason, they have placed all their desire rather on mortifying their body than on slaying their self-will. These people feed at the table of penitence and are good and perfect; but unless they have a great humility and conform themselves not wholly to judge according to the will of God and not according to that of men, they often wrong their perfection, making themselves judges of those who do not walk in the same way in which they do.

This happens to them because they have put more thought and desire on mortifying their body than on slaying their self-will. Such men as these always want to choose times and places and mental consolations to suit themselves; also, worldly tribulations, and their battles with the devil; saying, through self-deceit, beguiled by their own will--which is called spiritual self-will--"I should like this consolation, and not these assaults or battles with the devil; not for my own sake, but to please God, and possess Him more fully, because I seem to possess Him better in this way than in that." Many a time, in such a way as this, the soul falls into suffering and weariness, and becomes unendurable to itself through them, and thus wrongs its state of perfection. The odour of pride clings to it, and this it does not perceive. For, were it truly humble and not presumptuous, it would see well that the Sweet Primal Truth gives conditions, time and place, and consolation and tribulation, according as is needful to our perfection, and to fulfil in the soul the perfection to which it is chosen. It would see that everything is given through love, and therefore with love.

All things ought to be received with reverence, as is done by the second class of people, who abide in this sweet and glorious light, who are perfect in whatever condition they are, and, in so far as God permits them, hold everything in due reverence, esteeming themselves worthy of sufferings and scandals in the world, and of missing their consolations. As they hold themselves worthy of sufferings, so they hold themselves unworthy of the reward which follows suffering. These have known and tasted in the light the eternal will of God, which wishes naught but our good, and that we be sanctified in Him, therefore giving His gifts. When the soul has known this will, it is arrayed therein, and cares for nothing save to see in what wise it can grow, and preserve its condition perfect, for glory and praise of the Name of God. Therefore, it opens the eye of the mind upon its object, Christ crucified, who is rule and way and doctrine for perfect and imperfect: and sees the loving Lamb, Who gives it the doctrine of perfection, which seeing it loves.

Perfection is this: that the Word, the Son of God, fed at the table of holy desire for the honour of God and for our salvation; and with this desire ran with great zeal to the shameful death of the Cross, avoiding neither toil nor labour, not drawing back for the ingratitude and ignorance of us men who did not recognize His benefits, nor for the persecution of the Jews, nor for mockery or insults or criticism of the people, but underwent them all, like our captain and true knight, who was come to teach us His way and rule and doctrine, opening the door with the keys of His precious Blood, shed with ardent love and hatred against sin. As says this sweet, loving Word, "Behold, I have made you a way, and opened the door with My blood. Be you then not negligent to follow it, and do not sit yourselves down in self-love, ignorantly failing to know the Way, and presumptuously wishing to choose it after your own fashion, and not after Mine who made it. Rise up then, and follow Me: for no one can go to the Father but by Me. I am the Way and the Door."

Then the soul, enamoured and tormented with love, runs to the table of holy desire, and sees not itself in itself, seeking private consolation, spiritual or temporal, but, as one who has wholly destroyed his own will in this light and knowledge, refuses no toil from whatever side it comes. Nay, in suffering, in pain, in many assaults from the devil and criticisms from men, it seeks upon the table of the Cross the food of the honour of God and the salvation of men. And it seeks no reward, from God or from fellow-creatures; such men serve God, not for their own joy, and the neighbour not for their own will or profit, but from pure love. They lose themselves, divesting them of the old man, their fleshly desires, and array them in the new man, Christ sweet Jesus, following Him manfully. These are they who feed at the table of holy desire, and have more zeal for slaying their self-will than for slaying and mortifying the body. They have mortified the body, to be sure, but not as a chief aim, but as the tool which it is, to help in slaying self-will; for one's chief aim ought to be and is to slay the will; that it may seek and wish naught save to follow Christ crucified, seeking the honour and glory of His Name, and the salvation of souls. Such men abide ever in peace and quiet; there are none who can offend them, because they have cast away the thing that gives offence--that is, self-will. All the persecutions which the world and the devil can inflict run away beneath their feet; they stand in the water, made fast to the twigs of eager desire, and are not submerged. Such a man as this rejoices in everything; he does not make himself a judge of the servants of God, nor of any rational creature; nay, he rejoices in every condition and every type that he sees, saying, "Thanks be to Thee, eternal Father, that Thou hast many mansions in Thy House." And he rejoices more in the different kinds of men that he sees than he would do in seeing them all walk in the same way, for so he sees the greatness of God's goodness more manifest. He joys in everything, and gets from it the fragrance of roses. And even as to a thing which he may expressly see to be sin, he does not pose as a judge, but regards it rather with holy true compassion, saying, "To-day it is thy turn, and to-morrow mine, unless it be for divine grace which preserves me."

Oh, holy minds, who feed at the table of holy desire, who have attained in great light to nourish you with holy food, clothed with the sweet raiment of the Lamb, His love and charity! You do not lose time in accepting false judgments, either of the servants of God or of the servants of the world; you do not take offence at any criticism, either against yourselves or others. Your love toward God and your neighbour is governed well, and not ungoverned. And because it is governed, such men as these, dearest son, never take offence at those whom they love; for appearances are dead to them, and they have submitted themselves not to be guided by men, but only by the Holy Spirit. See then, these enjoy in this life the pledge of life eternal.

I wish you and the other ignorant sons to reach this light, for I see that this perfection is lacking to you and to others. For were it not lacking to you, you would not have fallen into such criticism and offence and false judgment, as to say and believe that another man was guided and mastered by the will of the creature and not of the Creator. My soul and my heart grieve to see you wrong the perfection to which God has called you, under pretence of love and odour of virtue. Nevertheless, these are the tares which the devil has sowed in the field of the Lord; he has done this to choke the seed of holy desire and doctrine sowed in your fields. Will then to do so no more, since God has of grace given you great lights; the first, to despise the world; the second, to mortify the body; the third, to seek the honour of God. Do not wrong this perfection with spiritual self-will, but rise from the table of penance and attain the table of the desire of God, where the soul is wholly dead to its own will, nourishing itself without suffering on the honour of God and the salvation of souls, growing in perfection and not wronging it.

Therefore, considering that this condition cannot be had without light, and seeing that you had it not, I said that I desired and desire to see you in true and perfect light. Thus I pray you, by the love of Christ crucified--you and Brother Antonio and all the others--that you struggle to win it, so that you may be numbered among the perfect and not among the imperfect. I say no more. Remain in the holy and sweet grace of God. I commend me to all of you. Bathe you in the Blood of Christ crucified. Sweet Jesus, Jesus Love.

TO DANIELLA OF ORVIETO CLOTHED WITH
THE HABIT OF ST. DOMINIC

Thou seest, then, that such men enjoy in this life the pledge of life eternal. They receive, not the payment, but the pledge--not waiting to receive it till the enduring life, where is life without death, satiety without disgust, and hunger without pain. For far is the pain of hunger, since they have completely what they desire; and far is the disgust of satiety, since that is the Food of Life without any lack. It is true that in this life one begins to enjoy the pledge, in this way, that the soul begins to be an-hungered for the food of the honour of God and the salvation of souls. As it is an-hungered, so it feeds thereon; yes, the soul nourishes itself on charity for the neighbour, for whom it has a hungry desire. That is a food which never satisfies those nourished on it. It never satiates, and therefore hunger lasts for ever. As a pledge is a beginning of surety given to a man, through which he expects to receive payment (not that the pledge is perfect in itself, but it gives assurance through one's trust, that fulfilment will come), so the soul enamoured of Christ, which has already received in this life the pledge of love for God and its neighbour, is not perfect in itself, but awaits the perfection of the life immortal. I say that this pledge is not perfect--that is, the soul which enjoys it has not yet reached such perfection as not to feel sufferings, in itself or others: in itself, from the wrong it does to God, through the perverse law which is bound into our members; and in others, from the wrong of the neighbour. It is, to be sure, perfect in grace, but it has not the perfection of the saints, who are in the eternal life, as I said; since their desires are free from suffering and ours are not. Dost thou know how it is with the true servant of God, who nourishes him at the table of holy desire? He is blessed and grieving, as was the Son of God upon the wood of the Most Holy Cross: for the flesh of Christ was grieved and tortured, and the soul was blessed, through its union with the Divine Nature. So, through the union of our desire with God, ought we to be blessed, and clothed with His sweet will; and grieving, through compassion for our neighbour, casting from us sensuous joys and comforts and mortifying our flesh.

But listen, daughter and dearest sister. I have spoken to thee and me in general, but now I shall speak to thee and me in particular. I want us to do two special things, in order that ignorance may not hinder our perfection, to which God calls us; that the devil, under cloak of virtue and love of the neighbour, may not nourish the root of presumption within our soul. For from this we shall fall into false judgments; seeming to ourselves to judge aright, we shall judge crookedly: often, if we followed our own impressions, the devil would make us see many truths to lead us into falsehood; and this, because we make ourselves judges of the minds of our fellow-creatures, which are for God alone to judge.

This is one of the two things from which I wish that we should free ourselves completely. But I want the lesson to be learned reasonably. This is the reasonable way: if God expressly, not only once or twice, but more often, reveals the fault of a neighbour to our mind, we ought never to tell it in particular to the person whom it concerns, but to correct in common the vices of all those whom it befalls us to judge, and to implant virtues, tenderly and benignly. Severity in the benignity, as may be needed. And should it seem that God showed us repeatedly the faults of another, yet unless there were, as I said, a special revelation, keep on the safer side, that we may escape the deceit and malice of the devil; for he would catch us with this hook of desire. On thy lips, then, let silence abide, and holy talk of virtues, and disdain of vice. And any vice that it may seem to thee to recognize in others, do thou ascribe at once to them and to thyself, using ever a true humility. If that vice really exists in any such person, he will correct himself better, seeing himself so gently understood, and will say that to thee which thou wouldest have said to him. And thou wilt be safe, and wilt close the way to the devil, who will be unable to deceive us or to hinder the perfection of thy soul. Know that we ought not to trust in any appearances, but to put them behind our backs, and abide only in the perception and knowledge of ourselves. And if it ever happened that we were praying particularly for some fellow- creatures, and in prayer we saw some light of grace in one of those for whom we were praying, and none in another, who was also a servant of God-- but thou didst seem to see him with his mind abased and sterile--do not therefore assume to judge that there is grave fault or lack in him, for it might be that thy opinion was false. For it happens sometimes that when one is praying for the same person, one occasion will find him in such light and holy desire before God that the soul will seem to fatten on his welfare; and on another occasion thou shalt find him when his soul seems so far from God, and full of shadows and temptations, that it is toil to whoso prays for him to hold him in God's presence. This may happen sometimes through a fault of him for whom one is praying, but more often it is due not to a fault, but to God's having withdrawn Himself from this soul--that is, He has withdrawn Himself as to any feeling of sweetness and consolation, though not as to grace. So the soul will have stayed sterile, dry, and full of pain--which God makes that soul which is praying for it perceive. And God does this in mercy to that soul which receives the prayer, that thou mayest aid Him to scatter the cloud. So thou seest, sweet my sister, how ignorant and worthy of rebuke our opinion would be, if simply from these appearances we judged that there was vice in this soul. Therefore, if God showed it to us so troubled and darkened, when we have already seen that it was not deprived of grace, but only of the sweetness of feeling God's presence--I beg thee, then, thee and me and every servant of God, that we apply us to knowing ourselves perfectly, that we may more perfectly know the goodness of God; so that, illumined, we may abandon judging our neighbour, and adopt true compassion, hungering to proclaim virtues and reprove sin in both ourselves and them, in the way we spoke of before.

We have spoken of one thing, but now I tell thee of the other, which I beg that we rebuke in ourselves: if sometimes the devil or our own very evil construction of matters tormented us by making us want to send or see all the servants of God walking in the same way that we are walking in ourselves. For it frequently happens that a soul which sees itself advance by way of great penance, would like to send all people by that same way; and if it sees that they do not walk there, it is displeased and shocked, feeling that they are not doing right: while sometimes it will happen that the man is doing better and being more virtuous than his critic, although he does not do as much penance. For perfection does not consist in macerating or killing the body, but in killing our perverse self-will. And in this way, of the will destroyed, submitted to the sweet Will of God, we ought indeed to desire all men to walk. Good is penance and the maceration of the body; but do not show me these as a rule for every one, since all bodies are not alike, and also since it often happens that a penance begun has to be given up from many accidents that may occur. If, then, we made ourselves or others build on penance as a foundation, it might come to nothing, and be so imperfect that consolation and virtue would fail the soul; for, deprived of the thing which it loved and had made of prime importance, it would seem to be deprived of God, and so would fall into weariness and very great sadness and bitterness, and would lose in the bitterness the activity and fervent prayer to which it was accustomed. So thou seest what evil would follow from making penance alone one's chief concern: we should be ignorant, and should fall into a critical attitude, and become weary and very bitter; we should strive to give only a finished work to God, who is Infinite Good that demands from us infinite desire. We ought, then, to build our foundation on killing and destroying our own perverse will; with that will submitted to the will of God, we shall devote sweet, hungry, infinite desire to the honour of God and the salvation of souls. Thus shall we feed at the table of that holy desire which never takes offence either at itself or at its neighbour, but rejoices and finds fruit in everything. Miserable woman that I am, I mourn that I never followed this true doctrine; nay, I have done the contrary, and therefore I feel that I have often fallen into irritation and a judicial attitude toward my neighbour. Wherefore I pray thee, by the love of Christ Crucified, that for this and for my every other infirmity, healing may be found; so that thou and I may begin to-day to walk in the way of truth, enlightened to build our true foundation on holy desire, and not trusting in appearances and impressions; so that we may not lightly neglect ourselves and judge the faults of our neighbours, unless by way of compassion or general rebuke.

This we shall do if we nourish us at the table of holy desire: otherwise we cannot. For from desire we have light, and light gives us desire; so one nourishes the other. Therefore I said that I desired to see thee in the true light. I say no more. Remain in the holy and sweet grace of God. Sweet Jesus, Jesus Love.

TO MONNA AGNESE WIFE OF FRANCESCO,
A TAILOR OF FLORENCE

In the Name of Jesus Christ crucified and of sweet Mary:

Dearest daughter in Christ sweet Jesus: I Catherine, servant and slave of the servants of Jesus Christ, write to thee in His precious Blood, with desire to see thee clothed in true and perfect humility--for that is a little virtue which makes us great in the sweet sight of God. This is the virtue which constrained and inclined God to make His most sweet Son incarnate in the Womb of Mary. It is as exalted as the proud are humbled; it shines in the sight of God and men; it binds the hands of the wicked, it unites the soul with God, it purifies and laves away the soil of our sin, and calls on God to show us mercy. I will then, sweetest daughter, that thou strive to embrace this glorious virtue, so that thou mayest pass over the stormy sea of this world free from storm and peril.

Now comfort thee in this sweet and sincere virtue, and bathe thee in the Blood of Christ crucified. And when thou canst empty thy time for prayer, I pray thee to do it. And love tenderly every rational being. Then, I beg and command thee not to fast, except, when thou canst, on the days commanded by Holy Church. And when thou dost not feel strong enough to fast then, do not observe them. At other times, do not fast, except when thou feelest able, on Saturday. When this heat is over, fast on the days of Holy Mary, if thou canst, and no more. And drink something beside water every day. Labour hard to increase thy holy desire, and let these other things alone for the future. Do not be anxious or depressed over us, for we are all well. When it shall please the Divine Goodness, we shall see one another again. I say no more to thee. Remain in the holy and sweet grace of God. Comfort my sweet daughters, Ursula and Ginevra. Sweet Jesus, Jesus Love.

LETTERS IN RESPONSE TO CERTAIN CRITICISMS

Catherine had ample opportunity to suffer from those keenly critical instincts of the respectable which she reproved in the last group of letters. Her life was full of eager unconventionalities that drew down on her the frequent distrust of her co-religionists and fellow-townsmen. We cannot tell what special cause had excited the indignation of the loyal friends to whom the following note is written; but we may enjoy the spirit of fresh and pure humility in which Catherine gives them the difficult injunction to acquiesce in any criticism made upon her.

The very matters which were later to be considered as proofs of her sanctity, were during her lifetime grounds of suspicion. Some unknown, exercised in his mind over the reports of her extraordinary abstinence, took evidently what would to-day appear the somewhat impertinent course of writing her a letter of remonstrance. Catherine's inability or reluctance to eat as much as others was one of the most interesting marvels of her life to her simple contemporaries. It is clear, that partly from the extreme mortification which according to mediaeval custom she inflicted on her flesh from childhood, her condition became at an early age thoroughly abnormal. Salads and water were practically her only diet; the curious are referred to the copious details furnished by her biographers. Meantime, the present letter shows how reasonable was her own attitude in the matter. It shows also with what gentle dignity she received criticism. The little touch at the end--"I pray you not to be light in judging, if you are not surely illumined in the sight of God"--is the only hint at a natural impulse of resentment: unless one reads, as it is tempting to do, a delicate irony in the opening portion of the letter.

TO MONNA ORSA WIFE OF BARTOLO USIMBARDI AND TO MONNA AGNESE WIFE OF FRANCESCO DI PIPINO TAILOR OF FLORENCE

In the Name of Jesus Christ crucified and of sweet Mary:Dearest daughter in Christ sweet Jesus: I Catherine, servant and slave of the servants of Jesus Christ, write to you in His precious Blood: with desire to see you persevere in holy desire, so that you may never look back. For otherwise you would not receive your reward, and would transgress the word of the Saviour, which says that we are not to turn back to look at the furrow. Be persevering, then, and contemplate not what is done, but what you have to do. And what have we to do? To turn our affections constantly back toward God, despising the world with all its joys, and loving virtue, bearing with true patience what the divine goodness permits us; considering that whatever He gives is given for our good that we may be sanctified in Him. We shall find in the Blood that the truth is thus. So we ought to fill our memory with this glorious Blood, which shows us so sweet a truth, that we may never be without the recollection of it. Thus I want you to do, dearest daughters: that in this life you shall persevere until death, and at the close of your life shall receive the Eternal Vision of God. I say no more here.

I reprove thee, dearest my sweet daughter, because thou hast not kept in mind what I told thee--not to answer anyone who should say to thee anything about myself that seemed to thee less than good. Now I do not wish thee to do so any more, but I wish both of you to reply to anyone who narrated my faults to you in this wise--that they are not telling so many that a great many more might not be told. Tell them to be moved by compassion within their hearts in the sight of God, as they appear to be by their tongues--and to pray the Divine Goodness earnestly for me, that It will correct my life. Then say to them that it is the Highest Judge who will punish my every fault, and reward every labour that shall be borne for His

Name. As to Monna Paula, I do not wish thee to be in the least indignant with her: but think that she is acting like a good mother, who wants to test her daughter to see whether she has virtue or not. I confess truthfully that I have found little success in myself; but I have hope in my Creator, who will make me correct myself and change my way of life. Comfort you, and give yourselves no more pain; for we shall find ourselves united in the fire of divine Charity, a union that shall be taken from us neither by demon nor by creature. I say no more to you. Remain in the holy and sweet grace of God. Sweet Jesus, Jesus Love.

TO A RELIGIOUS MAN IN FLORENCE WHO WAS SHOCKED AT HER ASCETIC PRACTICES

In the Name of Jesus Christ crucified and of sweet Mary:

Dearest and most beloved father in Christ sweet Jesus: I Catherine, a useless servant of Jesus Christ, commend me to you: with the desire to see us united and transformed in that sweet, eternal and pure Truth which destroys in us all falsity and lying. I thank you cordially, dearest father, for the holy zeal and jealousy which you have toward my soul: in that you are apparently very anxious over what you hear of my life. I am certain that nothing affects you except desire for the honour of God and for my salvation, which makes you fear the assaults and illusions of devils. As to your special fear, father, concerning my behaviour about eating, I am not surprised; for I assure you, that not only do you fear, but I myself tremble, for fear of devilish wiles. Were it not that I trust in the goodness of God, and distrust myself, knowing that in myself I can have no confidence. For you sent, asking me whether or no I believed that I might be deceived, saying that if I did not believe so, that was a wile of the devil. I answer you, that not only about this, which is above the nature of the body, but about all my other activities also, I am always afraid, on account of my frailty and the astuteness of the devil, and think that I may be deceived; for I am perfectly well aware that the devil lost beatitude, but not wisdom, with which wisdom, as I said, I recognized that he might deceive me. But then I turn me, and lean against the Tree of the Most Holy Cross of Christ crucified, and there will I fasten me; and I do not doubt that if I shall be nailed and held with Him by love and with profound humility, the devils will have no power against me--not through my virtue, but through the virtue of Christ crucified.

You sent me word to pray God particularly that I might eat. I tell you, my father, and I say it in the sight of God, that in all ways within my power I have always forced myself once or twice a day to take food. And I have prayed constantly, and do pray God and shall pray Him, that in this matter of eating He will give me grace to live like other creatures, if it is His will--for it is mine. I tell you, that often enough, when I have done what I could, I enter within myself, to recognize my infirmity, and God, who by most special grace has made me correct the sin of gluttony. I grieve much that I have not corrected that miserable fault of mine through love. I for myself do not know what other remedy to adopt, except that I beg you to pray that Highest Eternal Truth, that He give me grace, if it is more for His honour and the salvation of my soul, to enable me to take food if it please Him. And I am sure that the goodness of God will not despise your prayers. I beg you that if you see any remedy you will write me of it; and provided it be for the honour of God, I will accept it willingly. Also I beg you not to be light in judging, if you are not clearly illumined in the sight of God. I say no more to you. Remain in the holy and sweet grace of God. Sweet Jesus, Jesus Love.

TO BROTHER BARTOLOMEO DOMINICI OF THE ORDER OF THE PREACHERS WHEN HE WAS BIBLE READER AT FLORENCE

Belief in the wrath to come is sufficiently real to Catherine, and the current demonology of her day slips readily from her tongue. These things she accepted as she found them. But the atmosphere in which her spirit breathes is the perception of the love of God. The spiritual history of the race, from the creation to the coming of the Spirit and the perpetual support of the soul in the Sacrament of the Altar, is to her a revelation of the One encompassing Love, poured forth in fresh measure and under new forms at each stage in the movement of human destiny.

And so, in this little letter, she invites us to enter with her the "peaceful and profound sea" found in the words "God is Love." Elsewhere, both in her Dialogue and in a letter to one Brother Matteo Tolomei, she analyses with keen insight the relations which redeemed humanity can bear to the Loving God; she tells us how the servant, obedient through fear, may become the friend, obedient through gratitude and desire for spiritual blessings; and how these lower loves, through the operation of the Holy Spirit, may be transformed into the love of the son, who seeks God for His own sake, "with nothing between." And how shall human love, when it has reached this point, reflect the love of Him who "needs not man's work nor His own gifts?" How become, not merely receptive, but active and creative? Catherine gives the simple Christian answer: "God has loved us without being loved, but we love Him because we are loved.... We cannot be of any profit to Him, nor love Him with this first love. Yet God demands of us, that as He has loved us without any second thoughts, so He should be loved by us. In what way can we do this, then, since He demands it of us and we cannot give it to Him? I tell you: through a means which He has established by which we can love Him freely, and without the least regard to any profit of ours: we can be useful, not to Him, which is impossible, but to our neighbour.... To show the love we have to Him, we ought to serve and love every rational creature.... Every virtue receives life from love, and love is gained in love, that is, by raising the eye of our mind to behold how much we are beloved of God. Seeing ourselves loved, we cannot do otherwise than love.... So thou seest that we conceive virtues through God and bring them to the birth for our neighbour."

Thus do Catherine's loftiest meditations end on the practical note. Her fundamental thought, here as elsewhere, is strikingly akin to the thought of St. Bernard. Love yourself not for your own sake, but for God! she constantly repeats. To the same effect, Bernard describes at length the progress of the soul till it reaches the highest stage, in which self-love is so lost that even gratitude is left behind, and man loves himself and God for the sake of God alone.

In the Name of Jesus Christ crucified and of sweet Mary:

To you, most beloved and dear father, through reverence of the most sweet Sacrament, and son in Christ Jesus: I Catherine, servant and slave of the servants of Jesus Christ, write and send comfort in His precious Blood, with desire to see you kindled, on fire, and consumed in His most ardent charity, since I know that he who is on fire and consumed with this charity sees not himself. This, then, I will that you do. I summon you to enter through this most ardent charity, a sea that is peaceful and profound. This I have just now found anew--not that the sea is new, but that it is new to me in the feeling of my soul--in that word, God is Love. And in this word, as the mirror reflects the face of man, and the sun its light upon the earth, so it is reflected in my soul, that all His works whatsoever are Love alone, for they are not wrought of anything save love. Therefore He says, "I God am Love." From this a light is thrown on the unsearchable mystery of the Incarnate Word, who by force of love was given with such humility that it confounds my pride, and teaches us not to regard His works, but the burning devotion of the Word given to us. He says that we should do as he who loves: who, when his friend comes with a present, looks not at the hands for the gift which he brings, but opens the eye of love, and regards his heart and affection. So He wills that we should do, when the Highest eternal goodness of God, sweet above all things, visits our soul. It visits us then with measureless benefits. Let memory act swiftly to receive the intention in the divine charity: and let the will arise with most ardent desire, and receive and behold the sacrificed Heart of sweet and good Jesus the Giver: and thus you shall find you kindled and clothed with fire, and with the gift of the Blood of the Son of God; and you shall be free from all pain and disease. This it was which took away the pain of the holy disciples, when it behoved them to leave Mary and one another, and gladly they endured that separation, to sow the word of God. Run then, run, run.

Concerning the affairs of Benincasa, I cannot reply unless I am at Siena. Thank Messer Nicolao for the charity which he has shown for them. Alessa and I and Cecca, poor women, commend ourselves to you a thousand thousand times. May God be ever in your soul, amen. Jesus, Jesus.

Catherine, servant of the servants of God.

TO BROTHER MATTEO DI FRANCESCO TOLOMEI OF THE ORDER OF THE PREACHERS

In the Name of Jesus Christ crucified and of sweet Mary:

Dearest son in Christ sweet Jesus: I Catherine, servant and slave of the servants of Jesus Christ, write to you in His precious Blood, with desire to see you seek God in truth, not through the intervention of your own fleshliness or of any other creature, for we cannot please God through any intervening means. God gave us the Word, His Only-Begotten Son, without regard to His own profit. This is true, that we cannot be of any profit to Him; but the reverse is not the case, because, although we do not serve God for our profit, nevertheless we profit just the same. To Him belongs the flower of honour, and to us the fruit of profit. He has loved us without being loved, and we love because we are loved: He loves us of grace, and we Him of duty, because we are bound to love Him. We cannot be of any profit to God just as we cannot love Him of grace, without duty. For we are bound to Him, and not He to us, because before He was loved, He loved us, and therefore created us in His Image and Likeness. There it is, then: we cannot be of any profit to Him, nor love Him with this first love. Yet I say that God demands of us, that as He has loved us without any second thoughts, so He should be loved by us. In what way can we do this, then, since He demands it of us, and we cannot give it Him? I tell you: through a means which He has established, by which we can love Him freely, and without the least regard to any profit of ours; that is, we can be useful, not to Him, which is impossible, but to our neighbour. Now by this means we can obey what He demands of us for the glory and praise of His Name; to show the love that we have for Him, we ought to serve and love every rational creature, and extend our charity to good and bad, to every kind of people, as much to one who does us ill service and criticises us as to one who serves us. For God is no respecter of persons, but of holy desires, and His charity extends over just men and sinners.

One man, to be sure, He loves as a son, and one as a friend, and another as a servant, and another as a person who has departed from Him, for whose return He longs--these last are the wicked sinners who are deprived of grace. But wherein does the Highest Father show His love to these? In lending them time, and in time He gives them many opportunities, either to repent of their sins, taking from them place and power to do as much ill as they would, or He has many other ways to make them hate vice and love virtue, the love of which takes away the wish to sin. And so, through the time which God gave them in love, from foes they are made friends, and have grace and are fit to become the Father's heirs.

He loves as sons those who serve Him in truth without any servile fear, who have annulled and killed their self-will, and are through God obedient till death to every rational creature: no mercenaries they, who serve Him for their own profit, but sons; and they despise consolations and joy in tribulations, and seek only in what way they can conform them to Christ crucified, and nourish them on His shames and labours and sorrows. Such men seek not God nor serve Him for sweetness or consolation, spiritual or temporal, which they receive from God or the fellow-creature; they seek not God for their own sakes, nor the neighbour, but God for God, inasmuch as He is worthy of being loved, and themselves for God, for the glory and praise of His Name; and they serve their neighbour for God, being of what profit they may to Him. These men follow the footsteps of the Father, rejoicing wholly in charity toward their neighbour, loving the servants of God through the love with which they love their Creator; and they love imperfect men through love that they should reach perfection, devoting to them holy desire and continual prayers. They love wicked men, who lie in the death of mortal sin, because they are rational beings, created by God, and bought by the same Blood as they, wherefore they mourn over their condemnation, and to rescue them would give themselves to bodily death. As to the persecutors and slanderers and judges who take offence at them, they love these both because they are creatures of God, as I said, and also because they are the means and cause of testing their virtue, and helping them reach perfection--especially as to that royal virtue patience, a sweet virtue, which is never offended or disturbed, nor cast down by any contrary wind or any molesting of men. Such men are those who seek God with nothing between, and love Him truly as dear and lawful sons; and He loves them as a true father, and shows them the secret of His charity, to make them heirs of His eternal kingdom, wherefore they run, refreshed by the Blood of Christ, kindled by the fire of divine charity, by which they are perfectly illumined. Such men do not run in the path of virtue after their own fashion, nay, but after the fashion of Christ crucified, following in His steps. Were it possible for them to serve God and win virtue without labour, they would not wish it. These men do not act like the second kinds of men, the friend and the servant, for the service of these last has some ulterior thought. Sometimes it has regard to the man's own profit; one can reach great friendship in this way, when he knows his need, and his benefactor, who, as he sees, can and will help him. Yet first he was a servant, for he knew his own wrong-doing, on which followed punishment; so from the fear of punishment he drives out his sin, and lovingly embraces virtue, serving his Lord, whom he has wronged; and he begins to draw hope from His benignity, considering that He wills not the death of a sinner, but that he be converted and live. If the man abode in fear alone, it would not suffice to give him life, nor would he attain to the perfect favour of his Lord; but he would be a mercenary servant. Nor ought he to remain only in the love of the fruit and the consolation which he might receive from his Lord, after he has been made a friend; for this kind of love would not be strong, but would fail when it was deprived of sweetness or consolation and joy of mind, or else when some contrary wind struck it, of persecution or temptation from the devil; then at once it would fail under temptations of the devil or vexations of the flesh. So it would fall into confusion through being deprived of mental consolation; and in the persecutions and insults wrought against it by fellow- creatures, it would fall into impatience.

So you see, that this kind of love is not strong. Nay, he who loves with this love does as St. Peter, who before the Passion loved Christ tenderly; but he was not strong, therefore he failed in the time of the Cross: but then, after the coming of the Holy Spirit, he separated him from the love of sweetness, and lost fear, and reached a love strong, and tried in the fire of many tribulations. Thence, having reached the love of a son, he bore all such with true patience--nay, ran under them in great gladness, as he had been going to a marriage feast and not to torment. This was because he had been made a son. But had Peter remained absorbed in the sweetness and the fear which he felt in the Passion and after the Passion of Christ, he would not have reached such perfection as to be a son and champion of Holy Church, a lover and seeker of souls. But note the way that Peter took, and the other disciples, to gain power to lose their servile fear and love of consolations, and to receive the Holy Spirit, as had been promised them by the Sweet Primal Truth. Therefore says the Scripture that they shut them in the house, and stayed there in vigil and continual prayers; they stayed ten days, and then came the Holy Spirit.

Now this is the teaching which we and every rational creature ought to receive; to shut ourselves into the house, and remain in vigil and continual prayer: to stay ten days, and then we shall receive the plenitude of the Holy Spirit. Who, when He was come, illumined them with truth; and they saw the secret of the immeasurable love of the Word, with the will of the Father, who willed naught but our sanctification. This has been shown us by the Blood of that sweet and enamoured Word: who was restored to His disciples, when the plenitude of the Holy Spirit came. He came with the power of the Father, the wisdom of the Son, the mercy and clemency of the Holy Spirit; so the truth of Christ is fulfilled, which He spake to His disciples: I shall go and shall return to you. Then did He return, because the Holy Spirit could not come without the Son and the Father, because He was one thing with them. Thus He came, as I said, with the power that is assigned to the Father, and the wisdom that is assigned to the Son, and the benevolence and love that is assigned to the Holy Spirit. Well did the Apostles show it, for suddenly through love they lost their fear. So in true wisdom they knew the truth, and went with great power against the infidels; they threw idols to the ground and drove out devils. This was not with the power of the world, nor with bodily fortitude, but with strength of spirit and the power of God, which they had received through Divine grace. Now thus it will happen to those who have arisen from the filth of mortal sin and the misery of this world, and begin to taste the Highest Good and enamour themselves of His sweetness. But as I have said, by remaining in fear alone, one would not escape hell; but would do like the thief, who does not steal, because he is afraid of the gallows; but he would not abstain from stealing if he did not expect to be punished. It is just such a case when one loves God for the sweetness of it; that is, one would not be strong and perfect, but weak and imperfect.

The way to arrive at perfection is that of the disciples, as I said. That is, as Peter and the others shut themselves into the house, so those have done and should do who have attained the love of the Father, who are sons. Those who wish to reach this state should enter the house, and shut themselves in; that is, the house of the knowledge of themselves, which is the cell that the soul should inhabit. Within this cell another cell is found, that of the knowledge of the goodness of God in Himself. So from knowledge of self the soul draws true humility, with holy hatred of the wrong which it has done to its Creator, and by this it attains to true and holy patience. And from the knowledge of God, which it finds in itself, it wins the virtue of most ardent charity: whence it draws holy and loving desires. In this wise it finds vigil and continual prayer--that is, while it abides enclosed in so sweet and glorious a thing as is the knowledge of itself and of God. It keeps vigil, I say, not only with the eye of the body, but with the eye of the soul; that is, the eye of the intellect never sees itself closed, but remains opened upon its Object and ineffable Love, Christ crucified: and there it finds love, and its own guilt. For that guilt, Christ gave us His Blood. Then the soul uplifts itself with deepest devotion, to love what God loves and to hate what He hates. And it directs all its works in God, and does everything to the glory and praise of His Name. This is the continual prayer of which Paul says, "Pray without ceasing." Now this is the way to rise from being only a servant and a friend--that is, from servile fear and from tender love of one's own consolation--and to arrive at being a true servant, true friend, true son. For when one is truly made a son, he does not therefore lose being a servant and true friend; but is a servant and friend in truth, without any regard to himself, or to anything except pleasing God alone.

We said that they abode ten days, and then came the Holy Spirit. So the soul, which wishes to arrive at this perfection, must observe ten days, that is the ten commandments of the law. And with the legal commandments it will observe the Counsels; for they are bound together, and the one cannot be observed without the other. True, those who are in the world must observe the Counsels mentally, through holy desire, and those who are freed from the world must observe them both mentally and actually. Thus, if the soul receives the abundance of the Holy Spirit, with true wisdom of true and perfect light and knowledge, and with fortitude and power to make it strong in every battle, it becomes mighty chiefly against itself, lording it over its own fleshly nature. But all this you could not do if you went roaming about, in much conversation, keeping far from the cell, and neglecting the choir. Whence, considering this, I said to you when you left me that you should study to flee conversation and to visit the cell, and not to abandon the choir or the refectory (so far as might be possible to you), and to keep vigil with humble prayer: and thus to fulfil my desire, when I told you that I desired to see you seek God in truth, without anything between. I say no more to you. Remain in the holy and sweet grace of God. Sweet Jesus, Jesus Love.

TO A MANTELLATA OF SAINT DOMINIC CALLED CATARINA DI SCETTO

In the Name of Jesus Christ crucified and of sweet Mary:

My dearest sister and daughter in Christ sweet Jesus. I Catherine, servant and slave of the servants of Jesus Christ, write to thee in His precious Blood, with desire to see thee a true servant and bride of Christ crucified. Servants we ought to be, because we are bought with His blood. But I do not see that we can be of any profit to Him by our service; we ought, then, to be of profit to our neighbour, because he is the means by which we test and gain virtue. Thou knowest that every virtue receives life from love; and love is gained in love, that is, by raising the eye of our mind to behold how much we are beloved of God. Seeing ourselves loved, we cannot do otherwise than love; loving Him, we shall embrace virtue through the force of love, and shall hate vice and spurn it.

So thou seest that we conceive virtues through God, and bring them to the birth for our neighbour. Thou knowest well that for the necessity of thy neighbour thou bringest forth the child charity that is within thy soul, and patience in the wrongs which thou receivest from him. Thou givest him prayer, particularly to those who have done thee wrong. And thus we ought to do; if men are untrue to us, we ought to be true to them, and faithfully to seek their salvation; loving them of grace, and not by barter. That is, do thou beware not to love thy neighbour for thine own profit; for that would not be faithful love, and thou wouldst not respond to the love which God bears thee. For as God has loved thee of grace, so He wills that since thou canst not return this love to Him, thou return it to thy neighbour, loving him of grace and not by barter, as I said. Neither if thou art wronged, nor if thou shouldst see love toward thee, or thy joy or profit lessened, must thou lessen or stint love toward thy neighbour; but love him tenderly, bearing and enduring his faults; and beholding with great consolation and reverence the servants of God.

Beware lest thou do like mad and foolish people who want to set themselves to investigate and judge the deeds and habits of the servants of God. He who does this is entirely worthy of severe rebuke. Know that it would not be different from setting a law and rule to the Holy Spirit if we wished to make the servants of God all walk in our own way--a thing which could never be done. Let the soul inclined to this kind of judgment think that the root of pride is not yet out, nor true charity toward the neighbour planted--that is, the loving him by grace and not by barter. Then let us love the servants of God, and not judge them. Nay, it befits us to love in general every rational creature: those who are outside of grace we must love with grief and bitterness over their fault, because they wrong God and their own soul. Thus thou shalt be in accord with that sweet enamoured Paul, who mourns with those who mourn, and joys with those who joy; thus thou shalt mourn with those who are in mournful state, through desire for the honour of God and for their salvation; and thou shalt joy with the servants of God who rejoice, possessing God through loving tenderness.

Thou seest, then, that through charity to God we conceive virtues, and through charity toward our neighbours they are brought to the birth. Being thus--loving thy neighbour sincerely, without any falsity of love or heart, freely, without any regard to thine own profit, spiritual or temporal--thou shalt be a true servant, and respond by means of thy neighbour to the love which thy Creator bears thee; thou shalt be a faithful, not a faithless bride. Then does the bride fail in faith to her bridegroom, when she gives to another creature the faith which she ought to give to him. Thou art a bride, for Christ in His circumcision showed that He would wed the human race. Thou, beholding love so ineffable, shouldst love Him without any means that might be apart from God. Thus art thou made the servant of thy neighbour, serving him in all things to the measure of thy power. Verily thou art the bride of Christ, and shouldst be the servant of thy neighbour. If thou art a faithful bride, since we can neither be of profit nor of service to God by the love which we bear Him, we ought, as I said, to serve our neighbour with true and heartfelt love. In no other way nor wise can we serve Him. Therefore I said to thee that I desired to see thee the true servant and bride of Christ crucified. I say no more. Remain in the holy and sweet grace of God. Sweet Jesus, Jesus Love.

LETTERS TO NERI DI LANDOCCIO DEI PAGLIARESI

Neri di Landoccio dei Pagliaresi is one of the attractive group of Catherine's secretaries, which included also Stefano Maconi and Barduccio Canigiani. There is something very charming, wholly Italian and mediaeval, in the thought of the three highly-born and gently-bred young Tuscans, who, without leaving the world or taking religious vows, attached themselves with a pure and passionate devotion to the person of the Beata Populana, dedicated their time and powers to her service, caught the fire of her ideals, and after her death followed her wishes for their future. The faces that appear a little later in such pictures as Botticelli's "Adoration of the Magi," help us to understand the type of these young men.

Of the three secretaries, Neri was the first to enter Catherine's service. It was he who introduced to her most of the people who later became her disciples, and many letters yet extant from one and another show that he was devotedly loved by the little group. He was of a sensitive, subtle, and despondent temperament--a reader of Dante, himself a poet, a man given to self-torment, and, as his later life showed, with a tendency to melancholia. He must have possessed tact, force, and probably charm, for Catherine more than once sent him on important embassies-- once as harbinger of her own coming to Pope Gregory at Avignon, and again, at a later time, to the corrupt and brilliant court of Queen Giovanna at Naples. In obedience to the dying wish of his spiritual mother--who probably well understood his needs--he became a hermit after her death.

Catherine writes to this fine but fearful soul with an exquisite tenderness. "Confusion of mind," with its inhibiting sadness and helplessness, is of all evils in the world the one most abhorrent to her clear, decisive, intuitive nature. Against this, his besetting danger, she seeks with all her customary vigour to protect her beloved disciple. The love rather than the wrath of God was, as we have seen, ever the chief burden of Catherine's teaching. Never did she dwell on it more earnestly than here, as with searching insight into the unfathomable depths of the Divine mercy, she writes firmly: "His truth is this, that He created us to give us life eternal." Her words must have brought reassurance to any darkened vision, while her practical counsels were never more adapted to individual need than in these peculiarly gentle letters, written to one whose temptations and spiritual perils were far different from her own.

In the Name of Jesus Christ crucified and of sweet Mary:

Dearest son in Christ sweet Jesus. I Catherine, servant and slave of the servants of Jesus Christ, write to thee in His precious Blood: with desire to see thee in the true light, that in the light may be known the truth of thy Creator. His truth is this, that He created us to give us life eternal. But because man rebelled against God, this truth was not fulfilled, and therefore He descended to the greatest depths to which descent is possible, when Deity assumed the vesture of our humanity. So we see in this glorious light that God has been made man, and this He has done to fulfil His truth in us: and He has shown this to us verily by the Blood of the Loving Word, inasmuch that what we held by faith is proved to us with the price of that Blood. The creature that has reason in itself cannot deny that this is so.

I will, then, that thy confusion be consumed and vanish in the hope of the Blood, and in the fire of the immeasurable Love of God; and that nothing remain but the true knowledge of thyself, in which thou shalt humble thee and grow, and nourish light in thy soul. Is not He more ready to pardon than we to sin? And is not He the Physician and we the sick, the Bearer of our iniquities? And does not He hold confusion of mind as worse than all other faults? Yes, truly. Then, dearest son, open the eye of thine intellect in the light of most holy faith, and behold how much thou art beloved of God. And from beholding His love, and the ignorance and coldness of thy heart, do not fall into confusion; but let the flame of holy desire increase, with true knowledge and humility, as I said. And the more thou seest that thou hast not responded to such great favours as thy Creator has shown thee, humble thyself the more, and say with holy resolution: "What I have not done to-day, I will do now." Thou knowest that confusion is wholly discordant with the doctrine which has always been given thee. It is a leprosy that dries up soul and body, and holds them in continual affliction, and binds the arms of holy desire, and does not let one do what one would; and it makes the soul unendurable to itself, disposing the mind to conflicts and varying fantasies; it robs the soul of supernatural light, and darkens its natural light. So one falls into great faithlessness, because one does not know the truth of God, in which He has created us--that is, that He created us in truth to give us life eternal. Then with living faith, with holy desire, and with hope in the Blood of Christ, let the devil of confusion be defeated.

I say no more. Remain in the holy and sweet grace of God. I pray Him to give thee His sweet benediction. Sweet Jesus, Jesus Love.

In the Name of Jesus Christ crucified and of sweet Mary:

Dearest and sweetest son in Christ sweet Jesus. I Catherine, servant and slave of the servants of Jesus Christ, write to thee in His precious Blood: with desire to see in thee the light of most holy faith, in order that thou mayest never be shocked by anything that may happen to thee; but may thy mind be pacified concerning all the mysteries of God, as thou beholdest the ineffable love which moved Him to draw forth from Himself reasonable creatures, and to give us His image and likeness, and to buy us with the Blood of the humble and spotless Lamb. Thus doing, thou wilt hold all that happens to thee in due reverence, and in true humility thou wilt deny mere appearances, when sometimes through the illusion of the devil things seem to thee to get out of their right proportion, through thy many mental occupations and sweet physical torments. I say no more. Remain in the holy and sweet grace of God. May Christ the Blessed give thee His eternal benediction. Sweet Jesus, Jesus Love.

In the Name of Jesus Christ crucified and of sweet Mary:

Dearest and sweetest son in Christ sweet Jesus. I Catherine, servant and slave of the servants of Jesus Christ, write to thee in His precious Blood: with desire to see thee ever grow from virtue to virtue, till I behold thee return to that sea of peace where thou shalt never have any fear of being separated from God. For the foul perverse law that fights against the Spirit shall be left on earth, and shall have rendered its due thereto. I will, sweet my son, that while thou livest in this life thou exert thee to live dead to all self-will, and in such death thou shalt win virtue. Thus living, thou shalt resign to earth the law of perverse desire. So thou shalt not fear lest God permit in thy case what He permitted in that other, nor shalt thou suffer, because for a little while the human part of thee is separated from me and from the rest of the family. Comfort thee, and may that which Truth says abide in thy mind--

that not one person shall be lost out of His hands. I say out of His hands, because all things are His. And I know that thou understandest me without many words. I say no more. Remain in the holy and sweet grace of God. Sweet Jesus, Jesus Love.

TO MONNA GIOVANNA AND HER
OTHER DAUGHTERS IN SIENA

Teach us, O Lord, and enable us to live the life of saints and angels!" cried Cardinal Newman. There is a lovely parallel to Catherine's prayer in the Paternoster of Dante's blessed souls in Purgatory: "Come del suo voler gli angeli tuoi   Fan sacrificio a te, cantando osanna,   Cosi facciano gli uomini de' suoi." From the gentle thoughts on non-resistance with which this letter opens, Catherine turns with transition as fine as sudden to the splendid figure of the holy soul as a horse without bridle, running most swiftly "from grace to grace, from virtue to virtue." One is accustomed by Plato--not to speak of Browning in "The Two Poets of Croisic"--to the image of the soul as a charioteer. Catherine's metaphor is less familiar but not less forceful. The will, to her, is only free when pure: impure and sinful desires, far from being the sign of liberty, are the bit and bridle that hinder its fiery course toward God. The same thought, less vividly put, is found in a modern theologian--Dr. Moberly. "The real consummation of either moral or immoral character," he writes, "would exclude the ambiguity which was offered as the criterion of free will.... Full power to sin is not the key to freedom. On the contrary, all inherent power to do wrong is a direct infringement of the reality of free-will.... Free- will is not the independence of the creature, but rather his self- realisation in perfect dependence. Freedom is self-identity with goodness."

In the Name of Jesus Christ crucified and of sweet Mary:

Dearest and most beloved daughters in Christ sweet Jesus: I Catherine, servant and slave of the servants of Jesus Christ, and your mother in Christ, write to you and comfort you in the Precious Blood of the Son of God, who was a gentle Lamb, spotless and slain not by power of nails or lance, but by power of love and measureless charity which He felt and still feels to His creatures. Oh, charity unspeakable of our God! Thou hast taught me, Love most sweet, and hast shown me, not by words alone-- for Thou sayest that Thou dost not delight in many words--but by deeds, in which Thou sayest that Thou dost delight, and which Thou dost demand from Thy servants. And what hast Thou taught me, O Love Uncreate? Thou hast taught me that I should bear, patiently like a lamb, not only harsh words, but even blows harsh and hard and injury and loss. And with this Thou dost will that I be innocent and spotless, harmful to no one of my neighbours and brethren; not only in case of those who do not persecute us, but in that of those who injure us; Thou dost will that we pray for them as for special friends who give us a good and great gain. And Thou dost will that we be patient and meek not only in injuries and temporal losses, but universally, in everything that may be contrary to my will: as Thou didst not will Thine own will to be done in anything, but the will of Thy Father. How then shall we lift up our head against the goodness of God, wishing that our perverted wills should be fulfilled? How shall we not will that the will of God be fulfilled?

O Jesus, Most Sweet Love, make Thy will to be fulfilled in us ever, as in Heaven by Thy Angels and saints! Dearest my daughter in Christ, this is the meekness which our sweet Saviour wants to find in us: that we, with hearts wholly peaceful and tranquil, be content with everything which He plans and does concerning us, and wish neither times nor seasons in our own way, but in His alone. Then the soul, so divested of its every wish and clothed with the will of God, is very pleasing to God. Like an unbridled horse, it runs most swiftly from grace to grace, from virtue to virtue; for it has no bridle that holds or prevents it from running, since it has severed from itself every inordinate appetite and impulse of its own self-will, which are bands and bridles that do not allow the souls of spiritual men to run.

The affairs of the Crusade are going constantly better and better, and the honour of God is increasing every day. Increase constantly in virtue, and furnish the ship of your soul, for our time draws near. Comfort and bless Francesca, from Jesus Christ and me; and tell her to be zealous that I may find her increased in virtue when I shall return. Bless and comfort all my sons in Christ. Now this very day the ambassador of the Queen of Cyprus came and talked to me. He is going to the Holy Father, Christ on earth, to urge him concerning the affairs of the holy Crusade. And, moreover, the Holy Father has sent to Genoa to urge them concerning the same thing.

Our sweet Saviour give you His eternal benediction! Remain in the holy and sweet grace of God. Sweet Jesus, Jesus Love.

TO MESSER JOHN THE SOLDIER OF FORTUNE AND HEAD OF THE COMPANY THAT CAME IN THE TIME OF FAMINE

Which letter is one of credentials, certifying that he may put faith in all things said to him by Fra Raimondo of Capua. Wherefore the said Fra Raimondo went to the said Messer John, and the other captains, to induce them to go over and fight against the infidels should it happen that others should go. And before leaving he had from them and from Messer John a promise on the sacrament that they would go, and they signed it with their hands and sealed it with their seals.

So runs the old heading to this letter. It is piquant to contemplate Catherine writing to that picturesque gentleman, Sir John Hawkwood. Her attitude of friendly and almost sisterly sympathy with the audacious free- lance appears in her unwonted addition of the word "glory" to her usual formula, "The honour of God and the salvation of souls," in the last sentence. We are told that the letter and Fra Raimondo produced a real impression, and that Hawkwood not only vowed himself to the Crusade, but that, no Crusade occurring, he from this time bore arms only in regular warfare. He who follows the Englishman's subsequent career may perhaps wonder a little what "regular warfare" meant to his mind. Yet let us remember to his credit that Hawkwood protested against the massacre of Cesena--nor was this the only occasion on which his nature flashed for a moment a chivalrous light. May his bones rest in peace in the Duomo of Florence, that city to the gates of which he brought terror and dismay, but which bore him no grudge, and at the end decreed him splendid funerals, and sepulchre among her honoured sons!

In the Name of Jesus Christ crucified and of sweet Mary:

To you, most beloved and dear brothers in Christ Jesus: I Catherine, servant and slave of the servants of Jesus Christ, write in His precious Blood: with desire to see you a true son and knight of Christ, in such wise that you may desire to give your life a thousand times, if need were, in service of sweet and good Jesus. This is a gift which would pay off all our sins, which we have committed against our Saviour. Dearest and sweetest brother in Christ Jesus, it would be a great thing now if you would withdraw a little into yourself, and consider, and reflect how great are the pains and anguish which you have endured by being in the service and pay of the devil. Now my soul desires that you should change your way of life, and take the pay and the cross of Christ crucified, you and all your followers and companions; so that you may be Christ's company, to march against the infidel dogs who possess our Holy Place, where rested the Sweet Primal Truth and bore death and pains for us. I beg you, then, gently in Christ Jesus, that since God and also our Holy Father have ordered a crusade against the infidels, and you take such pleasure in war and fighting, you should not make war against Christians any more--for this is a wrong to God; but go against the infidels! For it is a great cruelty that we who are Christians, and members bound in the Body of Holy Church, should persecute one another. We are not to do so; but to rise with perfect zeal, and to uplift ourselves above every evil thought.

I marvel much that you, having, as I heard, promised to be willing to go to die for Christ in this holy crusade, are wanting to make war in these parts. This is not that holy disposition which God demands from you if you are to go to so holy and venerable a place. It seems to me that you ought now, at this present time, to dispose you to virtue, until the time shall come for us and the others who shall be ready to give their lives for Christ: and thus you shall show that you are a manly and true knight.

There is coming to you this father and son of mine, Brother Raimondo, who brings you this letter. Trust in what he tells you; because he is a true, faithful servant of God, and will advise you and say to you nothing except what will be to the honour of God and the safety and glory of your soul. I say no more. I beg you, dearest brother, to keep in memory the shortness of your time. Remain in the holy and sweet grace of God. Sweet Jesus, Jesus Love.

TO MONNA COLOMBA IN LUCCA

Let us hope that the frivolous Monna Colomba listened to Catherine's gentle but very explicit exhortations and turned away from her levities. If she had a sense of humour--and it is a not uncommon possession of light-minded elderly widows--she must have been lovingly entertained at the pale virgin's identification of herself with those who "walk in the way of luxuries and pleasures," and "set themselves up as an example of sin and vanity." But Catherine's use of the first person in this connection, strained though it may appear, is more than a figure of speech, to soften the severity of her rebuke. We learn from the legend that till the end of her life she never ceased to repent, bitterly and with tears, for having at the age of twelve allowed an older sister to dress her prettily, and blanch her hair after the fashion of the day. The reason for this terrible lapse, as she told her confessor, was simply a delight in beautiful things--but she always looked back on it with horror.

The application of the finding of Christ in the Temple, in this letter, is curious, but not devoid of grace.

In the Name of Jesus Christ crucified and of sweet Mary:

To you, dearest sister and daughter in Christ sweet Jesus: I Catherine, servant and slave of the servants of Jesus Christ, write in His precious Blood, with desire that I might see you a fruitful field, receiving the seed of the Word of God, and bringing forth fruit for yourself and others. I want to see you, who are now getting to be an old woman, and who are free from worldly ties, a mirror of virtue to younger women, who are still bound to the world by the tie of their husbands.

Alas, alas, I perceive that we are unfruitful ground, for we are letting the Word of God be smothered by the inordinate affections and desires of the world, and are walking in the way of its luxuries and pleasures, studying to please our fellow-beings rather than our Creator. And there is a more wretched thing yet, for our own evil-doing is not enough for us; where we ought to be an example of virtue and modesty, we set ourselves up as an example of sin and vanity. And as the devil was not willing to fall alone, but wanted a large company with him, so we are enticing other people to those same vanities and amusements that we indulge in ourselves. You ought to withdraw, by love of virtue and your salvation, from vain diversions and worldly weddings--for they do not suit your condition--and try to keep others away, who would like to be there. But you talk bad talk, and entice young women, who are wanting to withdraw from going to these things through love of virtue, because they see that it is wronging God. I do not wonder, then, if no fruit appears, since the seed is smothered as I said. Perhaps you would find some excuse in saying, "Still, I have to condescend to my friends and relatives by doing this, so that they will not be annoyed and irritated with me." So fear and perverted self-indulgence sap our life, and often kill us; rob us of the perfection to which God chose and calls us. This excuse is not acceptable to God; for we ought not to condescend to people in a matter which wrongs God and our own soul; nor to love or serve them, except in those matters which come from God and befit our condition.

Oh me, miserable! Was it our relatives or friends or any fellow-being who bought us? No; Christ crucified alone was the Lamb who with love unsearchable sacrificed His Body, making Him our Purification and Healing, our Food and Raiment, and the Bed where we can rest. He had no regard to love of self nor fleshly joy, but abased Himself in pain, enduring shames and insults, seeking the honour of the Father and our salvation. It ill befits that we poor miserable men should hold by another way than that held by the Sweet Primal Truth.

You know that God is not found in luxuries and pleasures. We perceive that when Our Saviour was lost in the Temple, going to the Feast, Mary could not find Him among friends or relatives, but found Him in the Temple disputing with the doctors. And this He did to give us an example--for He is our Rule, and the Way we should follow. Notice that it says that He was lost when going to the Feast. Know, most beloved sister, that, as was said, God is not found at feasts or balls or games or weddings or places of recreation. Nay, going there is a very sure means of losing Him, and falling into many sins and faults, and inordinate frivolous self- indulgence. Since this is the reason that has made us lose God by grace, is there any way to find Him again? Yes; to accompany Mary. Let us seek Him with her, in bitterness and pain and distaste for the fault committed against our Creator, to condescend to the will of men. It befits us then to go to the Temple, and there He is found. Let our hearts, our minds, and desires be lifted up with this Company of Bitterness, and let us go to the Temple of our soul, and there we shall know ourselves. Then the soul, recognizing itself not to be, will recognize the goodness of God towards it, who is He who is. Then the will shall be uplifted with zeal, and shall love what God loves and hate what God hates. Then, as it enters into reason with itself, it will rebuke the memory which has held in itself the gaieties and pleasures of the world, and has nor held nor retained the favours and gifts and great benefits of God, who has given Himself to us with so great fire of love. It will rebuke the mind, which has given itself to understand the will of fellow-creatures, and the shows and observances of the world, rather than the will of its Creator, and therefore will and fleshly love have turned them to love and desire those gross things of sense, which pass like the wind. The soul should not do thus, but should note and know the will of God, which seeks and wants naught but our sanctification, and has therefore given us life.

God has not set you free from the world, for you are smothered and drowned in the world by your affections and inordinate desires. Now, have you more than one soul? No. If you had two, you might give one to God and the other to the world. Nor have you more than one body, and this gets tired over every little thing.

Be a dispenser to the poor of your temporal substance. Submit you to the yoke of holy and true obedience. Kill, kill your own will, that it may not be so tied to your relatives, and mortify your body, and do not so pamper it in delicate ways. Despise yourself, and have in regard neither rank nor riches, for virtue is the only thing that makes us gentlefolk, and the riches of this life are the worst of poverty when possessed with inordinate love apart from God. Recall to memory what the glorious Jerome said about this, which one can never repeat often enough, forbidding that widows should abound in daintiness, or keep their face anointed, or their garments choice or delicate. Nor should their conversation be with vain or dissolute young women, but in the cell: they should do like the turtle-dove, who, when her companion has died, mourns for ever, and keeps to herself, and wants no other company. Limit your intercourse, dearest and most beloved Sister, to Christ crucified; set your affection and desire on following Him by the way of shame and true humility, in gentleness, binding you to the Lamb with the bands of charity.

This my soul desires, that you may be a true daughter, and a bride consecrated to Christ, and a fruitful field, not sterile, but full of the sweet fruits of true virtues. Hasten, hasten, for time is short and the road is long. And if you gave all you have in the world, time would not pause for you from running its course. I say no more. Remain in the holy and sweet grace of God. Pardon me if I have said too many words, for the love and zeal that I have for your salvation have made me say them. Know that I would far rather do something for you than merely talk. May God fill you with His most sweet Favour. Sweet Jesus, Jesus Love.

TO BROTHER RAIMONDO OF CAPUA OF THE ORDER OF THE PREACHERS

The following is one of the famous letters of the world. The record in art and literature of the scene which it depicts has carried knowledge of Catherine to many who otherwise would have but the vaguest idea of her personality. The letter has been frequently translated, but most of the translators have avoided the opening and closing paragraphs, with their amazing, confused, and to our modern taste almost shocking metaphors. Surely, however, we want the whole just as Catherine poured it out; full of intense excitement, her emotions clearer than her ideas, lifted into a region where taste and logic have no meaning, and using, to convey the inexpressible feelings quickened by the events she describes, homeliest figures of speech, such as her commercial surroundings naturally suggest to her. For the matter of that, modern congregations sing with no distress:

"Jesus let me still abide   In Thy heart and Wounded Side."

The reiteration of the figure of the Blood is here psychologically inevitable. Catherine writes still quivering from close contact with the victim of a mediaeval execution.

A young gentleman from Perugia, Niccolo Tuldo by name, had been condemned to death for speaking critically of the Sienese Government. It does not appear that he was a serious political conspirator, but simply a young man whose aristocratic sympathies led him thoughtlessly to the use of haughty or bitter speech. But a *parvenu* Government is always sensitive. We hear of a man at this time being condemned and executed because he had not invited one of the Riformatori to a feast!

Death was lightly inflicted in those days: probably it was no more lightly suffered than in our own. We have vivid accounts of the incredulity with which Niccolo Tuldo received his sentence--incredulity leading to horror, to rage, to rebellion, to black despair. Then Catherine went to him; her own words tell the rest. As one reads of the wonderful effect of her soothing presence, as one sees the terrified youth becoming quiet and subdued, clinging wistfully to the spiritual strength of this frail woman, and catching at the end not only her spirit of calm submission, but even something of her exaltation, one is irresistibly reminded of another scene--George Eliot's marvellous description in "Adam Bede" of Dinah's ministry to Hetty in the prison. But this scene is real, that only imagined; and here no third person, but the consoler herself, reveals the meaning of the experience to her own spirit.

In bringing Niccolo Tuldo to so illumined an end that he recognized the judgment-place as holy, and died in full accord with the will of God, Catherine achieved a great marvel which only Christianity can compass: she lifted one of those seemingly purposeless and cruel accidents of destiny which stagger faith, into unity with the organic work of the world's redemption.

In the Name of Jesus Christ crucified and of sweet Mary:

Most beloved and dearest father and dear my son in Christ Jesus: I Catherine, servant and slave of the servants of Jesus Christ, write to you, commending myself to you in the precious Blood of the Son of God; with desire to see you inflamed and drowned in that His sweetest Blood, which is blended with the fire of His most ardent charity. This my soul desires, to see you therein, you and Nanni and Jacopo my son. I see no other remedy by which we may reach those chief virtues which are necessary to us. Sweetest father, your soul, which has made itself food for me--(and no moment of time passes that I do not receive this food at the table of the sweet Lamb slain with such ardent love)--your soul, I say, would not attain the little virtue, true humility, were it not drowned in the Blood. This virtue shall be born from hate, and hate from love. Thus the soul is born with very perfect purity, as iron issues purified from the furnace.

I will, then, that you lock you in the open side of the Son of God, which is an open treasure-house, full of fragrance, even so that sin itself there becomes fragrant. There rests the sweet Bride on the bed of fire and blood. There is seen and shown the secret of the heart of the Son of God. Oh, flowing Source, which givest to drink and excitest every loving desire, and givest gladness, and enlightenest every mind and fillest every memory which fixes itself thereon! so that naught else can be held or meant or loved, save this sweet and good Jesus! Blood and fire, immeasurable

Love! Since my soul shall be blessed in seeing you thus drowned, I will that you do as he who draws up water with a bucket, and pours it over something else; thus do you pour the water of holy desire on the head of your brothers, who are our members, bound to us in the body of the sweet Bride. And beware, lest through illusion of the devils--who I know have given you trouble, and will give you--or through the saying of some fellow-creature, you should ever draw back: but persevere always in the hour when things look most cold, until we may see blood shed with sweet and enamoured desires.

Up, up, sweetest my father! and let us sleep no more! For I hear such news that I wish no more bed of repose or worldly state. I have just received a Head in my hands, which was to me of such sweetness as heart cannot think, nor tongue say, nor eye see, nor the ears hear. The will of God went on through the other mysteries wrought before; of which I do not tell, for it would be too long. I went to visit him whom you know: whence he received such comfort and consolation that he confessed, and prepared himself very well. And he made me promise by the love of God that when the time of the sentence should come, I would be with him. So I promised, and did. Then in the morning, before the bell rang, I went to him: and he received great consolation. I led him to hear Mass, and he received the Holy Communion, which he had never before received. His will was accorded and submitted to the will of God; and only one fear was left, that of not being strong at the moment. But the measureless and glowing goodness of God deceived him, creating in him such affection and love in the desire of God that he did not know how to abide without Him, and said: "Stay with me, and do not abandon me. So it shall not be otherwise than well with me. And I die content." And he held his head upon my breast. I heard then the rejoicing, and breathed the fragrance of his blood; and it was not without the fragrance of mine, which I desire to shed for the sweet Bridegroom Jesus. And, desire waxing in my soul, feeling his fear, I said: "Comfort thee, sweet my brother; since we shall soon arrive at the Wedding Feast. Thou shalt go there bathed in the sweet Blood of the Son of God, with the sweet Name of Jesus, which I will never to leave thy memory. And I await thee at the place of justice." Now think, father and son, his heart then lost all fear, and his face changed from sorrow to gladness; and he rejoiced, he exulted, and said: "Whence comes such grace to me, that the sweetness of my soul will await me at the holy place of justice?" See, that he had come to so much light that he called the place of justice holy! And he said: "I shall go wholly joyous, and strong, and it will seem to me a thousand years before I arrive, thinking that you are awaiting me there." And he said words so sweet as to break one's heart, of the goodness of God.

I waited for him then at the place of justice; and waited there with constant prayer, in the presence of Mary and of Catherine, Virgin and martyr. But before I attained, I prostrated me, and stretched my neck upon the block; but my desire did not come there, for I had too full consciousness of myself. Then up! I prayed, I constrained her, I cried "Mary!" for I wished this grace, that at the moment of death she should give him a light and a peace in his heart, and then I should see him reach his goal. Then my soul became so full that although a multitude of people were there, I could see no human creature, for the sweet promise made to me.

Then he came, like a gentle lamb; and seeing me, he began to smile, and wanted me to make the sign of the Cross. When he had received the sign, I said: "Down! To the Bridal, sweetest my brother! For soon shalt thou be in the enduring life." He prostrated him with great gentleness, and I stretched out his neck; and bowed me down, and recalled to him the Blood of the Lamb. His lips said naught save Jesus! and, Catherine! And so saying, I received his head in my hands, closing my eyes in the Divine Goodness, and saying, "I will!"

Then was seen God-and-Man, as might the clearness of the sun be seen. And He stood wounded, and received the blood; in that blood a fire of holy desire, given and hidden in the soul by grace. He received it in the fire of His divine charity. When He had received his blood and his desire, He also received his soul, which He put into the open treasure-house of His Side, full of mercy; the primal Truth showing that by grace and mercy alone He received it, and not for any other work. Oh, how sweet and unspeakable it was to see the goodness of God! with what sweetness and love He awaited that soul departed from the body! He turned the eye of mercy toward her, when she came to enter within His Side, bathed in blood which availed through the Blood of the Son of God. Thus received by God through power--powerful is He to do! the Son also, Wisdom the Word Incarnate, gave him and made him share the crucified love with which He received painful and shameful death through the obedience which he showed to the Father, for the good of the human race. And the hands of the Holy Spirit locked him within.

But he made a gesture sweet enough to draw a thousand hearts. And I do not wonder, for already he tasted the divine sweetness. He turned as does the Bride when she has reached the threshold of her bridegroom, who turns back her head and her look, bowing to those who have accompanied her, and with the gesture she gives signs of thanks.

When he was at rest, my soul rested in peace and in quiet, in so great fragrance of blood that I could not bear to remove the blood which had fallen on me from him.

Ah me, miserable! I will say no more. I stayed on the earth with the greatest envy. And it seems to me that the first new stone is already in place. Therefore do not wonder if I impose upon you nothing save to see yourselves drowned in the blood and flame poured from the side of the Son of God. Now then, no more negligence, sweetest my sons, since the blood is beginning to flow, and to receive the life. Sweet Jesus, Jesus Love.

TO GREGORY XI

This is the first letter to Gregory which has come down to us; it may or may not have been the first which Catherine wrote him. That she had had relations with him earlier seems fairly certain. As early as 1372 we find her writing to Gerard du Puy, a relative of the Pope and Papal Legate in Tuscany. This letter is evidently a reply, and contains passages which she apparently expected du Puy to share with Gregory. Perhaps Gregory had made approaches to her through his cousin. There was nothing unlikely at that time in such action on the part of a great churchman, who, man of the world though he was, retained a sincere reverence for humble men and women.

Be this as it may, Catherine in her letter to Gerard du Puy writes concerning the condition of the Church in the strain of indignant sorrow which she was to hold till her death: "In reply to the first of the three things you ask me, I will say that I believe that our sweet Christ on earth should do away entirely with two things which ravage the Bride of Christ. The first is the over-great tenderness and care for relatives, which ought to be entirely mortified. The other is that over-great good nature which is founded on too great mercy.... Christ holds three vices as especially evil--impurity, avarice, and swollen pride, which reign in the Bride of Christ among the prelates, who care for nothing but luxuries and honours and vast riches. A strong justice is needed to correct them, for too great pity is the greatest cruelty. As to the other question, I say: When I told you that you should toil for Holy Church, I was not thinking only of the labours you should assume about temporal things, but chiefly that you and the Holy Father ought to toil and do what you can to get rid of the wolfish shepherds who care for nothing but eating and fine palaces and big horses. Oh me, that which Christ won upon the wood of the Cross is spent with harlots! I beg that if you were to die for it, you tell the Holy Father to put an end to such iniquities. And when the time comes to make priests or cardinals, let them not be chosen through flatteries or moneys or simony; but beg him, as far as you can, that he notice well if virtue and a good and holy fame are found in the man; and let him not prefer a gentleman to a tradesman, for virtue is the thing that makes a man gentle." Savonarola could hardly say more.

This present letter must date from 1375, for the rebellion of the Tuscan cities was gathering when she wrote. It is evident that Catherine at the time had never met the Pope personally. She must, however, have gained from hearsay a fairly just idea of his character; in the letter--one of the most carefully composed which we have from her--we see her approaching him with frankness, dignity, and courage, and also with a rare degree of tact. It was one thing to speak her mind out through Gerard du Puy: it must have been another to speak directly to the Head of Christendom. How Catherine acquits herself the reader may judge. The hint that the "sweet Christ on earth," the father of the faithful, lacks self-knowledge, is made so delicately that offence could not be taken; yet as she proceeds the indirect suggestion becomes unmistakable. Gregory is that weak prelate in whom through self-indulgence holy justice is dead or dying; the smooth, peaceable man, who to avoid incurring displeasure, shuts his eyes to the corruption of the Church and the sins of her priests; he is the indolent physician who anoints when he should cauterize. As soon as she deems his mind prepared, comes the direct statement: "I hope by the goodness of God, venerable father mine, that you will quench this [self-love] in yourself, and will not love yourself for your own sake, nor your neighbour, nor God." Nor does she shrink from more specific mention of the dangers which beset him, in his devotion to the interests of "friends and parents," and considerations of temporal policy.

It is with relief, here as ever, that Catherine passes from criticism implied or explicit to a strain of high enthusiasm by which she tries to rouse the soul to all of latent manhood it may possess. She heartens Gregory with stirring appeal to the memories of his great predecessors-- yet more with impassioned reminder of that mystery of divine love and sacrifice from which their strength was drawn. All that was possible to them is possible to him, "for the same God is now that was then." "And if up to this time we have not stood very firm," she says--associating herself, as usual, with the weakness she would condemn--"I wish and pray in truth that you deal manfully with the moment of time which remains, following Christ, whose

vicar you are." Gentle encouragement, and a curious tone of almost maternal tenderness, pervade the rest of the letter. In dealing with the political situation which
Gregory confronted, Catherine speaks without reserve. The suggestions concerning
practical matters with which the letter closes are lucid and to the point. Altogether,
it is a masterly document which the daughter of Jacopo Benincasa despatches to the
Head of Christendom. Reading it, one finds no difficulty in understanding the influence which, as the sequel shows, she established over the sensitive and religious if
weak spirit of Gregory XI.

In the Name of Jesus Christ crucified and of sweet Mary:

To you, most reverend and beloved father in Christ Jesus, your unworthy, poor,
miserable daughter Catherine, servant and slave of the servants of Jesus Christ,
writes in His precious Blood; with desire to see you a fruitful tree, full of sweet and
mellow fruits, and planted in fruitful earth--for if it were out of the earth the tree
would dry up and bear no fruit--that is, in the earth of true knowledge of yourself.
For the soul that knows itself humbles itself, because it sees nothing to be proud of;
and ripens the sweet fruit of very ardent charity, recognizing in itself the unmeasured goodness of God; and aware that it is not, it attributes all its being to Him who
Is. Whence, then, it seems that the soul is constrained to love what God loves and
to hate what He hates.

Oh, sweet and true knowledge, which dost carry with thee the knife of hate,
and dost stretch out the hand of holy desire, to draw forth and kill with this hate
the worm of self-love--a worm that spoils and gnaws the root of our tree so that it
cannot bear any fruit of life, but dries up, and its verdure lasts not! For if a man loves
himself, perverse pride, head and source of every ill, lives in him, whatever his rank
may be, prelate or subject. If he is lover of himself alone--that is, if he loves himself
for his own sake and not for God--he cannot do other than ill, and all virtue is dead
in him. Such a one is like a woman who brings forth her sons dead. And so it really
is; for he has not had the life of charity in himself, and has cared only for praise and
self-glory, and not for the name of God. I say, then: if he is a prelate, he does ill, because to avoid falling into disfavour with his fellow-creatures--that is, through self-
love--in which he is bound by self-indulgence--holy justice dies in him. For he sees
his subjects commit faults and sins, and pretends not to see them and fails to correct
them; or if he does correct them, he does it with such coldness and lukewarmness

that he does not accomplish anything, but plasters vice over; and he is always afraid of giving displeasure or of getting into a quarrel. All this is because he loves himself. Sometimes men like this want to get along with purely peaceful means. I say that this is the very worst cruelty which can be shown. If a wound when necessary is not cauterized or cut out with steel, but simply covered with ointment, not only does it fail to heal, but it infects everything, and many a time death follows from it.

Oh me, oh me, sweetest "Babbo" mine! This is the reason that all the subjects are corrupted by impurity and iniquity. Oh me, weeping I say it! How dangerous is that worm we spoke of! For not only does it give death to the shepherd, but all the rest fall into sickness and death through it. Why does that shepherd go on using so much ointment? Because he does not suffer in consequence! For no displeasure visits one and no ill will, from spreading ointment over the sick; since one does nothing contrary to their will; they wanted ointment, and so ointment is given them. Oh, human wretchedness! Blind is the sick man who does not know his own need, and blind the shepherd-physician, who has regard to nothing but pleasing, and his own advantage--since, not to forfeit it, he refrains from using the knife of justice or the fire of ardent charity! But such men do as Christ says: for if one blind man guide the other, both fall into the ditch. Sick man and physician fall into hell. Such a man is a right hireling shepherd, for, far from dragging his sheep from the hands of the wolf, he devours them himself. The cause of all this is, that he loves himself apart from God: so he does not follow sweet Jesus, the true Shepherd, who has given His life for His sheep. Truly, then, this perverse love is perilous for one's self and for others, and truly to be shunned, since it works too much harm to every generation of people. I hope by the goodness of God, venerable father mine, that you will quench this in yourself, and will not love yourself for yourself, nor your neighbour for yourself, nor God; but will love Him because He is highest and eternal Goodness, and worthy of being loved; and yourself and your neighbour you will love to the honour and glory of the sweet Name of Jesus. I will, then, that you be so true and good a shepherd that if you had a hundred thousand lives you would be ready to give them all for the honour of God and the salvation of His creatures. O "Babbo" mine, sweet Christ on earth, follow that sweet Gregory (the Great)! For all will be possible to you as to him; for he was not of other flesh than you; and that God is now who was then: we lack nothing save virtue, and hunger for the salvation of souls. But there is a remedy for this, father: that we flee the love spoken of above, for ourselves and every creature apart from God. Let no more note be given to friends or parents or one's temporal needs, but only to virtue and the exaltation of things spiritual. For temporal things are failing you from no other cause than from your neglect of the spiritual.

Now, then, do we wish to have that glorious hunger which these holy and true shepherds of the past have felt, and to quench in ourselves that fire of self-love? Let us do as they, who with fire quenched fire; for so great was the fire of inestimable and ardent charity that burned in their hearts and souls, that they were an-hungered and famished for the savour of souls. Oh, sweet and glorious fire, which is of such power that it quenches fire, and every inordinate delight and pleasure and all love of self; and this love is like a drop of water, which is swiftly consumed in the furnace! Should one ask me how men attained that sweet fire and hunger--inasmuch as we are surely in ourselves unfruitful trees--I say that those men grafted themselves into the fruitful tree of the most holy and sweet Cross, where they found the Lamb, slain with such fire of love for our salvation as seems insatiable. Still He cries that He is athirst, as if saying: "I have greater ardour and desire and thirst for your salvation than I show you with My finished Passion." O sweet and good Jesus! Let pontiffs shame them, and shepherds, and every other creature, for our ignorance and pride and self-indulgence, in the presence of so great largess and goodness and ineffable love on the part of our Creator! He has revealed Himself to us in our humanity, a Tree full of sweet and mellow fruits, in order that we, wild trees, might graft ourselves in Him. Now in this wise wrought that enamoured Gregory, and those other good shepherds: knowing that they had no virtue in themselves, and gazing upon the Word, our Tree, they grafted themselves in Him, bound and chained by the bands of love. For in that which the eye sees does it delight, when the thing is fair and good. They saw, then, and seeing they so bound them that they saw not themselves, but saw and tasted everything in God. And there was neither wind nor hail nor demons nor creatures that could keep them from bearing cultivated fruits: since they were grafted in the substance of our Tree, Jesus. They brought forth their fruits, then, from the substance of sweet charity, in which they were united. And there is no other way.

This is what I wish to see in you. And if up to this time, we have not stood very firm, I wish and pray in truth that the moment of time which remains be dealt with manfully, following Christ, whose vicar you are, like a strong man. And fear not, father, for anything that may result from those tempestuous winds that are now beating against you, those decaying members which have rebelled against you. Fear not; for divine aid is near. Have a care for spiritual things alone, for good shepherds, good rulers, in your cities--since on account of bad shepherds and rulers you have encountered rebellion. Give us, then, a remedy; and comfort you in Christ Jesus, and fear not. Press on, and fulfil with true zeal and holy what you have begun with a holy resolve, concerning your return, and the holy and sweet crusade. And delay no longer, for many difficulties have occurred through delay, and the devil has risen up to prevent these things being done, because he perceives his own loss. Up, then, father, and no more negligence! Raise the gonfalon of the most holy Cross, for with the fragrance of the Cross you shall win peace. I beg you to summon those who have rebelled against you to a holy peace, so that all warfare may be turned against the infidels. I hope by the infinite goodness of God that He will swiftly send His aid. Comfort you, comfort you, and come, come, to console the poor, the servants of God, your sons! We await you with eager and loving desire. Pardon me, father, that I have said so many words to you. You know that through the abundance of the heart the mouth speaketh. I am certain that if you shall be the kind of tree I wish to see you, nothing will hinder you.

I beg you to send to Lucca and to Pisa with fatherly proposals, as God shall instruct you, supporting them so far as can be, and summoning them to remain firm and persevering. I have been at Pisa and at Lucca, up to now, influencing them as much as I can not to make a league with the decaying members that are rebelling against you: but they are in great perplexity, because they have no comfort from you, and are constantly urged to make it and threatened from the contrary side. However, up to the present time, they have not wholly consented. I beg you also to write emphatically to Messer Piero: and do it zealously, and do not delay. I say no more.

I have heard here that you have appointed the cardinals. I believe that it would honour God and profit us more if you would take heed always to appoint virtuous men. If the contrary is done, it will be a great insult to God, and disaster to Holy Church. Let us not wonder later if God sends us His disciplines and scourges; for the thing is just. I beg you to do what you have to do manfully and in the fear of God.

I have heard that you are to promote the Master of our Order to another benefice. Therefore I beg you, by the love of Christ crucified, that if this is so you will take pains to give us a good and virtuous Vicar. The Order has need of it, for it has run altogether too wild. You can talk of this with Messer Niccola da Osimo and the Archbishop of Tronto; and I will write them about it.

Remain in the sweet and holy grace of God. I ask you humbly for your blessing. Pardon my presumption, that I presume to write to you. Sweet Jesus, Jesus Love.

TO GREGORY XI

There is less formality here than in the first letter to Gregory. Catherine in writing to the Pope soon felt herself as much at home as a child in her earthly father's house. The little pet name, "Babbo," which she habitually uses to him, could be translated only by "Daddy"--which would sound so strange in English ears that it seems best to let the Italian stand. There is something touching as well as entertaining in the spirit of childlike freedom to which such a term bears witness.

The Anti-Papal League has become a grim reality. The un-Christian pomp and arrogance of ruling prelates, the mean cruelty of William of Noellet in refusing to allow corn to be imported from the Papal States in Tuscany in time of famine, the harshness and lack of tact in the policy of Gregory toward his unsatisfactory children, were all forces potent to destroy among the rebels any strong sense of committing a religious crime in their opposition to the Church. Catherine stands as mediator between the two parties. Not for a moment condoning the sin of a re-bellion heinous indeed in her eyes, she yet does not allow the Pope to forget that the chief cause of the trouble has been the unjust and iniquitous things which the Florentines have endured from the Legates--men "whom you know yourself"-- so she writes with vigorous plebeian candour--"whom you know yourself to be incar-nate demons"! Let God's vicegerent, then, show forth the love of God, and find in the divine attitude toward rebellious man an example for his own attitude toward his rebellious cities. Conciliation is to her mind the only wisdom. There is practi-cal sagacity in her remark in another letter: "On with benignity, father! For know that every rational creature is more easily conquered by love and benignity than by anything else: and especially these Italians of ours in these parts. I do not see any other way in which you can conquer them, but if you do this you can do anything you like with them."

The beautiful opening meditation on the Love of God as shown in creation and redemption is then no mere general exordium, but in close dramatic unity with the sequel of the letter. The Augustinian theology, however alien to our modern modes of thought, has, as she puts it, a nobility not to be ignored. As presented briefly here, and more grandly by Dante in the seventh canto of the *Paradiso*, it represents the supreme effort of the law-reverencing mind of the Latin Church to formulate the methods of Infinite Love. In the curious figure of the Tournament, we have a characteristic play of mediaeval fancy. As Langland puts it, a little differently:

"Then was Faith in a fenestre, and cryed: Ah! Fili David!
As doth an heraude of armes when adventrous cometh to jousts.
Olde Jewes of Jerusalem for joy they sungen,
  Benedictus qui venit in nomine Domini.
Then I frayned at Faith what all that fare meant,
And who should joust in Jerusalem: 'Jesus,' he said,
'And fetch that the fiend claimeth: Piers' fruit the Plowman.'
'Is Piers in this place?' quoth I: and he winked at me,--
'This Jesus of His gentrice will joust in Piers' armes,
In his helme and in his habergeon, humana natura.'"

In the Name of Jesus Christ crucified and of sweet Mary:

Most holy and most reverend my father in Christ Jesus: I Catherine your poor unworthy daughter, servant and slave of the servants of Christ, write to you in His precious Blood; with desire to see you a good shepherd. For I reflect, sweet my "Babbo," that the wolf is carrying away your sheep, and there is no one found to help them. So I hasten to you, our father and our shepherd, begging you on behalf of Christ crucified to learn from Him, who with such fire of love gave Himself to the shameful death of the most holy Cross, to rescue that lost sheep, the human race, from the hands of the demons; because, through man's rebellion against God, they were holding it for their own possession.

Then comes the Infinite Goodness of God, and sees the evil state and the loss and the ruin of these sheep, and sees that they cannot be won back by wrath or war. So, notwithstanding that it has been wronged by them--since man deserved an infinite penalty for his disobedient rebellion against God--Highest and Eternal Wisdom will not do thus; but finds an attractive way, the most gentle and loving possible to find. For it sees that the heart of man is in no wise so drawn as by love, because he was made by love. This seems to be the reason why he loves so much, that he was made by nothing but love, both his soul and his body. For by love God created him in His Image and Likeness, and by love his father and mother gave him substance, conceiving and bearing a son. God, therefore, seeing that man is so ready to love, throws the book of love straight at him, giving him the Word His Only-Begotten Son, who takes our humanity, to make a great peace. But justice wills that vengeance should be wrought for the wrong that has been done to God: so comes Divine Mercy and unspeakable Charity, and to satisfy justice and mercy condemns His Son to death, having clothed Him in our humanity--that is, with the clay of Adam, who sinned. So by His death the wrath of the Father is pacified, having wrought justice on the person of His son: so He has satisfied justice and has satisfied mercy, releasing the human race from the hands of demons. This sweet Word jousted in His arms upon the wood of the most holy Cross, death making a tournament with life, and life with death: so that by His death He destroyed our death, and to give us life He sacrificed the life of His body. So then with love He has drawn us, and has conquered our malice with His benignness, in so much that every heart should be drawn to Him: since greater love one cannot show--and this He Himself said--than to give one's life for one's friend. And if He commends the love which gives one's life for a friend, what, then, shall we say of that most burning and complete love which gave its life for its foe? For we through sin had been made foes of God. Oh, sweet and amorous Word, who with love hast found thy flock once more, and with love hast given Thy life for them, and hast brought them back into the fold, restoring to them the Grace which they had lost!

Holiest sweet "Babbo" mine, I see no other way for us, and no other help in winning back your sheep, which have left the fold of Holy Church in rebellion, not obedient nor subject to you, their father. I pray you therefore, on behalf of Christ crucified, and I will that you do me this grace, to overcome their malice with your benignity. Yours we are, father! I know and recognize that they all feel that they have done wrong; but although they have no excuse for their evil deeds, nevertheless it seemed to them that they could not do otherwise on account of the many sufferings and unjust and iniquitous things that they endured from bad shepherds and governors. For, breathing the stench of the life of many rulers whom you know yourself to be incarnate demons, they fell into the worst of fears, so that they did like Pilate, who, not to lose the government, killed Christ; so did they, for not to lose the state, they persecuted you. I ask you, then, father, to show them mercy. Do not have regard to the ignorance and pride of your sons; but with the food of love and of your benignity, inflicting such sweet discipline and benign reproof as shall please your Holiness, restore peace to us miserable children who have done wrong. I tell you, sweet Christ on earth, on behalf of Christ in Heaven, that if you do thus, without any strife or tempest, they will all come, grieving for the wrong they have done, and will put their heads in your bosom. Then you will rejoice, and we shall rejoice, because by love you have restored the wandering sheep to the fold of Holy Church. And then, sweet my "Babbo," you will fulfil your holy desire and the will of God, by making the holy Crusade, which I summon you in His Name to do swiftly and without negligence. They will turn to it with great eagerness; they are ready to give their life for Christ. Ah me, God, sweet Love! Raise swiftly, "Babbo," the gonfalon of the most holy Cross, and you will see the wolves become lambs. Peace, peace, peace, that war may not delay this happy time! But if you will wreak vengeance and justice, take them upon me, poor wretch, and give me any pain and torment that may please you, even to death. I believe that through the stench of my iniquities many evils have happened, and many misfortunes and discords. On me, then, your poor daughter, take any vengeance that you will. Ah me, father, I die of grief and cannot die! Come, come, and resist no more the will of God that calls you; and the hungry sheep await your coming to hold and possess the place of your predecessor and champion, Apostle Peter. For you, as the Vicar of Christ, should rest in your own place. Come, then, come, and delay no more; and comfort you, and fear not for anything that might happen, since God will be with you. I ask humbly your benediction, for me and for all my sons; and I beg you to pardon my presumption. I say no more. Remain in the holy and sweet grace of God. Sweet Jesus, Jesus Love.

TO GREGORY XI

"Ahi, Constantin, di quanto mal fu matre,
 Non la tua conversion, ma quella dote
  Che da te prese il primo ricco patre!"

For ever since Holy Church has aimed more at temporal than at spiritual things, matters have gone from bad to worse." Catherine's sorrowful denunciations of the sins of the Church recall the thought of Dante, the thought of Petrarch--which is also the thought of all the great saints, seers, and loyal Catholics, to whom through the Christian ages the shortcoming of their spiritual mother has meant grief beyond words. The lovely conception of Holy Church as a garden, borrowed though it be from Holy Writ, she has made peculiarly her own by constant repetition. We recognize in it the womanly imagination which, we are told, always found refreshment in wreathing fragrant flowers and walking abroad through the fields and woods.

Catherine in this letter presents explicitly her threefold policy: reform of the Church, return to Rome, the initiation of a Crusade. In her little letter to Sir John Hawkwood, we have already seen her devotion to this last cause. A Crusade in the fourteenth century was not to be. Nevertheless, Catherine never showed more political wisdom than in this matter, and it was the one aim of her life in which she wholly failed. We have in the Legenda Minore a racy account of a personal interview with Gregory on the subject, in which she presented cogent considerations to him. She shrewdly suggested that the mercenary troops who ravaged Italy, and were "the very cause and nourishment of war," would gladly turn their arms against the infidel, "For there are few people so wicked that they are not willing to serve God by indulging their taste: all men would gladly expiate their sins by doing what they enjoy." Behind all such considerations of policy, however, lay, as we clearly see, the intense desire that the infidels should be saved. And not for their own sake only. Desperate and desolate as she beheld the worldliness of Christian folk, and their remoteness from the faith and ardour of an earlier time, Catherine ventured to dream that new converts, won from the peoples that sat in darkness, might revive the spiritual life of Christendom by the infusion of spiritual passion strong in young purity. "Oh, what joy it would be," she wrote to Gregory, "could we see the Christian people convert the Infidel! For when they had once received the Light, they might reach great perfection, like a young plant which has escaped the wintry cold of faithlessness, and expands in the warmth and light of the Holy Spirit; so they might bear flowers and fruits of virtue in the mystical body of Holy Church; so that the fragrance of their virtue might help us to drive away the sins and vice, the pride and impurity, which abound to- day among the Christian people, and above all among those high in Holy Church."

It was a strange dream, and hopeless; but it was the dream of a saint.

In the Name of Jesus Christ crucified and of sweet Mary:

Most holy and dear and sweet father in Christ sweet Jesus: I your unworthy daughter Catherine, servant and slave of the servants of Jesus Christ, write to you in His precious Blood. With desire have I desired to see in you the fulness of divine grace, in such wise that you may be the means, through divine grace, of pacifying all the universal world. Therefore, I beg you, sweet my father, to use the instrument of your power and virtue, with zeal, and hungry desire for the peace and honour of God and the salvation of souls. And should you say to me, father--"The world is so ravaged! How shall I attain peace?" I tell you, on behalf of Christ crucified, it befits you to achieve three chief things through your power. Do you uproot in the garden of Holy Church the malodorous flowers, full of impurity and avarice, swollen with pride: that is, the bad priests and rulers who poison and rot that garden. Ah me, you our Governor, do you use your power to pluck out those flowers! Throw them away, that they may have no rule! Insist that they study to rule themselves in holy and good life. Plant in this garden fragrant flowers, priests and rulers who are true servants of Jesus Christ, and care for nothing but the honour of God and the salvation of souls, and are fathers of the poor. Alas, what confusion is this, to see those who ought to be a mirror of voluntary poverty, meek as lambs, distributing the possessions of Holy Church to the poor: and they appear in such luxury and state and pomp and worldly vanity, more than if they had turned them to the world a thousand times! Nay, many seculars put them to shame who live a good and holy life. But it seems that Highest and Eternal Goodness is having that done by force which is not done by love; it seems that He is permitting dignities and luxuries to be taken away from His Bride, as if He would show that Holy Church should return to her first condition, poor, humble, and meek as she was in that holy time when men took note of nothing but the honour of God and the salvation of souls, caring for spiritual things and not for temporal. For ever since she has aimed more at temporal than at spiritual, things have gone from bad to worse. See therefore that God, in judgment, has allowed much persecution and tribulation to befall her. But comfort you, father, and fear not for anything that could happen, which God does to make her state perfect once more, in order that lambs may feed in that garden, and not wolves who devour the honour that should belong to God, which they steal and give to themselves. Comfort you in Christ sweet Jesus; for I hope that His aid will be near you, plenitude of divine grace, aid and support divine in the way that I said before. Out of war you will attain greatest peace; out of persecution, greatest unity; not by human power, but by holy virtue, you will discomfit those visible demons, wicked men, and those invisible demons who never sleep around us.

But reflect, sweet father, that you could not do this easily unless you accomplished the other two things which precede the completion of the other: that is, your return to Rome and uplifting of the standard of the most holy Cross. Let not your holy desire fail on account of any scandal or rebellion of cities which you might see or hear; nay, let the flame of holy desire be more kindled to wish to do swiftly. Do not delay, then, your coming. Do not believe the devil, who perceives his own loss, and so exerts himself to rob you of your possessions in order that you may lose your love and charity and our coming be hindered. I tell you, father in Christ Jesus, come swiftly like a gentle lamb. Respond to the Holy Spirit who calls you. I tell you, Come, come, come, and do not wait for time, since time does not wait for you. Then you will do like the Lamb Slain whose place you hold, who without weapons in His hand slew our foes, coming in gentleness, using only the weapons of the strength of love, aiming only at care of spiritual things, and restoring grace to man who had lost it through sin.

Alas, sweet my father, with this sweet hand I pray you, and tell you to come to discomfit our enemies. On behalf of Christ crucified I tell it you: refuse to believe the counsels of the devil, who would hinder your holy and good resolution. Be manly in my sight, and not timorous. Answer God, who calls you to hold and possess the seat of the glorious Shepherd St. Peter, whose vicar you have been. And raise the standard of the holy Cross; for as we were freed by the Cross--so Paul says--thus raising this standard, which seems to me the refreshment of Christians, we shall be freed--we from our wars and divisions and many sins, the infidel people from their infidelity. In this way you will come and attain the reformation, giving good priests to Holy Church. Fill her heart with the ardent love that she has lost; for she has been so drained of blood by the iniquitous men who have devoured her that she is wholly wan. But comfort you, and come, father, and no longer make to wait the servants of God, who afflict themselves in desire. And I, poor, miserable woman, can wait no more; living, I seem to die in my pain, seeing God thus reviled. Do not, then, hold off from peace because of the circumstance which has occurred at Bologna, but come; for I tell you that the fierce wolves will put their heads in your bosom like gentle lambs, and will ask mercy from you, father. I say no more. I beg you, father, to hear and hark that which Fra Raimondo will say to you, and the other sons with him, who come in the Name of Christ crucified and of me; for they are true servants of God and sons of Holy Church. Pardon, father, my ignorance, and may the love and grief which make me speak excuse me to your benignity. Give me your benediction. Remain in the holy and sweet grace of God. Sweet Jesus, Jesus Love.

TO BROTHER RAIMONDO OF CAPUA AT AVIGNON

The last letter tells us that Catherine had sent to the Pope her beloved Confessor, who was later to become her biographer--Fra Raimondo of Capua. It is evident that the simple Italian priest and his companions have become somewhat daunted by the conditions they have encountered at Avignon; and, indeed, the subtlest temptations and most perplexing problems that Europe could furnish were doubtless focussed at the Papal Court. Just what the difficulties were which Raimondo had confided to Catherine and which called forth this spirited answer, we do not know, but we can easily imagine their nature. A holy man of considerable learning, Fra Raimondo was also of mild disposition, much inclined to sigh over dangers and blench before exposure. Catherine, on more than one occasion, showed herself the better man of the two. There was a militant strain in her bright nature; she was really the "Happy Warrior"--

> "Whose powers shed round him in the common strife
> Or mild concerns of ordinary life
> A constant influence, a peculiar grace;
> But who if he be called upon to face
> Some awful moment to which Heaven has joined
> Great issues, good or bad for human kind,
> Is happy as a Lover; and attired
> With sudden brightness, like a man inspired;
> And, through the heat of conflict, keeps the law
> In calmness made, and sees what he foresaw."

So, in this letter, we find the daughter encouraging the father, with reflections much in the temper of Browning:

"Was the trial sore,
 Temptation sharp? Thank God a second time!
 Why come temptations but for man to meet,
 And master, and make crouch beneath his feet,
 And so be pedestalled in triumph!"

In the Name of Jesus Christ crucified and of sweet Mary:

Reverend father in Christ sweet Jesus: I Catherine, servant and slave of the servants of Jesus Christ, write to you in His precious Blood: with desire to see you and the other sons clothed in the wedding garment that covers all our nakedness. That is a protection which does not let the blows of our adversary the devil pierce our flesh with mortal wound, but makes us rather strengthened than weakened by every blow of temptation or molesting of devils or fellow-creatures or our own flesh, rebellious to the spirit. I say that these blows not only do not hurt us, but they shall be precious stones and pearls placed on this garment of most burning charity.

Now suppose there should be a soul that did not have to endure many labours and temptations, from whatever direction and in whatever wise God may grant them. No virtue would be tested in it; for virtue is tested by its opposite. How is purity tested and won? Through the contrary--that is, through the vexations of uncleanliness. For were a man unclean already, there would be no need for him to be molested by unclean reflections, but because it is evident that his will is free from all depraved consenting, and purified from every spot by his holy and true desire to serve his Creator, therefore the devil, the world, and the flesh molest him. Yes, everything is driven out by its opposite. See how humility is won through pride. When a man sees himself molested by that vice of pride, at once he humbles himself, recognizing himself to be faulty--proud: while had he not been so molested he would not have known himself so well. When he has humbled and seen himself, he conceives hatred in such wise that he joys and exults in every pain and injury that he bears. Such a one is like a manful knight, who does not avoid blows. Nay, he holds him unworthy of so great grace, as it seems to him to be, to bear pain, temptations and vexations for Christ crucified. All is through the hate he has for himself, and the love he has conceived for virtue.

So you see that we are not to flee nor to grieve in the time of darkness, since from the darkness light is born. O God, sweet Love, what sweet doctrine Thou givest, that through the contrary of virtue, virtue is won! Out of impatience is won patience; for the soul that feels the vice of impatience becomes patient over the injury received, and is impatient toward the vice of impatience, and is more hurt because it is hurt than over anything else. And so out of the very contrary its perfection comes to be won. It is not aware of this; it finds itself become perfect in many storms and temptations. In no other wise does one ever arrive at the harbour of perfection.

Yea, meditate on this: that the soul can never receive nor desire virtue, unless it has cravings, vexations and temptations to endure with true and holy patience for the love of Christ crucified. We ought, then, to joy and exult in the time of conflicts, vexations and shadows, since from them proceeds such virtue and delight. Oh me, my son given me by Mary that sweet mother, I do not want you to fall into weariness or confusion through any vexations that you might feel in your mind; but I want you to keep that good and holy and true faithful will which I know that God in His mercy has given you. I know that you would rather die than offend Him mortally. Yes, I want that out of the shadows should issue knowledge of yourself, free from confusion; out of your goodwill should issue knowledge of the infinite goodness and unspeakable charity of God; and in this knowledge may our soul abide and fatten. Reflect that through love He keeps your will good, and does not let it run by its own consent or pleasure after the suggestions of the devil. And so, through love, He has permitted to you and me and His other servants, the many vexations and deceits of the devil and fellow-creatures and our own flesh, solely in order that we might rise from negligence, and reach perfect zeal, true humility and most ardent charity: humility which comes from knowledge of self, and charity which comes from knowledge of the goodness of God. There is the soul inspired and consumed by love.

Joy, father, and exult; and comfort you, without any servile fear, and fear not, for any thing that you should see happen. But comfort you: for perfection is near you. And answer the devil saying: "That power against you did not work through me, since it was not in me; it works through grace of the infinite pity and mercy of God." Yes, through Christ crucified you shall be able to do all things. Carry on all your works with living faith; and do not wonder should you see some contrary circumstance present itself which seemed to oppose your work. Comfort you, comfort you, because the Sweet Primal Truth has promised to fulfil your and my desire for you. Slay yourself through your burning desire, with the Lamb that was slain; rest you upon the Cross with Christ crucified. Rejoice in Christ crucified; rejoice in pains; steep yourself in shames for Christ crucified; graft your heart and your affection into the tree of the most holy Cross with Christ crucified, and make in His wounds your habitation. And pardon me, cause and instrument that I am of your every pain and imperfection; for were I an instrument of virtue, you and others would breathe the fragrance of virtue. And I do not say these words because I want you to suffer, for your suffering would be mine; but that you may have compassion, you and the other sons, upon my miseries. I hope and firmly hold, through the grace of the Holy Spirit, that He will put limit and end to all those things that are apart from the will of God.

Reflect that I, poor miserable woman, abide in the body, and find me through desire continually away from the body. Oh me, sweet and good Jesus! I die and cannot die, my heart breaks and cannot break, from the desire that I have of the renewal of Holy Church, for the honour of God and the salvation of every creature; and to see you and the others arrayed in purity, burned and consumed in His most ardent charity!

Tell Christ on earth not to make me wait longer; and when I shall see him, I shall sing with Simeon, that sweet old man: "Nunc dimittis servum tuum, Domine, secundum verbum tuum, in pace." I say no more; for did I follow my wish, I should begin again at once. Make me see and feel you bound and fastened into Christ sweet Jesus, in such wise that nor demon nor creature can ever separate you from so sweet a bond. Love, love, love one another. Remain in the holy and sweet grace of God. Sweet Jesus, Jesus Love.

TO CATARINA OF THE HOSPITAL AND GIOVANNA DI CAPO

From the comparative quiet of her home Catherine looks off to far horizons, surveying the religious and political world. She can encourage Fra Raimondo, yet the sword has pierced her heart. This letter is full of sickening recognition of evils that hold grave prevision of worse disaster. Even now we see clearly formed in Catherine's mind that strange sense of responsibility for the sins of her time, so illogical to the natural, so inevitable to the spiritual vision. "I believe that I am the wretched woman who is the cause of so great evils!" Thus she cries, not in rhetorical figure of speech, but in deep conviction. It is a conviction destined to grow more intense till it leads direct to her spiritual martyrdom.

Out of her pain she turns to the simple women, her daughters and companions in faith, calling on them to join her in the life of intercession and expiation. Then her thought fastens on one little lamb of the flock--one who had strayed and been rescued, and was in danger of straying again; and in care for this one soul needing shelter and strength she finds comfort. Catherine's sense of proportion is that of the spiritual man so finely presented by Browning in the person of Lazarus. Let Andrea be saved, and the corruption of the Church will seem less painful! She can say as her last word, "Sweet daughters, now is the time for toils, which must be our consolations in Christ crucified."

In the Name of Jesus Christ crucified and of sweet Mary:

Dearest daughters in Christ sweet Jesus: I Catherine, servant and slave of the servants of Jesus Christ, write to you in His precious Blood, with desire to see you established in true patience and deep humility, so that you may follow the sweet and Spotless Lamb, for you could not follow Him in other wise. Now is the time, my daughters, to show if we have virtue, and if you are daughters or not. It behoves you to bear with patience the persecutions and detractions, slanders and criticisms of your fellow- creatures, with true humility, and not with annoyance or impatience;

nor must you lift up your head in pride against any person whatever. Know well that this is the teaching which has been given us, that it behoves us to receive on the Cross the food of the honour of God and the salvation of souls, with holy and true patience. Ah me, sweetest daughters, I summon you on behalf of the Sweet Primal Truth to awaken from the sleep of negligence and selfish love of yourselves, and to offer humble and continual prayers, with many vigils, and with knowledge of yourselves, because the world is perishing through the crowding multitude of iniquities, and the irreverence shown to the sweet Bride of Christ. Well, then, let us give honour to God, and our toils to our neighbour. Ah, me, do not be willing, you or the other servants of God, that our life should end otherwise than in mourning and in sighs, for by no other means can be appeased the wrath of God, which is evidently falling upon us.

Ah, me, misfortunate! My daughters, I believe that I am the wretched woman who is the cause of so many evils, on account of the great ingratitude and other faults which I have committed toward my Creator. Ah, me! ah, me! Who is God, who is wronged by His creatures? He is Highest and eternal Goodness, who in His love created man in His image and likeness, and re- created him by grace, after his sin, in the Blood of the immaculate and enamoured Lamb, His Only-Begotten Son. And who is mercenary and ignorant man, who wrongs his Creator? We are those who are not ourselves by ourselves, save in so far as we are made by God, but by ourselves we are full of every wretchedness. It seems as if people sought nothing except in what way they could wrong God and their fellow-creatures, in contempt of the Creator. We see with our wretched eyes that Blood which has given us life persecuted in the holy Church of God. Then let our hearts break in torment and grieving desire; let life stay in our body no more, but let us rather die than behold God so reviled. I die in life, and demand death from my Creator and cannot have it. Better were it for me to die than to live, instead of beholding such disaster as has befallen and is to befall the Christian people.

Let us draw the weapons of holy prayer, for other help I see not. That time of persecution has come upon the servants of God when they must hide in the caves of knowledge of themselves and of God, craving His mercy through the merits of the Blood of His Son. I will say no more, for if I did according to my choice, my daughters, I should never rest until God removed me from this life.

To thee now I say, Andrea, that he who begins only never receives the crown of glory, but he who perseveres till death. O daughter mine, thou hast begun to put thy hand to the plough of virtue, leaving the parbreak of mortal sin; it behoves thee, then, to persevere, to receive the reward of thy labour, which thy soul endures, choosing to bridle its youth, that it may not run to be a member of the devil. Ah me, my daughter! And hast thou not reflection that thou wast once a member of the devil, sleeping in the filth of impurity, and that God by His mercy drew thee from that great misery in which thou wast, thy soul and thy body? It does not befit thee, then, to be ungrateful nor forgetful, for evil would befall thee, and the devil would come back with seven companions stronger than at first. Then thou shalt show the grace thou hast received by being grateful and mindful, when thou shalt be strong in battles with the devil, the world, and thy flesh, which vexes thee; thou must be persevering in virtue. Cling, my daughter, if thou wilt escape such vexations, to the Tree of the most holy Cross, in bodily abstinence, in vigil and in prayer, bathing thee by holy desire in the blood of Christ crucified. So thou shalt attain the life of grace, and do the will of God, and fulfil my desire, which longs to have thee a true servant of Christ crucified. I beg thee therefore not to be a child any longer, and to choose for Bridegroom Christ crucified, who has bought thee with His Blood. If thou yet wishest the life of the world, it befits thee to wait long enough so that the way can be found of giving it to thee in a way that shall be for the honour of God and for thy good. Be subject and obedient till death, and do not contradict the will of Catarina and Giovanna, who I know will never counsel thee or tell thee anything that is not for the honour of God and the salvation of thy soul and body. If thou dost not behave so, thou wilt displease me very much, and do thyself little good. I hope in the goodness of God that thou wilt so act that He will be honoured, and thou shalt have thy reward and give me great consolation.

I tell thee, Catarina and Giovanna, to work till death for the honour of God and her salvation. Sweet daughters, now is the time for toils, which must be our consolations in Christ crucified. I say no more. Remain in the holy and sweet grace of God. Sweet Jesus, Jesus Love.

TO SISTER DANIELLA OF ORVIETO CLOTHED WITH THE HABIT OF SAINT DOMINIC WHO NOT BEING ABLE TO CARRY OUT HER GREAT PENANCES HAD FALLEN INTO DEEP AFFLICTION

Catherine's beloved sister Daniella is in trouble. As happened to many others leading the dedicated life in the middle ages, she has carried her scorn of the body past all bounds of reason, has fallen ill and been obliged to care for her poor physical nature. Catherine, who is perpetually trying to raise Fra Raimondo and others in her spiritual family to more heroic heights, recognizes the different needs of this over-eager soul. She writes her friend, therefore, a long and tender letter, one of the most elaborate among her many analyses of the means that lead to perfection, urging upon her discretion and a sense of proportion in spiritual things. It is noteworthy that Catherine's exhortations to impassioned sacrifice are almost always delivered in connection with the claims of active service, to the Church or fellow-men. When writing to "contemplatives" absorbed in the ecstasies and trials of the interior life, her habitual warnings are against excess, her constant plea, as here, for a perception of relative values. She ranks, herself, alike as a great "contemplative" and as a great woman of action: both phases of experience relate to something deeper. Her soul was athirst for the Infinite, and well she knew that neither in deeds nor in ascetic ecstasy, but only in "holy desire," in the life of ceaseless aspiration "which prays for ever in the presence of God," can our mortality attain to untrammelled union with Infinite Being.

In the Name of Jesus Christ crucified and of sweet Mary:

Dearest daughter and sister in Christ sweet Jesus: I Catherine, servant and slave of the servants of Jesus Christ, write to thee in His precious Blood, with desire to see in thee the holy virtue of discretion, which it is necessary for us to have if we wish to be saved. Why is it so necessary? Because it proceeds from the knowledge of ourselves and of God; in this house its roots are planted. It is really an offspring of charity, which, properly speaking, is discretion--an illumined knowledge which the soul has, as I said, of God and itself. The chief thing it does is this: having seen, in a reasonable light, what it ought to render and to whom, it renders this with perfect discretion at once. So it renders glory to God and praise to His Name; the soul achieves all its works by this light and to this end. It renders to God His due of honour--not like an indiscreet robber, who wants to give honour to himself, and, seeking his own honour and pleasure, does not mind insulting God and harming his neighbour. When the roots of inclination in the soul are rotted by indiscretion, all its works, relating to others or to itself, are rotten. All relating to others, I say: for it imposes burdens indiscreetly, and lays down the law to other people, seculars or spiritual, or of whatever rank they may be. If such a person admonishes or advises, he does it indiscreetly, and wants to load everyone else with the burden which he carries himself. The discreet soul, that sees its own need and that of others reasonably, does just the opposite. When it has rendered to God His due of honour, it gives its own due to itself--that is, hatred of sin and of its own fleshliness. What is the reason? The love of virtue, which it loves in itself. It renders its due to the neighbour with the same light as to itself, and therefore I said, in relation to itself and to others. So it gives goodwill to its neighbour, as it is bound to do, loving virtue in him and hating sin. It loves him as a being created by the Highest Eternal Father. And it gives him loving charity more or less perfectly, according as it has this in itself. Yes, this is the principal result which the virtue of discretion achieves in the soul: it has seen clearly what due it ought to render, and to whom.

These are three chief branches of that glorious discretion which springs from the tree of charity. From this tree spring infinite fruits, all mellow and very sweet, which nourish the soul in the life of grace, when it plucks them with the hand of free will, and eats them with holy eager desire. Whatever condition a person may be in, he tastes these fruits, if he has the light of discretion, in diverse ways, according to his state. He who is placed in the world, and has this light, gathers the fruit of obedience to the commands of God, and distaste for the world, of which he divests himself in mind, although he may be clothed with it in fact. If he has children, he plucks the fruit of the fear of God, and nourishes them with this holy fear. If he is a nobleman, he plucks the fruit of justice, discreetly wishing to render to everyone his due--so he punishes the unjust man rigorously, and rewards the just, tasting the fruit of reason, and for no flatteries or servile fear deserts this way. If he is a subject, he gathers the fruit of obedience and reverence toward his lord, avoiding any cause or means by which he might offend him. Had he not seen these things by the light, he would not have avoided them. If men are monks or prelates, they get from the tree the sweet and pleasing fruit of observing their Rule, enduring one another's faults, embracing shames and annoyances, placing on their shoulders the yoke of obedience. The prelate takes desire for the honour of God and the salvation of souls, seeking to win them by doctrine and exemplary life. In what different ways and by what different people these fruits are gathered! It would take too long to tell them the tongue could not express it.

But let us see, dearest daughter (now we will speak in particular, and so we shall be speaking in general too), what rule that virtue of discretion imposes on the soul. That rule seems to me to apply both to the soul and body of people who wish to live spiritually, in deed and thought. To be sure, it regulates every person in his rank and place: but let us now talk to ourselves. The first rule it gives to the soul is that we have mentioned--to render honour to God, goodwill to one's neighbour, and to oneself, hatred of sin and of one's own fleshliness. It regulates this charity toward the neighbour; for it is not willing to sacrifice the soul to him, since, in order to do him good or pleasure, it is not willing to offend God; but it flees from guilt discreetly, yet holds its body ready for every pain and torment, even to death, to rescue a soul, and as many souls as it can, from the hands of the devil. Also, it is ready to give up all its temporal possessions to help and rescue the body of its neighbour. Charity does this, when enlightened with discretion; for discretion should regulate one's charity to one's neighbour. The indiscreet man does just the contrary, who does not mind offending God, or sacrificing his soul, to serve or please his neighbour--sometimes by keeping him company in wicked places, sometimes by bearing false witness, or in many other ways, as happens every day. This is the rule of indiscretion, which proceeds from pride and perverse self-love and the blindness of not having known oneself or God.

And when measure and rule have been found in regard to charity to the neighbour, discretion regulates also the matter which keeps the soul in that charity, and makes it grow--that is, in faithful, humble, and continual prayer; robing the soul in the cloak of desire for virtue, that it may not be injured by lukewarmness, negligence, or self-love, spiritual or temporal: therefore it inspires the soul with this desire for virtue, that its desire may not be placed on anything by which it might be deceived.

Also, it rules and orders the creature physically, in this way: the soul which is prepared to wish for God makes its beginning as we have said; but because it has the vessel of its body, enlightened discretion must impose a rule on this, as it has done upon the soul, since the body ought to be a means for the increase of virtue. The rule withdraws it from the indulgences and luxuries of the world, and the conversation of worldlings; gives it conversation with the servants of God; takes it from dissolute places, and keeps it in places that stimulate devotion. It imposes restraint on all the members of the body, that they be modest and temperate: let the eye not look where it should not, but hold before itself earth, and heaven; let the tongue flee idle and vain speech, and be disciplined to proclaim the word of God for the salvation of the neighbour, and to confess its sins: let the ear flee agreeable, flattering, dissolute words, and any words of detraction that might be said to it; and let it hearken for the word of God, and the need of the neighbour, willingly listening to his necessity. So let the hand be swift in touching and working, and the feet in going: to all, discretion gives a rule. And that the perverse law of the flesh that fights against the spirit may not throw these tools into disorder, it imposes a rule upon the body, mortifying it with vigil, fast, and the other exercises which are all meant to bridle our body.

But note, that all this is done, not indiscreetly, but with enlightened discretion. How is this shown? In this: that the soul does not place its chief desire in any act of penance. That it may not fall into such a fault as to take penance for its chief desire, enlightened discretion takes pains to robe the soul in the desire for virtue. Penance to be sure must be used as a tool, in due times and places, as need may be. If the flesh, being too strong, kicks against the spirit, penance takes the rod of discipline, and fast, and the cilice of many buds, and mighty vigils; and places burdens enough on the flesh, that it may be more subdued. But if the body is weak, fallen into illness, the rule of discretion does not approve of such a method. Nay, not only should fasting be abandoned, but flesh be eaten; if once a day is not enough, then four times. If one cannot stand up, let him stay on his bed; if he cannot kneel, let him sit or lie down, as he needs. This discretion demands. Therefore it insists that penance be treated as a means and not as a chief desire.

Dost thou know why it must not be chief? That the soul may not serve God with a thing that can be taken from it and that is finite: but with holy desire, which is infinite, through its union with the infinite desire of God; and with the virtues which neither devil nor fellow-creature nor weakness can take from us, unless we choose. Herein must we make our foundation, and not in penance. Nay, in weakness the virtue of patience may be tested; in vexing conflicts with devils, fortitude and long perseverance; and in adversities suffered from our fellow-beings, humility, patience, and charity. So as to all other virtues--God lets them be tested by many contraries, but never taken from us, unless we choose. Herein must we make our foundation, and not in penance. The soul cannot have two foundations: either the one or the other must be overthrown. Let the thing which is not the chief, be used as a means. If I find my chief principle in bodily penance, I build the city of my soul upon the sand, so that each little breeze throws it to the earth, and no building can be erected on it. But if I build upon the virtues, founded upon the Living Stone, Christ sweet Jesus, there is no building so great that it will not stand firmly, nor wind so contrary that it can ever blow it down.

From these and many other difficulties that arise, it has not been meant that penance should be used otherwise than as a means. I have already seen many penitents who have been neither patient nor obedient, because they have studied to kill their bodies, but not their wills. The rule of indiscretion has wrought this. Dost thou know the result? All their consolations and desires centre in carrying out their penance to suit themselves, and not to suit anyone else. Therein they nourish their will. While they can fulfil their penance, they have consolation and gladness, and seem to themselves full of God, as if they had accomplished everything; and they do not perceive that they fall into a mere personal estimate, and into a judicial attitude. For if all people do not walk in the same way, they seem to them in a state of damnation, an imperfect state. They indiscreetly want to measure all bodies by one same measure, by that with which they measure themselves. And if one wants to withdraw them from this, either to break their will or from some necessity of theirs, they hold their will harder than a diamond; living in such wise, that at the time of test by a temptation or injury, they find themselves, from indulgence in this wrong will, weaker than straw.

Indiscretion taught them that penance bridled wrath, impatience, and the other sinful impulses that come into the heart; it is not so. This glorious light teaches thee that thou shalt kill sin in thy soul, and draw out its roots, with hatred and displeasure against thyself, loading thy fault with rebuke, with the consideration of who God is whom thou wrongest, and who thou art who wrongest Him, with the memory of death and the longing for virtue. Penance cuts off, yet thou wilt always find the root in thee, ready to sprout again; but virtue pulls up. Earth in which sins have been planted is always ready to receive them again if self-will puts them there with free choice; not otherwise, when once the root is pulled up.

It may happen that a sick body is obliged perforce to give up its habits of life; then it falls at once into weariness and confusion of mind, deprived of all gladness: it thinks itself condemned and confounded, and finds no sweetness in prayer, such as it seemed to have in the time of its penance. And whither is this sweetness gone? Lost, with the personal will on which it was built! This cannot be gratified, and so the soul suffers. And why art thou fallen into such confusion and almost despair? And where is the hope which thou hadst in the Kingdom of God? All lost, by means of that very penance through which the soul hoped to have eternal life! Capable of this no more, it thinks itself deprived of the other.

These are the fruits of indiscretion. Had the soul the light of discretion, it would see that nothing but being without virtues deprived it of God; and it has eternal life through virtue, by the Blood of Christ. Then let us rise above all imperfection, and set our heart, as I said, on true virtues, which are of such joy and gladsomeness as tongue could not tell. There is none who can give pain to the soul founded on virtue, or take from it the hope of heaven; for it has put its self-will to death in spiritual things as in temporal, and its affections are not set on penance, or private consolations or revelations, but on endurance through Christ crucified and the love of virtue. So it is patient, faithful, hopes in God and not in itself or its works: is humble and obedient, believing others rather than itself, because it does not presume. It stretches wide the arms of mercy, and thereby drives forth confusion of mind. In shadows and conflicts it uplifts the light of faith, labouring manfully, with true and profound humility; and in gladness it enters into itself, that the heart may not fall into vain glee. It is strong and persevering, because it has put to death its own will, which made it weak and inconstant. All times are the right time for it; all places the right place. If it is in a season of penance, this is a time of gladness and consolation to it, using penance as a means; and if, by necessity or obedience, penance has to be abandoned, it rejoices; because its chief foundation, in the love of virtue, cannot be and is not taken from it; and because it sees the contradiction of its own will, which it has been enlightened to perceive must always be resisted with great diligence and zeal.

It finds prayer in every place, for it bears ever with it the place wherein God lives by grace, and where we ought to pray--that is, the house of our soul wherein holy desire prays constantly. This desire is uplifted by the light of the mind to be reflected in itself and in the immeasurable flame of divine love, which it finds in the Blood shed for us, which by largess of love it finds in the vase of the soul. This it cares and should care to know, that it may drink deep of the Blood, and therein consume its self-will--and not simply to accomplish the count of many paternosters. So we shall make our prayer continuous and faithful; because in the fire of His love we know that He is powerful to give us what we ask. He is Highest Wisdom, who knows how to give and discern what we need; He is a most piteous and gracious Father, who wishes to give us more than we desire, and more than we know how to ask for our need. The soul is humble, for it has recognized its own defects and that in itself it is not. This is the kind of prayer through which we attain virtue, and preserve in our souls the longing for it.

What is the beginning of so great good? Discretion, the daughter of charity, as I said. And it presents straightway to its neighbour the good which it has itself. So it seeks to present to its fellow-creature the foundation it has found, and the love and the teaching it has received, and shows these by example of life and doctrine, advising when it sees need or when advice were asked of it. It comforts the soul of its neighbour, and does not confound him by leading him into despair when he has fallen into some fault; but tenderly it makes itself ill with that soul, giving him what healing it can, and enlarging in him hope in the Blood of Christ crucified.

The virtue of discretion gives this and infinitely many other fruits to the neighbour. Then, since it is so useful and necessary, dearest and most beloved daughter and sister mine in Christ sweet Jesus, I summon thee and me to do what in past time I confess not to have done with that perfection which I should. It has not happened to thee as to me, to have been and to be very faulty, or over-lax and easy-going in my life, instead of strict, through my fault; but thou, as one who has wished to subdue her youthful body that it be not rebel to the soul, hast chosen a life so extremely strict that apparently it is out of all bounds of discretion; in so much that it seems to me that indiscretion is trying to make thee feel some of its results, and is quickening thy self-will in this. And now that thou art leaving what thou art accustomed to do, the devil apparently is trying to make it seem to thee that thou art damned. I am very much distressed at this, and I believe that it is a great offence against God. Therefore I will and I beg thee that our beginning and foundation be in the love of virtue, as I said. Kill thy self-will, and do what thou art made to do; pay attention rather to how things look to others than to thyself. Thou dost feel thy body weak and ill; take every day the food that is needed to restore nature. And if thy illness and weakness are relieved, undertake a regular life in moderation, and not intemperately. Do not consent to let the little good of penance hinder the greater; nor array thyself therein as thy chief affection--for thou wouldst find thyself deceived: but wish that we may haste in sincerity upon the beaten road of virtue, and that we may guide others on this same road, breaking and shattering our own wills. If we have the virtue of discretion in us, we shall do it; otherwise, not.

Therefore I said that I desired to see in thee the holy virtue of discretion. I say no more. Remain in the holy and sweet grace of God. Forgive me should I have talked too presumptuously; the love of thy salvation, through the honour of God, is my reason. Sweet Jesus, Jesus Love.

TO BROTHER RAIMONDO OF CAPUA OF THE ORDER OF THE PREACHERS
AND TO MASTER JOHN III. OF THE ORDER OF THE HERMIT BROTHERS OF
ST. AUGUSTINE AND TO ALL THEIR COMPANIONS WHEN
THEY WERE AT AVIGNON

Catherine's interest in public affairs is rising and widening. This letter marks an inner crisis. Her thoughts and deeds have, as we have seen, been already busied for some time with the dissension between the Pope and his rebellious Tuscan people: now the hour has come when she is to feel herself solemnly dedicated, by a divine command, to the great task of reconciliation. We overhear her, as it were, thinking out in her Master's presence and with His aid the deepest questions which the situation suggests: and as we listen to that colloquy, so natural, so sweetly familiar, so deeply reverent, we feel that no problems, however sorrowful and perplexing, could be hopeless there. From communion with her Lord, she went forth strong and reassured into the stormy action of her time. Christ Himself, so she tells us, placed the Cross upon her shoulder and the olive in her hand, changed her mourning into a high and rapturous hope, and bade her go, strong in the faith, to bear His message of joy "to one and the other people." Thus she should be shown in art--Cross-bearer like her Lord, and holding to the world the sign of reconciliation. Thus did she start upon the Via Dolorosa of the peace-maker; from now on we shall follow her in her letters, as she treads that way of sorrows which was also the way of life.

The experience here described fell on the first of April, 1376. Early in May, the Florentines, knowing of her holy fame, sent for her to come to their city and give them counsel. For to defy the Vicar of Christ was a fearsome thing, and many hearts were uneasy in the rebellious town.

In the Name of Jesus Christ crucified and of sweet Mary:

Dearest my sons in Christ Jesus. I your poor mother have longed passionately to see your hearts and affections nailed to the Cross, held together by the bond which grafted God into man and man into God. So my soul longs to see your affections grafted into the Incarnate Word Christ Jesus, in such wise that nor demons nor creatures can divide you. For if you are held and enkindled by sweet Jesus, I do not fear that all the devils of hell with all their wiles can separate you from so sweet love and union. So I wish, because there is mighty need, that you should never cease from throwing fuel on the fire of holy desire--the fuel of the knowledge of yourselves. For that is the fuel which feeds the fire of divine charity: charity which is won by knowledge of the inestimable love of God, and then unites the soul with its neighbour. And the more material one gives to the flame--that is, the more fuel of self-knowledge--the more the warmth of the love of Christ and one's neighbour increases. Abide, then, hidden in the knowledge of yourselves, and do not live superficially, lest Devil Malatasca catch you with many illusions and reflections against one another: this he would do to take from you your union in divine charity. So I will and command you that the one be subject to the other, and each bear the faults of the other; learning from the Sweet Primal Truth, who chose to be the least of men, and humbly bore all our faults and iniquities. So I will that you do, dearest sons; love, love, love one another. And joy and exult, for the summer-tide draws near.

For the first of April, especially in the night, God opened His secrets, showing His marvellous things in such a wise that my soul did not seem to be in the body, and received such joy and plenitude as the tongue does not suffice to tell. He explained and made clear part by part the mystery of the persecution which Holy Church is now enduring, and of her renewal and exaltation, which shall be in time to come: saying that the present crisis is permitted to restore her to her true condition. The Sweet Primal Truth quoted two words which are in the Holy Gospel--"It must needs be that offences come into the world": and then added: "But woe to him by whom the offence cometh." As if He said: "I permit this time of persecution, to uproot the thorns, with which My bride is wholly choked; but I do not permit the evil thoughts of men. Dost thou know what I do? I am doing as I did when I was in the world, when I made the scourge of cords, and drove out those who sold and bought in the Temple, not choosing that the House of God should be made a den of thieves. So I tell thee that I am doing now. For I have made a scourge out of human beings, and with that scourge I drive out the impure traffickers, greedy, avaricious, and swollen with pride, who buy and sell the gifts of the Holy Spirit." Yes, He was driving them forth with the scourge of the persecutions of their fellow-beings-- that is, by force of tribulation and persecution He put an end to their disorderly and immodest living.

And, the fire growing in me, I gazed and saw the Christian people and the infidel enter into the side of Christ crucified; and I passed through the midst of them, by my loving and longing desire, and entered with them into Christ Sweet Jesus, accompanied by my father St. Dominic, and John the Single, with all my sons together. Then He placed the Cross on my shoulder and the olive in my hand, almost as if I had asked for them, and said that thus I should bear them, to the one and to the other people. And He said to me: "Tell them, I bring you tidings of great joy." Then my soul became more full; it was lost to itself among the true believers who feed upon the Divine Substance, by the uniting force and longing of love. And so great was the delight of my soul, that it no longer realized its past affliction from seeing God wronged; nay! I said: "O blessed and fortunate wrong!" Then sweet Jesus smiled, and said: "Is sin fortunate, which is nothing at all? Dost thou know what St. Gregory meant when he said, 'Blessed and fortunate fault'? What element is it that thou holdest as fortunate and blessed, and that Gregory calls so?" I replied as He made me reply, and said: "I see well, sweet my Lord, and well I know, that sin is not worthy of good fortune, and is not fortunate nor blessed in itself; but the fruit may be, which comes from sin. It seems to me that Gregory meant this: that through the sin of Adam, God gave us the Word, His only- begotten Son, and the Word gave His Blood, so that, giving His life, He restored life with a great fire of love. So, then, sin is fortunate, not through the sin itself, but from the fruit and the gift we receive by that sin." Now, so it is. Thus from the wrong done by the wicked Christians who persecute the Bride of Christ, spring her exaltation, her light, and the fragrance of her virtues. This was so sweet that there seemed no comparison between the wrong, and the unsearchable goodness and benignity of God, which He showed toward His Bride. Then I rejoiced and exulted, and was so arrayed in assurance of the time to come that I seemed to possess and taste it. And I said then with Simeon: "Nunc dimittis servum tuum, Domine, secundum verbum tuum, in pace." So many mysteries were wrought in me as tongue cannot suffice to tell nor heart to think nor eye to see.

Now, what tongue could suffice to tell the wonderful things of God? Not mine, poor wretch that I am. Therefore I choose to keep silence, and to give me wholly to seeking the honour of God and the salvation of souls and the renewal and exaltation of Holy Church, and through grace and power of the Holy Spirit to persevere even unto death. With this desire I called our Christ on earth, and I will call him, with great love and compassion, and you, father, and all my dear sons; I made and was granted your petition. Rejoice, then, rejoice and exult. O sweet God our Love, fulfil quickly the desires of thy servants! I will say no more--and I have said nothing. I die, delayed in my desires. Have compassion on me. Pray the divine Goodness and Christ on earth that there be no more loitering. Remain in the holy and sweet grace of God. Drown you in the Blood of Christ crucified; and on no account faint, but rather take comfort. Rejoice, rejoice, in your sweet labours. Love, love, love one another. Sweet Jesus, Jesus Love.

TO SISTER BARTOLOMEA DELLA SETA NUN IN THE CONVENT OF SANTO STEFANO AT PISA

The conflicts of the cloister and of the court are not dissimilar; and the first, to Catherine, are as real and significant as the second. She writes in a familiar strain to Sister Bartolomea. The truths on which she is insisting have been reiterated in every age by guides to the spiritual life. But whenever, as here, they come from the depths of personal experience, they possess peculiar freshness and force; and, indeed, this Colloquy of the Saint of Siena with her Lord has become a *locus classicus* in the literature of the interior life.

One likes to note, in passing, how frequently Catherine urges frail, cloistered women, sheltered from all the din and storm of outer life, to "manfulness." "Virile," "virilmente"--they are among her especial words. And, indeed, they well befit her own spirit, singularly vigorous and fearless for a woman whose feminine sensitiveness is evident in every letter she writes.

In the Name of Jesus Christ crucified and of sweet Mary:

Dearest daughter in Christ Jesus. I Catherine, servant and slave of the servants of Jesus Christ, write to you in His precious Blood: with desire to see you a true bride, consecrated to the eternal Bridegroom. It belongs to a bride to make her will one with that of her bridegroom; she cannot will more than he wills, and seems unable to think of anything but him. Now do you so think, daughter mine, for you, who are a bride of Christ crucified, ought not to think or will anything apart from Him--that is, not to consent to any other thoughts. That thoughts should not come, this I do not tell thee--because neither thou nor any created being couldst prevent them. For the devil never sleeps; and God permits this to make His bride reach perfect zeal and grow in virtue. This is the reason why God sometimes permits the mind to remain sterile and gloomy, and beset by many perverse cogitations, so that it seems unable to think of God, and can hardly remember His Name.

Beware, when thou mayest feel this in thyself, lest thou fall into weariness or bewildered confusion, and do not give up thy exercises nor the act of praying, because the devil may say to thee: "How does this prayer uplift thee, since thou dost not offer it with any feeling or desire? It would be better for thee not to make it." Yet do not give up, nor fall for this into confusion, but reply manfully: "I would rather exert myself for Christ crucified, feeling pain, gloom and inward conflicts, than not exert myself and feel repose." And reflect, that this is the state of the perfect; if it were possible for them to escape Hell, and have joy in this life and joy eternal beside, they do not want it, because they delight so greatly in conforming themselves to Christ crucified; nay, they want to live rather by the way of the Cross and pain, than without pain. Now what greater joy can the bride have than to be conformed to her bridegroom, and clothed with like raiment? So, since Christ crucified in His life chose naught but the Cross and pain, and clothed Him in this raiment, His bride holds herself blessed when she is clothed in this same raiment; and because she sees that the Bridegroom has loved her so beyond measure, she loves and receives Him with such love and desire as no tongue can suffice to tell. Therefore the Highest and Eternal Goodness, to make her attain most perfect love and possess humility, permits her many conflicts and a dry mind, that the creature may know itself and see that it is not. For were it anything, it would free itself from pain when it chose, but being naught it cannot. So, knowing itself, it is humbled in its non-existence, and knows the goodness of God, which, through grace, has given it being, and every grace that is founded upon being.

But thou wilt say to me: "When I have so much pain, and suffer so many conflicts and such gloom, I can see nothing but confusion; and it does not seem as if I could take any hope, I see myself so wretched." I reply to thee, my daughter, that if thou shalt seek, thou shalt find God in thy goodwill. Granted that thou feel many conflicts, do thou not therefore feel thy will deprived of wishing God. Nay, this is the reason why the soul mourns and suffers, because it fears to offend God. It ought then to joy and exult, and not to fall into confusion through its conflicts, seeing that God keeps its will good, and gives it hatred of mortal sin.

I remember that I heard this said once to a servant of God, and it was said to her by the Sweet Primal Truth, when she was abiding in very great pain and temptation, and among other things, felt the greatest confusion, in so much that the devil said: "What wilt thou do? for all the time of thy life thou shalt abide in these pains, and then thou shalt have hell." She then answered with manly heart, and without any fear, and with holy hatred of herself, saying: "I do not avoid pains, for I have chosen pains for my refreshment. And if at the end He should give me hell, I will not therefore abandon serving my Creator. For I am she who am worthy of abiding in hell, because I wronged the Sweet Primal Truth; so, did He give me hell, He would do me no wrong, since I am His." Then our Saviour, in this sweet and true humility, scattered the shadows and torments of the devil, as it happens when the cloud passes that the sun remains; and suddenly came the Presence of Our Saviour. Thence she melted into a river of tears, and said in a sweet glow of love: "O sweet and good Jesus, where wast thou when my soul was in such affliction?" Sweet Jesus, the Spotless Lamb, replied: "I was beside thee. For I move not, and never leave My creature, unless the creature leave Me through mortal sin." And that woman abode in sweet converse with Him, and said: "If Thou wast with me, how did I not feel Thee? How can it be that being by the fire, I should not feel the heat? And I felt nothing but freezing cold, sadness, and bitterness, and seemed to myself full of mortal sins." He replied sweetly, and said: "Dost thou wish Me to show thee, daughter mine, how in those conflicts thou didst not fall into mortal sin, and how I was beside thee? Tell me, what is it that makes sin mortal? Only the will. For sin and virtue consist in the consent of the will; there is no sin nor virtue, unless voluntarily wrought. This will was not in thee; for had it been, thou wouldst have taken joy and delight in the suggestions of the devil; but since the will was not there, thou didst grieve over them, and suffer for fear of doing wrong. So thou seest that sin and virtue consist in choice-- wherefore I tell thee that thou shouldst not, on account of these conflicts, fall into disordered confusion. But I will that from this darkness thou derive the light of self-knowledge, in which thou mayest gain the virtue of humility, and joy and exult in a good will, knowing that then I abide in thee secretly. The will is a sign to thee that I am there; for hadst thou an evil will, I should not be in thee by grace. But knowest thou how I thus abide in thee? In the same way in which I hung upon the wood of the Cross. And I take the same way with you that my Father took with Me. Reflect, daughter mine, that upon the Cross I was blessed and was sorrowful; blessed I was by the union of the divine and the human nature, and nevertheless the flesh endured pain, because the Eternal Father withdrew His power to Himself, letting Me suffer; but He did not withdraw the union in which He was for ever united with Me. Reflect that in this way I abide in the soul; for often I withdraw to myself feeling, but do not withdraw grace, since grace is never lost, except by mortal sin, as I said. But knowest thou why I do this? Only to make the soul reach true perfection. Thou knowest that the soul cannot be perfect unless borne on these two wings, humility and charity. Humility is won through the knowledge of itself, into which it enters in the time of darkness; and charity is won by seeing that I, through love, have kept its will holy and good. Wherefore, I tell thee, that the wise soul, seeing that from this experience proceeds such profit, reassures itself (and for no other cause do I permit the devil to give you temptations), and will hold this time dearer than any other. Now I have told thee the way I take. And reflect, that such experience is very necessary to your salvation; for if the soul were not sometimes pressed by many temptations, it would fall into very great negligence, and would lose the exercise of continual desire and prayer. Because in the hour of battle it is more alert, through fear of its foes, and provisions the rock of its soul, having recourse to Me who am its Fortitude. But this is not the intention of the devil--for I permit him to tempt you that he may make you attain virtue, though he, on his part, tempts you to make you attain despair. Reflect that the devil will tempt a person who is dedicated to My service, not because he believes that the man may actually fall into that sin, for he sees at once that he would choose death rather than actually to do wrong. But what does he do? He exerts himself to make the man fall into confusion, saying: 'No good is of any use to you, on account of these thoughts and impulses that come to you.' Now thou seest how great is the malice of the devil; for, not being able to conquer in the first battle, he often conquers in the second, under guise of virtue. Wherefore I do not want thee ever to follow his malicious will; but I want thee to assume My will, as I have told thee. This is the rule which I give thee, and which I wish thee to teach others when there is need."

Now thus I tell thee, dearest my daughter, that I want thee to do. And be for me a mirror of virtue, following the footsteps of Christ crucified. Bathe thee in the Blood of Christ crucified, and so live, as is my will, that thou nor seek nor will aught but the Crucified, like a true bride, bought with the Blood of Christ crucified. Well seest thou that thou art a bride, and that He has wedded thee and every creature, not with a ring of silver, but with the ring of His Flesh. O depth and height of

Love unspeakable, how didst Thou love this Bride, the human race! O Life through which all things do live, Thou hast plucked it from the hands of the devil, who possessed it as his own; from his hands Thou hast plucked it, catching the devil with the hook of Thy humanity, and hast wedded it with Thy flesh. Thou hast given Thy Blood for a pledge, and at the last, sacrificing Thy body, Thou hast made the payment. Now drink deep, my daughter, and fall not into negligence, but arise with true zeal, and by this Blood may the hardness of thy heart be broken in such wise that it never may close again, for any ignorance or negligence, nor for the speech of any creature. I say no more. Remain in the holy and sweet grace of God. Sweet Jesus, Jesus Love.

TO GREGORY XI

Catherine, sent by the Florentines as their representative to the Pope, has reached Avignon and seen the Holy Father. Far from being overawed in his presence, she has evidently felt toward him a mingling of sympathy and tenderness not untouched by compassion. She is impressed by the sensitiveness of the man--by the strength of the adverse influences continually playing upon him from his own household; above all, by his extreme timidity. The gentle, reassuring tone of this letter is almost like that of a mother encouraging a dear but weak-spirited child to make his own decisions and to abide by them. Catherine's sweetness of nature preserves her from viewing Gregory with any tinge of contempt; but we cannot help feeling the contrast between this frail woman of heroic soul and the hesitating figure of the Pope.

In the Name of Jesus Christ crucified and of sweet Mary:

Most holy and blessed father in Christ sweet Jesus: your poor unworthy little daughter Catherine comforts you in His precious Blood, with desire to see you free from any servile fear. For I consider that a timorous man cuts short the vigour of holy resolves and good desire, and so I have prayed, and shall pray, sweet and good Jesus that He free you from all servile fear, and that holy fear alone remain. May ardour of charity be in you, in such wise as shall prevent you from hearing the voice of incarnate demons, and heeding the counsel of perverse counsellors, settled in self- love, who, as I understand, want to alarm you, so as to prevent your return, saying, "You will die." And I tell you on behalf of Christ crucified, most sweet and holy father, not to fear for any reason whatsoever. Come in security: trust you in Christ sweet Jesus: for, doing what you ought, God will be above you, and there will be no one who shall be against you. Up, father, like a man! For I tell you that you have no need to fear. You ought to come; come, then. Come gently, without any fear. And if any at home wish to hinder you, say to them bravely, as Christ said when St. Peter, through tenderness, wished to draw Him back from going to His passion; Christ turned to him, saying, "Get thee behind Me, Satan; thou art an offence to Me, seeking the things which are of men, and not those which are of God. Wilt thou not that I fulfil the will of My Father?" Do you likewise, sweetest father, following Him as His vicar, deliberating and deciding by yourself, and saying to those who would hinder you, "If my life should be spent a thousand times, I wish to fulfil the will of my Father." Although bodily life be laid down for it, yet seize on the life of grace and the means of winning it for ever. Now comfort you and fear not, for you have no need. Put on the armour of the most holy Cross, which is the safety and the life of Christians. Let talk who will, and hold you firm in your holy resolution. My father, Fra Raimondo, said to me on your behalf that I was to pray God to see whether you were to meet with an obstacle, and I had already prayed about it, before and after Holy Communion, and I saw neither death nor any peril. Those perils are invented by the men who counsel you. Believe, and trust you in Christ sweet Jesus. I hope that God will not despise so many prayers, made with so ardent desire, and with many tears and sweats. I say no more. Remain in the holy and sweet grace of God. Pardon me, pardon me. Jesus Christ crucified be with you. Sweet Jesus, Jesus Love.

TO THE KING OF FRANCE

Catherine's letters to great personages whom she did not know are, as would be expected, less searching and fresh than the many written with a more personal inspiration, but they afford at least an interesting testimony to the breadth of her interests. This letter to Charles V. was evidently written during her stay at Avignon, where she formed relations with the Duke of Anjou, and received his promise to lead in the prospective Crusade. Avignon was a centre of intellectual life and of European politics, and Catherine must have been quickened there to think more than ever before in large terms and on great issues. To think of a matter is always, for her, to feel a sense of responsibility toward it; she writes, accordingly, to Charles V., urging him to make peace with his brother monarch: "For so," says the maid of Siena serenely to the great King--"So you will fulfil the will of God and me."

In the Name of Jesus Christ crucified and of sweet Mary:

Dearest lord and father in Christ sweet Jesus: I Catherine, servant and slave of the servants of Jesus Christ, write to you in His precious Blood: with desire to see you observe the holy and sweet commands of God, since I consider that in no other way can we share the fruit of the Blood of the Spotless Lamb. Sweet Jesus, the Lamb, has taught us the Way: and thus He said: "Ego sum Via, Veritas et Vita." He is the sweet Master who has taught us the doctrine, ascending the pulpit of the most holy Cross. Venerable father, what doctrine and what way does He give us? His way is this: pains, shames, insults, injuries, and abuse; endurance in true patience, hunger and thirst; He was satiate with shame, nailed and held upon the Cross for the honour of the Father and our salvation. With His pains and shame He gave satisfaction for our guilt, and the reproach in which man had fallen through the sin committed. He has made restitution, and has punished our sins on His own Body, and this He has done of love alone and not for debt.

This sweet Lamb, our Way, has despised the world, with all its luxuries and dignity, and has hated vice and loved virtue. Do you, as son and faithful servant of Christ crucified, follow His footsteps and the way which He teaches you: bear in true patience all pain, torment, and tribulation which God permits the world to inflict on you. For patience is not overcome, but overcomes the world. Be, ah! be a lover of virtue, founded in true and holy justice, and despise vice. I beg you, by love of Christ crucified, to do in your state three especial things. The first is, to despise the world and yourself and all its joys, possessing your kingdom as a thing lent to you, and not your own. For well you know that nor life nor health nor riches nor honour nor dignity nor lordship is your own. Were they yours, you could possess them in your own way. But in such an hour a man wishes to be well, he is ill; or living, and he is dead; or rich, and he is poor; or a lord, and he is made a servant and vassal. All this is because these things are not his own, and he can only hold them in so far as may please Him who has lent them to him. Very simple-minded, then, is the man who holds the things of another as his own. He is really a thief, and worthy of death. Therefore I beg you that, as The Wise, you should act like a good steward, made His steward by God; possessing all things as merely lent to you.

The other matter is, that you maintain holy and true justice; let it not be ruined, either for self-love or for flatteries, or for any pleasing of men. And do not connive at your officials doing injustice for money, and denying right to the poor: but be to the poor a father, a distributer of what God has given you. And seek to have the faults that are found in your kingdom punished and virtue exalted. For all this appertains to the divine justice to do.

The third matter is, to observe the doctrine which that Master upon the Cross gives you; which is the thing that my soul most desires to see in you: that is, love and affection with your neighbour, with whom you have for so long a time been at war. For you know well that without this root of love, the tree of your soul would not bear fruit, but would dry up, abiding in hate and unable to draw up into itself the moisture of grace. Alas, dearest father, the Sweet Primal Truth teaches it to you, and leaves you for a commandment, to love God above everything, and one's neighbour as one's self. He gave you the example, hanging upon the wood of the most holy Cross. When the Jews cried "Crucify!" He cried with meek and gentle voice: "Father, forgive those who crucify Me, who know not what they do." Behold His unsearchable love! For not only does He pardon them, but excuses them before His Father! What example and teaching is this, that the Just, who has in Him no poison of sin, endures from the unjust the punishment of our iniquities!

Oh, how the man should be ashamed who follows the teaching of the devil and his own lower nature, caring more to gain and keep the riches of this world, which are all vain, and pass like the wind, than for his soul and his neighbour! For while abiding in hate with his neighbour, he has hate by his side, since hate deprives him of divine charity. Surely he is foolish and blind, for he does not see that with the sword of hate to his neighbour he is killing himself.

Therefore I beg you, and will that you follow Christ crucified, and love your neighbour's salvation: proving that you follow the Lamb, who for hunger of His Father's honour and the salvation of souls chose bodily death. So do you, my lord! Care not if you lose from your worldly substance; for loss will be gain to you, provided that you can reconcile your soul with your brother. I marvel that you are not willing to devote to this, not only temporal things, but even, were it possible, life itself: considering how great destruction of souls and bodies there has been, and how many Religious and women and children have been injured and exiled by this war. No more, by love of Christ crucified! Do you not reflect of how great harm you are cause, if you fail to do what you can? Harm to the Christians, and harm to infidels. For your strife has obstructed the mystery of the Holy Crusade, and is doing so still. If no other harm than this followed, it seems to me that we ought to expect the divine judgment. I beg you that you be no longer a worker of so great harm and an obstructer of so great good as the recovery of Holy Land and of those poor wretched souls who do not share in the Blood of the Son of God. Of which thing you ought to be ashamed, you and the other Christian rulers: for this is a very great confusion in the sight of men and abomination in the sight of God, that war should be made against one's brother, and the enemy left alone, and that a man should want to take away another person's possessions and not to win his own back again. No more such folly and blindness! I tell you, on behalf of Christ crucified, that you delay no longer to make this peace. Make peace, and direct all your warfare to the infidels. Help to encourage and uplift the standard of the most holy Cross, which God shall demand from you and others at the point of death--demanding also from you account for such ignorance and negligence as has been committed and is committed every day.

Sleep no more, for love of Christ crucified, and for your own profit, during the little time that remains to us: for time is short, and you are to die, and know not when.

May the flame of holy desire to follow this holy Cross and to be reconciled with your neighbour, increase in you! In this wise you will follow the way and doctrine of the Lamb slain and abandoned on the Cross, and you will observe the commandments. You will follow the way, enduring with patience the injuries that have been offered you; the doctrine, being reconciled with your neighbour; and the love of God, which you will manifest by following the most holy Cross in the holy and sweet Crusade. As to this matter, I think that your brother, Messer the Duke of Anjou, will undertake the labour of this holy enterprise, for the love of Christ. There would be reason for self-reproach did so sweet and holy a mystery remain unfulfilled through you. Now in this wise you will follow the footsteps of Christ crucified, you will fulfil the will of God and me, and His commands: as I told you that I wished to see you observe the holy commands of God. I say no more. Pardon my presumption. Remain in the holy and sweet grace of God. Sweet Jesus, Jesus Love.

LETTERS TO FLORENCE

The Florentines played with Catherine as history shows that subtle folk to have played with more than one of the friends whose services they accepted; the story of their dealings with her strongly recalls the situation in Browning's *Luria*. Having been despatched ostensibly with full powers as harbinger of the formal embassy to be sent later, Catherine carried through her part of the negotiations with expedition, prudence and entire success. It shows how such unconventional democracy and matter-of- fact respect for spiritual values existed in the later middle ages, that no one seems to have been surprised at the situation. Apparently it was considered quite natural that a powerful republic should send as its representative to the papal court a young woman, the daughter of simple tradespeople, whose life had been quietly passed in her father's house. Gregory bore himself to Catherine with compunctious deference. On the third day after her arrival she spoke in full consistory, pleading the cause of peace. The result she records in this letter: the Pope put the whole matter in her hands. To the young Dominican were left the terms of reconciliation between the two rival powers.

All now depended upon the arrival of the Florentine ambassadors; but these gentlemen failed to appear, while Florence continued to pursue a contumacious policy. The insult, alike to the Pope and to Catherine, was obvious. Avignon jested, shrugged shoulders, finally sneered. Gregory gently told Catherine the truth--that her friends had played her false. Few more mortifying situations than that in which she found herself could be conceived.

The spirited letter which follows was written ten days after her arrival. She speaks, as usual, without reserve, but it is noteworthy that the letter contains no word of personal reproof beyond the quiet statement: "You might bring great shame and reproach upon me. For nothing but shame and confusion could result if I told the Pope one thing and you another." When at last the ambassadors arrived, they brought small comfort, for they refused to confer with Catherine. In the second letter, written after they had come to a personal friend in Florence, she tells the situation frankly, and with dignity, but still with remarkable freedom from personal bitterness. In this time of test, no lower element than sorrow for the failure of her cause appears to have been present in her mind.

TO THE EIGHT OF WAR CHOSEN BY THE COMMUNE OF FLORENCE, AT WHOSE INSTANCE THE SAINT WENT TO POPE GREGORY XI

In the Name of Jesus Christ crucified and of sweet Mary: Dearest fathers and brothers in Christ Jesus: I Catherine, servant and slave of the servants of Jesus Christ, write to you in His precious Blood: with desire to see you true sons, humble and obedient to your father in such wise that you may never look back, but feel true grief and bitterness over the wrong that you have done to your father. For if he who does wrong does not rise in grief above the wrong he has done, he does not deserve to receive mercy. I summon you to true humiliation of your hearts; not looking back, but going forward, following up the holy resolutions which you began to take, and growing stronger in them every day, if you wish to be received in the arms of your father. As sons who have been dead, do you ask for life; and I hope by the goodness of God that you shall have it, if you are willing really to humble yourselves and to recognize your faults.

But I complain strongly of you, if it is true what is said in these parts, that you have imposed a tax upon the clergy. If this is so, it is a very great evil for two reasons. The first is that you are wronging God by it, for you cannot do it with a good conscience. But it seems to me that you are losing your conscience and everything good; it seems as if you cared for nothing but transitory things of sense, that pass like the wind. Do you not see that we are mortal, and must die, and know not when? Therefore it is great folly to throw away the life of grace, and to bring death on one's own self. I do not wish you to do so any more, for if you did you would be turning back, and you know that it is not he who begins who deserves glory, but he who perseveres to the end. So I tell you that you would never reach an effective peace, unless by perseverance in humility, no longer insulting or offending the ministers and priests of Holy Church.

This is the other thing that I was telling you was harmful and bad. For beside the evil I spoke of that comes from wronging God, I tell you that such action is ruin to your peace. For the Holy Father, if he knew it, would conceive greater indignation against you.

That is what some of the cardinals have said, who are seeking and eagerly desiring peace. Now, hearing this report, they say: "It doesn't seem true that the Florentines want to have peace made; for if it were true, they would beware of any least action that was against the will of the Holy Father and the habits of Holy Church." I believe that sweet Christ on earth himself may say these and like words, and he has excellent reason to say them if he does.

I tell you, dearest fathers, and I beg you, not to choose to hinder the grace of the Holy Spirit, which by no merits of yours He by His clemency is disposed to give you. You might bring great shame and reproach upon me. For nothing but shame and confusion could result if I told the Holy Father one thing and you did another. I beg you that it may not be so any more. Nay, do you exert yourselves to show in word and deed that you wish peace and not war.

I have talked to the Holy Father. He heard me graciously, by God's goodness and his own, showing that he had a warm love of peace; like a good father, who does not consider so much the wrong the son has done to him, as whether he has become humble, so that he may be shown full mercy. What peculiar joy he felt my tongue could not tell. Having discussed with him a good length of time, at the end of our talk he said that if your case were as I presented it to him, he was ready to receive you as sons, and to do what seemed best to me. I say no more here. It seems to me that absolutely no other answer ought to be given to the Holy Father until your ambassadors arrive. I marvel that they are not here yet. When they shall have come, I shall talk to them, and then to the Holy Father, and as I shall find things disposed I will write you. But you, with your taxes and frivolities, are spoiling all that is sown. Do so no more, for the love of Christ crucified and for your own profit. I say no more. Remain in the holy and sweet grace of God. Sweet Jesus, Jesus Love.

Given in Avignon, the 28th day of June, 1376.

TO BUONACCORSO DI LAPO IN FLORENCE WRITTEN WHEN THE SAINT WAS AT AVIGNON

In the Name of Jesus Christ crucified and of sweet Mary: Dearest brother in Christ sweet Jesus: I Catherine, servant and slave of the servants of Jesus Christ, write to you in His precious Blood: with desire to see you and the others your lords, pacify your heart and soul in His most sweet Blood, wherein all hate and warfare is quenched, and all human pride is lowered. For in the Blood man sees God humbled to his own level, assuming our humanity, which was opened and nailed and fastened on the Cross, so that it flows from the wounds of the Body of Christ crucified, and pours over us the Blood which is ministered to us by the ministers of Holy Church. I beg you by the love of Christ crucified to receive the treasure of the Blood given you by the Bride of Christ. Be reconciled, be reconciled to her in the Blood; recognize your sins and offences against her. For he who recognizes his sin, and shows that he does so by his deeds, and humbles him, always receives mercy. But he who shows repentance only in speech, and goes no further in works, never finds it. I do not say this so much for you as for others who might fall into this fault.

Oh me, oh me, dearest brother! I mourn over the methods which have prevailed in asking the Holy Father for peace. For words have been more in evidence than deeds. I say this because when I came yonder into the presence of you and your lords, they seemed by their words to have repented for their wrong, and to be willing to humble themselves and to ask mercy from the Holy Father. And when I said to them: "See, gentlemen, if you intend to show all possible humility in deed and speech, and wish me to offer you like dead children to your father, I will take all the trouble you wish in this matter, otherwise I will not go yonder," they answered me that they were content. Alas, alas! dearest brothers, this was the way and the door by which you ought to have entered, and there is no other. Had this way been followed in deed as in word, you would have had the most glorious peace that anyone ever gained. And I do not say this without reason, for I know what the Holy Father's disposition was; but since we began to leave that path, following the astute ways of the world, doing differently from what our words had previously implied, the Holy Father has had reason, not for peace, but for more disturbance. For when your ambassadors came into these parts, they did not hold to the right way which the servants of God indicated to them. You went on in your own ways. And I never had a chance to confer with them, as you told me that you would direct when I asked for a letter of credentials, so that we might confer together about everything, and you said: "We do not believe that this thing will ever be accomplished by any other hands than those of the servants of God." Exactly the contrary has been done. All is because we have not yet true recognition of our faults. I perceive that those humble words proceeded rather from fear and policy than from a real impulse of love and virtue; for had the wrong done really been recognized, deeds would have corresponded to the sound of words, and you would have trusted your needs and what you wished from the Holy Father to the hands of the true servants of God. They would so have conducted your affairs and those of the Holy Father that you would have reached a good understanding. You have not done it; wherefore I have felt great bitterness, over the wrong done to God and over our loss.

But you do not see what evil and what great misfortunes come from your obstinacy, and clinging fast to your resolution! Oh me, oh me! loose yourselves from the bond of pride, and bind you to the humble Lamb; and do not scorn or oppose His Vicar. No more thus! For the love of Christ crucified! Hold not His Blood cheap! That which has not been done in past time, do it now. Do not feel bitter or scornful should it seem to you that the Holy Father demanded what appeared very hard and impossible to do. Nevertheless he will not wish anything but what is possible to you. But he does as a true father, who beats his son when he does wrong. He reproves him very severely, to make him humble, and cognizant of his fault; and the true son does not grow angry with his father, for he sees that whatever he does is done for love of him; therefore the more the father drives him off, the more he returns to him, ever asking for mercy. So I tell you, on behalf of Christ crucified, that the more times you should be spurned by our father Christ on earth, so many times you are to flee to him. Let him do as he will, for he is right.

Behold that now he is coming to his bride, that is to hold the seat of St. Peter and St. Paul. Do you run to him at once, with true humility of heart and amendment of your sins, following the holy principle with which you began. So doing, you shall have peace, spiritual and bodily. And if you do in any other way, our ancestors never had so many woes as we shall have, for we shall call down the wrath of God upon us, and shall not share in the Blood of the Lamb.

I say no more. Be as urgent as you can, now that the Holy Father is to be at Rome. I have done, and shall do, what I can, until death, for the honour of God and for your peace, in order that this obstacle may be removed, for it hinders the holy and sweet Crusade. If no other ill should come from it, we are worthy of a thousand hells. Comfort you in Christ our sweet Jesus, for I hope by His goodness that if you will keep in the way you should you will have a good peace. Remain in the holy and sweet grace of God. Sweet Jesus, Jesus Love.

TO GREGORY XI

The attempt to reconcile Gregory with the Florentines miscarried through their own fault. Catherine, far from being daunted by mortification or failure, bent herself with new energy to the cause which she had even more deeply at heart--the return of the Pope to Rome. The ascendency which she obtained over his sensitive spirit was soon evident to everyone, and no sooner was it realized than counter influences were set to work. Other people beside this woman of Siena could write letters, and, since Gregory proved superstitious and susceptible to the influence of holy fools, why, there were ecstatics enough in Europe! The Pope, as is obvious from this reply of Catherine's, had received an anonymous epistle, craftily wrought, purporting to come from a man of God, working on his well-known love for his family and timidity of nature, warning him of poison should he venture to return to Rome. Whether Catherine's surmise that the letter was a forgery proceeding from the papal court was justified we do not know; the episode is of interest to us now chiefly because it called forth a reply which shows how sardonic the meek of the earth can be. Catherine's trenchant exposure of the weakness of the anonymous correspondent shows her in a new aspect. Terrible is the scorn of the gentle. "He who wrote it does not seem to me to understand his trade very well; he ought to put himself to school," writes she, and proceeds with analysis so convincing and exhortation so invigorating that even the vacillating Gregory must have been magnetized afresh with power to resolve. One feels in the letter that Catherine is as near impatience with him and with the situation as is permitted to a saint. Gregory must have felt the sting in her words when she tells him plainly that his correspondent treats him like a coward or a frightened child, and adds on her own part, "I pray you on behalf of Christ crucified that you be no longer a timorous child, but manly. Open your mouth, and swallow down the bitter for the sake of the sweet." If anyone could hold a weak nature true to its better self, it would be this woman, endued as she was with a vitality that tingles through her words down the centuries.

In the Name of Jesus Christ crucified and of sweet Mary:

Most holy and reverend sweet father in Christ sweet Jesus: your poor unworthy daughter Catherine, servant and slave of the servants of Jesus Christ, writes to your Holiness in His precious Blood, with desire to see you so strong and persevering in your holy resolve that no contrary wind can hinder you, neither devil nor creature. For it seems that your enemies are disposed to come, as Our Saviour says in His holy gospel, in sheeps' raiment, looking like lambs, while they are ravening wolves. Our Saviour says that we should be on our guard against such. Apparently, sweet father, they are beginning to approach you in writing; and beside writing, they announce to you the coming of the author, saying that he will arrive at your door when you know it not. The man sounds humble when he says, "If it is open to me, I will enter and we will reason together"; but he puts on the garment of humility only that he may be believed. And the virtue in which pride cloaks itself is really boastful.

So far as I have understood, this person has treated your Holiness in this letter as the devil treats the soul, who often, under colour of virtue and compassion, injects poison into it. And he uses this device especially with the servants of God, because he sees that he could not deceive them with open sin alone. So it seems to me that this incarnate demon is doing who has written you under colour of compassion and in holy style, for the letter purports to come from a holy and just man, and it does come from wicked men, counsellors of the devil, who cripple the common good of the Christian congregation and the reform of Holy Church, self-lovers, who seek only their own private good. But you can soon discover, father, whether it came from that just man or not. And it seems to me that, for the honour of God, you must investigate.

So far as I can understand, I do not think the man a servant of God, and his language does not so present him--but the letter seems to me a forgery. Nor does he who wrote it understand his trade very well. He ought to put himself to school--he seems to have known less than a small child.

Notice, now, most Holy Father: he has made his first appeal to the tendency that he knows to be the chief frailty in man, and especially in those who are very tender and pitiful in their natural affections, and tender to their own bodies--for such men as these hold life dearer than any others. So he fastened on this point from his first word. But I hope, by the goodness of God, that you will pay more heed to His honour and the safety of your own flock than to yourself, like a good shepherd, who ought to lay down his life for his sheep.

Next, this poisonous man seems on the one hand to commend your return to Rome, calling it a good and holy thing; but, on the other hand, he says that poison is prepared for you there; and he seems to advise you to send trustworthy men to precede you, who will find the poison on the tables-- that is, apparently, in bottles, ready to be administered by degrees, either by the day, or the month, or the year. Now I quite agree with him that poison can be found--for that matter, as well on the tables of Avignon or other cities as on those of Rome: and prepared for administration slowly, by the month, or the year, or in large quantities, as may please the purchaser: it can be found everywhere. So he would think it well for you to send, and delay your return for this purpose he proposes that you wait till divine judgment fall by this means on those wicked men who, it would seem, according to what he says, are seeking your death. But were he wise, he would expect that judgment to fall on himself, for he is sowing the worst poison that has been sown for a long time in Holy Church, inasmuch as he wants to hinder you from following God's call and doing your duty. Do you know how that poison would be sown? If you did not go, but sent, as the good man advises you, scandal and rebellion, spiritual and temporal, would be stirred up--men finding a lie in you, who hold the Seat of Truth. For since you have decided on your return and announced it, the scandal and bewilderment and disturbance in men's hearts would be too great if they found that it did not happen. Assuredly he says the truth: he is as prophetic as Caiphas when he said: "It is necessary for one man to die that the people perish not." He did not know what he was saying, but the Holy Spirit, who spoke the truth by his mouth, knew very well--though the devil did not make him speak with this intention. So this man is likely to be another Caiphas. He prophesies that if you send, men will find poison. Truly so it is; for were your sins so great that you stayed and they went, your confidants will find poison bottled in their hearts and mouths, as was said. And not only enough for one day, but it would last the month and the year before it was digested. Much I marvel at the words of this man, who commends an act as good and holy and religious, and then wants this holy act to be given up from bodily fear! It is not the habit of the servants of God ever to be willing to give up a spiritual act or work on account of bodily or temporal harm, even should life itself be spent: for had they done thus, none of them would have reached his goal. For the perseverance of holy and good desire into good works, is the thing which is crowned, and which merits glory and not confusion.

Therefore I said to you, Reverend Father, that I desired to see you firm and stable in your good resolution (since on this will follow the pacification of your rebellious sons and the reform of Holy Church) and also to see you fulfil the desire felt by the servants of God, to behold you raise the standard of the most holy Cross against the infidels. Then can you minister the Blood of the Lamb to those wretched infidels: for you are cupbearer of that Blood, and hold the keys of it.

Alas, father, I beg you, by the love of Christ crucified, that you turn your power to this swiftly, since without your power it cannot be done. Yet I do not advise you, sweet father, to abandon those who are your natural sons, who feed at the breasts of the Bride of Christ, for bastard sons who are not yet made lawful by holy baptism. But I hope, by the goodness of God, that if your legitimate sons walk with your authority, and with the divine power of the sword of holy Writ, and with human force and virtue, these others will turn to Holy Church the Mother, and you will legalize them. It seems as if this would be honour to God, profit to yourself, honour and exaltation to the sweet Bride of Christ Jesus, rather than to follow the foolish advice of this just man, who propounds that it would be better for you and for other ministers of the Church of God to live among faithless Saracens than among the people of Rome and Italy.

I am pleased by the commendable hunger that he has for the salvation of the infidels, but I am not pleased that he wishes to take the father from his lawful sons, and the shepherd from the sheep gathered in the fold. I think he wants to treat you as the mother treats the child when she wants to wean him: she puts something bitter on her bosom, that he may taste the bitterness before the milk, so that he may abandon the sweet through fear of the bitter; because a child is more easily deluded by bitterness than by anything else. So this man wants to do to you, suggesting to you the bitterness of poison and of great persecution, to delude the childishness of your weak sensuous love, that you may leave the milk through fear: the milk of grace, which follows on your sweet return. And I beg of you, on behalf of Christ crucified, that you be not a timorous child, but manly. Open your mouth, and swallow down the bitter for the sweet. It would not befit your holiness to abandon the milk for the bitterness. I hope by the infinite and inestimable goodness of God, that if you choose He will show favour to both us and to you; and that you will be a firm and stable man, unmoved by any wind or illusion of the devil, or counsel of devil incarnate, but following the will of God and your good desire, and the counsel of the servants of Jesus Christ crucified.

I say no more. I conclude that the letter sent to you does not come from that servant of God named to you, and that it was not written very far away; but I believe that it comes from very near, and from the servants of the devil, who have little fear of God. For in so far as I might believe that it came from that man, I should not hold him a servant of God unless I saw some other proof. Pardon me, father, my over-presumptuous speech. Humbly I ask you to pardon me and give me your benediction. Remain in the holy and sweet grace of God. I pray His infinite Goodness to grant me the favour soon, for His honour, to see you put your feet beyond the threshold in peace, repose, and quiet of soul and body. I beg you, sweet father, to grant me audience when it shall please your Holiness, for I would find myself in your presence before I depart. The time is short: therefore, wherever it may please you, I wish that it might be soon. Sweet Jesus, Jesus Love.

TO MONNA LAPA HER MOTHER BEFORE SHE RETURNED FROM AVIGNON

Catherine succeeded in her great aim. In September, 1376, Gregory actually started for Rome. Her mission being ended, Catherine set forth on her homeward journey on the same day as the Pope, though by a different route. But her progress was interrupted at Genoa, where, owing to illness among her companions, she was detained for a month in the house of Madonna Orietta Scotta. Her prolonged absence seems to have been too much for the patience of Monna Lapa, who was always unable to understand in the least the actions of her puzzling though beloved child. Catherine, though lifted into the region of great anxieties and great triumphs, was yet always tenderly mindful of the claims of home. Very daughterly, very gently wise, is this little letter to the lonely and fretful mother, written when the saint had just passed through those exciting and decisive months at the Papal court.

In the Name of Jesus Christ crucified and of sweet Mary:

Dearest mother in Christ sweet Jesus: Your poor, unworthy daughter Catherine comforts you in the precious Blood of the Son of God. With desire have I desired to see you a true mother, not only of my body but of my soul; for I have reflected that if you are more the lover of my soul than of my body, all disordinate tenderness will die in you, and it will not be such a burden to you to long for my bodily presence; but it will rather be a consolation to you, and you will wish, for the honour of God, to endure every burden for me, provided that the honour of God be wrought. Working for the honour of God, I am not without the increase of grace and power in my soul. Yes, indeed, it is true that if you, sweetest mother, love my soul better than my body, you will be consoled and not disconsolate. I want you to learn from that sweet mother, Mary, who, for the honour of God and for our salvation, gave us her Son, dead upon the wood of the most holy Cross. And when Mary was left alone, after Christ had ascended into Heaven, she stayed with the holy disciples; and although Mary and the disciples had great consolation together, and to separate was sorrow, nevertheless, for the glory and praise of her Son, for the good of the whole universal world, she consented and chose that they should go away. And she chose the burden of their departure rather than the consolation of their remaining, solely through the love that she had for the honour of God and for our salvation. Now, I want you to learn from her, dearest mother. You know that it behoves me to follow the will of God; and I know that you wish me to follow it. His will was that I should go away; which going did not happen without mystery, nor without fruit of great value. It was His will that I should come, and not the will of man; and whoever might say the opposite, it is not the truth. And thus it will behove me to go on, following His footsteps in what way and at what time shall please His inestimable goodness. You, like a good, sweet mother, must be content, and not disconsolate, enduring every burden for the honour of God, and for your and my salvation. Remember that you did this for the sake of temporal goods, when your sons left you to gain temporal wealth; now, to gain eternal life, it seems to you such an affliction that you say that you will go and run away if I do not reply to you soon. All this happens to you because you love better that part which I derived from you--that is, your flesh, with which you clothed me--than what I have derived from God. Lift up, lift up your heart and mind a little to that sweet and holiest Cross where all affliction ceases; be willing to bear a little finite pain, to escape the infinite pain which we merit for our sins. Now, comfort you, for the love of Christ crucified, and do not think that you are abandoned either by God or by me. Yet shall you be comforted, and receive full consolation; and the pain has not been so great that the joy shall not be greater. We shall come soon, by the mercy of God; and we should not have delayed our coming now, were it not for the obstacle we have had in the serious illness of Neri. Also Master Giovanni and Fra Bartolommeo have been ill.... I say no more. Commend us.... Remain in the holy and sweet grace of God. Sweet Jesus, Jesus Love!

TO MONNA GIOVANNA DI CORRADO MACONI

Monna Lapa was evidently not the only mother in Siena who fretted over the long absence from home of Catherine and her spiritual children. Monna Giovanna, of the noble family of the Maconi, longed for the presence of Catherine's secretary, her beloved son Stefano. This is the second letter which Catherine wrote in the effort to reconcile her. We cannot be surprised if she murmured. Stefano had known Catherine for a few months only when she bore him off with her to Avignon. Their relations dated from January, 1376, when at his entreaty she healed a feud of long standing between the Maconi and the rival house of the Tolomei. From this time he attached himself to her person, and his devotion to her made him an object of ridicule to his bewildered former friends. He was, by all accounts, a singularly attractive and lovable young man-- sunny, light-hearted, and popular wherever he went. Catherine from the first loved him, as she avows in this letter, with especial tenderness. She made him her trusted intimate, and from now until shortly before her death he was in almost constant attendance upon her, or when away was still occupied in her affairs. Catherine was evidently on intimate and affectionate terms with the rest of the Maconi family also; but it is not strange if Monna Giovanna developed a little motherly jealousy, as she saw her brilliant son not only absorbed by this new friendship, but borne away to distant lands. Catherine's letter is as applicable to-day as then, to all parents whose misguided tenderness would seek to hinder their children in a high vocation.

In the Name of Jesus Christ crucified and of sweet Mary:

To you, dearest sister and daughter in Christ Jesus: I Catherine, servant and slave of the servants of Jesus Christ, write in His precious Blood, with desire to see you clothed in the wedding garment. For I consider that without this garment the soul cannot please its Creator, nor take its place at the Marriage Feast in the enduring life. I wish you, therefore, to be clothed in it; and in order that you may clothe you the better, I wish you to divest yourself of all self-love according to nature and the senses, which you feel for yourself, your children, and any other created thing. You ought to love neither yourself nor anything else apart from God; for it is impossible that a man can serve two masters; if he serve the one, he does not give satisfaction to the other. And there is no one who can serve both God and the world, for they have no harmony with each other. The world seeks honour, rank, wealth, sons in high place, good birth, sensuous pleasure and indulgence, all rooted in perverted pride; but God seeks and wants exactly the opposite. He wants voluntary poverty, a humbled heart, disparagement of self and of every worldly joy and grace; that personal honour be not sought, but the honour of God and the salvation of one's neighbour. Let a man seek only in what way he may clothe him in the fire of most ardent charity with the ornament of sweet and sincere virtue, with true and holy patience; let him take no revenge on another for any injury his neighbour may show him, but endure all in patience, seeking only to pass sentence on himself, because he sees that he has wronged the Sweet Primal Truth. And what he loves, let him love in God, and apart from God love nothing.

And did you say to me, "In what way should I love?" I answer you that children and everything else should be loved for love of Him who created them, and not for love of one's self or the children; and that God should never be wronged for their sake or any other. That is, do not love through regard to any utility, nor as your own thing, but as a thing lent to you: since whatever is given us in this life is given for use, as a loan, and is left to us so long only as pleases the Divine Goodness which gave it us. You should use everything, then, as a steward of Christ crucified, spending your temporal substance so far as is possible to you for the poor, who stand in the place of God; and so you ought to spend your children, nourishing and educating them ever in the fear of God, and wishing that they should die rather than wrong their Creator. Oh, make a sacrifice of yourself and them to God! And if you see that God is calling them, offer no resistance to His sweet will: but if they welcome it with one hand, do you reach out both like a true loving mother, who loves their salvation; do not desire to shape their lives to suit yourself--for this would be a sign that you loved them apart from God--but with any state to which God calls them, with that be you content. For a mother who loves her children according to the wickedness of the world, says many a time: "It pleases me well that my children should please God; they can serve Him in the world as well as anywhere else." But it happens often to these simple mothers, who want to plunge their children in the world, that later they possess those children neither in the world nor in God. And it is a just thing that they should be deprived of them, spirit and body, since such ignorance and pride reigns in them that they want to lay down law and rule to the Holy Spirit, who is calling them. Such people do not love their children in God, but with sensuous self-love apart from God, for they love their bodies more than their souls. Never, dearest sister and daughter in Christ sweet Jesus, could he clothe himself in Christ crucified who had not first divested him of this. I hope by the goodness of God that all this will not apply to you, but that you will give yourself and them to the honour and glory of the Name of God, like a true good mother, and so shall you be clothed in the Wedding Garment. But in order that you may clothe you the better, I want that you should lift your desire and heart above the world and all its doings, and that you should open the eye of the mind to know what love God bears to you, who has given you, for love, the Word, His Only-Begotten Son; and the Son in burning love has given you life, and has sacrificed His Body that He might cleanse us with His Blood. Ignorant are we and wretched who nor know nor love so great a benefit! But all this is because our eyes are closed; for were they open, and had they fastened themselves on Christ crucified, they would not be ignorant nor ungrateful in presence of so great grace. Therefore I say to you, keep your eyes ever open, and fasten them fixedly on the Lamb that was slain, in order that you may never fall into ignorance.

Up, sweetest daughter, let us delay no more! Let us recover the time we have lost, with true and perfect love; so that, clothing ourselves in this life with the garment I spoke of, we may joy and exult at the Marriage Feast in the enduring life-- you and your husband and your children together. And comfort you sweetly, and be patient, and do not grow disturbed because I have kept Stefano so long: for I have taken good care of him, for by love and tenderness I have become one thing with him, therefore I have treated your things as if they were my own. I think you have not taken this in bad part. I wish to do whatever I can for him and for you, even to death. You, mother, bore him once; and I wish to bear him and you and all your family, in tears and sweats, by continual prayers and desire for your salvation.

I say no more. Commend me to Currado, and bless all the rest of the family, and especially my little new plant, that has just been planted anew in the Garden of Holy Church. Be it commended to you, and do you bring it up for me virtuously, so that it may shed fragrance among the other flowers. God fill you with His most sweet favour. Remain in the holy and sweet grace of God. Sweet Jesus, Jesus Love.

TO MESSER RISTORO CANIGIANI

Apart from her relations with Religious seeking to follow the Counsels, Catherine directed the life of a number of devout laymen. Among these was Ristoro Canigiani, an honourable citizen of Florence, whose younger brother, Barduccio, became one of her secretaries, and was with her at her death. In the first letter to Ristoro here given, we see that he had already become Catherine's disciple. He had evinced his sincerity by forgiving his enemies--a feat more practical and difficult for most men in those days than now--by withdrawing in a measure from society-- (ecclesiastical, one notes, as well as secular)--and by embracing the simple life, selling his superfluous possessions. In the second letter given, he has evidently advanced in experience. Like many religious souls since his day, he suffers from scruples lest he be unworthy to receive the Holy Communion. Catherine handles his difficulties tenderly and wisely, in words which all anxious souls would do well to take to heart. She has no reproofs for this excellent man, only applause and encouragement. It is noteworthy that neither in these letters nor in any others does she seek to induct Ristoro into that region of ecstatic mystery where she herself lived, and whither she was wont to expect--often in vain--certain of her friends to follow her. The standard which she sets for this devout layman could not be better summed up than in the familiar words: "A sober, godly, and righteous life."

In other letters to Ristoro she seeks to inspire him with a fervour of charity by very beautiful meditations, in which she presents the love of friends and family as sanctified and glorified by its relation to the all- enfolding Love from which all pure human affection must proceed. In her attitude toward the natural world and its claims, Catherine again recalls St. Bernard, who, in naming the degrees of love, starts from an hypothesis which sets forth natural things, not as evil and destroying, but good, and waiting their transfiguration. Like poor Francesca, but with a conception more pure, Catherine rings the changes on the words "amore," "amare." "Perocche, condizione e del' amore d' amare quando si sente amare, d' amare tutte le cose che ama colui ch' egli ama. E pero, a mano che l' anima ha conosciuto l' amore del suo Creatore verso di lui, l' ama: e amandolo, ama tutte quelle cose che Dio ama." "For it is of the nature of love, to love when it feels itself loved, and to love all things loved of its beloved. So when the soul has by degrees known the love of its Creator toward it, it loves Him, and, loving Him, loves all things whatsoever that God loves." ... As we read, we recognize once more how far is this great Mystic from the cold asceticism that has sometimes been attributed to her.

In the Name of Jesus Christ crucified and of sweet Mary:

Dearest brother in Christ sweet Jesus: I Catherine, servant and slave of the servants of Jesus Christ, write to you in His precious Blood, with desire to see you constant and persevering in virtue; for it is not he who begins who is crowned, but only he who perseveres. For Perseverance is the Queen who is crowned; she stands between Fortitude and true Patience, but she alone receives a crown of glory. So I want you, dearest brother, to be constant and persevering in virtue, that you may receive the reward of your every labour. I hope in the great goodness of God that He will fortify you in such wise that neither demon nor fellow-creature can make you look back to your vomit.

You seem, according to what you write me, to have made a good beginning, in which I rejoice greatly for your salvation, seeing your holy desire. First, you say that you have forgiven every man who had wronged you or wished to wrong you. This is a thing which is very necessary, if you wish to have God in your soul through grace, and to be at rest even according to the world. For he who abides in hate is deprived of God and is in a state of condemnation, and has in this life the foretaste of hell; for he is always gnawing at himself, and hungers for vengeance, and abides in fear. Believing to slay his enemy, he has first killed himself, for he has slain his soul with the knife of hate. Such men as these, who think to slay their enemy, slay themselves. He who truly forgives through the love of Christ crucified, has peace and quiet, and suffers no perturbation; for the wrath that perturbs is slain in his soul, and God the Rewarder of every good gives him His grace and at the last eternal life. What joy the soul, then, receives, and gladness and rest in its conscience, the tongue could never tell. And even according to the world, very great honour is given to the man who through love of virtue and magnanimity does not greedily desire to wreak vengeance on his enemy. So I summon you and comfort you, to persevere in this holy resolution.

To demand and obtain your own in a reasonable way, this you can do with good conscience; whoever wants to can do it: for a man is not bound to abandon his possessions more than he chooses; but he who would choose to abandon them would reach a much greater perfection. It is well and excellent not to go to the Bishop's house nor to the palace, but to stay peaceably at home. For if other people get excited, we are weak, and often we find our own soul excited, and doing unjust and irrational things, one to show that he knows more than another, and one from appetite for money. Yes, it is better to keep away from the place.

But I add one thing: that when such poor men and women as are clearly in the right, and have no one to help them, show us the reason why they have no money, it would be greatly to the honour of God for you to undertake their cause, from the impulse of charity, like St. Ives, who in his time was the lawyer of the poor. Consider that the deed of pity, and ministering to the poor with those faculties which God has given you, is very pleasing to God, and salvation to your soul. Therefore St. Gregory says that it is impossible that a pitiful man should perish with an evil, that is, an eternal death. This, then, pleases me much, and I beg you to do it.

In all your works put God before your eyes, saying to yourself when intemperate appetite would lift its head against the resolution you have made: "Consider, my soul, that the eye of God is upon thee, and sees the secret of thy heart. Thou art mortal, for thou must die, and knowest not when; and it shall befit thee to render account before the highest Judge of what thou shalt do--a Judge who punishes every fault and rewards every good deed." In this wise, if you put on the bit it will not slip off, separating from the will of God.

You ought to give satisfaction to your soul as soon as you can, and unburden your conscience of what you feel it burdened with. Give it satisfaction, either for the trouble it has felt in giving up temporal possessions, or for the other annoyances that others have given it. And have pardon asked fully from everyone, in order that you may always remain in the joy of charity with your neighbour. As for selling the goods which you have over and above, and the showy garments (which are very harmful, dearest brother, and a means of penetrating the heart with vanity, and nourishing it with pride, since they make a man seem to be more and bigger than others, boasting of what one ought not to boast of; so it is great shame to us, false Christians, to see our Head tormented, and to abide ourselves in such luxuries: so St. Bernard says, that it is not fitting for limbs to be delicate beneath a thorn-crowned Head),--I say that you do very well to find a remedy for this. But clothe you as you need, modestly, at no immoderate price, and you will greatly please God. And, so far as you can, make your wife and your sons do the same; so that you may be to them example and teacher, as the father should be, who should educate his sons with the words and deeds of virtue.

I add one thing; that you abide in the state of marriage, with fear of God, and treat it with reverence as a sacrament, and not with intemperate desire. Hold in due reverence the days ordered by Holy Church, like a reasonable man, and not a brute beast. Then from yourself and her, like good trees, you will bring forth good fruits.

You will do very well to refuse offices; for a man seldom fails to give offence in them. It ought to weary you simply to hear them mentioned. Let the dead, then, bury themselves, and do you exert yourself, in liberty of heart, to please God, loving Him above everything in the desire of virtue, and your neighbour as yourself, fleeing the world and its delights. Renounce your sins and your own fleshly instincts, ever bringing back to memory the favours of God, and especially the favour of the Blood, shed for us with such fire of love.

Again, it is needful for you, if you wish your soul to preserve grace and grow in virtue, to make your holy confession often for your joy, that you may wash your soul's face in the Blood of Christ. At least once a month, since indeed we soil it every day. If more, more; but less it seems to me ought not to be done. And rejoice in hearing the Word of God. And when the season shall come that we are reconciled with our Father, do you communicate on the solemn Feasts, or at least once a year: rejoicing in the Office, and hearing Mass every day; and if you cannot every day, at least you must make an effort, just as far as you can, on the days which are ordered by Holy Church, to which we are bound.

Prayer must not be far from you. Nay, on the due and ordered hours, so far as you can, seek to withdraw a little, to know yourself, and the wrongs done to God, and the largess of His goodness, which has worked and is working so sweetly in you; opening the eye of your mind in the light of most holy faith, to behold how beyond measure God loves us; love which He shows us through the means of His only-begotten Son. And I beg that, if you are not saying it already, you should say every day the office of the Virgin, that she may be your refreshment and your advocate before God. As to ordering your life, I beg you to do it. Fast on Saturday, in reverence for Mary. And never give up the days commanded by Holy Church, unless of necessity. Avoid being at intemperate banquets, but live moderately, like a man who does not want to make a god of his belly. But take food for need, and not for the wretched pleasure it gives. For it is impossible that any man who does not govern himself in eating should keep himself innocent.

But I am sure that the infinite goodness of God, as regards this and all the rest, will make you yourself adopt that rule which will be needful for your salvation. And I will pray, and will make others pray, that He grant you perfect perseverance until death, and illumine you concerning that which you have to do for your salvation. I say no more to you. Remain in the holy and sweet grace of God. Sweet Jesus, Jesus Love.

In the Name of Jesus Christ crucified and of sweet Mary:

Dearest son in Christ sweet Jesus: I Catherine, servant and slave of the servants of Jesus Christ, write to you in His precious Blood: with desire to see you free from every particle of self-love, so that you may not lose the light and knowledge which come from seeing the unspeakable love which God has for you. And because it is light which makes us know this, and false love is what takes light from us, therefore I have very great desire to see it quenched in you. Oh, how dangerous this self-love is to our salvation! It deprives the soul of grace, for it takes from it the love of God and of its neighbour, which makes us live in grace. It deprives us of light, as we said, because it darkens the eye of the mind, and when the light is taken away we walk in darkness, and do not know what we need.

What do we need to know? The great goodness of God, and His unspeakable love toward us; the perverse law which always fights against the Spirit, and our own wretchedness. In this knowledge the soul begins to render His due to God; that is, glory and praise to His Name, loving Him above everything, and the neighbour as one's self, with eager desire for virtue; and the soul bestows hate and displeasure on itself, hating in itself vice, and its own sensuousness, which is the cause of every vice. The soul wins all virtue and grace in the knowledge of itself, abiding therein with light, as was said. Where shall the soul find the wealth of contrition for its sins, and the abundance of God's mercy? In this House of Self- Knowledge.

Now let us see whether we find it in ourselves or not. Let us talk somewhat about it. For, as you wrote me, you have a desire to feel contrition for your sins, and not being able to feel it, you give up for this reason Holy Communion. Now we shall see whether you ought to give it up for this.

You know that God is supremely good, and loved us before we were: and is Eternal Wisdom, and His Power in virtue is immeasurable: so for this reason we are sure that He has power, knowledge, and will to give us what we need. Well we see, in proof, that He gives us more than we know how to ask, and that which was not asked by us. Did we ever ask Him that He should create us reasonable creatures, in His own image and likeness, rather than brute beasts? No. Or that He should create us by Grace by the Blood of the Word, His only-begotten Son, or that He should give us Himself for food, perfect God and perfect Man, flesh and blood, body and soul, united to Deity? Beyond these most high gifts, which are so great, and show such fire of love toward us, that there is no heart so hard that its hardness and cold- ness would not melt by considering them at all: infinite are the gifts and graces which we receive from Him without asking.

Then, since He gives so much without our asking--how much the more will He fulfil our desires when we shall desire a just thing of Him? Nay, who makes us desire and ask it? Only He. Then, if He makes us ask it, it is a sign that He means to fulfil it, and give us what we seek.

But you will say to me: "I confess that He is what thou sayest. But how comes it that many a time I ask, both contrition and other things, and they seem not to be given me?" I answer you: It may be it is through a defect in him who asks, asking imprudently, with words alone and not with his whole heart--and of such as these Our Saviour said that they call Him Lord, Lord, but shall not be known of Him-- not that He does not know them, but for their fault they shall not be known of His mercy. Or, the man who prays asks for something which, if he had it, would be injurious to his salvation. So that, when he does not have what he asks, he really has it, because he asks for it thinking that it would be for his good; but if he had it, it would be to his harm, and it is for his good not to have it; so God has satisfied the intention with which he asked it. So that on God's side we always have our prayer; but this is the case, that God knows the secret and the open, and is aware of our imperfection; so He sees that if He gave us the grace at once as we ask it, we should do like an unclean creature, who, rising from the sweetest honey, does not mind afterwards lighting on a fetid object. God sees that we do so many a time. For, receiving His graces and benefits, sharing the sweetness of His charity, we do not mind afterward alighting on miserable things, turning back to the filth of the world. Therefore, God sometimes does not give us what we ask as soon as we should like, to make us increase in the hunger of our desire, because He rejoices and pleases Himself in seeing the hunger of His creatures toward Him.

Sometimes He will do us the grace by giving it to us in effect though not in feeling. He uses this means with foresight, because He knows that if a man felt himself to possess it, either he would slacken the pull of desire, or would fall into presumption; therefore He withdraws the feeling, but not the grace. There are others who both receive and feel, according as it pleases the sweet goodness of our Physician to give to us sick folk; and He gives to everyone in the way that our sickness needs. You see, then, that in any case the yearning of the creature, with which it asks of God, is always fulfilled. Now we see what we ought to seek, and how prudently.

It seems to me that the Sweet Primal Truth teaches us what we ought to seek when in the holy Gospel, reproving man for the intemperate zeal which he bestows on gaining and holding the honours and riches of the world, He said: "Take no thought for the morrow. Its own care suffices for the day." Here He shows us that we should consider prudently the shortness of time. Then He adds: "Seek first the Kingdom of Heaven; for your heavenly Father knows well that you have need of these lesser things." What is this kingdom, and how is it sought? It is the kingdom of eternal life, and the kingdom of our own soul, for this kingdom of the soul, unless it is possessed through reason, never becomes part of the kingdom of God. With what is it sought? Not only with words--we have already said that such as these are not recognized by God--but with the yearning of true and real virtues. Virtue is what seeks and possesses this kingdom of heaven; virtue, which makes a man prudent, so that he works for the honour of God and the salvation of himself and his neighbour, with prudence and maturity. Prudently he endures his neighbour's faults; prudently he rules the impulse of charity, loving God above everything, and his neighbour as himself. This is the rule: that he hold him ready to give bodily life for the salvation of souls, and temporal goods to help the body of his neighbour. Such a rule is set by prudent charity. Were he imprudent, it would be just the opposite as with many who use a foolish and crazy sort of charity, who many a time, to help their neighbour--I speak not of his soul, but of his body--are ready to betray their own souls, by publishing abroad lies, giving false witness. Such men as these lose charity, because it is not built upon prudence.

We have seen that we must seek the kingdom of Heaven prudently: now I answer you about the attitude we should hold toward the Holy Communion, and how it befits us to take it. We should not use a foolish humility, as do secular men of the world. I say, it befits us to receive that sweet Sacrament, because it is the food of souls without which we cannot live in grace. Therefore no bond is so great that it cannot and must not be broken, that we may come to this sweet Sacrament. A man must do on his part as much as he can, and that is enough. How ought we to receive it? With the light of most holy faith, and with the mouth of holy desire. In the light of faith you shall contemplate all God and all Man in that Host. Then the impulse that follows the intellectual perception, receives with tender love and holy meditation on its sins and faults, whence it arrives at contrition, and considers the generosity of the immeasurable love of God, who in so great love has given Himself for our food. Because one does not seem to have that perfect contrition and disposition which he himself would wish, he must not therefore turn away; for goodwill alone is sufficient, and the disposition which on his part exists.

Again I say, that it befits us to receive as was imaged in the Old Testament, when it was commanded that the Lamb should be eaten roasted and not seethed; whole and not in part; girded and standing, staff in hand; and the blood of the Lamb should be placed on the stone of the threshold. Thus it befits us to receive this Sacrament: to eat it roasted, and not seethed; for were it seethed there would be interposed earth and water-- that is, earthly affections and the water of self-love. Therefore it must be roasted, so that there shall be nothing between. We take it so when we receive it straight from the fire of divine charity. And we ought to be girt with the girdle of conscience, for it would be very shocking that one should advance to so great cleanliness and purity with mind or body unclean. We ought to stand upright, that is, our heart and mind should be wholly faithful and turned toward God; with the staff of the most holy Cross, where we find the teaching of

Christ crucified. This is the staff on which we lean, which defends us from our foes, the world, the devil, and the flesh. And it befits us eat it whole and not in part: that is, in the light of faith, we should contemplate not only the Humanity in this sacrament, but the body and soul of Christ crucified, wrought into unity with Deity, all God and all Man. We must take the Blood of this Lamb and put it upon our forehead--that is, confess it to every rational being, and never deny it, for pain or for death. Thus sweetly it befits us to receive this Lamb, prepared in the fire of charity upon the wood of the Cross. Thus we shall be found signed with the seal of Tau, and shall never be struck by the avenging angel.

I said that it did not befit us, nor do I wish you, to do as many imprudent laymen, who pass over what is commanded them by Holy Church, saying: "I am not worthy of it." Thus they spend a long time in mortal sin without the food of their souls. Oh, foolish humility! Who does not see that thou art not worthy? At what time dost thou await worthiness? Do not await it; for thou wilt be just as worthy at the end as at the beginning. For with all our just deeds, we shall never be worthy of it. But God is He who is worthy, and makes us worthy with His worth. His worth grows never less. What ought we to do? Make us ready on our part, and observe His sweet commandment. For did we not do so, giving up communion, in such wise believing to flee from fault, we should fall into fault.

Therefore I conclude, and will that such folly be not in you; but that you make you ready, as a faithful Christian, to receive this Holy Communion as I said. You will do it just as perfectly as you are in true knowledge of yourself; not otherwise. For if you abide in that knowledge, you will see everything clearly. Do not slacken your holy desire, for pain or loss, or injury or ingratitude of those whom you have served; but manfully, with true and long perseverance you shall persevere till death. Thus I beg you to do by the love of Christ crucified. I say no more. Remain in the holy and sweet grace of God. Sweet Jesus, Jesus Love.

TO THE ANZIANI AND CONSULS AND GONFALONIERI OF BOLOGNA

Catherine lays down admirable political principles, for the fourteenth or for the twentieth century. Yet times have changed, and we can hardly imagine a modern city council giving serious welcome to such a letter as this. It is a fair specimen of the letters which she was in the habit of sending to the governments of the Italian towns--direct, simple, high- minded presentations of the fundamental virtues on which the true prosperity of a State must rest. She was capable, as she showed during the Schism, of detailed political sagacity: but she never lost the womanly conviction that moral generalizations would convict men of sin and point them to the path of holiness. Nor was she wholly wrong. Her letters seem to have been received with respect, and not to have failed in effectiveness. On the present occasion, the authorities of Bologna have evidently sent asking her prayers. These she promises gladly, but adds that the Bolognese must not expect "the servants of God" to do all their work for them.

In the Name of Jesus Christ crucified and of sweet Mary:

Dearest brothers in Christ sweet Jesus: I Catherine, servant and slave of the servants of Jesus Christ, write to you in His precious Blood: with desire to see you divested of the old man and clothed with the new-- divested, that is, of the world and the fleshly self-love which is the old sin of Adam, and clothed with the new Christ sweet Jesus, and His tender charity. When this charity is in the soul, it seeks not its own, but is liberal and generous to render His due to God: to love Him above everything else, and to hate its own lower nature; and to love itself for God, rendering praise and glory to His Name: to render its neighbour benevolence, with fraternal charity and well-ordered love. For charity ought to be regulated: that is, a man must not wrong himself by sinning, in order to rescue one soul--nay more, in order, were it possible, to save the whole world; since it is not lawful to commit the least fault to achieve a great virtue. And our body should not be sacrificed to rescue the body of our neighbour; but we ought surely to sacrifice our bodily life for the salvation of souls, and temporal possessions for the welfare and life of our neighbour. So you see that this charity should be and is regulated in the soul.

But those who are deprived of charity and full of self-love do just the opposite; and as they are extravagant in their affections, so they are in all their works. Thus we see that men of the world serve and love their neighbour without virtue, and in sin; and to serve and please them, they do not mind disserving and displeasing God, and injuring their own souls. This is that perverted love which often kills soul and body--robs us of light and casts us into darkness, robs us of life and condemns us to death, deprives us of the conversation of the Blessed and leads us to that of Hell. And if a man does not correct himself while he has time, he destroys the shining pearls of holy justice, and loses the warmth of true charity and obedience.

Now on whatever side we turn, we see every kind of rational creature lacking in all virtue, and arrayed in this evil fleshly self-love. If we turn to the prelates, they devote themselves so much to their own affairs and live so luxuriously, that they do not seem to care when they see their subjects in the hands of demons. As to the subjects, it is just the same, they do not care to obey either the civil law or the divine, nor do they care to serve one another unless for their own profit. And yet this kind of love, and the union of those who are united by natural love and not by true charity, does not suffice; such friendship suffices and lasts only so long as pleasure and enjoyment lasts, and the personal profit derived from it.

So, when a man is lord, he fails in holy justice. And this is the reason: that he fears to lose his dignity, and, so as not to excite annoyance, he goes about cloaking and hiding men's faults, spreading ointment over a wound at the time when it ought to be cauterized. Oh, miserable my soul! When the man ought to apply the flame of divine charity, and burn out the fault with holy punishment and correction inflicted by holy justice, he flatters and pretends that he does not see. He behaves thus toward those who he sees might impair his dignity; but as to the poor, who count for little and whom he does not fear, he shows very great zeal for justice, and without any mercy or pity imposes most severe punishment for a little fault. What causes such injustice? Self-love. But the wretched men of the world, because they are deprived of truth, do not recognize truth, either as regards their salvation or as regards the true preservation of their lordship. For did they know the truth, they would see that only living in the fear of God preserves their state and the city in peace: they would preserve holy justice, rendering his due to every subject, they would show mercy on whoso deserved mercy, not by passionate impulse, but by regard for truth; and justice they would show on whoso deserved it, built upon mercy, and not on passionate wrath. Nor would they judge by hearsay, but by holy and true justice; and they would heed the common good, and not any private good, and would appoint officials and those who are to rule the city, not by party or prejudice, not for flatteries or bribery, but with virtue and reason alone; and they would choose men mature and excellent, and not mere children--such as fear God and love the Commonwealth and not their own particular advantage. Now in this way, their state and the city is preserved in peace and unity. But unjust deeds, and living in cliques, and the appointment to rule and government of men who do not know how to rule themselves or their families--unjust and violent, passionate lovers of themselves--these are the methods that make them lose both the state of spiritual grace and their temporal state. To such as these it may be said: "In vain thou dost labour to guard thy city if God guard it not: if thou fear not God, and hold Him not before thee in thy works."

So you see, dearest brothers and lords, that self-love ruins the city of the soul, and ruins and overturns the cities of earth. I will that you know that nothing has so divided the world into every kind of people as self-love, from which injustice is for ever born.

Apparently, dearest brothers, you have a desire to increase and preserve the welfare of your city; and this desire moved you to write to me, poor wretch that I am, full of faults. I heard and saw that letter with tender love, and with wish to satisfy your desires, and to exert me, with what grace God shall give me, to offer you and your city before God with continual prayer. If you shall be just men, and carry on your government as I said above, not in passion nor for self-love or your private good, but for the universal good founded on the Rock Christ sweet Jesus, and if you do all your works in His fear, then by means of prayer you shall preserve the state, the peace and unity of your city. Therefore I beg you by the love of Christ crucified--for there is no other way--that since you have the help of the prayers of the servants of God, you should not fail on your side in what is needful. For did you fail you might to be sure be helped a little by the prayers, but not so much that it would not soon come to nothing; because you ought to help, on your part, to bear this weight.

So, considering that if you were clothed in fleshly and personal love, you could not help the servants of God, and that he who does not help himself with virtue and holy zeal for justice, cannot help his brothers' city, I say that it is needful for you to be clothed with the New Man, Christ sweet Jesus, and His immeasurable charity. But we cannot be clothed therein unless first we divest us--nor could I divest me unless I see how harmful it is to me to hold my old sin, and how useful the new garment of divine charity. For when man has seen his sin, he hates it, and strips it off; and loves, and in love arrays him in the garment of virtue woven with the love of the New Man. Now this is the Way. Therefore I said to you that I desired to see you divested of the old man and clothed with the New Man, Christ crucified; and in this way you shall win and keep the state of grace and the state of your city, and you will never fail in the reverence due to Holy Church, but with pleasing manner will render your due and keep your state. I say no more. Remain in the holy and sweet grace of God. Sweet Jesus, Jesus Love.

TO NICHOLAS OF OSIMO

Ardour is the first trait which one feels in approaching the character of Catherine; but the second is fidelity. Neither the one nor the other flagged till the hour of her death. In the grave and tranquil words of this letter we can see, yet more clearly, perhaps, than in the fervid utterances of hours of excitement or crisis, how profound was her conception of the Church, how fixed her resolution to sacrifice herself for "that sweet Bride." Gregory has returned to Italy, and Catherine is knowing a brief respite from public responsibilities in the comparative retirement of Siena. But peace is not yet made with Florence, nor is the reform of the Church even begun. Her heart, however, refuses to harbour discouragement, and seeking as ever to hold others to the same steady pitch of faith and consecration which she herself maintained, she writes to the secretary of the Pope. He appears to have been a holy man who shared her aspirations, but he was evidently disheartened by the apparent failure of his efforts and by the necessary absorption in external things of a life dedicated to public affairs. Catherine's keen analysis leaves Nicholas of Osimo no excuse for indolence. Her letter, especially in the earlier portion, reads like a paraphrase of Newman's fine verses on "Sensitiveness":--

"Time was, I shrank from what was right
　For fear of what was wrong:
I would not mingle in the fight
　Because the foe was strong:
"But now I cast that finer sense
　And sorer shame aside:
Such dread of sin was indolence,
　Such aim at heaven was pride.

"So, when my Saviour calls, I rise,
  And calmly do my best,
 Leaving to Him, with silent eyes
  Of hope and fear, the rest.
"I step, I mount, where He has led;
  Men count my haltings o'er;
 I know them; yet, though self I dread,
  I love His precept more."

In the Name of Jesus Christ crucified and of sweet Mary:

Dearest and most reverend father in Christ sweet Jesus: I Catherine, servant and slave of the servants of Jesus Christ, write to you in His precious Blood: with desire to see you a firm pillar, that shall never move, except in God; never avoiding or refusing the toils and labours laid on you in the mystical body of Holy Church, the sweet Bride of Christ-- neither for the ingratitude and ignorance you found among those who feed in that garden, nor from the weariness that might afflict us from seeing the affairs of the Church get into a disorderly state. For it often happens that when a man is spending all his efforts on something, and it does not come about in the way or to the end that he wants, his mind falls into weariness and sadness, as if he reflected and said: "It is better for thee to give up this enterprise which thou hast begun and worked on so long, and it is not yet come to an end: and to seek peace and quiet in thy own mind." Then the soul ought to reply boldly, hungering for the honour of God and the salvation of souls, and decline personal consolation, and say: "I will not avoid or flee from labour, for I am not worthy of peace and quiet of mind. Nay, I wish to remain in that state which I have chosen, and manfully to give honour to God with my labour, and my labour to my neighbour." Yet sometimes the devil, to make our enterprises weary us, when we feel little peace of mind, will make a suggestion to the man, saying in his thought: "I am doing more harm in this thing than I am deserving good. So I would gladly run away from it, not on account of the labour, but because I do not want to do harm." Oh, dearest father, do not yield either to yourself or the devil, nor believe him, when he puts such thoughts into your heart and mind; but embrace your labour with gladness and ardent desire, and without any servile fear.

And do not be afraid to do wrong in this; for wrong is shown to us in a dis-ordered and perverse will. For when the will is not settled in God, then one does wrong. The time of the soul is not lost because it may be deprived of consolations, and of saying its office and many psalms, and cannot say them at the right time or place, or with that peace of mind which it would itself wish. Nay, it is occupied wholly for God. So it ought not to feel pain in its mind--especially when it is la-bouring and working for the Bride of Christ. For in whatever way or concerning whatever matter we are labouring for her, it is so deserving and gives such pleasure to God, that our intellect does not suffice to see or imagine it.

I recall, dearest father, a servant of God to whom it was shown how pleasing this service is to Him; I tell this that you may be encouraged to bear labours for Holy Church. This servant of God, as I understood, having one time among others an intense desire to shed her blood and her life and annihilate her very consciousness for Holy Church, the Bride of Christ, lifted the eye of her mind to know that she had no being in herself, and to know the goodness of God toward her--that is, to see how God through love had given her being and all gifts and graces that follow from being. So, seeing and tasting such love and such depths of mercy, she saw not how she could respond to God except by love. But because she could be of no use to Him, she could not show her love; therefore she gave herself to considering whether she found anyone to love through Him, by whom she might show love. So she saw that God loved supremely His rational creatures, and she found the same love to all that was given to herself, for all are loved of God. This was the means she found (which showed whether she loved God or not) by which she could be of use. So then she rose ardently, full of charity to her neighbours, and conceived such love for their salvation that she would willingly have given her life for it. So the service which she could not render to God she desired to render to her neighbour. And when she had realized that it befitted her to respond by means of her neighbour, and thus to render Him love for love--as God by means of the Word, His Son, has shown us love and mercy--so, seeing that by means of desire for the salvation of souls, giving honour to God and labour to one's neighbour, God was well pleased--she looked then to see in what garden and upon what table the neighbour might be enjoyed.

Then Our Saviour showed her, saying: "Dearest daughter, it befits thee to eat in the garden of my Bride, upon the table of the most holy Cross, giving thy suffering, and crucified desire, and vigils and prayers, and every activity that thou canst, without negligence. Know that thou canst not have desire for the salvation of souls without having it for Holy Church; for she is the universal body of all creatures who share the light of holy faith, who can have no life if they are not obedient to My Bride. Therefore, thou oughtest to desire to see thy Christian neighbours, and the infidels and every rational creature, feeding in this garden, under the yoke of holy obedience, clothed in the light of living faith, and with good and holy works--for faith without works is dead. This is the common hunger and desire of that whole body. But now I say and will that thou grow yet more in hunger and desire, and hold thee ready to lay down thy life, if need be, in especial, in the mystical body of Holy Church, for the reform of My Bride. For when she is reformed, the profit of the whole world will follow. How? Because through darkness, and ignorance, and self- love, and impurities, and swollen pride, darkness and death are born in the souls of her subjects. So I summon thee and my other servants to labour in desire, in vigils, and prayer, and every other work, according to the skill which I give you; for I tell thee that the labour and service offered her are so pleasing to me, that not only they shall be rewarded in My servants who have a sincere and holy intention, but also in the servants of the world, who often serve her through self-love, though also many a time through reverence for Holy Church. Wherefore I tell thee that there is no one who serves her reverently--so good I hold this service-- who shall not be rewarded; and I tell thee that such shall not see eternal death. So, likewise, in those who wrong and serve ill and irreverently My Bride, I shall not let that wrong go unpunished, by one way or another."

Then, as she saw such greatness and generosity in the goodness of God, and perceived what ought to be done to please Him more, the flame of desire so increased that had it been possible for her to give her life for Holy Church a thousand times a day, and from now till the final judgment day, it seemed to her that it would be less than a drop of wine in the sea. And so it really is.

I wish you, then, and summon you, to labour for her as you have always done; yea, you are a pillar, who have placed yourself to support and help this Bride. So you ought to be, as I said--so that neither tribulation nor consolation should ever stir you. Nor because many contrary winds are blowing to hinder those who walk in the way of truth, ought we for any reason to look back. Therefore I said that I desired to see you a firm pillar. Up, then, dearest and sweetest father: because it is our hour to give for that Bride honour to God and labour to her. I beg you, by the love of Christ crucified, to pray the holy father that he adopt zealously, without negligence, every remedy which can be found consistent to his conscience for the reform of Holy Church and peace to this great war which is damning so many souls, since for all negligence and lukewarmness God will rebuke Him most severely, and will demand the souls who through this are perishing. Commend me to him; and I ask him humbly for his benediction. I say no more. Remain in the holy and sweet grace of God. Sweet Jesus, Jesus Love.

TO MISSER LORENZO DEL PINO OF BOLOGNA, DOCTOR IN DE-CRETALS (WRITTEN IN TRANCE)

The familiar but ever-noble theology with which this letter opens, leads first to a severe description of the unworthy and mercenary man, which is followed by a temperately wise discussion of the true use of worldly pleasures and goods. "Whatever God has made is good and perfect," says Catherine--"except sin, which was not made by Him, and so is not worthy of love." The modern religious Epicureanism which would applaud this sentiment would, however, be less contented with the sequel; for Catherine never forgets the anti-modern position that, though possession be legitimate to the Christian, it is, after all, "more perfect to renounce than to possess," and that the man who has preserved true detachment of mind towards this world's goods will, by inevitable logic, come to hunger, sooner or later, for detachment in deed.

It is a curiously tranquil letter to have been written in trance. Whatever the mysterious condition may have been, it evidently did not rob Catherine of her mental sanity and sobriety. The Doctor of Laws to whom it was addressed was a person of considerable importance in the public and legal life of his time. One cannot help suspecting a personal bearing in the severe description of the hard man--evidently a lawyer--who makes the poor wait before giving them counsel: yet, perhaps, the suspicion is unwarranted, and the letter carried to Misser Lorenzo nothing more searching than a general account of the temptations to which his profession was subject.

In the Name of Jesus Christ crucified and of sweet Mary:

Dearest brother and son in Christ sweet Jesus: I Catherine, servant and slave of the servants of Jesus Christ, write to you in His precious Blood: with desire to see you a lover and follower of truth and a despiser of falsehood. But this truth cannot be possessed or loved if it is not known. Who is Truth? God is the Highest and

Eternal Truth. In whom shall we know Him? In Christ sweet Jesus, for He shows us with His Blood the truth of the Eternal Father. His truth toward us is this, that He created us in His image and likeness to give us life eternal, that we might share and enjoy His Good. But through man's sin this truth was not fulfilled in him, and therefore God gave us the Word His Son, and imposed this obedience on Him, that He should restore man to grace through much endurance, purging the sin of man in His own Person, and manifesting His truth in His Blood. So man knows, by the unsearchable love which he finds shown to him through the Blood of Christ crucified, that God nor seeks nor wills aught but our sanctification. For this end we were created; and whatever God gives or permits to us in this life, He gives that we may be sanctified in Him. He who knows this truth never jars with it, but always follows and loves it, walking in the footsteps of Christ crucified. And as this sweet loving Word, for our example and teaching, despised the world and all delights, and chose to endure hunger and thirst, shame and reproach, even to the shameful death on the Cross, for the honour of the Father and our salvation, so does he who is the lover of the truth which he knows in the light of most holy faith, follow this way and these footsteps. For without this light it could not be known; but when a man has the light, he knows it, and knowing it, loves it, and becomes a lover of what God loves, and hates what God hates.

There is this difference between him who loves the truth and him who hates it. He who hates the truth, lies in the darkness of mortal sin. He hates what God loves, and loves what God hates. God hates sin, and the inordinate joys and luxuries of the world, and such a man loves it all, fattening himself on the world's wretched trifles, and corrupting himself in every rank. If he has an office in which he ought to minister in some way to his neighbour, he serves him only so far as he can get some good for himself out of it, and no farther, and becomes a lover of himself. Christ the Blessed gave His life for us, and such a man will not give one word to serve his neighbour unless he sees it paid, and overpaid. If the neighbour happens to be a poor man who cannot pay, he makes him wait before telling him the truth, and often does not tell it to him at all, but makes fun of him; and where he ought to be pitiful and a father of the poor, he becomes cruel to his own soul because he wrongs the poor. But the wretched man does not see that the Highest Judge will return to him nothing else than what he receives from him, since every sin is justly punished and every good rewarded. Christ embraced voluntary poverty and was a lover of continence; the wretched man who has made himself a follower and lover of falsehood does just the contrary; not only does he fail to be content with what he has, or to refrain through love of virtue, but he robs other people. Nor does he remain content in the state of marriage, in which, if it is observed as it should be, a man can stay with a good conscience; but he plunges into every wretchedness, like a brute beast, without moderation, and as the pig rolls in filth, so does he in the filth of impurity.

But we might say: "What shall I do, who have riches, and am in the state of marriage, if these things bring damnation to my soul?" Dearest brother, a man can save his soul and receive the life of grace into himself, in whatever condition he may be; but not while he abides in guilt of mortal sin. For every condition is pleasing to God, and He is the acceptor, not of men's conditions, but of holy desire. So we may hold to these things when they are held with a temperate will; for whatever God has made is good and perfect, except sin, which was not made by Him, and therefore is not worthy of love. A man can hold to riches and worldly place if he likes, and he does not wrong God nor his own soul; but it would be greater perfection if he renounced them, because there is more perfection in renunciation than in possession. If he does not wish to renounce them in deed, he ought to renounce and abandon them with holy desire, and not to place his chief affections upon them, but upon God alone; and let him keep these things to serve his own needs and those of his family, like a thing that is lent and not like his own. So doing, he will never suffer pain from any created thing; for a thing that is not possessed with love is never lost with sorrow. So we see that the servants of the world, lovers of falsehood, endure very great sufferings in their life, and bitter tortures to the very end. What is the reason? The inordinate love they have for themselves and for created things, which they love apart from God. For the Divine Goodness has permitted that every inordinate affection should be unendurable to itself.

Such a man as this always believes falsehood, because there is no knowledge of truth in him. And he thinks to hold to the world and abide in delights, to make a god of his body, and of the other things that he loves immoderately a god, and he must leave them all. We see that either he leaves them by dying, or God permits that they be taken from him first. Every day we see it. For now a man is rich, and now poor; to-day he is exalted in worldly state, and to-morrow he is cast down; now he is well, and now ill. So all things are mutable, and are taken from us when we think to clasp them firmly; or we are snatched away from them by death.

So you see that all things pass. Then, seeing that they pass, they should be possessed with moderation in the light of reason, loved in such wise as they should be loved. And he who holds them thus will not hold them with the help of sin, but with grace; with generosity of heart, and not with avarice; in pity for the poor, and not in cruelty; in humility, not in pride; in gratitude, not in ingratitude: and will recognize that his possessions come from his Creator, and not himself. With this same temperate love he will love his children, his friends, his relatives, and all other rational beings. He will hold the condition of marriage as ordained, and ordained as a Sacrament; and will have in respect the days commanded by Holy Church. He will be and live like a man, and not a beast; and will be, not indeed ascetic, but continent and self-controlled. Such a man will be a fruitful tree, that will bear the fruits of virtue, and will be fragrant, shedding perfume although planted in the earth; and the seed that issues from him will be good and virtuous.

So you see that you can have God in any condition; for the condition is not what robs us of Him, but the evil will alone, which, when it is set on loving falsehood, is ill-ordered and corrupts a man's every work. But if he loves truth, he follows the footsteps of truth; so he hates what truth hates and loves what truth loves, and then his every work is good and perfect. Otherwise it would not be possible for him to share the life of grace, nor would any work of his bear living fruit.

So, knowing no other way, I said that I desired to see you a lover and follower of truth and despiser of falsehood; hating the devil the father of lies, and your own lower nature, that follows such a parent; and loving Christ crucified, who is Way, Truth and Life. For He who walks in Him reaches the Light, and is clothed in the shining garment of charity, wherein are all virtues found. Which charity and love unspeakable, when it is in the soul, holds itself not content in the common state, but desires to advance further. Thus from mental poverty it desires to advance to actual, and from mental continence to actual; to observe the Counsels as well as the Commandments of Christ; for it begins to feel aversion for the dunghill of the world. And because it sees the difficulty of being in filth and not defiled, it longs with breathless desire and burning charity to free itself by one act from the world so far as possible. If it is not able to escape in deed, it studies to be perfect in its own place. At least, it does not lack desire.

Then, dearest brother, let us sleep no more, but awaken from slumber. Open the eye of the mind in the light of faith, to know, to love, to follow that truth which you shall know through the Blood of the humble and loving Lamb. You shall know that Blood in the knowledge of yourself, that the face of your soul may be washed therein. And it is ours, and none can take it from us unless we choose. Then be negligent no more; but like a vase, fill yourself with the Blood of Christ crucified. I say no more. Remain in the holy and sweet grace of God. Sweet Jesus, Jesus Love.

LETTERS WRITTEN FROM ROCCA D'ORCIA

These informal little notes were written probably in the autumn of 1377 while Catherine was making a visit to the feudal stronghold of the Salimbeni family, about twenty-three miles from Siena, among the foothills of Monte Amiata. The young "populana" was admitted to the intimate counsels of these great nobles, leaders of the opposition to the popular government with which her own sympathies would naturally have lain. It must have been a new experience to the town-bred girl--life in this castle-eyrie among the hills, where mercenary troops and rude peasants thronged the courtyard, and manners, one surmises, must have been at once more artful and more brutal than among her bourgeois friends. We hear of picturesque scenes, where men and women afflicted of demons are brought writhing into her presence, to be welcomed, cared for, and healed. She had the comfort of the company of several confessors; the first of these letters shows them labouring with homely eagerness, quaintly expressed, for the religious welfare of the wild soldiery. Absorbed, as ever, in the inward life, Catherine was as tranquilly at home here in the mountains, among the great ladies of the Salimbeni family, as in Siena or in the papal court.

Meantime, good Monna Lapa grumbled as of old over the separation from her daughter; and evidently Catherine's sister mantellate were also disconsolate. She writes them very gently, very simply, trying to reconcile them by the reminder of like sorrows borne by that first group of disciples to whom she and her friends loved to compare themselves. To her beloved Alessa she expresses herself more freely, giving just the details of health and mental state that intimate love would crave. These were sad days in her private life; for she had parted from Fra Raimondo, who had been called to other service. Her words to Alessa reflect her sadness, and also her entire submission. It is noticeable that she respects the secrets of her hosts with dignity, giving no hint on the matters that occupied her beyond the reticent statement to her mother: "I believe that if you knew the circumstances you yourself would send me here."

This is not the only time by any means that Catherine had to meet similar complaints. Wherever she bore her strong vitality, limitless sympathy and peculiar charm, new friends gathered around her and clung to her with an unreasoning devotion that cried out in exacting hunger for her presence, and often proved to her a real distress. For Catherine, swiftly responsive as she was to individual affections, perfect in loyalty as she always showed herself, moved, nevertheless, in a region where unswerving service of a larger duty might at any moment force her to refuse to gratify, at least in outward ways, the personal claim. This was very hard for her friends to understand; one is sorry for them. At the same time, one feels more than a little pathos in her efforts to bring these simpler minds into understanding sympathy with that high sense of vocation which underlay all her doings: "Know, dearest mother, that I, your poor little daughter, am not put on earth for anything else than this; to this my Creator has chosen me. I know you are content that I should obey Him." But Monna Lapa never was quite content--not to the very end.

TO MONNA LAPA HER MOTHER AND TO MONNA CECCA IN THE MONASTERY OF SAINT AGNES AT MONTEPULCIANO, WHEN SHE WAS AT ROCCA

In the Name of Jesus Christ crucified and of sweet Mary: Dearest mother and daughter in Christ sweet Jesus: I Catherine, servant and slave of the servants of Jesus Christ, write to you in His precious Blood: with desire to see you so clothed in the flames of divine charity that you may bear all pain and torment, hunger and thirst, persecution and injury, derision, outrage and insult, and everything else, with true patience; learning from the Lamb suffering and slain, who ran with such burning love to the shameful death of the Cross. Do you then keep in companionship with sweetest Mother Mary, who, in order that the holy disciples might seek the honour of God and the salvation of souls, following the footsteps of her sweet Son, consents that they should leave her presence, although she loved them supremely: and she stays as if alone, a guest and a pilgrim. And the disciples, who loved her beyond measure, yet leave her joyously, enduring every grief for the honour of God, and go out among tyrants, enduring many persecutions. And if you ask them: "Why do you carry yourselves so joyously, and you are going away from Mary?" they would reply: "Because we have lost ourselves, and are enamoured of the honour of God and the salvation of souls." Well, dearest mother and daughter, I want you to do just so. If up to now you have not been, I want you to be now, kindled in the fire of divine charity, seeking always the honour of God and the salvation of souls. Otherwise you would fall into the greatest grief and tribulation, and would drag me down into them. Know, dearest mother, that I, your poor little daughter, am not put on earth for anything else; to this my Creator has elected me. I know you are content that I should obey Him. I beg you that if I seemed to stay away longer than pleased your will, you will be contented; for I cannot do otherwise. I believe that if you knew the circumstances you yourself would send me here. I am staying to find help if I can for a great scandal. It is no fault of the Countess, though; therefore do you all pray God and that glorious Virgin to send us a good result. And do you, Cecca, and Giustina, drown yourselves in the Blood of Christ crucified; for now is the time to prove the virtue in your soul. God give His sweet and eternal benediction to you all. I say no more. Remain in the holy and sweet grace of God. Sweet Jesus, Jesus Love.

TO MONNA CATARINA OF THE HOSPITAL AND TO GIOVANNA DI CAPO IN SIENA

In the Name of Jesus Christ crucified and of sweet Mary:

Dearest daughters in Christ sweet Jesus: I Catherine, servant and slave of the servants of Jesus Christ, write to you in His precious Blood: with desire to see you obedient daughters, united in true and perfect charity. This obedience and love will dissipate all your suffering and gloom; for obedience removes the thing which gives us suffering, that is our own perverse will, which is wholly destroyed in true holy obedience. Gloom is scattered and consumed by the impulse of charity and unity, for God is true charity and highest eternal light. He who has this true light for his guide, cannot miss the road. Therefore, dearest daughters, I want, since it is so necessary, that you should study to lose your own will and to gain this light.

This is the doctrine which I remember has always been given you, although you have learned little of it. That which is not done, I beg you to do, dearest daughters. If you did not, you would abide in continual sufferings, and would drag poor me, who deserve every suffering, into them too.

We must do for the honour of God as the holy apostles did. When they had received the Holy Spirit, they separated from one another, and from that sweet mother Mary. Although it was their greatest delight to stay together, yet they gave up their own delight, and sought the honour of God and the salvation of souls. And although Mary sends them away from her, they do not therefore hold that love is diminished, or that they are deprived of the affection of Mary. This is the rule that we must take to ourselves. I know that my presence is a great consolation to you. Nevertheless, as truly obedient, you should not seek your own consolation, for the honour of God and the salvation of souls: and do not give place to the devil, who makes it look to you as if you were deprived of the love and devotion which I bear to your souls and bodies. Were it otherwise, true love would not be built on you. I assure you that I do not love you otherwise than in God. Why do you fall into such unregulated suffering over things which must necessarily be so? Oh, what shall we do when it shall befit us to do great deeds if we fail so in the little ones? We shall have to be together or separated according as things shall befall. Just now our sweet Saviour wills and permits that we be separated for His honour.

You are in Siena, and Cecca and Grandma are in Montepulciano. Frate Bartolomeo and Frate Matteo will be there and have been there. Alessa and Monna Bruna are at Monte Giove, eighteen miles from Montepulciano; they are with the Countess and Monna Lisa. Frate Raimondo and Frate Tommaso and Monna Tomma and Lisa and I are at Rocca among the Free-lances. And so many incarnate demons are being eaten up that Frate Tommaso says that his stomach aches over it! With all this they cannot be satisfied, and they are hungry for more, and find work here at a good price. Pray the Divine Goodness to give them big, sweet and bitter mouthfuls! Think that the honour of God and the salvation of souls is being sweetly seen. You ought not to want or desire anything else. You could do nothing more pleasing to the highest eternal will of God, and to mine, than feeling thus. Up, my daughters, begin to sacrifice your own wills to God! Don't be ready always to stay nurselings--for you should get the teeth of your desire ready to bite hard and musty bread, if needs be.

I say no more. Bind you in the sweet bands of love, so you will show that you are daughters--not otherwise. Comfort you in Christ sweet Jesus, and comfort all the other daughters. We will come back as soon as we can, according as it shall please the Divine Goodness. Remain in the holy and sweet grace of God. Sweet Jesus, Jesus Love.

TO MONNA ALESSA CLOTHED WITH THE HABIT OF SAINT DOMINIC, WHEN SHE WAS AT ROCCA

In the Name of Jesus Christ crucified and of sweet Mary: Dearest daughter in Christ sweet Jesus: I Catherine, servant and slave of the servants of Jesus Christ, write to thee in His precious Blood: with desire to see thee follow the doctrine of the Spotless Lamb with a free heart, divested of every creature-love, clothed only with the Creator, in the light of most holy faith. For without the light thou couldst not walk in the straight way of the Slain and Spotless Lamb. Therefore my soul desires to see thee and the others clean and virile, and not blown about by every wind that may befall. Beware of looking back, but go on steadily, holding in mind the teaching that has been given thee. Be sure to enter every day anew into the garden of thy soul with the light of faith to pull up every thorn that might smother the seed of the teaching given thee, and to turn over the earth; that is, every day do thou divest thy heart. It is necessary to divest it over and over; for many a time I have seen people who seemed to have divested themselves, whom I have found clothed in sin, by evidence rather of deed than of words. The opposite might appear by their words, but deeds showed their affections. I want, then, that thou shouldst divest thy heart in truth, following Christ crucified. And let silence abide on thy lips. I have taken note; for I believe that the other woman holds to it very little. I am very sorry for that. If it is so, as it seems to me, my Creator wills that I should bear it, and I am content to do so: but I am not content with the wrong done to God.

Thou didst write me that God seemed to constrain thee in thy orisons to pray for me. Thanks be to the Divine Goodness, who shows such unspeakable love to my poor soul! Thou didst tell me to write thee if I were suffering and had my usual infirmities at this time. I reply that God has cared for me marvellously, within and without. He has cared very much for my body this Advent, causing the pains to be diverted by writing; it is true that, by the goodness of God, they have been worse than they used to be. If He made them worse, He saw to it that Lisa was cured as soon as Frate Santi fell ill--for he has been at the point of death. Now, almost miraculously, he has grown so much better that he can be called cured. But apparently my Bridegroom, Eternal Truth, has wished to put me to a very sweet and genuine test, inward and outward, in the things which are seen and those which are not--the latter beyond count the greater. But while He was testing us, He has cared for us so gently as tongue could not tell. Therefore I wish pains to be food to me, tears my drink, sweat my ointment. Let pains make me fat, let pains cure me, let pains give me light, let pains give me wisdom, let pains clothe my nakedness, let pains strip me of all self-love, spiritual and temporal. The pain of lacking consolations from my fellow-creatures has called me to consider my own lack of virtue, recognizing my imperfection, and the very perfect light of Sweet Truth, who gives and receives, not material things, but holy desires: Him who has not withdrawn His goodness toward me for my little light or knowledge, but has had regard only to Himself, the One supremely Good.

I beg thee by the love of Jesus Christ crucified, dearest my daughter, do not slacken in prayer: nay, redouble it--for I have greater need thereof than thou seest--and do thou thank the Goodness of God for me. And pray Him to give me grace that I may give my life for Him, and to take away, if so please Him, the burden of my body. For my life is of very little use to anyone else; rather is it painful and oppressive to every person, far and near, by reason of my sins. May God by His mercy take from me such great faults, and for the little time that I have to live, may He make me live impassioned by the love of virtue! And may I in pain offer before Him my dolorous and suffering desires for the salvation of all the world and the reformation of Holy Church! Joy, joy in the Cross with me! So may the Cross be a bed where the soul may rest: a table where may be tasted heavenly food, the fruit of patience with quietness and assurance.

Thou didst send to me saying ... I was consoled by this thing, both by her life, hoping that she is correcting herself and living with less vanity of heart than she has done till now, and also by the children's having been brought to the light of Holy Baptism. May God give them His sweetest grace, and grant them death if they are not to be good! Bless them, and comfort her, in Christ sweet Jesus: and tell her to live in the holy and sweet fear of God, and to recognize the grace she has received from God, which has not been small but very great. Were she to be ungrateful, it would much displease God, and perhaps He would not leave her unpunished.

I commend to thee ... I have had no news at all of them, I do not know why. The will of God be done! Our Saviour has put me on the Island, and the winds beat from every side. Let everyone rejoice in Christ crucified, however far one from the other. Shut thee into the house of self- knowledge. I say no more. Remain in the holy and sweet grace of God. Sweet Jesus, Jesus Love.

TO GREGORY XI

There is no evidence as to the date of this letter, but the tone is such that Catherine's latest editor is probably right in placing it after the return of the Pope to Italy. It suggests that a long relation is drawing to a close, and closing, so far as Catherine is concerned, in disappointment. Never, in her earlier relations with Gregory, would she have gone such lengths as here, in her amazing hint that he would better resign the Papacy if he finds himself unable to sustain the moral burdens it imposes. The Pope is at Rome, but he has changed his sky and not his mind. Catherine's letter is a brief and powerful summary of oft-reiterated pleas. In the solemnity and authority of its adjurations, in the distinctness of its accusations, it is surely one of the most surprising epistles ever written by a devout and wholly faithful subject to her acknowledged head. Such a letter proceeds, indeed, from a spiritual region where all earthly distinctions--ecclesiastical as well as intellectual or social--are lost to sight, and the illiterate daughter of the dyer can rebuke and exhort as by her natural right him whom with unwavering faith she believed to be the God-appointed father of all Christian people. Catherine's patience, one feels, is near the breaking point: and heart- break for her is in truth not many years away.

In the Name of Jesus Christ crucified and of sweet Mary:

Most holy and sweet father, your poor unworthy daughter Catherine in Christ sweet Jesus, commends herself to you in His precious Blood: with desire to see you a manly man, free from any fear or fleshly love toward yourself, or toward any creature related to you in the flesh; since I perceive in the sweet Presence of God that nothing so hinders your holy, good desire and so serves to hinder the honour of God and the exaltation and reform of Holy Church, as this. Therefore, my soul desires with immeasurable love that God by His infinite mercy may take from you all passion and lukewarmness of heart, and re-form you another man, by forming in you anew a burning and ardent desire; for in no other way could you fulfil the will of God and the desire of His servants. Alas, alas, sweetest "Babbo" mine, pardon my presumption in what I have said to you and am saying; I am constrained by the Sweet Primal Truth to say it. His will, father, is this, and thus demands of you. It demands that you execute justice on the abundance of many iniquities committed by those who are fed and pastured in the garden of Holy Church; declaring that brutes should not be fed with the food of men. Since He has given you authority and you have assumed it, you should use your virtue and power: and if you are not willing to use it, it would be better for you to resign what you have assumed; more honour to God and health to your soul would it be.

Another demand that His will makes is this: He wills that you make peace with all Tuscany, with which you are at strife; securing from all your wicked sons who have rebelled against you whatever is possible to secure without war--but punishing them as a father ought to punish a son who has wronged him. Moreover, the sweet goodness of God demands from you that you give full authority to those who ask you to make ready for the Holy Crusade--that thing which appears impossible to you, and possible to the sweet goodness of God, who has ordained it, and wills that so it be. Beware, as you hold your life dear, that you commit no negligence in this, nor treat as jests the works of the Holy Spirit, which are demanded from you because you can do them. If you want justice, you can execute it. You can have peace, withdrawing from the perverse pomps and delights of the world, preserving only the honour of God and the due of Holy Church. Authority also you have to give peace to those who ask you for it. Then, since you are not poor but rich--you who bear in your hand the keys of Heaven, to whom you open it is open, and to whom you shut it is shut--if you do not do this, you would be rebuked by God. I, if I were in your place, should fear lest divine judgment come upon me. Therefore I beg you most gently on behalf of Christ crucified to be obedient to the will of God, for I know that you want and desire no other thing than to do His will, that this sharp rebuke fall not upon you: "Cursed be thou, for the time and the strength entrusted to thee thou hast not used." I believe, father, by the goodness of God, and also taking hope from your holiness, that you will so act that this will not fall upon you.

I say no more. Pardon me, pardon me; for the great love which I bear to your salvation, and my great grief when I see the contrary, makes me speak so. Willingly would I have said it to your own person, fully to unburden my conscience. When it shall please your Holiness that I come to you, I will come willingly. So do that I may not appeal to Christ crucified from you; for to no other can I appeal, for there is no greater on earth. Remain in the holy and sweet grace of God. I ask you humbly for your benediction. Sweet Jesus, Jesus Love.

TO RAIMONDO OF CAPUA OF THE ORDER OF THE PREACHERS

This letter confirms what history elsewhere indicates--that Gregory, after his return to Italy, turned against Catherine. She no longer addresses her "dear Babbo" personally, with the old happy familiarity; rather, she sends through Fra Raimondo formal and almost tremulous messages to "his Holiness, the Vicar of Christ." Raimondo, apparently from his connection with her, is evidently included in the papal displeasure. Catherine writes to give him courage and comfort; in her touching advice as to the best way of preparing one's self to meet contentions and injustice, we may recognize the secret source of her own rare self-control.

Catherine's attitude toward the angered Pope is a compound of contrition and firmness. No words could express swifter readiness to accept rebuke or a more passionate humility: none could more vigorously maintain the unwelcome convictions which had given offence. There are various surmises as to the exact occasion of the misunderstanding to which this letter refers: were we to add one, we might suspect that the audacity of the preceding letter had been too much, even for Gregory. But the general situation speaks for itself. Gregory was strong enough, under her inspiration, to make the great physical and moral effort of returning to Italy: he was, as we have seen, not strong enough to cope with what he found there. Enfeebled by ill-health, hampered by his lack of knowledge of Italian, rendered desperate by the difficulties he encountered, it is small wonder that, as many another weak nature would have done, he turned in rage or cold displeasure against the instrument of his return. There is a story that Gregory on his deathbed warned the bystanders against Catherine, and whether it be true or not, it suggests the contemporary impression as to his tone toward her during his last days. Here is sad ending to a relation that during its earlier phases possessed a singular beauty. How sorely Catherine must have been hurt we may well imagine. Her brief triumph was all turned to bitterness: less, we may be sure, from her personal loss of the Pope's confidence--though she was human enough to feel this keenly--than from the utter failure of the hopes she had built on his return.

In this letter her genuine self-abasement before Gregory's displeasure changes with dramatic suddenness to another tone. The accuser becomes the judge once more, and speaks with the old authority: "God demands that you do this--as you know that you were told." Her personal feeling for the man breaks forth in the appeal: "To whom shall I have recourse should you abandon me? Who would help me?" But in the same breath comes her magnificent assurance, that though she may offend Christ's Vicar, the Head of the Church, she may yet flee with confidence to Christ Himself, and rest secure upon the bosom of His Bride.

In the Name of Jesus Christ crucified and of sweet Mary:

Dearest and sweetest father in Christ sweet Jesus: I Catherine, servant and slave of the servants of Jesus Christ, write to you in His precious Blood: with desire to see you a true combatant against the wiles and vexations of the devil, and the malice and persecution of men, and against your own fleshly self-love, which is an enemy that, unless a man drives it away by virtue and holy hate, prevents him from ever being strong in the other battles which we encounter every day. For self-love weakens us, and therefore it is imperative that we drive it away with the strength of virtue, which we shall gain in the unspeakable love that God has shown us, through the Blood of His only-begotten Son. This love, drawn from the divine love, gives us light and life; light, to know the truth when necessary to our salvation and to win great perfection, and to endure with true patience and fortitude and constancy until death--for by such fortitude, won from the light that makes us know the truth, we win the life of divine grace. Drink deep, then, in the Blood of the Spotless Lamb, and be a faithful servant, not faithless, to your Creator. And fear not, nor turn back, for any battle or gloom that may come upon you, but persevere in faith till death; for well you know that perseverance will give you the fruit of your labours.

I have understood from a certain servant of God who holds you in continual prayer before Him, that you have met very great battles, and that gloom has fallen upon your mind through the crafts and wiles of the devil, who wishes to make you see wrong as right and right as wrong; this he does in order that you may fail in your going and not reach the goal. But comfort you, for God has provided and shall provide, and His providence shall not be lacking. Be sure that in all things you have recourse to Mary, embracing the holy Cross, and never let yourself fall into confusion of mind, but sail in a stormy sea in the ship of divine mercy. I understand: if from men religious or secular, even in the mystical body of Holy Church, you have suffered persecution or displeasure, or have been visited with the indignation of the Vicar of Christ, either on your own account, or if you have had something to bear on my account with all these people-- you are not to resist, but bear it patiently, leaving at once, and going into your cell, there to know yourself in holy meditation; reflecting that God is making you worthy to endure for the love of truth, and to be persecuted for His Name, deeming yourself in true humility worthy of punishment and unworthy to gain results. And do all the things that you have to do prudently, holding God before your eyes; do and say what you have to say and do in the Presence of God and of your own thought with the help of holy prayer. There shall you find the Master, the Holy Spirit, rich in clemency, who shall pour upon you a light of wisdom that shall make you discern and choose what shall be to his honour. This is the doctrine given to us by the Sweet Primal Truth, caring for our need with measureless love.

If it happened, dearest father, that you found yourself in the presence of his Holiness the Vicar of Christ, our very sweet and holy father, humbly commend me to him. I hold myself in fault before his Holiness for much ignorance and negligence which I have committed against God, and for disobedience against my Creator, who summoned me to cry aloud with passionate desire, and to cry before Him in prayer, and to put myself in word and in bodily presence close to His Vicar. In all possible ways I have committed measureless faults, on account of which, yes, on account of my many iniquities, I believe that he has suffered many persecutions, he and Holy Church. Wherefore if he complains of me he is right, and right in punishing me for my defects. But tell him that up to the limits of my power I shall strive to correct my faults, and to fulfil more perfectly his obedience. So I trust by the divine goodness that He will turn the eyes of His mercy upon the Bride of Christ and His Vicar, and upon me, freeing me from my defects and ignorance; but upon His Bride, by giving her the refreshment of peace and renewal, with much endurance (for in no way without toils can be uprooted the many thorny faults that choke the garden of Holy Church), and that God will give him grace in those parts where he wants to be a manly man, and not to look back, for any toil or persecution that may befall him from his wicked sons; constant and persevering, let him not avoid weariness, but let him throw himself like a lamb into the midst of the wolves, with hungry desire for the honour of God and the salvation of souls, putting far from him care for temporal things, and watching over spiritual things alone. If he does so, as divine goodness demands of him, the lamb will lord it over the wolves, and the wolves will turn into lambs; and thus we shall see the glory and praise of the name of God, the good and peace of Holy Church. In no other way can these be won; not through war, but through peace and benignity, and such holy spiritual punishment as a father should inflict on a son who does wrong.

Alas, alas, alas, most holy father! The first day that you came to your own place, you should have done so. I hope in the goodness of God and in your holiness that what is not done you will do. In this way both temporalities and spiritualities are won back. God demanded that you do this--as you know that you were told--that you care for the reformation of Holy Church, punishing its sins and establishing good shepherds; and that you make holy peace with your wicked sons in the best way and most pleasing to God that could be done; so that then you might see to uplifting with your arms the standard of the most holy Cross against the infidels. I believe that our negligence and our not doing what could be done--not cruelly nor quarrelsomely, but in peace and benignity--(always punishing a man who has done wrong, not in proportion to his deserts, for he could not endure what he deserves, but in proportion to what the sick man is in a condition to bear)--are, perhaps, the reason why such disaster and loss and irreverence toward Holy Church and her ministers has befallen. And I fear that unless a remedy is found by doing what has been left undone, our sins may deserve so much that we shall see greater misfortunes; such I say as would grieve us much more than to lose temporal possessions. Of all these evils and sorrows, wretched I am the cause, through my little virtue and my great disobedience.

Most holy father, look in the light of reason and truth at your displeasure against me, not as punishment, but as displeasure. To whom shall I have recourse should you abandon me? Who would help me? To whom do I flee, should you cast me out? My persecutors pursue me, and I flee to you, and to the other sons and servants of God. Should you abandon me, assuming displeasure and wrath against me,

I will hide me in the wounds of Christ crucified, whose Vicar you are: and I know that He will receive me, for He wills not the death of a sinner. And, when I am received by Him, you will not drive me out; nay, we shall abide in our own place to fight manfully with the weapons of virtue for the sweet Bride of Christ. In her I wish to end my life, with tears, with sweats, with sighs, giving my blood and the marrow of my bones. And should all the world drive me out, I will not care, reposing with plaints and great endurance on the breast of that sweet Bride. Pardon, most holy father, all my ignorance, and the wrong that I have done to God and to your Holiness. It is Truth that excuses me and sets me free; Truth Eternal. Humbly I ask your benediction.

To you, dearest father (Raimondo), I say: when it is possible to you, keep a manly heart in the presence of his Holiness, without any pain or servile fear; remain first a while in your cell, in the presence of Mary and of the most holy Cross, in holy and humble prayer, in true knowledge of yourself, with living faith and will to endure; and then go (to the Pope) in security. And do what you can for the honour of God and the salvation of souls, to the point of death. Announce to him what I write you in this letter as the Holy Spirit shall guide you. I say no more. Remain in the holy and sweet grace of God. Sweet Jesus, Jesus Love.

TO URBAN VI

In March, 1378, Gregory died, and was succeeded by the Archbishop of Bari, who took the name of Urban VI. The sensitive, cultured, vacillating Frenchman gave place to a Neapolitan of coarse physique--a man personally virtuous, but, as history shows us, extraordinarily harsh and violent in disposition. "It seems," the Prior of the Island of Gorgona wrote with alarming candour to Catherine, "that our new Christ on earth is a terrible man."

Catherine was at Florence at the time--having been sent thither by Gregory, who, however alienated from her personally, seems till the end to have valued her services. The following is the first letter from her to Urban which we possess. It is evident that she has as yet little knowledge of the new Pope at first hand. She writes to him in much the same strain as that in which she was accustomed to address his predecessor; only the sense of a new hearer inspires her, after the rather dull opening of the letter, with fresh fervour in recapitulating the sins and woes of the Church. Possibly, also, there is a little more insistence than usual on the plea that mercy temper justice, in the case of the rebellious Tuscan cities. The sensible policy for such a situation could hardly be better summed up than in her concise phrase: "Receive from a sick man what he can give you."

In the Name of Jesus Christ crucified and of sweet Mary:

Most holy and dear father in Christ sweet Jesus: I Catherine, servant and slave of the servants of Jesus Christ, write to you in His precious Blood: with desire to see you founded upon true and perfect charity, so that, like a good shepherd, you may lay down your life for your sheep. And truly, most holy father, only he who is founded upon charity is ready to die for the love of God and the salvation of souls: because he is free from self-love. For he who abides in self-love is not ready to give his life; and not to speak of his life, apparently he is not willing to bear the least little pain: for he is always afraid for himself, lest he lose his bodily life and his private consolations. So he does whatever he may do imperfectly and corruptly, because his chief impulse, through which he acts, is corrupt. In whatever state he may be, shepherd or subject, he shows little virtue. But the shepherd who is established in true charity does not do so; his every work is good and perfect, because his impulse is absolutely one with the perfection of divine charity. Such a man as this fears neither the devil nor his fellow-beings, but only his Creator; he does not mind the detractions of the world, nor shames, nor insults, nor jests, nor the criticisms of his subordinates; who take offence, and turn to criticizing when they are reproved by their prelate. But like a manly man, clothed in the fortitude of charity, he does not care.

Nor, therefore, does he suppress the flame of holy desire, nor cast from him the pearl of justice, lucid and one with mercy, which he bears upon his breast. Were justice without mercy, it would abide in the shadows of cruelty, and would turn into injustice. And mercy without justice toward one's subordinate would be like ointment on a wound that ought to be cauterized: if ointment is applied without cauterizing it rots more than it heals. But when both are joined they give life to the prelate who uses them, and health to the subject if he is not a member of the devil, entirely unwilling to correct himself. However, if the subject failed to correct himself a thousand times over, the prelate ought not to give up correcting him, and his virtue will be none the less because that wicked man does not profit by it. In this way works the pure and clean charity of a soul that cares for itself not for its own sake, but for God, and seeks God for the glory and praise of His name, in so far as it sees that He is worthy of being loved for His infinite goodness--nor seeks its neighbour for its own sake, but for God, wishing to render him that service which it cannot render to God. For it recognizes that He is our God, who has no need of us. Therefore it studies with great zeal to be useful to its neighbour, and especially to the subjects committed to it. And it does not draw back from pursuing the salvation of their souls and bodies for any ingratitude found in them, nor for the threats or flatteries of man; but, in truth, clothed in the wedding garment, follows the doctrine of the Spotless Humble Lamb, that gentle and good Shepherd who, as one enamoured, ran for our salvation to the shameful death of the most holy Cross. The unspeakable love which the soul has conceived for Christ crucified does all this. Most holy father, God has placed you as a shepherd over all His sheep who belong to the whole Christian religion; He has placed you as the minister of the Blood of Christ crucified, whose Vicar you are; and He placed you in a time in which wickedness abounds more among your inferiors than it has done for a long time, both in the body of Holy Church, and in the universal body of the Christian religion. Therefore it is extremely necessary for you to be established in perfect charity, wearing the pearl of justice, as I said; that you may not mind the world, nor poor people used to evil, nor any injuries of theirs; but manfully correct them, like a true knight and just shepherd, uprooting vices and implanting virtues, ready to lay down your life if needs be. Sweetest father, the world cannot bear any more; vices are so abundant, especially among those who were put in the garden of Holy Church to be fragrant flowers, shedding the fragrance of virtue; and we see that they abound in wretched, hateful vices, so that they make the whole world reek! Oh me! where is the purity of heart and perfect charity which should make the incontinent continent by contact with them? It is quite the contrary: many a time the continent and the pure are led by their impurities to try incontinence. Oh me! where is the generosity of charity, and the care of souls, and distribution to the poor and to the good of the Church, and their necessities? You know well that men do quite the contrary. Oh me miserable! With grief I say it --your sons nourish themselves on the wealth they receive by ministering the Blood of Christ, and are not ashamed of being as money-changers, playing with those most sacred anointed hands of yours, you Vicar of Christ: without speaking of the other wretched deeds which they commit. Oh me! where is that deep humility with which to confound that pride of sensuality of theirs, by which in their great avarice they commit simonies, buying benefices with gifts, or flatteries, or money, dissolute and vain adornments, not as clerics, but worse than seculars! Oh me, sweet my Babbo, bring us a remedy! And give refreshment to the desperate desires of the servants of God, who die and cannot die. They wait with great desire that you as a true shepherd should put your hand to correcting these things, not only with words but with deeds, while the pearl of justice, joined to mercy, shines on your breast; correcting in truth, without any servile fear, those who nourish them at the breast of the sweet Bride of Christ, the ministers of the Blood.

But truly, most holy father, I do not see how this can be well done if you do not make over anew the garden of your Bride, stocking it with good virtuous plants; taking pains to choose a troop of very holy men, in whom you find virtue and no fear of death. Do not aim at grandeur, but let them be shepherds who rule their flocks with zeal. And a troop of good cardinals, who may be upright columns of yours, helping you to bear the weight of many burdens, with divine help. Oh, how blessed will be my soul then, when I shall see that which is hers given back to the Bride of Christ, and those nourished at her breast regarding not their own good, but the glory and praise of the Name of God, and feeding on the food of souls at the table of the holy Cross. I have no question that then your lay subjects will correct themselves--for they will not be able to help it, constrained by the holy and pure life of the clergy. We are not, then, to sleep over it, but manfully and without negligence to do what you can, even unto death, for the glory and praise of the Name of God.

Next I beg you, and constrain you by the love of Christ crucified, as to those sheep who have left the fold--I believe, for my sins--that by the love of that Blood of which you are made minister, you delay not to receive them in mercy, and with your benignity and holiness force their hardness; give them the good of bringing them back into the fold, and if they do not ask it in true and perfect humility, let your Holiness fulfil their imperfection. Receive from a sick man what he can give you. Oh me, oh me, have mercy on so many souls that perish! Do not consider the scandal which occurred in this city, in which surely the devils of hell busied themselves, to hinder the peace and quiet of souls and bodies: but Divine Goodness saw to it that no great harm came from the great evil, but your sons pacified themselves, and now ask of you the oil of mercy. Grant that it seems to you, most holy father, that they do not ask it in those conciliatory ways nor with that heartfelt distaste for the sin they committed which they should, as it would please your Holiness to have them--yet, oh me, do not give up! For they will make better sons than other people. Oh me, Babbo mine, I do not want to stay here any longer! Do with me then what you will. Show me this grace and favour, poor wretch that I am, knocking at your door. Do not deny me the easy little things that I ask you for your sons; so that, having made peace, you may raise the standard of the most holy Cross. For you see well that the infidels have come to summon you. I hope by the sweet goodness of God that He will fill you with His burning charity, so that you shall know the loss of souls, and how much you are bound to love them: and so you shall increase in eager zeal to set them free from the hands of the devil, and shall seek to heal the mystical body of Holy Church, and the body of the universal Christian religion; and especially to reconcile your sons, winning them with benignity, with as much use of the rod of justice as they are fit to bear, and no more. I am certain that unless we have the virtue of charity, this will not be done; and therefore I said that I wished to see you established in true and perfect charity. Not that I do not believe that you are in charity, but because we can grow in the perfection of charity since we are always pilgrims and strangers in this life, I said that I wished this perfection in you, that you feed it constantly with the flame of holy desire, and shed it upon your subjects, like a good shepherd. I beg you to do so. And I will stay, and labour till I die, in prayer and in whatever way I can, for the honour of God and for your peace and that of your sons.

I say no more to you. Remain in the holy and sweet grace of God. Pardon my presumption, most holy father; but love and grief are my excuse before your Holiness. I ask you humbly for your benediction. Sweet Jesus, Jesus Love.

TO HER SPIRITUAL CHILDREN IN SIENA

Catherine turned without difficulty from public cares to the needs and problems of the little group of disciples in the restricted life of Siena. To her eyes, there was no great nor small; the one drama was as important as the other, since both were God's appointed schools of character. She was, as we have already seen, wise in the lore of Christian friendship. How thoroughly she understood the tendencies likely to appear in a limited group of good people, bound closely together in faith and life, these letters, among others, bear witness. Not only in religious communities, but wherever such a group exists, similar conditions arise. The life of the affections becomes of leading importance; too often it is unregulated, and runs to morbid extremes; on the other hand, the peculiarly provincial temptation to carping mutual scrutiny as well as to overwrought sensitiveness, is sure to be at play. All her life long Catherine combated these dangers, in the strength at once of a large mind and of a gentle heart. The first of these letters puts in beautiful form the ideal of a truly consecrated affection. The second repeats her familiar warning against a critical temper, and her favourite plea for that generous tolerance which puts the highest possible construction on one's neighbour's conduct. Tolerance, one surmises, was to her peculiarly swift and lofty spirit one of the most difficult among the virtues. Yet, or rather therefore, no one has ever presented more emphatically the relief afforded by the great permission and command, "Judge not."

TO BROTHER WILLIAM AND TO MESSER MATTEO OF THE MISERICORDIA AND TO BROTHER SANTI AND TO HER OTHER SONS

In the Name of Jesus Christ crucified and of sweet Mary: Dearest sons in Christ sweet Jesus: I Catherine, servant and slave of the servants of Jesus Christ, write to you in His precious Blood, with desire to see you bound in the bands of charity, for I consider that without this bond we cannot please God. This is the sweet sign by which the servants and sons of Christ are recognized. But think, my sons, that this bond must be clean, and not spotted by self-love. If thou lovest thy Creator, love and serve Him in so far as He is highest and eternal good, worthy of being loved, and not for thine own profit, for that would be a mercenary love, like a miser who loves money because of his avarice. So let your love for your neighbour be clean. Love, love one another; you are neighbours one of the other. But be on your guard, for if your love were founded in your own profit or in the private affection which you might have for one another, it would not endure, but would fail, and your soul would find itself empty. The love which is founded in God must be of such a sort that it has to love with regard to virtue, and inasmuch as the friend is a creature made in the image of God. For while delight in him whom I love, or profit from him may grow less, if one abides in God love does not fail, because one loves with regard to virtue and the honour of God, and not to one's own personality. I say that if one abides in God, even if virtue should fail in him who loves, yet love does not turn away. The love of the virtue which is not there fails to be sure; but it does not fail in so far as a man is a creature of God, His member, bound in the mystical body of the Holy Church. Nay, there grows within one a love made up of great and true compassion, and with desire he brings his friend to the birth, with tears and sighs and continual prayers in the sweet Presence of God. Now this is the affection which Christ left to His disciples, which never lessens or grows languid, and is not impatient for any injury it receives; there is no spirit of criticism in it nor displeasure, because it loves the friend, not for himself, but for God. It does not judge nor want to judge the will of men, but the will of its Creator, which seeks and wills naught but our sanctification. And it joys in what God permits, of whatsoever kind it be, since it seeks naught but the honour of its Creator and the salvation of its neighbour. Truly may we say that such men are bound in the bond of charity with the band which held God-and-Man fast and nailed on the wood of the most holy and sweet Cross.

But think, sons mine, that you would never reach this perfect union did you not hold as your object Christ crucified, and follow His footsteps. For in Him you will find this love, who has loved you by grace and not by duty. And because He loves by grace, He has never grown languid in His love, neither for our ingratitude nor ignorance nor pride nor vanity, but ever persevering, even to the shameful death of the Cross, freeing us from death and giving us life. Now so do you, my sons, learn--learn from Him. Love, love one another, with pure and holy love, in Christ sweet Jesus. I say no more, because I hope to see you again soon, when it shall please the divine goodness. Remain in the holy and sweet grace of God. Sweet Jesus, Jesus Love.

TO SANO DI MACO AND ALL HER OTHER SONS IN SIENA

In the Name of Jesus Christ crucified and of sweet Mary:

Dearest sons in Christ sweet Jesus: I Catherine, servant and slave of the servants of Jesus Christ, write to you in His precious Blood: with desire to see you strong and persevering till the end of your life. For I consider that without perseverance no one can please God, or receive the crown of reward. He who perseveres is always strong, and fortitude makes him persevere.

We have absolute need of the gift of fortitude, for we are besieged by many foes. The world, with its delights and deceits; the devil, with many vexing temptations, who lights upon the lips of men, making them say insulting and critical things, and who often makes us lose our worldly goods--and this he does solely to recall us from devoted charity to our neighbour; the flesh, astir in our own senses, seeking to war against the spirit. Yes, truly, all these foes of ours have besieged us; yet we need feel no servile fear, because they are discomfited through the Blood of the Spotless Lamb. We ought bravely to reply to the world and resist it, disparaging its delights and honours, judging it to have in itself no abiding stability whatever. It shows us long life, with youth a-blossom and great riches; and they are all seen to be vanity, since from life we come to death, from youth to age, from wealth to poverty; and thus we are always running toward the goal of death. Therefore we need to open the eye of the mind, to see how miserable he is who trusts in the world. In this wise one will come to despise and hate what first he loved. To the wiles of the devil we can reply manfully, seeing his weakness; for he can conquer no one who does not wish to be conquered. One can reply to him then with lively faith and hope, and with holy hatred of one's self. For in such hate one will become patient toward every tempting vexation and tribulation of the world, and will bear these things with true patience, from what side soever they come, if one shall hate one's own fleshliness and love to abide on the Cross with Christ crucified.

From living faith one will derive a will in accord with that of God, and will quench in heart and mind the human instinct of judging. The will of God alone shall judge, which seeks and wills naught but our sanctification. In this wise one is not shocked at his neighbour and does not criticize him. Nor does he pass judgment on a man who talks against him: he condemns himself alone, seeing that it is the will of God which permits such men to vex him for his good. Ah, how blessed is the soul which clothes itself in a judgment so gentle! He does not condemn the servants of this world who do him injury; nor does he condemn the servants of God, wishing to drive them in his own way, as many presumptuous, proud men do, who under cloak of the honour of God and the salvation of souls, are shocked by the servants of God, and assume a critical attitude under cover of this cloak, saying: "Such words do not please me." And so a man becomes disturbed in himself, and also makes others disturbed with his tongue, claiming that he speaks through the force of love--and so he thinks he does. But if he will open his eyes, he will find the serpent of presumption under a false aspect, which plays the judge, judging in its own fashion, and not according to the mysteries and the holy and diverse ways in which God works with His creatures. Let human pride be ashamed, and consent to see that in the House of the Eternal Father are many mansions. Let it not seek to impose a rule upon the Holy Spirit: for He is the Rule itself, Giver of the Rule: nor let it measure Him who cannot be measured. The true servant of God, arrayed in His highest eternal will, will not do thus; nay, he will hold in reverence the ways and deeds and habits of God's servants, since he judges them fixed not by man, but by God. For, just because things are not pleasing to us and do not go according to our habits, we ought to be predisposed to believe that they are pleasing to God. We ought not to judge anything at all, nor can we, except what is manifest and open sin. And even this the soul enamoured of God and lost to itself does not assume to judge, except in displeasure for the sin and wrong done to God; and with great compassion for the soul of him who sins, eagerly willing to give itself to any torture for the salvation of that soul.

Now I summon you to this perfection, dearest sons; do you study with true and holy zeal to acquire it. And reflect that every stage in perfection which you reach will advance you in this holy and true judgment, free from offence or pain. So, on the contrary, false judgment betrays you into every sort of pain, and fault-finding and ruinous faithlessness toward the servants of God. All this proceeds from the personal passion and rooted pride which impels us to judge the will of our fellow-man. So such a man is always looking back, and does not persevere in gracious love of his neighbour, and never has strong and persevering love. Nay, his is like the imperfect love felt by the disciples of Christ before the Passion; for they loved Him, rejoicing much in His presence; but because their love was not founded in truth, but pleasure and self-indulgence were in it, it failed when His presence was taken away; and they did not know how to bear pain with Christ, but fled in fear. Beware, beware, lest this happen to you. You rejoice much in the presence of a friend, and in absence you make a fire of straw; for when the presence is taken away, every little wind and rain quenches it, and nothing remains except the black smoke of a dark conscience. All this happens because we have made ourselves judges of the will of our fellows, and the habits and ways of the servants of God, not according to His sweet will. Now no more thus, for love of Christ crucified! but be faithful sons, strong and persevering in Christ sweet Jesus. Thus shall you discomfit the temptation of the devil, and the words which he says, lighting on the lips of men.

Our last enemy--that is, our miserable flesh with its sense-appetites--is overcome by the flesh of Christ, scourged and nailed on the wood of the most holy Cross, by mastering it with fast and vigil and continuous prayer, with burning sweet and loving desire. Thus sweetly shall we conquer and discomfit our foes by the power of the Blood of Christ. Thus shall you fulfil His will and my desire, which grieves when it beholds your imperfection. I hope by His infinite goodness that He will console my desire in you. Therefore I beg that you be not negligent, but zealous; do not shift about in the wind like a leaf, but be firm, stable, and constant; loving one another with true brotherly charity, bearing one another's faults. By this I shall perceive whether you love God and me, who desire naught but to see you in true unity. Drown you in the Blood of Christ crucified and hide you in His sweetest Wounds. I say no more.

Let the convent of Santa Maria degli Angeli be commended to you. And never mind because I am not there, for good sons do more when the mother is not present than when she is, because they want to show the love they have for her, and to enter more fully into her favour.

I beg you, Sano, to read this letter to all the children. And do you all pray God for us, that He grant us to complete what is begun to His honour and the salvation of souls; for we wish no other desire nor work, in despite of any who may wish to hinder it. Remain in the holy and sweet grace of God. May God fill you with His sweetest favour. Sweet Jesus, Jesus Love.

TO BROTHER RAIMONDO OF CAPUA OF
THE ORDER OF THE PREACHERS

With all her longing to suffer for her faith, Catherine was only once, so far as we know, exposed to physical violence. This was on the occasion of which she is here speaking. She is still in Florence, faithful under the new Pope as under the old to her efforts to bring about the passionately desired peace. In a tumult in the disordered city, it came to pass that her life was threatened, and she took refuge with her "famiglia," in a garden without the walls. Hither her enemies pursued her, but as they drew near, fell back of a sudden, awestruck, as she herself here tells us, by her words and bearing. The danger was averted, and Catherine had met one of the disappointments of her life[1]. There is an almost childlike simplicity in her account of the inner side of the experience. Nothing could be more genuine than her grief that the crown of martyrdom was not granted her--few things more lovely than her confiding account of the fine joys which the mere hope of martyrdom, brief and frustrated though it were, awakened in her spirit. Nor can she know even so supremely isolated an experience without insisting that it be shared by those she loves, and returning thanks for the great mercy which her "dear sons and daughters" have received.

In the Name of Jesus Christ crucified and of sweet Mary:

Dearest father in Christ sweet Jesus: I Catherine, servant and slave of the servants of Jesus Christ, write to you in His precious Blood: with desire to see you a faithful servant and bridegroom of truth, and of sweet Mary, that we may never look back for any reason in the world, nor for any tribulations which God might send you: but with firm hope, with the light of most holy faith, pass through this stormy sea in all truthfulness; and let us rejoice in endurance, not seeking our own glory,

---

1 As she herself expresses it, "The Eternal Bridegroom played a great joke on me."

but the glory of God and the salvation of souls, as the glorious martyrs did, who for the sake of truth made them ready for death and for all torments, so that with their blood, shed for love of the Blood, they built the walls of Holy Church. Ah, sweet Blood, that dost raise the dead! Thou givest life, thou dost dissolve the shadows that darken the minds of reasonable creatures, and dost give us light! Sweet Blood, thou dost unite those who strive, thou dost clothe the naked, thou dost feed the hungry and give to drink to those who thirst for thee, and with the milk of thy sweetness thou dost nourish the little ones who have made themselves small by true humility, and innocent by true purity. Oh, holy Blood, who shall receive thee amiss? The lovers of themselves, because they do not perceive thy fragrance.

So, dearest and sweetest father, let us divest us and clothe us in truth, so we shall be faithful lovers. I tell you that today I will to begin again, in order that my sins may not hold me back from such a good as it is to give one's life for Christ crucified. For I see that in the past, through my faults, this has been denied me. I had desired very much, with a new intensity, increased in me beyond all custom, to endure without fault for the honour of God and the salvation of souls and the reformation and good of Holy Church, so that my heart was melting from the love and desire I had to lay down my life. This desire was blessed and grievous; blessed it was for the union that I felt with truth, and grievous it was for the oppression which I felt from the wrong against God, and the multitude of demons who overshadowed all the city, dimming the eye of the mind in human beings. Almost it seemed that God was letting them have their way, through justice and divine discipline. Therefore my life could not but dissolve in weeping, fearful for the great evil which seemed on the point of coming, and because peace was hindered for this reason. But in this great evil, God, who despises not the desire of His servants, and that sweet mother Mary, whose name was invoked with pained and dolorous and loving desires, granted that in all the tumult and the great upheaval that occurred, we may almost say that there were no human deaths, except those which justice inflicted. So the desire I had that God would show His providence and destroy the power of the demons that they might not do so much harm as they were ready to do, was fulfilled; but my desire to give my life for the Truth and the sweet Bride of Christ was not fulfilled. But the Eternal Bridegroom played a great joke on me, as Christopher will tell you more fully by word of mouth. So I have reason to weep, because the multitude of my iniquities was so great that I did not deserve that my blood should give life, or illumine darkened minds, or reconcile the sons with the father, or cement a stone in the mystical body of Holy Church. Nay, it seemed that the hands of him who wanted to kill me were bound. My words, "I am she. Take me, and let this family be," were a sword that pierced straight through his heart. O Babbo mine, feel a wonderful joy in yourself, for I never experienced in myself such mysteries, with so great joy! There was the sweetness of truth in it, the gladness of a clean and pure conscience; there was the fragrance of the sweet providence of God; there was the savour of the times of new martyrs, foretold as you know by the Eternal Truth. Tongue would not suffice to tell how great the good is that my soul feels. I seem to be so bound to my Creator that if I gave my body to be burned I could not satisfy the great mercy which I and my cherished sons and daughters have received.

All this I tell you that you may not conceive bitterness; but may feel an unspeakable delight, with softest gladness; and that you and I may begin to sorrow over my imperfection, because so great a good was hindered by my sin. How blessed my soul would have been had I given my blood for the sweet Bride, and for love of the Blood and the salvation of souls! Now let us rejoice and be faithful lovers.

I will not say more on this subject; I let Christopher tell this and other things. Only I want to say this: do you pray Christ on earth not to delay the peace because of what has happened, but make it all the more promptly, so that then the other great deeds may be wrought which he has to do for the honour of God and the reformation of Holy Church. For the condition of things has not been changed by this--nay, for the present the city is pacified suitably enough. Pray him to act swiftly; and I ask him this in mercy, for infinite wrongs against God which happen through the situation will thus be put an end to. Tell him to have pity and compassion on these souls which are in great darkness: and tell him to release me from prison swiftly; for unless peace is made it does not seem as if I could get out; and I would wish then to come where you are, to taste the blood of the martyrs, and to visit his Holiness, and to find myself with you once more, telling of the admirable mysteries which God has wrought at this time; with gladness of mind, and joyousness of heart, and increase of hope, in the light of most holy faith. I say no more to you. Remain in the holy and sweet grace of God. Sweet Jesus, Jesus Love.

TO URBAN VI

By this time Catherine has evidently more than an inkling of the character of the man she is addressing. Gregory had been, if anything, only too susceptible to influences from varying quarters: Urban's arbitrary and headstrong nature resented any interference. He was making extraordinary blunders in tact and policy; but woe to the audacious person who sought to point them out!

Catherine's letters to this new Pope, if less familiarly affectionate than those to the old, show the same amazing combination of candour and reverence. True to her constant principles in the interpretation of character, she insists on putting the best possible construction on his actions, ascribing his impatient vehemence and bad temper to a noble and partially impersonal cause. One suspects that Urban had lost his temper with poor Fra Bartolomeo because the friar had used too great freedom of speech rather than too little, as Catherine suggests. Despite her generosity, however, she can rebuke pungently enough, as this letter shows. On another occasion, we find her sending to Urban a tangible allegory in the form of bitter oranges, candied within and gilded without, doubtless by her own hands, with a pretty letter to point the moral. And again she wrote: "Mitigate a little, for the love of Christ crucified, those sudden impulses which nature forces on you. In holy virtue, throw nature aside. As God has given you a great heart naturally, so I beg and want you to make it great supernaturally: with zealous desire for virtue and the reform of Holy Church, do you establish the manly heart you have gained in true humility. In this way you will have both natural and supernatural gifts--for the one without the other would avail little, but would rather inspire us with wrath and pride: and when it came to correcting our intimates it would slacken its pace and become cowardly."

In the Name of Jesus Christ crucified and of sweet Mary:

Most holy and sweet father in Christ sweet Jesus: I Catherine, servant and slave of the servants of Jesus Christ, write to you in His precious Blood: with desire to see you a true and royal ruler of your flock, whom you have to nourish with the Blood of Christ crucified. Your Holiness has to see to it with great diligence to whom you administer that Blood, and by what means it is given; that is, I say, most holy father, that when shepherds are to be appointed in the garden of Holy Church, let them be people who seek God, and not benefices: and let the means of asking for the post be such as act openly in the truth and not in falsehood.

Most holy father, have patience when you are talked to about these things. For they are only said to you for the honour of God and for your salvation, as a son ought to speak who loves his father tenderly, and cannot bear that anything should be done which should turn to the loss or shame of his father; but watches constantly, with intent earnestness, because he sees well that his father, who has to rule a large family, can see no more than one man sees. So if his lawful sons were not earnest in caring for his honour and welfare, he would be deceived many a time and oft. So it stands, most holy father. You are father and lord of the universal body of the Christian religion; we are all under the wings of your Holiness: as to authority, you can do everything, but as to seeing, you can do no more than one man; so your sons must of necessity watch and care with clean hearts and without any servile fear over what may be for the honour of God and the safety and honour of you and the flocks that are beneath your crook. And I know that your Holiness is very desirous of having people to help you; but you must be patient in listening to them.

I am certain that two things must give you pain and make your mind angry, and I am not in the least surprised. The one is that when you hear that sins are committed, it hurts you that God should be wronged, for the wrong and the faults displease you, and you experience a piercing of your heart. In this case we ought not to be patient, or to refrain from grieving over the wrongs that are shown to God. No; for so it would seem as if we conformed us to these same vices. The other thing that might hurt you is when the son who comes to tell you what he feels to be turning into wrong against God and loss to souls and little honour to your holiness, commits such ignorance that he conscientiously obliges himself, in the presence of your Holiness, not to tell you clearly the absolute truth as it is; for nothing should be secret nor hidden from you.

I beg you, holy father, that when your ignorant son offends in this point, your pain should be without any excitement on your part: correct him in his ignorance. I say this, because according to what Master Giovanni told me of Brother Bartolomeo, he annoyed you and made you angry by his faults and his scrupulous conscience; for which he and I have been extremely sorry, since he thought that he had offended your Holiness. I beg you, by the love of Christ crucified, to punish in me every pain that he may have given you; I am ready for any discipline and correction which shall please your Holiness. I believe that my sins were the reason why he showed himself so ignorant, therefore I ought to bear the penalty; and he is very desirous to come penitently to you wherever it might please your Holiness. Have patience to bear his faults and mine. Bathe you in the Blood of Christ crucified; comfort you in the sweet flame of His charity. Pardon my ignorance.

I ask you humbly for your benediction. I thank the Divine Goodness and your Holiness for the favour that you granted me on the day of St. John. Remain in the holy and sweet grace of God. Sweet Jesus, Jesus Love.

TO DON GIOVANNI OF THE CELLS OF VALLOMBROSA

Catherine has missed her chance at martyrdom. Schism is threatening, and she knows it: "I seem to have heard that discord is arising yonder between Christ on earth and his disciples: from which thing I receive an intolerable grief.... For everything else, like war, dishonour, and other tribulations, would seem less than a straw or a shadow in comparison with this. Think! For I tremble only to think of it ... I tell you, it seemed as if my heart and life would leave their body through grief." So she writes, out of trance, to the Cardinal Pietro di Luna--himself destined to become later the antipope Benedict XIII.

The present sorrowful letter is to a hermit who had sinned violently in youth, and repented passionately through many years of strictest discipline. Catherine pours out her heart to him. The words in which Shelley's Fury drives home to the agonizing Prometheus the apparent tragedy of existence were fulfilled before her eyes:

> "Hypocrisy and custom make their minds
> The fanes of many a worship now outworn:
>   *   *   *   *
> The good want power but to weep barren tears,
> The powerful goodness want--worse need for them:
> The wise want love; and those who love want wisdom;
> And all best things are thus confused to ill."

With unflinching clear-sightedness she presents the situation, turning in vain to every quarter whence help might come. To the whole body of the priesthood; to the timid monastic orders; to pious laymen honestly devout, yet touched by no flame of sacrificial passion such as she felt might bring salvation. It is never the sins of the world that most torture Catherine: always, as here, the sins of the Church. She does not pause till she comes to the terrible climax: "I see the Christian religion lying like a dead man, and I neither mourn nor weep over him." It is the very light of most holy faith that has confused the vision of men. And again we hear the familiar refrain, "I believe that my iniquities are the cause of it."

In the Name of Jesus Christ crucified and of sweet Mary:

Dearest father in Christ sweet Jesus: I Catherine, servant and slave of the servants of Jesus Christ, write to you in His precious Blood: with desire to see you an hungered for souls, on the table of the most holy Cross, in company with the humble and immaculate Lamb. I do not see, father, that this sweet food can be eaten anywhere else. Why not? Because we cannot eat it truly without enduring much; it must be eaten with the teeth of true patience and the lips of holy desire, on the Cross of many tribulations, from whatsoever side they may come--complaints, or the scandals in the world; and we must endure all things till death. Now is the time, dearest father, to show whether we are lovers of Christ crucified and rejoice in this food or not. It is time to give honour to God and our toils to our neighbour: toils, I say, of the body, with much endurance, and toils of the mind, with grief and bitterness offering tears and sweats, humble and continual prayer, and suffering desire, before God. For I do not see that in any other way the wrath of God may be pacified toward us, and His mercy inclined, and through His mercy the many sheep recovered who are perishing in the hands of devils, unless in the way I said, through great grief and compassion of heart, and the very greatest devotion in prayer.

Therefore I invite you, dearest father, on behalf of Christ crucified, to begin anew with me to lose ourselves, and to seek only the honour of God in the salvation of souls, without any slavish fear: never to slacken our steps either on account of our sufferings, or in order to please our fellow-creatures, or because we might have to bear death, or for any other reason; but let us run, as inebriate with love and grief over the persecution that is wrought upon the Blood of Christ crucified. For on whatever side we turn we see it persecuted. If I turn me toward ourselves, rotten members that we are, we are persecuting it with our many faults, and such stench of mortal sins and empoisoned self-love as poisons the whole world. And if I turn me to the ministers of the Blood of the sweet and humble Lamb, my tongue cannot even narrate their faults and sins. If I turn me to the ministers who are under the yoke of obedience, I see them so imperfect--the accursed root of self-love not being yet dead in them-- that not one has come to the point of wishing to give his life for Christ crucified; but they have encouraged fear of death and pain rather than holy fear of God and reverence for the Blood. And if I turn me to the secular people who have already released their affections from the world, they have not exercised virtue enough to leave the place where they were, or suffer death rather than to do that which ought not to be done. They have behaved so through imperfection, or else they are doing so through prudence. If I had to teach them prudence, I should advise them that if they wanted to reach perfection they should rather choose death, and if they felt themselves weak, they should flee the place and cause of sin, just as far as we can. This same counsel, if any chance came in your way, I should think that you and every servant of God ought to give. For you know that it is never lawful for us to commit a little sin in any way, surely not for fear of suffering or death, since not even for accomplishing some great good. So, then, on whatever side we turn us, we find nothing but faults. For I do not doubt that if one single person had had perfection enough to give his life, during the events which have happened and are happening every day, the Blood would have called for mercy, and bound the hands of divine justice, and broken those Pharaoh- hearts which are hard as diamond stone; and I see no way in which they can break other than through blood.

Ah me, ah me, misfortunate my soul! I see the Christian religion lying a dead man, and I neither weep nor mourn over him. I see darkness invading the light, for by the very light of most holy faith, received in the Blood of Christ, I see men's sight become confused and the pupil of their eye dried up; so that we see them fall as blind men into the ditch, into the mouth of the wolf of Hell, stripped of virtue and dead by cold; being stripped of the love of God and their neighbour, and released from the bond of love, and lost to all reverence for God and for the Blood. Ah me! I believe that my iniquities have been the cause of it.

So I beg you, dearest father, to pray God for me, that He take from me so great iniquities, and that I be not the cause of so great ill: or may He give me death. And I beg you to lift these sons of ours as dead up to the table of the most holy Cross, and there do you eat this food, bathed in the Blood of Christ crucified. I tell you that if you and the other servants of God, and all of us, do not persuade ourselves with many prayers, and others, to correct themselves of evils so great, divine judgment will come, and divine justice will draw forth its rod. Indeed, if we open our eyes, one of the greatest judgments that we can know in this life is already befallen--that is, that we are deprived of light, and do not see the loss and ill of soul and body. He who does not see cannot correct himself, because he does not hate evil or love true good. So, not correcting himself, he falls from bad to worse. So it seems to me that we are doing, and we are at a worse point now than the first day. It is essential, then, that we should never stop, if we are true servants of God, in our much endurance and true patience, and in giving our toils to our neighbour, and honour to God, with many prayers and grieving desire; let sighs be food to us and tears our drink, upon the table of the Cross; for another way I do not see. Therefore I said to you that I desired to see you an hungered for souls upon the table of the most holy Cross.

I beg that your and my dearest sons be commended to you--those yonder, and those here. Nourish them and make them grow in great perfection, so far as your power goes. And let us strive to run, dead to all self-will, spiritual and temporal; that is, not seeking our own spiritual consolations, but only the food of souls, rejoicing in the Cross with Christ crucified and giving our life, if need be, for the glory and praise of His Name. I for my part die and cannot die, hearing and seeing the insults to my Lord and Creator; therefore I ask an alms from you, that you pray God for me, you and the others. I say no more to you. Remain in the holy and sweet grace of God. Sweet Jesus, Jesus Love.

LETTERS ANNOUNCING PEACE

Amid the horrors which darkened Europe during her last years, one episode of pure joy was vouchsafed to Catherine. The decisiveness of Urban brought to an end the vacillating negotiations of the Papal See with the Florentines, and peace was proclaimed at last.

The first of these notes announces the first step toward a satisfactory end--the observance of the Interdict, placed by Gregory upon the city, and contumaciously broken by the rebels. In the second, the news of the establishment of peace has just been brought. Catherine's first impulse is to bid the friends at home rejoice with her in news great in itself, and greater because it may clear the way for the realization of wider hopes. It is noteworthy that the instant the end for which she has long been straining is achieved, her loyal and aspiring spirit reverts to her old dreams, and summons her companions to resume prayer for a Crusade.

The arrival of the olive of peace, of which Catherine sends a portion to her friends, is the fit close to the long drama which had opened when Christ placed the Cross on her shoulder and the olive in her hand, and sent her to bear His command of reconciliation "to one and to the other people."

TO MONNA ALESSA WHEN THE SAINT WAS AT FLORENCE

In the Name of Jesus Christ crucified and of sweet Mary:

Dearest daughter in Christ sweet Jesus: I Catherine, servant and slave of the servants of Jesus Christ, write to thee in His precious Blood: with desire to see thee and the others brides and faithful servants of Christ crucified, that you may constantly renew your wailing for the honour of God, the salvation of souls, and the reform of Holy Church. Now is the time for you to shut yourselves within self-knowledge, with continual vigil and prayer that the sun may soon rise; for the aurora has begun to dawn. The aurora has come in that the dusk of great mortal sins which were committed in the office being said and heard publicly, is now scattered, despite whoso would have hindered: and the interdict is observed. Thanks, thanks be to our sweet Saviour, who despises not humble prayer, nor the tears and burning desires of His servants! Since, then, He despises them not, nay, but accepts them, I summon you to pray and to have prayer offered to the Divine Goodness that He send us peace swiftly; that God may be glorified and so great an evil ended, and that we may find ourselves united, to tell the wonderful things of God.

Up! And sleep no more! Awaken, all of you, from the sleep of negligence! Have special prayers offered at such and such monasteries, and tell our Prioress to have all those daughters of hers offer special prayers for peace, that God may show mercy on us, and that I may not return without it. And for me, her poor daughter, that God will give me grace ever to love and to proclaim the truth, and that for that truth I may die. I say no more. Remain in the holy and sweet grace of God. Sweet Jesus, Jesus Love.

TO SANO DI MACO AND TO THE OTHER SONS IN CHRIST
WHILE SHE WAS IN FLORENCE

In the Name of Jesus Christ crucified and of sweet Mary:

Dearest sons in Christ sweet Jesus: I Catherine, servant and slave of the servants of Jesus Christ, write to you in His precious Blood: with desire to see you true sons, really serving our sweet Saviour, that you may give more zealously thanks and praise to His name.

Oh, dearest sons, God has heard the cry of His servants, who for so long have cried aloud before His face, and the lamentable cry which they have raised so long over the sons who were dead. Now are they risen again--from death they have come to life, and from blindness to light. Dearest sons, the lame walk, and the deaf hear, the blind eye sees and the dumb speak, crying aloud with a loud voice: "Peace, peace, peace!" with great gladness--seeing themselves return as sons into the obedience and favour of their father, their minds being reconciled. As people who now begin to see, they say: "Thanks be to Thee, Lord, who hast reconciled us with our holy father." Now the Lamb of God, sweet Christ on earth, is called holy, while before he was called a heretic and a Patarin. Now they receive him for a father, where before they refused him. I do not wonder, for the cloud is passed, and fair weather has come. Rejoice, rejoice, dearest sons, with very sweet weeping for thanksgiving, before the Highest Eternal Father, not calling yourselves content with this, but praying Him that soon may be raised the gonfalon of the most holy Cross. Rejoice, exult, in Christ sweet Jesus; let our hearts break, seeing the largess of the infinite goodness of God. Now peace is made, despite him who would hinder it. Discomfited is the devil of hell.

Saturday evening one olive came at one o'clock at night; and to-day at vespers came the other. And Saturday evening that friend of ours was caught with a companion, so that at one time heresy was thoroughly put an end to and peace came;

now he is in prison. Pray God for him, that He give him true light and knowledge. Drown you and bathe you in the Blood of Christ crucified. Love, love one another. I send you some of the olive of peace. Remain in the holy and sweet grace of God. Sweet Jesus, Jesus Love.

TO THREE ITALIAN CARDINALS

Catherine had ardently wished to see in the Seat of Peter a reformer, who should have courage to apply surgery to the festering wounds of the Church. She had her desire; Urban began at once a drastic policy of Church reform. But his domineering asperity proved unbearable to the College of Cardinals, and schism broke upon a horrified world.

This was the situation:--After the death of Gregory, the cardinals, of whom a large majority were French, when assembled in conclave in what was to them the barbarous city of Rome, had been terrified by the shouts of the populace demanding a Roman, or at least an Italian, for Pope. Resorting to stratagem, they reported as their choice the old Roman cardinal of San Pietro, who repudiated the false rumour with distress. Meantime, agreeing on compromise and finding a "dark horse," the Sacred College elected with all due solemnity the Archbishop of Bari, and by the usual formalities notified the Christian world of the election. They soon, as has been said, rebelled against the man of their choice, and, announcing that the election had been invalid because occasioned by fear, proceeded to appoint an antipope--Robert of Geneva, a man of personal charm but of evil life, known in history as Clement VII. The impudence of the reasons alleged by the cardinals for their action is well pointed out by Catherine. But Europe became divided in its allegiance, and war of words was soon followed by war of swords.

Catherine rose to the occasion. The rest of her tempestuous life was spent in the desperate defence of the cause of Urban--a man whom she rightly believed to be the lawful successor of Peter, yet concerning whose unlovely character she was, as we have already seen, under no illusions. The many letters which she wrote with the aim of convincing important personages of the validity of Urban's claims, are historical documents of high value. One feels in them all the amazement with which a woman whose native air was the mystical conception of an infallible Church, faced the realities of the ecclesiastical machine. But loyalty stood the test, and while never leaving the highest ground, Catherine proved herself capable of a statesmanlike treatment of the actual situation. The present letter is addressed to the three Italian members of the Sacred College, who, after holding at first by their countryman, were induced by the Frenchmen to betray him: it is a tissue of telling and convincing representations, interwoven with indignant rebuke and eloquent pleadings.

This was not the first time that a great Italian patriot had remonstrated with the churchmen of Italy. Catherine's letter invites inevitable comparison with that noble letter to Italian cardinals written by Dante on the occasion of the impending papal election that followed the death of Clement V. Dante, like Catherine, appealed to the cardinals on behalf of Rome and Italy: his plea, that they put an end to the Babylonian Captivity in Avignon and return to the Seat of Peter. That letter marked an early stage in the disgraceful abandonment of the Holy City; this of Catherine treats of the outcome of that great wrong. "Yet the wound will be healed," wrote Dante; "(though it cannot be otherwise than that the scar and brand of infamy will have burned with fire upon the Apostolic See and will disfigure her for whom heaven and earth had been reserved)--if ye who were the authors of this transgression will all with one accord fight manfully for the Bride of Christ, for the Throne of the Bride which is Rome, for our Italy, and that I may speak more fully, for the whole commonwealth of pilgrims upon this earth...." Over sixty years had passed since Dante wrote thus; they had been years of sin and shame. The words of Catherine, as she confronts a situation yet darker than he had faced, breathe a less assured courage. But her patriotism and her Christianity are of like temper with his own.

In the Name of Jesus Christ crucified and of sweet Mary:

Dearest brothers and fathers in Christ sweet Jesus: I Catherine, servant and slave of the servants of Jesus Christ, write to you in His precious Blood: with desire to see you turn back to the true and most perfect light, leaving the deep shadows of blindness into which you are fallen. Then you shall be fathers to me; otherwise not. Yes, indeed, I call you fathers in so far as you shall leave death and turn back to life (for, as things go now, you are parted from the life of grace, limbs cut off from your head from which you drew life), when you shall stand united in faith, and in that perfect obedience to Pope Urban VI., in which those abide who have the light, and in light know the truth, and knowing it love it. For the thing that is not seen cannot be known, and he who knows not loves not, and he who loves not and fears not his Creator loves himself with fleshly love, and whatever he loves, joys or honours and dignities of the world, he loves according to the flesh. Since man is created through love, he cannot live without love; either he loves God, or he loves himself and the world with the love that kills, fastening the eye of his mind darkened by self-love on those transitory things that pass like the wind. In this state he can recognize no truth nor goodness; he recognizes naught but falsehood, because he has not light. For truly had he the light, he would recognize that from such a love as this naught can result but pain and eternal death. It gives him a foretaste of hell in this life; for he who immoderately loves himself and the things of this world, becomes unendurable to himself.

Oh, human blindness! Seest thou not, unfortunate man, that thou thinkest to love things firm and stable, joyous things, good and fair? and they are mutable, the sum of wretchedness, hideous, and without any goodness; not as they are created things in themselves, since all are created by God, who is perfectly good, but through the nature of him who possesses them intemperately. How mutable are the riches and honours of the world in him who possesses them without God, without the fear of Him! for to-day is he rich and great, and to-day he is poor. How hideous is our bodily life, that living we shed stench from every part of our body! Simply a sack of dung, the food for worms, the food of death! Our life and the beauty of youth pass by, like the beauty of the flower when it is gathered from the plant. There is none who can save this beauty, none who can preserve it, that it be not taken, when it shall please the highest Judge to gather this flower of life by death; and none knows when.

Oh, wretched man, the darkness of self-love does not let thee know this truth. For didst thou know it, thou wouldst choose any pain rather than guide thy life in this way; thou wouldst give thee to loving and desiring Him who Is; thou wouldst enjoy His truth in firmness, and wouldst not move about like a leaf in the wind; thou wouldst serve thy Creator, and wouldst love everything in Him, and apart from Him nothing. Oh, how will this blindness be reproved at the last moment in every rational being, and much the more in those whom God has taken from the filth of the world, and assigned to the greatest excellence that can be, having made them ministers of the Blood of the humble and spotless Lamb! Oh me, oh me! what have you come to by not having followed up your dignities with virtue? You were placed to nourish you at the breasts of Holy Church; you were flowers planted to breathe forth the fragrance of virtue in that garden; you were placed as masts to strengthen this ship, and the Vicar of Christ on earth; you were placed as lights in a candlestick, to give light to faithful Christians, and to spread the faith. Well you know if you have done that for which you were created. Surely no; for self-love has prevented you from knowing that in truth alone, to fortify men and give a shining example of good and holy life, you were put in this garden. Had you known this you would have loved it, and clothed you in that sweet truth. Where is the gratitude which you ought to have for the Bride who has nourished you at her breast? I see in us naught but such ingratitude as dries up the fountain of pity. What shows me that you are ungrateful, coarse, and mercenary? The persecution which you, together with others, are inflicting on that sweet Bride, at a time when you ought to be shields, to ward off the blows of heresy. In spite of which, you clearly know the truth, that Pope Urban VI. is truly Pope, the highest Pontiff, chosen in orderly election, not influenced by fear, truly rather by divine inspiration than by your human industry. And so you announced it to us, which was the truth. Now you have turned your backs, like poor mean knights; your shadow has made you afraid. You have divided you from the truth which strengthens us, and drawn close to falsehood, which weakens soul and body, depriving you of temporal and spiritual grace. What made you do this? The poison of self-love, which has infected the world. That is what has made you pillars lighter than straw. Flowers you who shed no perfume, but stench that makes the whole world reek! No lights you placed in a candlestick, that you might spread the faith; but, having hidden your light under the bushel of pride, and become not extenders, but contaminators of the faith, you shed darkness over yourselves and others. You should have been angels on earth, placed to release us from the devils of hell, and performing the office of angels, by bringing back the sheep into the obedience of Holy Church, and you have taken the office of devils. That evil which you have in yourselves you wish to infect us with, withdrawing us from obedience to Christ on earth, and leading us into obedience to antichrist, a member of the devil, as you are too, so long as you shall abide in this heresy.

This is not the kind of blindness that springs from ignorance. It has not happened to you because people have reported one thing to you while another is so. No, for you know what the truth is: it was you who announced it to us, and not we to you. Oh, how mad you are! For you told us the truth, and you want yourselves to taste a lie! Now you want to corrupt this truth, and make us see the opposite, saying that you chose Pope Urban from fear, which is not so; but anyone who says it--speaking to you without reverence, because you have deprived yourselves of reverence-- lies up to his eyes. For it is evident to anyone who wished to see, who it is that you presented as your choice through fear--that was Messer di Santo Pietro. You might say to me, "Why do you not believe us? We know the truth as to whom we chose better than you." And I reply, that you yourselves have shown me that you deserted the truth in many ways, so that I ought not to believe you, that Pope Urban VI. is not the true Pope. If I turn to the beginnings of your life, I do not recognize in you so good and holy a life that you would shrink from a lie for conscience' sake. What shows me that your life is badly governed? The poison of heresy. If I turn to the election ordained by your lips, we knew that you chose him canonically and not through fear. We have already said that he whom you presented to the people through fear was Messer di Santo Pietro. What proves to me the regular election with which you chose Messer Bartolommeo, Archbishop of Bari, who to-day is made in truth Pope Urban VI.? In the solemnity with which his coronation was observed, this truth is clear to us. That the solemnity was carried out in good faith is shown by the reverence which you gave him and the favours asked from him, which you have used in all sorts of ways. You cannot deny this truth except with plain lies.

Ah, foolish men, worthy of a thousand deaths! As blind, you do not see your own wrong, and have fallen into such confusion that you make of your own selves liars and idolaters. For even were it true (which it is not; nay, I assert again that Pope Urban VI. is the true Pope), but were it true what you say, would you not have lied to us when you told us that he was the highest pontiff, as he is? And would you not falsely have shown him reverence, adoring him for Christ on earth? And would you not have practised simony, in trying for favours and using them unlawfully? Yes, indeed. Now they, and you with them, have made an antipope, as far as your action and outward appearance go, since you consented to remain on the spot, when the incarnate demons chose the demon!

You might say to me: "No, we did not choose him." I do not know how I can believe that. For I do not believe that you could have borne to stay there otherwise, had you given your life for it; at least the fact that you suppressed the truth, and did not burst out with it--for this would not have been within your power--makes me inclined to think so. Although, perhaps, you did less wrong than the others in your intention, yet you did do wrong with all the rest. What can I say? I can say that he who is not for the truth is against the truth; he who was not at that time for Christ on earth, Pope Urban VI., was against him. Therefore I tell you that you did wrong, with the antipope: and I may say that he was chosen a member of the devil; for had he been a member of Christ, he would have chosen death rather than consent to so great an evil, for he well knows the truth, and cannot excuse himself through ignorance. Now you have committed all these faults in regard to this devil: that is, to confess him as Pope, which he surely is not, and to show reverence to whom you should not. You have deserted the light, and gone into darkness: the truth, and joined you to a lie. On what side soever, I find nothing but lies. You are worthy of torture, which, I tell you in truth and unburden my conscience thereof, unless you return to obedience with true humility, will fall upon you.

O misery upon misery, and blindness upon blindness, which does not let its wrong be seen nor the loss to soul and body! For had you seen it, you would not have deserted the truth so lightly, in servile fear, passionate all, like proud people and arbitrary, accustomed to pleasant and soft dealings from men! You could not endure, not only an actual correction indeed, but even a harsh word of reproof made you lift up rebellious heads. This is the reason why you changed. And it clearly reveals the truth to us; for, before Christ on earth began to sting you, you confessed him and reverenced him as the Vicar of Christ that he is. But this last fruit that you bear, which brings forth death, shows what kind of trees you are; and that your tree is planted in the earth of pride, which springs from the self-love that robs you of the light of reason.

Oh me, no more thus for the love of God! Take refuge in humbling you beneath the mighty hand of God, in obedience to His Vicar, while you have time; for when the time is passed there will be no more help for us. Recognize your faults, that you may be humble, and know the infinite goodness of God, who has not commanded the earth to swallow you up, nor beasts to devour you; nay, but has given you time, that you may correct your soul. But if you shall not recognize this, what He has given you as a grace shall turn to your great judgment. But if you will return to the fold, and feed in truth at the breast of the Bride of Christ, you shall be received in mercy, by Christ in heaven and by Christ on earth, despite the iniquity you have wrought. I beg that you delay no more, nor kick against the prick of conscience that I know is perpetually stabbing you. And let not confusion of mind, over the evil that you have wrought, so overcome you, that you abandon your salvation in weariness and despair, as seeming unable to find help. Not so must you do; but in living faith, hold firm hope in your Creator, and return humbly to your yoke; for the last sin of obstinacy and despair would be the worst, and most hateful to God and the world. Arise, then, into the light! For without light you would walk in darkness, as you have done up to now.

My soul considering this, that we can neither know nor love the truth without light, I said and say that I desire intensely to see you arisen from darkness, and one with the light. This desire reaches out to all rational beings, but much more to you three, concerning whom I have had the greatest sorrow, and marvel more at your fault than at all the others who have shared it. For did all desert their father, you should have been such sons as strengthened the father, showing the truth. Notwithstanding that the father might have treated you with nothing but reproof, you ought not therefore to have assumed the lead, denying his holiness in any way. Speaking entirely in the natural sense--for according to virtue we ought all to be equal--speaking humanly, Christ on earth being an Italian, and you Italian, I see no reason but self-love why passion for your country could not move you as it did the Ultramontanes. Cast it to earth now, and do not wait for time, since time does not wait for you--trampling such selfishness underfoot, with hate of vice and love of virtue.

Return, return, and wait not for the rod of justice, since we cannot escape the hands of God! We are in His hands either by justice or by mercy; better it is for us to recognize our faults and to abide in the hands of mercy, than to remain in fault and in the hands of justice. For our faults do not pass unpunished, especially those that are wrought against Holy Church. But I wish to bind myself to bear you before God with tears and continual prayer, and to bear with you your penitence, provided that you choose to return to your father, who like a true father awaits you with the open wings of mercy. Oh me, oh me, avoid and flee it not, but humbly receive it, and do not believe evil counsellors who have given you over to death! Oh me, sweet brothers! Sweet brothers and fathers you shall be to me, in so far as you draw close to truth. Make no more resistance to the tears and sweats which the servants of God shed for you, but wash you in them from head to foot. For did you despise them, and the eager sweet and grieving desires which are offered by them for you, you would receive much greater rebuke. Fear God, and His true judgment. I hope by His infinite goodness that He will fulfil in you the desire of His servants.

Let it not seem hard to you if I pierce you with the words which the love of your salvation has made me write: rather would I pierce you with my living voice, did God permit me. His will be done. And yet you deserve rather deeds than words. I come to an end, and say no more; for did I follow my will I should not yet pause, so full is my soul of grief and sorrow to see such blindness in those who were placed for a light: no lambs they, who feed on the food of the honour of God and the salvation of souls, and the reform of Holy Church; but as thieves they steal the honour which they ought to give to God, and give it to themselves, and as wolves they devour the sheep, so that I have great bitterness. I beg you by love of that precious Blood shed with such fiery love for you, that you give refreshment to my soul, which seeks your salvation. I say no more to you. Remain in the holy and sweet grace of God: bathe you in the Blood of the Spotless Lamb, where you shall lose all servile fear, and enlightened, you shall abide in holy fear. Sweet Jesus, Jesus Love.

TO GIOVANNA QUEEN OF NAPLES

Giovanna of Naples was one of the most depraved, as well as one of the most romantic, figures of her time. In fascination, as in evil, she antici-pates the type of the women of the renascence. Her many crimes had never prevented Catherine Benincasa from yearning over her with a pe-culiar tenderness, and we have many letters written by the daughter of the dyer of Siena to the great Neapolitan queen. Some of the earlier among these letters seem, curiously enough, not to have been without effect; for Giovanna not only replied to them, but gave her promise to join in a Crusade.

Now that the Great Schism had broken forth, the adhesion of Giovanna to the cause of Urban, who was politically her subject, was of prime importance; and Catherine wrote her about the matter, not once, but many times. In her varied cor-respondence at this period, these letters have a peculiar interest, from the passionate personal feeling which pervades them. It is not only for the sake of the truth that Catherine pleads and argues, but for the sake of Giovanna's salvation; one would think that even the hardened old Queen must have been touched with the intense and tender solicitude of the following letter, even if she were not convinced by its irrefutable reasoning. As a matter of fact, Giovanna, after having for a time sided with Clement, did temporarily change her base and espouse the cause of Urban. Soon, however, she reverted to her former position. It is probable that for her, as for many European sovereigns, the matter was decided by considerations with which the naif question of the legitimacy of a papal election had little or nothing to do.

Dearest mother in Christ sweet Jesus: I Catherine, servant and slave of the servants of Jesus Christ, write to you in His precious Blood: with desire to see you grounded in the truth which we must know and love for our salvation. He who shall be grounded in the knowledge of the Truth, Christ sweet Jesus, shall win and enjoy peace and quiet of soul, in the ardour of that charity which receives the soul into this knowledge.

We should know this truth in two chief ways--although it befits us to know it in everything--that is, everything which exists should love itself in God and through God, who is Truth itself, and there is nothing without Him; otherwise it would escape from truth and would walk in falsehood, following the devil, who is the father thereof. I was saying that we ought to recognize truth especially in two ways. The first is, we should recognise the truth about God. He loves us unspeakably, and loved us before we were; nay, by love He created us--this was and is the truth--in order that we might have life eternal and enjoy His highest eternal good. What shows us that this is truly so? The Blood, shed for us with such fire of love. In the sweet Blood of the Word, the Son of God, we shall know the truth of His doctrine, which gives life and light, scattering every shadow of fleshly love and human self-indulgence, but knowing and following with pure heart the doctrine of Christ crucified, which is grounded in the truth. The second and last way is, that we ought to recognize the truth about our neighbour, whether he be great or humble, subject or lord. That is, when we see that men are doing some deed in which we might invite our neighbour to join, we ought to perceive whether it is grounded in truth or not, and what foundation he has who is impelled to do this deed. He who does not do this, acts as one mad and blind, who follows a blind guide, grounded in falsehood, and shows that he has no truth in himself, and therefore seeks not the truth. Sometimes it happens that people are so insane and brutal that they see themselves lose through such a deed the life of soul and body and their temporal possessions; and they do not care, for they are blinded, and do not know what they ought to know; they walk in darkness, with a feminine nature that lacks any firmness or stability.

Dearest mother,--in so far as you are a lover of truth and obedient to Holy Church I call you mother, but in no otherwise, nor do I speak to you with reverence, because I see a great change in your person. You who were a lady have made yourself a servant, and slave of that which is not, having submitted yourself to falsehood, and to the devil, who is its father; abandoning the counsels of the Holy Spirit and accepting the counsels of incarnate demons. You who were a branch of the true vine, have cut yourself off from it with the knife of self-love. You who were a legitimate daughter, tenderly beloved of her father, the Vicar of Christ on earth,

Pope Urban VI., who is really the Pope the highest pontiff, have divided yourself from the bosom of your mother, Holy Church, where for so long a time you have been nourished. Oh me! oh me! one can mourn over you as over a dead woman, cast off from the life of grace; dead in soul and dead in body, if you do not escape from such an error. It appears that you have not known God's truth in the way I spoke of; for had you known it, you would have chosen death rather than to offend God mortally. Nor have you known truth about your neighbour; but in great ignorance, moved by your own passion, you have followed the most miserable and insulting counsel--having acted according to it--that I ever heard of. What greater shame can be incurred than that one who was a Christian, held to be a Catholic and virtuous woman, should act like a Christian who denies her faith, and depart from good and holy customs and the due reverence she has observed? Oh me! open the eye of your mind, and sleep no more in so great misery. Do not await the moment of death-- after which it will not help you to make excuses, nor to say: "I thought to do good." For you know that you do ill, but like a sick and passionate woman, you let yourself be guided by your passions.

I am quite sure that the counsel came from someone beside yourself. Will, will to know the truth; who those men are, and why they make you see falsehood for truth, saying that Pope Urban VI. is not true Pope, and making you consider that the antipope, who is simply an antichrist, member of the devil, is Christ on earth. With what truth can they say that to you? Not with any; but they say it with entire falsity, lying over their heads. What can those iniquitous men say?--not men, but incarnate demons --since, on whatever side they turn, they must see that they have done nothing but ill. Even were it true--as it is not--that Pope Urban VI. was not the Pope, they would merit a thousand deaths for this alone, as liars discovered in their untruth; for had they chosen him through fear in the beginning, and not honestly with a regular election, and had presented him to us as a true Pope, see! they would have shown us a lie for truth, making us, and themselves at the same time, obey and reverence him whom we ought not. For they did do him reverence, and asked favours from him, and profited by them, as if they came from the highest pontiff, as they did. I say, that were it true that he was not the Pope--(which is not the case, by the great goodness of God, who has had mercy upon us)--for this reason alone they could not be too severely disciplined; but they deserve a thousand thousand deaths to pretend that they elected the Pope through fear, when it was not so. But they cannot speak the truth, being men founded in falsehood, for they cannot so hide it that its darkness and stench cannot be seen and felt. What they pretended is perfectly true: they did elect a Pope through fear after they had elected the true Pope, Messer Bartolomeo, Archbishop of Bari, who to-day is Pope Urban VI.: that was, Messer di Santo Pietro. But he, like a good man and just, confessed that he was not the Pope, but Messer Bartolomeo, Archbishop of Bari, who to-day is called Pope Urban VI., and revered by faithful Christians as highest pontiff and most just man, despite wicked men--not Christians, for they bear the name of Christ neither on their lips nor on their heart--but infidels who have deserted the faith and obedience of Holy Church and the Vicar of Christ on earth, branches cut off from the True Vine, sowers of schism and of greatest heresy.

Open, open the eye of your mind, and sleep no more in such blindness. You should not be so ignorant nor so separated from the true light as not to know the wicked life, with no fear of God, of those who have led you into so great heresy: for the fruits which they bear show you what kinds of trees they are. Their life shows you that they do not tell the truth; so do the counsellors they have about them, without and within, who may be men of knowledge, but they are not men of virtue, nor men whose life is praiseworthy, but rather to be blamed for many faults. Where is the just man whom they have chosen for antipope, if indeed our highest pontiff, Pope Urban VI., were not the true Vicar of Christ? What man have they chosen? A man of holy life? No, but an iniquitous man, a demon--and therefore he does the works of demons. The devil exerts himself to withdraw us from the truth, and he does the very same thing. Why did they not choose a just man? Because they knew well enough that a just man would have chosen death rather than to have accepted the papacy, since he would have seen no colour of truth in them. Therefore the demons took the demon, and the liars the lie. All these things show that Pope Urban VI. is truly Pope, and that they are without truth, lovers of the lie.

If you said to me, "My mind is not clear as to all these things," why do you not at least stay neutral? although it is as clear as can possibly be said. And if you are not willing to help the Pope with your temporal substance until you have more illumination--(help which you are in duty bound to give, because the sons ought to help the father when he is in need)--at least obey him in spiritual things, and in other things remain neutral. But you are behaving like a passionate woman; and hate, and spite, and the fear of losing him of whom you deprived yourself, which you caught from a cursed teller of tales, has robbed us of light and knowledge; for you do not know the truth, obstinately persevering in this evil; and in this obstinacy you do not see the judgment which is coming upon you.

Oh me! I say these words with heartfelt grief, because I tenderly love your salvation. If you do not change your ways, and correct your life, by abandoning this great error, and in regard to everything else, the highest Judge, who does not let sins pass unpunished unless the soul purifies them with contrition of heart and confession and satisfaction, will give you such a punishment that you will become a signal instance to cause anyone to tremble who should ever lift his head against the Holy Church. Wait not for this rod; for it will be hard for you to kick against the divine justice. You are to die, and know not when. Not riches, nor position, however great, nor worldly dignity, nor barons, nor people who are your subjects as to the body, shall be able to defend you before the highest Judge, nor hinder the divine justice. But sometimes God works through rascally men, in order that they may execute justice on His enemy. You have invited and invite the people and all your subjects to be rather against you than with you; for they have found little truth in your character--not the quality of a man with virile heart, but that of a woman without any firmness or stability, a woman who changes like a leaf in the wind.

They have well in mind that when Pope Urban VI., true Pope, was created by a great and true election, and crowned with great solemnity, you held a great and high festival, as the child should do over the exaltation of the father, and the mother over that of the son. For he was both son and father to you; father, through his dignity to which he had come, son because he was your subject--that is to say, of your kingdom. Therefore you did well. Further, you commanded everyone to obey his Holiness as the highest pontiff. Now I see that you have turned about, like a woman who has no decision, and you will them to do the contrary. Oh, miserable passion! That evil which you have in yourself you wish to impart to them. How do you suppose that they can love you and be faithful to you, when they see that you are responsible for separating them from life and leading them into death, and casting them from truth into falsehood? You separate them from Christ in heaven and from Christ on earth, and seek to bind them to the devil, and to antichrist--lover and prophet of lies that he is, he and you and the others who follow him.

No more thus for the love of Christ crucified! You are in every way calling down the divine judgment. I grieve for it. If you do not hinder the ruin that is coming upon you, you cannot escape from the hands of God. Either by justice or by mercy, you are in His hands. Correct your life, that you may escape the hands of justice, and remain in those of mercy. And do not wait for the time, for an hour comes when you shall wish and cannot. O sheep, return to your fold; let you be governed by the Shepherd: else the wolf of hell shall devour you! Take back for your guards the servants of God, who love you in truth more than you yourself, and good, mature and discreet counsellors. For the counsel of incarnate demons, with the inordinate fear into which they have thrown you through terror of losing your temporal state--(which passes like the wind with no permanence, for either it leaves us, or we it through death)--has brought you where you are. You shall yet weep, if you change not your ways, saying: "Alas, alas! I am one who has robbed herself, on account of the fear into which I was thrown by villainous counsellors!" But there is yet time, dearest mother, to avert the judgment of God. Return to the obedience of Holy Church: know the ill that you have wrought: humble you under the mighty hand of God; and God, who has regard to the humility of His handmaid, shall show mercy upon us: He will placate His wrath over your faults; through the mediation of the Blood of Christ, you shall be grafted and bound in Him with the chain of that charity in which you shall know and love the truth. The truth shall set you free from lie: it shall scatter all shadows, giving you light and knowledge in the mercy of God. In this truth you shall be freed; in other wise, never.

And because the truth sets us free, I, having desire for your salvation, said that I desired to see you established in the truth, that it be not wronged by falsehood. I beg you, fulfil in yourself the will of God and the desire of my soul, for with all the depth and all the strength of my soul I desire your salvation. And, therefore, constrained by the Divine Goodness which loves you unspeakably, I have moved me to write to you with great sorrow. Another time, also, I wrote you on this same matter. Have patience if I burden you too much with words, and if I speak with you boldly, irreverently. The love which I bear to you makes me speak with boldness: the fault which you have committed makes me depart from due reverence, and speak irreverently. I could wish far rather to tell you the truth by speech than by writing, for your salvation, and chiefly for the honour of God; and I would far rather deal in deeds than in words with him who is to blame for it all, although the blame and the reason is in yourself, since there is no one, neither demon nor creature, who can force you to the least fault unless you choose. Therefore I said to you that you are the cause of it. Bathe you in the Blood of Christ crucified. There are scattered the clouds of self-love and servile fear, and the poison of hate and self-scorn. I say no more to you. Remain in the holy and sweet grace of God. Sweet Jesus, Jesus Love.

TO SISTER DANIELLA OF ORVIETO

S ister Daniella has found herself in straits again; constrained, it would seem, by the Spirit, to action not endorsed by her religious superiors. Possibly she wished, following the example of Catherine, to leave her cloister and take part in the public life of her time. Catherine herself had been in like straits during much of her early life. Well she knew, as St. Francis knew before her, the suffering of that inward conflict, when the Voice of God summons one way, and the voices of men, reinforced by that instinct of humility and obedience which the middle ages held so dear, insist upon another. She writes to her friend with comprehending sympathy. Daniella, as we have already seen, was a woman who understood her and whom she understood. And it must have been a relief to Catherine, at this point in her career, for once to encourage ardour instead of rebuking sin or seeking to inspire timidity. Our saint is so constantly on the side of obedience, when, as not infrequently happens, some weak brother or sister is restless under the yoke of vows, that we are sure she must know her woman when she writes: "Fear and serve God, disregarding yourself; and then do not care what people say unless it is to feel compassion for them."

We see at the end of the letter that Catherine is on the point of going to Rome. In fact, Urban had summoned her thither, being evidently alive to the advantages of the support of one so famed for sanctity. In Rome the remainder of her life was to be passed.

In the Name of Jesus Christ crucified and of sweet Mary:

Dearest daughter in Christ sweet Jesus: I Catherine, servant and slave of the servants of Jesus Christ, write to you in His precious Blood: with desire to see thee in true and very perfect light, that thou mayest know the truth in perfection. Oh, how necessary this light is to us, dearest daughter! For without it we cannot walk in the Way of Christ crucified, a shining Way that brings us to life; without it we shall walk among shadows and abide in great storm and bitterness. But, if I consider aright, it behoves us to possess two orders of this light. There is a general light, that every rational creature ought to have, for recognizing whom he ought to love and obey--perceiving in the light of his mind by the pupil of most holy faith, that he is bound to love and serve his Creator, loving Him directly, with all his heart and mind, and obeying the commandments of the law to love God above everything, and our neighbour as ourselves. These are the principles by which all men beside ourselves are held. This is a general light, which we are all bound by; and without it we shall die, and shall follow, deprived of the life of grace, the darkened way of the devil. But there is another light, which is not apart from this, but one with it--nay, by this first, one attains to the second. There are those who, observing the commandments of God, grow into another most perfect light; these rise from imperfection with great and holy desire, and attain unto perfection, observing both commandments and counsels in thought and deed. One should use this light with hungry desire for the honour of God and the salvation of souls, gazing therewith into the light of the sweet and loving Word, where the soul tastes the ineffable love which God has to His creatures, shown to us through that Word, who ran as enamoured to the shameful death of the Cross, for the honour of the Father and for our salvation.

When the soul has known this truth in the perfect light, it rises above itself, above its natural instincts; with intense, sweet and loving desires, it runs, following the footsteps of Christ crucified, bearing pains, bearing shame, ridicule and insult with much persecution, from the world, and often from the servants of God under pretext of virtue. Hungrily it seeks the honour of God and the salvation of souls; and so much does it delight in this glorious food, that it despises itself and everything else: this alone it seeks, and abandons itself. In this perfect light lived the glorious virgins and the other saints, who delighted only in receiving this food with their Bridegroom, on the table of the Cross. Now to us, dearest daughter and sweet my sister in Christ sweet Jesus, He has shown such grace and mercy that He has placed us in the number of those who have advanced from the general light to the particular--that is, He has made us choose the perfect state of the Counsels: therefore we ought to follow that sweet and straight way perfectly, in true light, not looking back for any reason whatever; not walking in our own fashion but in the fashion of God, enduring sufferings without fault even unto death, rescuing the soul from the hands of devils. For this is the Way and the Rule that the Eternal Truth has given thee; and He wrote it on His body, not with ink, but with His Blood, in letters so big that no one is of such low intelligence as to be excused from reading. Well thou seest the initials of that Book, how great they are; and all show the truth of the Eternal Father, the ineffable love with which we were created--this is the truth--only that we might share His highest and eternal good. This our Master is lifted up on high upon the pulpit of the Cross, in order that we may better study it, and should not deceive ourselves, saying: "He teaches this to me on earth, and not on high." Not so: for He ascended upon the Cross, and uplifted there in pain, He seeks to exalt the honour of the Father, and to restore the beauty of souls. Then let us read heartfelt love, founded in truth, in this Book of Life. Lose thyself wholly; and the more thou shalt lose the more thou shalt find; and God will not despise thy desire. Nay, He will direct thee, and show thee what thou shouldst do; and will enlighten him to whom thou mightest be subject, if thou dost according to His counsel. For the soul that prays ought to have a holy jealousy, and let it always rejoice to do whatever it does with the help of prayer and counsel.

Thou didst write me, and as I understood from thy letter it seems that thou art troubled in heart. And this is not a slight feeling; nay, it is mighty, stronger than any other, when on the one side thou dost feel thyself called by God in new ways, and His servants put themselves on the contrary side, saying that this is not well. I have a very great compassion for thee; for I know not what burden is like that, from the jealousy the soul has for itself; for it cannot offer resistance to God, and it would also fulfil the will of His servants, trusting more in their light and knowledge than in its own; and yet it does not seem able to. Now I reply to thee simply according to my low and poor sight. Do not make up thy mind obstinately, but as thou feelest thyself called without thine own doing, so respond. So, if thou dost see souls in danger, and thou canst help them, do not close thine eyes, but exert thyself with perfect zeal to help them, even to death. And never mind about thy past resolutions to silence or anything else--lest it be said to thee later: "Cursed be thou, that thou wast silent." Our every principle and foundation is in the love of God and our neighbour alone; all our other activities are instruments and buildings placed on this foundation. Therefore thou shouldst not, for pleasure in the instrument or the building, desert the principal foundation in the honour of God and the love of our neighbour. Work, then, my daughter, in that field where thou seest that God calls thee to work; and do not get distressed or anxious in mind over what I have said to thee, but endure manfully. Fear and serve God, with no regard to thyself; and then do not care for what people may say, except to have compassion on them.

As to the desire thou hast to leave thy house and go to Rome, throw it upon the will of thy Bridegroom, and if it shall be for His honour and thy salvation, He will send thee means and the way when thou art thinking nothing about it, in a way that thou wouldst never have imagined. Let Him alone, and lose thyself; and beware that thou lose thee nowhere but on the Cross, and there thou shalt find thyself most perfectly. But this thou couldst not do without the perfect light; and therefore I said to thee that I desired to see thee in the true and most perfect light, beyond the common light we talked of.

Let us sleep no more! Let us wake from the slumber of negligence, groaning with humble continual prayers, over the mystical Body of Holy Church, and over the Vicar of Christ! Cease not to pray for him, that Christ may give him light and fortitude to resist the strokes of incarnate demons, lovers of themselves, who seek to contaminate our faith. It is a time for weeping.

As to my coming thy way, pray the highest eternal Goodness of God to do what may be for His honour and the salvation of the soul, and pray especially, for I am on the point of going to Rome, to fulfil the will of Christ crucified and of His Vicar. I do not know what way I shall take. Pray Christ sweet Jesus to send us by that way which is most to His honour, in peace and quiet of our souls. I say no more to thee. Remain in the holy and sweet grace of God. Sweet Jesus, Jesus Love.

TO STEFANO MACONI

To Stefano di Corrado Maconi, her ignorant and most ungrateful son": "To Stefano Maconi, her most ungrateful and unworthy son, when she was at Rome": so run the superscriptions to these letters. Doubtless, they headed copies made by the hand of Stefano himself. We have seen in connection with Catherine's letters to his mother how constantly after their first meeting this young disciple had been with her. Long before this, he had become the best-beloved of the "Famiglia," and next to herself its most important member. He did not, however, for some reason, accompany her to Rome, and Catherine's heart yearned over him during the last weary months. From the first, she had perceived in his frank and joyous temperament the germs of high spiritual perfection, and had sought to draw him to the monastic life. "Cut the bonds that hold thee, and do not merely loosen them," she wrote in one of the first letters to Stefano that we possess: "Resist no longer the Holy Spirit that is calling thee--for it will be hard for thee to kick against Him. Do not let thyself be withheld by thine own lukewarm heart, or by a womanish tenderness for thyself, but be a man, and enter the battlefield manfully." Stefano, however, despite his personal devotion to Catherine, felt for a long time no vocation for the cloister. She continued, as we see in these letters, to urge him with increasing insistence: but his hesitation was ended only by her death. He hastened to Rome at the last, urgently summoned, in time to see her living and to receive her last words. Her dying request did what her entreaties during life had failed to do; the brilliant young noble became a Carthusian monk. At a later time he was made General of the Order. Devotion to the memory of Catherine was the inspiration of his life after she left him.

The letters in this group were all written after Catherine had reached Rome. They form a strong contrast to the more formal and elaborate documents which she was at this time despatching to dignitaries, concerning the ecclesiastical situation.

Their serene spiritual fervour bears witness to the "central peace" subsisting at the heart of the "endless agitation" of her active life. In their intimate messages, moreover, to home friends and disciples, they throw a charming light on what may be called the domestic side of her character.

In the Name of Jesus Christ crucified and of sweet Mary:

Dearest son in Christ sweet Jesus: I Catherine, servant and slave of the servants of Jesus Christ, write to thee in His precious Blood: with desire to see thee a true guardian of the city of thy soul. Oh, dearest son, this city has many gates! They are three--Memory, Intellect, and Will, and our Creator allows all of them to be battered, and sometimes opened by violence, except one--that is, Will. So it happens at times that the intellect sees nothing but shadows; the memory is occupied with vain and transitory things, with many and varied reflections and impure thoughts; and likewise all the sensations of the body are ill-regulated and ravaging. So it is perfectly clear that no one of these gates is in our own free possession, except only the Gate of Will. This belongs to our liberties, and has for its Watch Free-will. And this gate is so strong that nor demon nor creature can open it if the watch does not consent. And while this gate is not open--that is, while it does not consent to what Memory and Intellect and the other gates experience--our city keeps its free privileges for ever. Let us, then, recognize, my son, let us recognize so excellent a benefit and so unmeasured a largess of charity as we have received from the Divine Goodness, that has put us in free possession of so noble a city.

Let us strive to hold good and zealous watch, keeping at the side of our Watch Free-will, the dog Conscience, who when anyone comes at the gate must awake Reason by its barking, that she may discern whether it be friend or foe: so that the watch may let friends enter, ordering good and holy inspirations to do their work, and may drive away the foes, locking the Gate of Will, that it consent not to admit the evil thoughts that come to the gate every day. And when thy city shall be demanded of thee by the Lord, thou canst give it up, sound, and adorned with true and royal virtues, thanks to His grace. I say no more here.

As I wrote on the first day of the month to all the sons in common, we arrived here on the first Sunday in Advent with much peace. Remain in the holy and sweet grace of God. Sweet Jesus, Jesus Love.

In the Name of Jesus Christ crucified and of sweet Mary:

Dearest son in Christ sweet Jesus: I Catherine, servant and slave of the servants of Jesus Christ, write to thee in His precious Blood: with desire to see thee risen above childishness, and become a manly man; risen from enjoying the milk of consolations, mental and actual, and set to eat the hard musty bread of many tribulations in mind and body, of conflicts with devils and injuries from thy fellows, and of any other kind that God might be pleased to grant thee. I desire to see thee rejoicing in such, and hasting to meet them with kindling desire and sweet gratitude to the divine goodness, when it may please Him to show thee such great gifts-- which will be whenever He shall see thee fit to receive them. Rouse thee, my son, rouse thee from thy lukewarmness of heart; steep it in the Blood, that it may burn in the furnace of divine charity, so that it may attain to abominate all childish deeds, and be on fire to be all manful, to enter on the battlefield to do great works for Christ crucified, fighting manfully. For Paul says that none shall be crowned save such as have manfully fought. So he who sees himself abide away from the Field has cause for weeping. Now I say no more here.

I had thy letter, and saw it gladly. Concerning the affair of the Proposal, I reply that thy disposition pleases me much; and we must be glad of the sweet games that our sweet God plays with His creatures, to persuade them to the end for which we were all created: so that when the sweet medicine and ointment of consolations does not help, He sends us tribulations, cauterizing the wound that it may not suppurate. I will willingly take pains about thy affair, for the love of God and thy salvation, as soon as these festivals and holy days are past.

I will try to obtain the Indulgences that thou askest me for with the first I shall demand. I do not know when--for I have worn out the clerks of the court. One must hold one's self a little back.

I am writing a letter to Matteo: give it to him. And comfort him, and go to find him sometimes, to warm him up to the enterprise that is begun. I have heard of the illness which God has sent ... and, considering his need, I beg and constrain thee as much as I can that thou and thy brothers bring it about that the Company of the Virgin Mary give him aid, as much as thou canst get. Catarina is very much to be pitied, to find herself alone and poor without any refuge; so be zealous to show this charity. I am writing of this to Pietro, too. Let me perceive that you have not shown any negligence.

I say no more to thee. Remain in the holy and sweet grace of God. All this family comfort thee in Christ, and be the negligent and ungrateful writer commended to thee. Sweet Jesus, Jesus Love.

In the Name of Jesus Christ crucified and of sweet Mary:

Dearest son in Christ sweet Jesus: I Catherine, servant and slave of the servants of Jesus Christ, write to thee in His precious Blood: with desire to see thee cut thy bonds, and not simply set thyself to loosening them, for it takes some time to loosen, and this thou art not sure of having, so swiftly it passes from thee. It is better, then, to cut them thoroughly, with a true and holy zeal. Oh, how blessed my soul will be when I shall see that thou hast cut thyself off from the world in deed and thought, and from thy own fleshly instincts, and hast united thyself to life eternal: a union that is of such joy and sweetness and suavity that it quenches all bitterness and renders light every heavy weight! Who, then, shall hold us from drawing the sword of hate and love, and cutting self from self with the hand of free will? As soon as this sword has cut, it is of such virtue that it unites. But thou wilt say to me, dearest son: "Where is this sword found and wrought?" I reply to thee, Thou findest it in the cell of self- knowledge, where thou dost conceive hatred of thine own sin and frailty, and love of thy Creator and thy neighbour, with true and sincere virtues. Where is it wrought? In the fire of divine charity, on the anvil of the Body of the sweet and loving Word, the Son of God. Then ignorant indeed, and worthy of great rebuke, is he who has weapons in his possession to defend himself with, and who throws them away.

I do not want thee to be of these ignorant people, but I want thee to hasten in thy whole manhood, and respond to Mary, who calls thee with greatest love. The blood of these glorious martyrs, buried here in Rome as to the body, who gave blood and life with so fiery love for the love of Life, is hot with longing, summoning thee and the others that you come to suffer, for glory and praise of the Name of God and Holy Church, and for the trial of your virtues. For to this Holy Land, wherein God revealed His dignity, calling it His garden, He has called His servants, saying: "Now is the time for them to come, to test the gold of virtue." Now let us not play the deaf man. Were our ears stopped by cold, let us cleanse us in the Blood, hot because it is mingled with fire, and all deafness shall be taken away. Hide thee in the Wounds of Christ crucified; flee before the world, leave thy father's house; flee into the refuge of the Side of Christ crucified, that thou mayest come to the Land of Promise. This same thing I say also to Pietro. Place you at the table of the Cross, and there, refreshed by the Blood, take the food of souls, enduring pains and shames, insults, ridicule, hunger, thirst, and nakedness: glorying, with that sweet Paul the Chosen Vessel, in the shame of Christ crucified. If thou shalt cut thee free, as I said, endurance shall be thy glory, otherwise not, but it shall be a pain to thee, and thy shadow will make thee afraid.

My soul, considering this, as an hungered for thy salvation. I desire to see thee cut thyself free, and not set thyself to loosen, that thou mayest run thee more swiftly. Clothe thee in the Blood of Christ crucified. I say no more to thee. Remain in the holy and sweet grace of God.

I had thy letters, and had great consolation from them, over Battista's being healed, because I have hope that he will yet be a good plant, and for the compassion I felt for Monna Giovanna. But I rejoiced very much more that God has sent thee a way of extricating thyself from the world, and also over the good disposition of which thou writest me, that the Lords and our other citizens have toward our sweet "Babbo," Pope Urban VI. May God by His infinite mercy preserve it, and increase ever their reverence and obedience toward him. While thou and the others shall be there, be zealous to sow the truth and confound falsehood as far as your power extends.

Commend me closely to Monna Giovanna and Currado. Comfort also Battista and the rest of the family. Comfort all those sons of mine, and tell them also particularly to pardon me if I do not write to them, because it seems somewhat difficult. Comfort Messer Matteo: tell him to send us word of what he wants, first, because I have forgotten it, and Fra Raimondo went away so soon that we could not get it from him. Then I will zealously do all I can. And tell Frate Tommaso that I do not write to him because I do not know whether he is there, but if he is there, comfort him, and tell him to give me his blessing. Our Lisa and all the family commend themselves to thee. Neri does not write thee because he has been at the point of death; but now he is cured.

May God give thee His sweet eternal blessing. Tell Pietro to come here if he can, for something that is of importance. Sweet Jesus, Jesus Love!

Give all these letters, or have them given. And pray God for us. As to these few letters bound by themselves, give them just as they are to Monna Catarina di Giovanni, and let her distribute them.

In the Name of Jesus Christ crucified and of sweet Mary:

Dearest son in Christ sweet Jesus: I Catherine, servant and slave of the servants of Jesus Christ, write to thee in His precious Blood: with desire to see thee arise from the lukewarmness of thy heart, lest thou be spewed from the mouth of God, hearing this rebuke, "Cursed are ye, the lukewarm! Would you had at least been ice-cold!" This lukewarmness proceeds from ingratitude, which comes from a faint light that does not let us see the agonizing and utter love of Christ crucified, and the infinite benefits received from Him. For in truth, did we see them, our heart would burn with the flame of love, and we should be famished for time, using it with great zeal for the honour of God and the salvation of souls. To this zeal I summon thee, dearest son, that now we begin to work anew.

I send thee a letter that I am writing to the Lords, and one to the Company of the Virgin Mary. See and understand them, and then give them; and then ... And talk to them fully concerning this matter that is contained in the letters, begging each of them, on behalf of Christ crucified and me, that they deal zealously, just so far as they can, with the Lords and whoever has to do with it, that the right thing may be done in regard to Holy Church, and the Vicar of Christ, Urban VI. It weighs upon me very much, for my part, that it should please them to have confidence in this matter, for the honour of God, and the spiritual and temporal profit of the city. Do thou be fervent and not tepid in this activity, and in quickening thy brothers and elders of the Company to do all they may in the affair of which I write. If you are what you ought to be, you will set fire to all Italy, and not only yonder.

I say no more to thee. Remain in the holy and sweet grace of God. Comfort ... all these, thy brothers, and thy sister, comfort thee in Christ, and all are waiting for thee. Sweet Jesus, Jesus Love.

TO CERTAIN HOLY HERMITS WHO HAD BEEN INVITED TO ROME BY THE POPE

From early years, Catherine had cherished the simple-hearted desire that the affairs of Christ's people be put in the hands of His truest followers. Now, in this last period of her life, surrounded by the corruption and intrigue of the papal court, her thoughts turned more and more wistfully to the reserves of spiritual passion and insight that lingered in the hearts of obscure "servants of God" living in monasteries or in hermits' cells.

To invite these holy men to Rome--to gather them around Urban, and so show by triumphant witness of those in nearest fellowship with God on which side lay God's truth--was doubtless the political idea of a very unworldly saint. Nevertheless, it commended itself to the Pope. At his request, then, though probably by her own suggestion, Catherine wrote to sundry of those eremites with whom she had long held spiritual converse, summoning them to the Holy City. Her letters were a thrilling call to the champions of Christ, to cast off timidity and indolence, and betake them swiftly to the field where difficulties and troubles, and it might be a martyr's death, was waiting them.

In the third of the letters that follow, Catherine gives a touching picture of two bewildered hermits--Dominican "dogs of the lord" from the gentle Umbrian plain--who obeyed the call. "Old men, and far from well, who have lived such a long time in their peace," they have made the laborious journey, and are now valiantly suppressing their homesickness, and unsaying their involuntary complaints. But not all the hermits summoned were equally docile. Visionary raptures could hardly be looked for in the streets of the metropolis: dear was the seclusion of wood and cell. Father William Flete, whom Catherine had always persisted in admiring, despite his failings, flatly declined to stir; so did his comrade, Brother Antonio. The Abbot of St. Antimo, another person for whom she had always entertained a deep respect, although he came, appears from her letters to have played the part of a coward.

We cannot be surprised if peaceable Religious who had lived their long days in unbroken quiet objected to enter the unpleasant whirlpool of Roman politics. A similar attitude on the part of eremites of culture is not unknown to-day. But their refusal was a blow to Catherine. She could hardly have drawn the natural conclusion that a recluse life unfitted men to fight for practical righteousness, but she did feel deeply troubled. From early youth she had been, as we have repeatedly seen, alive to the dangers of selfishness and indolence peculiarly incident to the contemplative life; at the same time she had firmly believed that, did the flame of intercession only burn bright enough, this life might be profoundly sacrificial. Now her best-beloved recluses did not stand the test in the hour of trial, and their naif egotism disappointed her unspeakably. Her grief, her amaze, her all but scathing contempt for a religion that declined to forego its inward comforts even at the dramatic summons of a crisis in the Church, find expression in these letters. Doubtless the "great refusal" thus offered by men whom she had trusted helped to darken her last months. Not even in the hearts of her intimates, not even among the elect of God, was Catherine to find here on earth a continuing city.

TO BROTHER WILLIAM OF ENGLAND AND
BROTHER ANTONIO OF NIZZA AT LECCETO

In the Name of Jesus Christ crucified and of sweet Mary:

Dearest sons in Christ sweet Jesus: I Catherine, servant and slave of the servants of Jesus Christ, write to you in His precious Blood: with desire to see you so lose yourselves that you shall seek nor peace nor quiet elsewhere than in Christ crucified, becoming an-hungered upon the table of the Cross, for the honour of God, the salvation of souls, and the reformation of Holy Church, whom to-day we see in so great need that to help her one must come out from one's wood and renounce one's self. If one sees that he can bear fruit in her, it is no time to stay still nor to say, "I should forfeit my peace." For now that God has given us the grace of providing Holy Church with a good and just shepherd, who delights in the servants of God, and wishes them near him, and expects to be able to purify the Church and uproot vices and plant virtues, without any fear of man, since he bears himself like a just and manly man, we others ought to help him. I shall perceive whether we have in truth conceived love for the reformation of Holy Church; for if it is really so, you will follow the will of God and of His Vicar, will come out of your wood, and make haste to enter the battlefield. But if you do not do it, you will be in discord with the will of God. Therefore I pray you, by the love of Christ crucified, that you respond swiftly without delay to the request that the Holy Father makes of you. And do not hesitate because of not having a wood, for there are woods and forests here. Up, dearest sons, and sleep no more, for it is time to watch! I say no more to you. Remain in the holy and sweet grace of God. Sweet Jesus, Jesus Love! In Rome, on the fifteenth day of December, 1378.

TO BROTHER ANDREA OF LUCCA TO BROTHER BALDO AND TO BROTHER LANDO SERVANTS OF GOD IN SPOLETO, WHEN THEY WERE SUMMONED BY THE HOLY FATHER

In the Name of Jesus Christ crucified and of sweet Mary: Dearest fathers in Christ sweet Jesus: I Catherine, servant and slave of the servants of Jesus Christ, write to you in His precious Blood: with desire to see you eager and ready to do the will of God, in obedience to His Vicar, Pope Urban VI., in order that by you and the other servants of God help may be brought to His sweet Bride. For we see her in such bitter straits that she is attacked on every side by contrary winds; and you see that she is especially attacked by wicked men, lovers of themselves, by the perilous and evil wind of heresy and schism, which can contaminate our faith. Was she ever in so great a need as now, when those who ought to help her have attacked her, and darkness is shed abroad by those whose task it is to enlighten? They should nourish us with the food of souls, ministering the Blood of Christ crucified which gives the life of grace; and they drag it from men's mouths, ministering eternal death, like wolves who feed not the flock, but devour them. And what shall the dogs do--the servants of God, who are placed in the world as guardians, that they may bark when they see the wolf come, to awaken the chief shepherd? What are they to bark with? With humble and continual prayer, and with the living voice. In this way they shall terrify the demons, visible and invisible, and the heart and mind of our chief Shepherd, Pope Urban VI., shall awaken; and when he shall be wakened, we do not doubt that the mystical body of Holy Church and the universal body of the Christian religion shall be helped, and the flock recovered, and saved from the hands of devils. You ought not to draw back for any reason: not for suffering that you expected, nor for shames nor persecution, nor ridicule that might be cast at you; not for hunger, thirst, or death a thousand times were it possible; not for desire of quiet, nor of your consolations, saying: "I wish my soul's peace, and I can cry out in prayer before the face of God (without going to Rome)"; nay, by the love of Christ crucified. For it is not now the hour to seek one's self for one's self, nor to flee pains in order to possess consolations; nay, it is the hour to lose one's self, since the Infinite Goodness and Mercy of God has seen to the necessity of Holy Church, and given her a just and good shepherd, who wishes to have these dogs around him, which shall bark constantly for the honour of God; fearing lest he sleep, and not trusting in his vigil, unless they are always ready to bark to waken him. You are among those whom he has chosen. Therefore I beg and constrain you in Christ sweet Jesus, that you come swiftly, to fulfil the will of God, who wills thus, and the holy will of the Vicar of Christ, that is calling you and the others.

You need not be afraid of luxuries or of great consolations; for you are coming to endure, and not to enjoy yourselves, except with the joy of the Cross. Lean your head out, and come forth into the Field, to fight genuinely for truth; holding before the eye of your mind the persecution wrought to the Blood of Christ, and the damnation of souls; in order that we may be more inspired for the battle, so that we may look back for no possible cause. Come, come! and do not linger, waiting for the hour, for the hour does not wait us. I am sure that the Infinite Goodness of God will make you know the truth. And yet I know that many, even among those who are servants of God, will go to you and oppose this holy and good work, thinking to speak well, in saying: "You will go, and nothing will be done." And I, like a presumptuous woman, say that something will be done; if our principal desire is not now to be fulfilled, at least the way will be cleared. And even if nothing at all should be done, we have shown in the sight of God and our fellow-men that we have done what we could; our own conscience has been aroused and unburdened. So that it is well in any case. The more opposition you shall have, the clearer sign it is to you that this is a good and holy work; since as we have seen, and continue to see constantly, great, holy, and good works meet more opposition than little ones, because they have larger results; and therefore the devil hinders them in every way he can, especially by means of the servants of God, through obscure deceits, under colour of virtue. I have said this to you in order that you should not give up coming for any reason, but should present yourselves with prompt obedience at the feet of his Holiness.

Drown you in the Blood of Christ, and may our own will die in all things. I say no more to you. Remain in the holy and sweet grace of God. Commend me to all the servants of God near you, that they may pray the Divine Goodness to give me grace to lay down my life for His Truth. Sweet Jesus, Jesus Love.

TO BROTHER ANTONIO OF NIZZA OF THE
HERMIT BROTHERS OF SAINT AUGUSTINE AT THE CONVENT
OF LECCETO NEAR SIENA

In the name of Jesus Christ crucified and of sweet Mary:

Dearest son in Christ sweet Jesus: I Catherine, servant and slave of the servants of Jesus Christ, write to you in His precious Blood: with desire to see you founded upon the Living Rock, Christ sweet Jesus, so that the building you shall raise on it may never be overthrown by any contrary wind that may strike you, but may endure wholly solid, firm, and stable, even till your death upon the Way of Truth. Oh, how we need this true and royal foundation--not known of my ignorance! for did I truly know it, I should not build upon myself, who am worse than sand, but upon that Living Rock I spoke of. Following Christ upon the way of shame and outrage and insult, I should deprive me of every consolation from whatever source, within or without, to conform myself with Him. I would not seek myself for my own sake, but would care only for the honour of God, the salvation of souls, and the reform of Holy Church, whom I see in so great need! Me miserable, who am doing quite the contrary! But though I do wrong, dearest son, I would not that you and the others did; nay, I desire to see you founded on this Rock. Now the hour is come that proves who is a servant of God, and whether men shall seek themselves for their own sake, and God for the private consolation they find in Him, and their neighbours for their own sake in so far as they see consolations in them--yes, or no, and whether we are to believe that God may be found only in one place and not in another. I do not see that this is so--but find that to the true servant of God every place is the right place and every time is the right time. So when the time comes to abandon his own consolations and embrace labours for the honour of God, he does it; and when the time comes to flee the wood for need of the honour of God, he does it, and betakes him to public places, as did the blessed St. Antony, who although he supremely loved solitude, yet deserted it many times to comfort the Christians. And so I might tell of many other saints. This has always been the habit of the true servants of God, to emerge in time of need and adversity, but not in the time of prosperity--nay, that they flee. There is no need to flee just now, through fear lest our great prosperity make our hearts sail away in the wind of pride and vainglory; for there is no one who can glory now otherwise than in labours. But light seems to be failing us, dazzled as we are by our consolations and the hope we place in special revelations-- things which do not let us know the truth rightly, though we act in good faith. But God, who is highest and eternal Goodness, gives us perfect and true light. I enlarge no more on this matter.

It appears, from the letter which Brother William has sent me, that neither he nor you is coming here. I do not intend to reply to this letter: but I grieve much over his simplicity, for little honour to God or edification to his neighbour results from it. For if he is unwilling to come from humility and fear of forfeiting his peace, he ought to exercise the virtue of humility, by asking permission from the Vicar of Christ humbly and with gentleness, entreating his Holiness graciously to permit him to stay in his wood, for his greater peace, nevertheless, as one truly obedient, submitting the matter to his will. Thus he would be more pleasing to God, and would secure his own good. But he seems to have done just the contrary, alleging that a person who is bound to divine obedience ought not to obey his fellow-creatures. As to other people, I should care very little; but that he should include the Vicar of Christ, this does grieve me much, to see him so discordant with truth. For divine obedience never prevents us from obedience to the Holy Father: nay, the more perfect the one, the more perfect is the other. And we ought always to be subject to his commands and obedient unto death. However indiscreet obedience to him might seem, and however it should deprive us of mental peace and consolation, we ought to obey; and I consider that to do the opposite is a great imperfection, and deceit of the devil. It appears from what he writes that two servants of God have had a great revelation, to the effect that Christ on earth, and whoever advised him to send for these servants of God, followed human and not divine counsel, and that it was rather the instigation of the devil than the inspiration of God that made them wish to drag their servants from their peace and consolations: adding that if you and the others came you would lose your spiritual life, and thus would be of no help in prayer, and unable to stand by the Holy Father in spirit. Now really, the spiritual life is quite too lightly held if it is lost by change of place. Apparently God is an acceptor of places, and is found only in a wood, and not elsewhere in time of need! Then what shall we say --we who, on the one hand, wish that the Church of God be reformed, the thorns uprooted, and the fragrant flowers the servants of God planted there; and, on the other hand, we are told that to send for them, and drag them from their mental peace and quiet in order that they may come to help that little Ship is a wile of the devil? At least, let a man speak for himself, and not speak of the other servants of God--for among the servants of the world we are not to count ourselves. Not thus have done Brother Andrea of Lucca, nor Brother Paolina, those great servants of God, old men and far from well, who have lived such a long time in their peace: but at once, with all their weariness and disabilities they put themselves on the road, and have come, and fulfilled their obedience: and although desire constrains them to return to their cells, they are not therefore willing to throw off the yoke, but say: "What I have said, be it unsaid!" --disregarding their self-will and their personal consolations. One comes here to endure: not for honours, but for the dignity of many labours, with tears, vigils and continual prayers; thus should one do. Now let us not weigh ourselves down with more words. May God by His mercy send us clear vision, and guide us in the way of truth, and give us true and perfect light, that we may never walk among shadows. I beg you, you and the Bachellor, and the other servants of God, to pray the Humble Lamb that He make me walk in His Way. Remain in the holy and sweet grace of God. Sweet Jesus, Jesus Love.

TO QUEEN GIOVANNA OF NAPLES (WRITTEN IN TRANCE)

Giovanna, recalcitrant, has failed to respond to the entreaties of Catherine. Her temporary espousal of the cause of Urban has made only more painful her reversion to the side of Clement. "You see your subjects pitted against each other like beasts through this unhappy division," writes Catherine in another letter. "Oh me! how is it that your heart does not burst, to endure that they should be divided by you, and one hold to the white rose and one the red, one to truth and one to falsehood? Misfortunate my soul! Do you not see that they are all created in that very pure rose, the eternal will of God, and re-created by grace in that very burning rose, crimson with the Blood of Christ, in which we were washed from sin in Baptism? Consider that nor you nor another ever so bathed them or gave them that glorious rose, but only our Mother, Holy Church, through the highest Pontiff who holds the keys, Pope Urban VI. How can your soul bear to take from them that which you cannot give? If this does not move you, are you not at least moved by the shame into which you are fallen in the sight of the world? This much more since your change than before; for lately you confessed the truth and your wrong, and showed yourself willing to throw yourself like a daughter upon the mercy of your father; and since then you have wrought worse than ever, whether because your heart was not pure, and feigned what was not there, or because justice willed that I should anew do penance for my ancient sins, that I do not merit to see you in peace and quiet, feeding at the breasts of Holy Church. It is such a pain to me, that I cannot bear a greater cross in this life, when I consider the letter which I received from you, in which you confessed that Pope Urban was the true highest father and priest, and said that you were willing to be obedient to him, and now I find the contrary."

In the present letter Catherine pours forth to the yet living woman a sorrowful elegy over the dead soul. She argues no longer; the political aspect of the situation is for the time being overshadowed by the grief with which she contemplates the hardened sin and coming doom of the woman to whom her heart had from her youth up gone out with an especial tenderness, and in whom she had hoped at one time to see a true Defender of the Faith. It will be noticed that she writes in trance. Whatever may have been the nature of that mysterious state, we may be sure that thoughts then uttered came from the depths of her being which lie below consciousness, and we may so gain an additional evidence of the intensity of her feeling concerning Giovanna.

In the Name of Jesus Christ crucified and of sweet Mary:

Dearest mother in Christ sweet Jesus: I, Catherine, servant and slave of the servants of Jesus Christ, write to you in His precious Blood, with desire to see you compassionate to your own soul and body. For if we are not merciful to our own souls, the mercy and pity of others would avail us little. The soul treats itself with great cruelty when of its own accord it puts the knife with which it can be killed in the hands of its foe. For our foes have no weapons with which they can hurt us. They would be very glad to, but they cannot, because will alone can hurt us; and as for the will, neither demon nor creature can move it, nor force it to one least fault more than it chooses. So the perverse will which consents to the malice of our foes is a knife which kills the soul that gives it into the hand of these foes with its own free choice. Which shall we call the more cruel--the foes or the very person who receives the blow? It is we who are more cruel, for we consent to our own death.

We have three chief foes. First, the devil, who is weak if I do not make him strong by consenting to his malice. He loses his strength in the power of the Blood of the humble and spotless Lamb. The world with all its honours and delights, which is our foe, is also weak, save in so far as we strengthen it to hurt us by possessing these things with intemperate love. In the gentleness, humility, poverty, in the shame and disgrace of Christ crucified, this tyrant the world is destroyed. Our third foe, our own frailty, was made weak; but reason strengthens it by the union which God has made with our humanity, arraying the Word with our humanity, and by the death of that sweet and loving Word, Christ crucified. So we are strong, and our foes are weak.

It is very true, then, that we are more cruel to ourselves than our foes are. For without our help they cannot kill nor hurt us, since God has not given them to us that we might be vanquished, but that we might vanquish them. Then our fortitude and constancy are proved. But I do not see that we can avoid such cruelty and become merciful without the light of most holy faith, opening the eye of the mind to behold how displeasing it is to God and harmful to soul and body, and how pleasing to God and useful to our salvation is mercy.

Dearest mother--mother I say in so far as I see you to be a faithful daughter of Holy Church--it seems to me that you have no mercy on yourself. Oh me! oh me! because I love you I grieve over the evil state of your soul and body. I would willingly lay down my life to prevent this cruelty. Many times I have written you in compassion, showing you that what is shown you for truth is a lie; and the rod of divine justice, which is ready for you if you do not flee so great wrong. It is a human thing to sin, but perseverance in sin is a thing of the devil. Oh me! there is none who tells you the truth, nor do you seek among the servants of God those who might tell it you, that you should not stay in a state of condemnation. Oh, how blessed my soul would be could I come into your parts, and lay down my life to restore to you the good of heaven and the good of earth; to take from you the knife of cruelty, with which you have killed yourself, and help to give you that of mercy, which kills vice; so that you should clothe you in the holy fear of God and love of truth, and bind you in His sweet will!

Oh me, do not await the time which you are not sure of having! Do not choose that my eyes should have to shed rivers of tears over your wretched soul and body--a soul which I hold as my own! If I consider that soul, I see that it is dead, because separated from its body; it persecutes, not Pope Urban VI., but our truth and faith. I expected, mother and daughter mine, as you used to write to me, that through you these should be spread among the infidels by means of divine grace, and declared and helped among us, defended when we should see a taint appear, from those who have been or were contaminated. Now I see quite the contrary appear in you, through the evil counsel which has been given you for my sins. You have received it as one merciless toward your salvation; and I see that there will be no human creature who can restore your loss, but you yourself must render this account before the highest Judge. You did not offend through ignorance, not knowing the right, for the truth was shown to you; but you do not know how to turn back from that which you have begun, because the knife of perverse and selfish will destroys knowledge and choice, making you hold that as shame which is your greatest honour. For perseverance in fault and in such an evil is greatest disgrace, and displays one as a sign of shame before the eyes of one's fellow-creatures; but to escape from them is greatest honour; and by honour and the odour of virtue, shame is escaped and the stench of vice extinguished.

And if I consider your condition as to those temporal and transitory goods that pass like the wind--you yourself have deprived yourself of them by right. You have only to receive the last sentence of being deprived of them by deed, and published a heretic. My heart breaks and cannot break, from the fear that I have lest the devil so obscure the eye of your mind that you endure that loss, and such shame and confusion as I should repute greater than the loss that you would suffer. And you cannot hide it with saying, "This would be done to me unjustly, and the thing which is unjustly inflicted casts no shame." That cannot be said; for it would be done justly, both because of the fault you have committed, and because he can do it as highest and true pontiff that he is, chosen by the Truth in truth. For were he not so, you would not have offended. So that it would be just. But he has refrained from doing this through love, as a benignant father who waits for his son to correct himself. Yet I fear that he may do it, constrained by justice, and by your long perseverance in evil. And I do not say this as one who does not know what she is saying.

And if you said to me, "I do not care about this, for I am strong and mighty, and I have other lords who will help me, and I know that he is weak"--I reply to you that he wearies himself in vain who will guard the city with force and with great zeal, if God guard it not. And can you say that you have God with you? We cannot say it, for you have put Him against you for putting yourself against truth; you have put you against Him, and it is truth that sets him free who holds thereto, and none there is who can confound it. Therefore you have reason to fear, and not to trust in your strength and power, had you yet more of them than you have. And he has reason to comfort his weakness in Christ sweet Jesus, whose place he holds, trusting in His strength and aid, who shall send him aid from such a side as we cannot imagine. And you know that if God is for you, none shall be against you.

Then let us fear God, and tremble beneath the rod of His justice. Let us correct us, and advance no further. Be merciful to yourself, and you shall call down the mercy of God upon you. Have compassion on the many souls who are perishing through you; of whom you will have to render account before God at the last extremity of death. There is yet healing for us, and time wherein we can return; and He will receive you with great benignity. I am sure that if you will be merciful and not cruel to your soul and also to your body, you will do this, and will have pity upon your subjects: in otherwise, no. Therefore I said that I desired to see you merciful and not cruel to your soul. And thus I pray you, through the love of Christ crucified, that at least you hold and will to be held, the truth which was announced to you and to the other lords of the world. And if you should say, "It is still doubtful to me," stay neutral till it is made clear to you, and do not do what you should not. Desire illumination and counsel from those whom you see to fear God, and not from members of the devil, who would counsel you ill in that which they do not hold for themselves. Fear, fear God, and place Him before your eyes, and think that God sees you, and His eye is upon you, and His justice wills that every fault be punished and every good rewarded. Be merciful, ah, be merciful to yourself! I say naught else to you. Remain in the holy and sweet grace of God. Sweet Jesus, Jesus Love.

TO BROTHER RAIMONDO OF THE PREACHING ORDER WHEN HE WAS IN GENOA

In more grievous ways than any yet noted, Catherine was to be wounded in the house of her friends. The letters already given have shown us how tenderly intimate, on the human as well as on the spiritual side, were her relations with the father of her soul, "given her by that sweet mother, Mary." One shares her affection for good Father Raimondo as one reads the legend. His figure might well have belonged to the trecento rather than to the more strenuous age that followed. He was the simplest, the most modest of men--albeit by no means lacking in homely shrewdness; he was also one of the least heroic. Catherine, like most uplifted natures, demanded heroism from those dear to her, as a matter of course. Others wish for their beloved ease, delights, the gratification of ambition and desire; Catherine sought for them sorrow, hardships, the opportunity to offer their lives in exalted sacrifice for the sins of the Church and the world. She craved for them only less passionately than for herself, the crowning grace of martyrdom. Now Fra Raimondo had no affinity whatever for martyrdom. His chance at it came, in the fortunes of those stern times, and was promptly rejected. Urban, perhaps at Catherine's instigation, had despatched him to the King of France, and Raimondo had bidden his spiritual daughter and mother a solemn farewell, surmising doubtless that he was to see her face no more. He proceeded to the port of Genoa, planning thence to set sail for France. But the galleys of the antipope sought to debar the passage; and Raimondo, accepting the obstacle (one imagines with much ease), allowed himself to give up the expedition.

Catherine wrote him two letters on the matter. The first is brief, and half-playful in tone: "Oh my naughty father" (*cativello padre mio*) she says, "How blessed your soul and mine would have been could you have sealed with your blood a stone in Holy Church! I do wish I could see you risen above your childishness--see you shed your milk teeth and eat bread, the mustier the better!" Evidently Raimondo had answered this letter, writing, one imagines, in a deprecating tone, fearing lest Catherine may love him the less for his failure, yet after all assuming--so strong is our expectation of finding our own attitude in our friends--that she will rejoice in his escape. In this her reply she tells her whole heart. Surely, few more pathetic revelations of disappointed yet faithful affection have drifted to us on the tide of the ages. Catherine was at this time far advanced upon her own Via Dolorosa. One of the stations of her sorrow had been the parting with her friend: "And you have left me here, and have gone away with God." Here was another station, marked by a deeper pain: "Faithful obedience would have done more in the sight of God and men than all human prudence; my sins have prevented me from seeing it in you." With a glad suffering she had given Raimondo up to the service of God; with a suffering that was bitterly shamed, she saw him false to his calling. She utters no vain reproaches. In her own way she begins with earnest self-accusations, and proceeds to comfort the weakness of the man who should have been her guide with tender and subtly-reasoned assurances of her unchanged affection. At the same time she does not flinch from uncondoning, scathing statement of his sin and of her disillusion. Considerate, delicate, even courteous to a degree, the letter yet reveals in every line the sense of solitude which the action of Raimondo had caused her. There is no rebellion in her spirit: "I hold me none the less in peace, because I am certain that nothing happens without mystery," she sighs. But we grieve with a new, awestruck perception of the loneliness of her great soul, as we realize that to Raimondo was to be given perforce her deepest confidence in the passion upon which she was even now entering.

In the Name of Jesus Christ crucified and of sweet Mary:

Dearest father in Christ sweet Jesus: I Catherine, servant and slave of the servants of Jesus Christ, write to you in His precious Blood: with desire to see in you the light of most holy faith. This is a light which shows us the way of truth, and without it no activity, or desire, or work of ours would come to fruition, or to the end for which we began it; but everything would become imperfect--slow we should be in the love of God and of our neighbour. This is the reason: seemingly love is as great as faith, and faith is as great as love. He who loves is always faithful to him whom he loves, and faithfully serves him till death. By this I perceive that in truth I do not love God, nor the creatures through God: for if in truth I loved Him, I should be faithful in such wise that I should give myself to death a thousand times a day, were it needful and possible, for the glory and praise of His Name, and faith would not fail me, since for the love of God and of virtue and of Holy Church I should set myself to endure. So I should believe that God was my help and my defender, as He was of those glorious martyrs who went with gladness to the place of martyrdom. Were I faithful I should not fear, but I should hold for sure that the same God is for me who was for them; and His power to provide for my necessities is not weakened as to capacity, knowledge, or will. But because I do not love, I do not really trust myself to Him, but the sensuous fear in me shows me that love is lukewarm, and the light of faith is darkened by faithlessness toward my Creator, and by trusting in myself. I confess and deny not that this root of evil is not yet up-rooted from my soul, and therefore those works are hindered which God wants to do or puts in my way, so that they do not reach the lucid and fruitful end for which God had them begun. Ah me, ah me, my Lord! Woe to me miserable! And shall I find myself thus every time, in every place, and in every state? Shall I always close with my faithlessness the way to Thy providence? Yes, truly, if indeed Thou by Thy mercy do not unmake me, and make me anew. Then, Lord, unmake me, and break the hardness of my heart, that I be not a tool which spoils Thy works!

And I beg you, dearest father, to pray earnestly that I and you both together may drown ourselves in the Blood of the humble Lamb, which will make us strong and faithful. We shall feel the fire of the divine charity: we shall be co-workers with His grace, and not undoers or spoilers of it. So we shall show that we are faithful to God, and trust in His help, and not in our knowledge nor in that of men.

With this same faith we shall love the creature; for as love of the neighbour proceeds from love of God, so with faith, in general and in particular; as there is a general faith corresponding to the love which we ought to feel in general to every creature, so there is a special faith belonging to those who love one another more intimately: like this, which beyond the common love has established between us two a close particular love, a love which faith manifests. So much love does it manifest that it cannot believe nor imagine that one of us wishes anything else than the other's good; and it believes earnestly, for it seeks this with great insistence in the sight of God and men, seeking ever in the other the glory of the name of God and the profit of his soul; constraining Divine Help, that as it adds burdens it may add fortitude and long perseverance. Such faith bears he who loves, and never lessens it for any reason, neither for speech of man nor illusion of the devil, nor change of place. If anyone does otherwise, it is a sign that he loves God and his neighbour imperfectly.

Apparently, as I understood by your letter, many diverse battles befell you, and troubled reflections, through the deceit of the devil and through your own sensuous passion, it seeming to you that a burden was imposed on you greater than you can bear. You did not seem to yourself strong enough for me to measure you with my measure, and on this account you were in doubt lest my affection and love to you were diminished. But you did not see aright, and it was you who showed that I had grown to love more, and you less; for with the love with which I love myself, with that I love you, in the lively faith that all which is lacking on your part, God will complete by His goodness. But this is not done yet, for you have known how to find ways to throw your load down to earth. You present us many scraps of excuses to cover up your faithless frailty, but not in such wise that I do not see it quite enough now, and good it will seem to me if it is not perceived by anyone but me. Yes, yes, I show you a love increased in me toward you, and not waning. But what shall I say? How could your ignorance give place to one of the least of those thoughts? Could you ever believe that I wished anything else than the life of your soul? Where is the faith that you always used to have and ought to have, and the certainty that you have had, that before a thing is done, it is seen and determined in the sight of God--not only this, which is so great a deed, but every least thing? Had you been faithful, you would not have gone about vacillating so, nor fallen into fear toward God and toward me; but like a faithful son, ready for obedience, you would have gone and done what you could. And if you could not have gone upright, you would have gone on all fours; if you could not have gone as a Frate, you would have gone as a pilgrim; if there is no money for us, one would have gone begging. This faithful obedience would have accomplished more in the sight of God and in the hearts of men than all human prudences. My sins have prevented me from seeing it in you.

Nevertheless I am quite sure, that although selfish passion was there, you yet had and have holy and good regard to fulfil better the will of God and that of Christ on earth, Pope Urban VI. Not that I would have had you stay, though; nay, but take to the road at once, in whatever fashion and by whatever way had been open to you. Day and night I was constrained by God concerning many other things also; which, through the carelessness of him who has to do them, but chiefly through my sins which hinder every good, are all coming to nothing. And thus, ah me! we see ourselves drowning, and offences against God increasing, with many torments; and I live in an agony of delay. May God, in His mercy, soon take me from this life of shadows!

We see in the kingdom of Naples that this last disaster is worse than the first; and so many evils are likely to happen there, that may God remedy them! But He in His pity showed the disaster, and the remedies that ought to be applied. But, as I said, the abundance of my faults hinders all good. I shall have a great deal to say to you about these matters, should I not receive the greatest grace, that of release from earth before I see you again.

Yes, as I say, I do entirely wish that you had gone. Nevertheless I hold me in peace, because I am certain that nothing happens without mystery; and also because I unburdened my conscience, doing what I could that a messenger should be sent to the King of France. May the clemency of the Holy Spirit achieve it! For we by ourselves are bad workmen.

As for going quickly to the King of Hungary, it is clear that the Holy Father would be well enough pleased, and he had planned that you should go with other companions. Now, I do not know why, he has changed his mind, and wishes you to stay where you are, and do what good you can. I beg you to be zealous about it.

Abandon yourself, and every personal pleasure and consolation; and let turfs be thrown upon those who are dead, and with the cords of humble desire and holy prayer let the hands of divine justice be bound, the devil, and fleshly appetite. We are offered dead in the garden of Holy Church, and to Christ on earth, the lord of that garden. Then let us do the works of the dead. The dead man does not see nor hear nor feel. Be strong to slay yourself with the knife of hate and love, that you may not hear the derision, the insults, the reproaches of the world, which the persecutors of Holy Church would offer you. Let not your eyes see things as impossible to do, nor the torment that may follow; but let them see with the light of faith that through Christ crucified you can do all things, and that God will not impose a greater burden than can be borne. Why, we are to rejoice in great burdens, because then

God gives us the gift of fortitude. With the love of endurance, fleshly sensitiveness is lost; and thus dead, dead, we may nourish ourselves in this garden. When I see this, I shall account my soul as blessed. I tell you, sweetest father, that whether we will or no, the times to-day summon us to die. Then be no more alive! End pains in pain, and increase the joy of holy desire in the pain; that our life may pass no otherwise than in crucified desire, and that we may give our bodies willingly to be eaten by beasts; that is, for the love of virtue let us willingly fling ourselves upon the tongues and hands of bestial men, as did those others who have worked, dead, in this sweet garden, and watered it with their blood, but first with their tears and sweats. And I--(grievous my life!)--because I have not given enough water to it, was refused permission to give it my blood. I will it to be no more thus, but be our life renewed and the fire of desire increased!

You ask me to pray the Divine Goodness to give you the fire of Vincent, of Lawrence, and of sweet Paul, and that of the charming John--saying that then you will do great things. And so I shall be glad. Surely I say the truth, that without this fire you would not do anything, neither little nor big, nor should I be glad in you.

Therefore, considering that it is so, and that I have seen it proved, an impulse has grown in me, with great zeal in the sweet sight of God. Were you near me in the body, truly I would show you that it is so, and would give you other than words. I rejoice, and I want you to rejoice; for, since this desire grows, He will fulfil it in you and me, because He accepts holy and true desires; provided that you open the eye of your mind in the light of holiest faith, that you may know the truth of the will of God. Knowing it you will love it, and loving it you will be faithful, and your heart will not be overshadowed by any wile of the devil. Being faithful, you will do every great thing in God: what He puts into your hands will be fulfilled perfectly; that is, it will not be hindered on your part from coming to perfection. With this light you will be cautious, modest, and weighty in speech and conversation and in all your works and way; but without it you would do quite the contrary in your ways and habits, and everything else would turn out contrary for you.

So, knowing that this is the case, I desired to see in you the light of most holy faith; and so I want you to have it. And because I want this, and love you immeasurably for your salvation, and desire with great desire to see you in the state of the perfect, therefore I pray you with many words--but I would do so more willingly in deed; and I use reproaches with you, in order that you may return continually to yourself. I have done my best, and I shall do so, to make you assume the burden of the perfect for the honour of God, and ask His goodness to make you reach the last state of perfection; that is, to shed your blood for Holy Church, whether your servant the flesh will it or no. Lose you in the Blood of Christ crucified, and bear my faults and words with good patience. And whenever your faults may be shown you, rejoice, and thank the Divine Goodness, which has assigned someone to labour over you, who watches for you in His sight.

As to what you write me, that antichrist and his members seek diligently to have you, do not fear; for God is strong to take away their light and their force, that they may not fulfil their desires. Beside, you ought to think that you are not worthy of so great a good, and so you need not fear. Take confidence; for sweet Mary and the Truth will be for you always.

I, vile slave, who am placed in the Field, where blood was shed for the love of Blood--(and you have left me here, and gone away with God)--shall never pause from working for you. I beg you so to do that you give me no matter for mourning, nor for shaming me in the sight of God. As you are a man in promising the will to do and bear for the honour of God, do not then turn into a woman when we come to the shutting of the lock; for I should appeal against you to Christ crucified and to Mary. Beware lest it happen later to you as to the abbot of St. Antimo, who, through fear and under colour of not tempting God, left Siena and came to Rome, supposing that he had escaped his prison and was safe; and he was thrown into prison, with the punishment that you know. So are pusillanimous hearts cured. Be, then, be all a man: that death may be granted you.

I beg you to pardon me whatever I might have said that was not honour to God and due reverence to yourself: let love excuse it. I say no more to you. Remain in the holy and sweet grace of God. I ask your benediction. Sweet Jesus, Jesus Love!

TO URBAN VI

This is the last letter to Urban that we possess. If, as seems likely, it is also the last that Catherine wrote to him, it must have been written on the Monday after Sexagesima, 1380, under circumstances which she describes for us in the next letter to be given. She had already at the time entered upon the mystical agony which preceded her *transitus*.

The letter alludes to historic details of which we have no knowledge and for which we do not care. Yet it has rare interest. That exquisite sweetness which often blends in so unique a way with Catherine's authoritative tone, was never more evident. Urban's impetuous inconsistencies, and the irrational gusts of anger which were by this time alienating even his friends, could not be more clearly nor more gently rebuked. One's heart aches at the thought of what manner of man he was to whom this sensitive and high-minded woman was forced by her faith to give not only allegiance but championship. Not once during Catherine's active life was she allowed to fight in a clear cause, or at least in a cause in which sympathies could be undivided; the pathos of the situation is evident in the meek and patient firmness of her tone. But the letter has a deeper interest, if it is really the last she wrote to him. Knowing the circumstances of its composition, we must be amazed at the lucidity of her thought and words, at the steady and definite wisdom with which she discusses the movement of events in the outer world. It is surely significant to the psychologist that a woman in the throes of such an experience as the next letters present, could write in such a strain. The whole life of Catherine, indeed, refutes the popular opinion that mystics cannot be trusted to sane judgment or sustained wisdom of action in the confused affairs of this world.

In the Name of Jesus Christ crucified and of sweet Mary:

Dearest and sweetest father in Christ sweet Jesus: I Catherine, your poor unworthy daughter, write to you with great desire to see a prudence and sweet light of truth in you, in such wise that I may see you follow the glorious St. Gregory, and govern Holy Church with such prudence that it may never be necessary to take back anything which may be ordered or done by your Holiness; even the least word; so that your firmness grounded in the truth may be evident in the sight of God and men, as ought to be the case with the true holy High Priest. I pray the inestimable charity of God that He clothe your soul in this; for it seems to me that light and prudence are very necessary indeed to us, and especially to your Holiness and to anyone else who might be in your place; most chiefly in these current times. Because I know that you have a desire to find these in yourself, I remind you of them, showing you the desire of your own soul.

I have heard, holy father, of the reply which the violence of the Prefect made; surely in violence of wrath and irreverence toward the Roman ambassadors. On which reply it seems that they are to hold a General Council, and then the heads of the wards and certain other good men are to come to you. I beg you, most holy father, that as you have begun so you will continue to meet with them often, and to bind them prudently with the bands of love. So I beg you that now, as to what they will say to you when the Council is held, you will receive them with as much gentleness as you can, showing them what your Holiness thinks must be done. Pardon me--for love makes me say what perhaps there is no need of saying, since I know that you must understand the temperament of your Roman sons, who are drawn and held more with gentleness than with any force or asperity of words; and also you recognize the great necessity in which you are, and Holy Church, to keep this people in obedience and reverence toward your Holiness; because the head and beginning of our faith is here. And I humbly beg you, that you will aim prudently always to promise that which it ought to be possible to you fully to perform, so that loss, shame, and confusion may not follow later. Pardon me, most sweet and holy father, for saying these words to you. I am confident that your humility and benignity are content that they should be said, and will not feel distaste or scorn for them because they come from the mouth of a most despicable woman; for the humble man does not consider who speaks to him, but pays note to the honour of God, and to truth and his own salvation.

Comfort you, and do not fear on account of any bad reply which this rebel against your Holiness may have made or may make, for God will care for this and for everything else, as Ruler and Helper of the ship of Holy Church, and of your Holiness. Be you manful for me, in the holy fear of God; wholly exemplary in your words, your habits, and all your deeds. Let all shine clear in the sight of God and men; as a light placed in the candlestick of Holy Church, to which looks and should look all the Christian people.

Also I beg you that you should bring us some help for what Leo told you; for this scandal grows greater every day, not only through the thing that was done to the Sienese ambassador, but also through the other things which are seen day by day, which are enough to provoke to wrath the feeble hearts of men. You do not need this person now, but someone who shall be a means of peace, and not of war. Although he may act with a good zeal for justice, there are many who do so with such disorder and such impulse of wrath that they depart from all reason and measure. Therefore I earnestly beg your Holiness to condescend to the infirmity of men, and provide a physician who shall know how to cure the infirmity better than he. And do not wait so long that death shall follow: for I tell you that if no other help is found, the infirmity will grow.

Then recall to yourself the disaster that fell upon all Italy, because bad rulers were not guarded against, who governed in such wise that they were the cause of the Church of God being despoiled. I know that you are aware of this: now let your Holiness see what is to be done. Comfort you, comfort you sweetly; for God does not despise your desire, nor the prayer of His servants. I say no more to you. Remain in the holy and sweet Grace of God. Humbly I ask your benediction. Sweet Jesus, Jesus Love.

LETTERS DESCRIBING THE EXPERIENCE PRECEDING DEATH

Fightings and fears within, without," had long been Catherine's portion. Now the end was at hand. From girlhood she had confronted a great contradiction. The sharpest trial to Christian faith throughout the ages is probably the spectacle presented by the visible Church of Christ. This abiding parable of the contrast between ideal and actual was perhaps never more painful to the devout soul than in Catherine's time, and perhaps we are safe in saying that no one ever suffered from it more than she. Her whole life was an Act of Faith: faith the more heroic because maintained against the recurrent attacks of spiritual doubt and despair. At more than one point in her career we see her, overwhelmed by the seeming failure of the divine purpose, lifting her whole being into the Presence of God, there to receive reassurance, none the less satisfying to her vigorous intellect because conveyed through the channel of mystic ecstasy.

One such experience may be quoted here. It dates apparently from the time of her greatest disappointment in Gregory; we can judge of its significance and depth from the fact that she afterward recorded it more fully, and used it as the basis for the first book of her "Dialogue." "Comfort you, dearest father," she writes to Raimondo: "Concerning the sweet Bride of Christ: for the more she abounds in tribulations and bitterness, so much the more Divine Truth promises to make her abound in sweetness.... When I had thoroughly understood your letters, I begged a servant of God to offer tears and sweats before God, for the Bride and because of the 'Babbo's' weakness.

"Whence instantly, by divine grace, there grew in her a desire and gladness beyond all measure. She waited for the morning to have Mass, it being the Day of Mary; and when the hour of Mass had come, took her place with true self-knowledge, abasing herself before God for her imperfection. And rising above herself with eager desire, and gazing with the eye of her mind into Eternal Truth, she made four petitions there, holding herself and her father in the Presence of the Bride of Truth.

"First, the reform of Holy Church. Then God, letting Himself be constrained by tears and bound by the cords of her desire, said: 'Sweetest My daughter, thou seest how she has soiled her face with impurity and self-love, and become swollen by the pride and avarice of those who feed at her bosom. But take thy tears and sweat, drawing them from the fountain of My divine charity, and cleanse her face. For I promise thee that her beauty shall not be restored to her by the sword, nor by cruelty or war, but by peace, and humble continual prayers, tears and sweats, poured forth from the grieving desires of My servants. So thy desire shall be fulfilled in long abiding, and My providence shall in no wise fail you.'

"Although the salvation of all the whole world was contained in this, nevertheless the prayer reached out more in particular, entreating for the whole world. Then God showed in how great love He had created man, and He said: 'Now thou seest that every one is striking at Me. See, daughter, with what diverse and many sins they strike at Me, and especially with their wretched abominable self-love, whence issues every evil, with which they have poisoned the whole world. Do you then, My servants, adorn you in My Presence with many prayers, and so you shall mitigate the wrath of divine justice. And know that no one can escape from My Hands. Open the eye of thy mind and gaze upon My Hand.' And lifting her eyes she saw held in His grasp all the universal world. Then He said: 'I will that thou know that no one can be taken from Me; for all are under either justice or mercy; therefore all are Mine. And because they came forth from Me, I love them unspeakably, and shall show them mercy by means of My servants.' Then, the flame of desire increasing, that woman abode as one blessed and grieving, and gave thanks to the Divine Goodness: as perceiving that God had showed her the faults of His creatures that she might be constrained to arise with more zeal and greater desire. And so greatly increased the holy fire of love, that she despised the sweat of water she poured forth, through her great desire to see a sweat of blood pour from her body: and she said to herself, 'Soul mine, thou hast wasted thy whole life. Therefore have so great losses and evils fallen on the world and on Holy Church, in general and in particular. So now I wish thee to atone with sweat of blood.' Then that soul, spurred on by holy desire, arose much higher, and opened the eye of her mind, and gazed into the Divine Charity: where she saw and felt how much we are bound to seek the glory and praise of the Name of God in the salvation of souls."

In this remarkable passage we see Catherine's high and increasing sense of responsibility. Her tears and sweats are to cleanse the face of the Church, and through the grieving desire of the servants of God, redemption is to be accomplished. She was never, as we know, one of those Christian fatalists whose optimism leads them to inaction. From the day when, reluctant, she left her little cell, she threw her power with unwearied constancy and courage into the life of her day, repugnant though its problems might be to her natural temper. Catherine was, however, profoundly convinced that social salvation was to be wrought, not by work alone, but also by prayer; or rather, for the antithesis is false, that the forces which re-create society are set in motion in the invisible sphere. Constant intercession, and the uplifting of that "holy desire" which is the watchword of her teaching into a sacrificial passion--these are the means from which she hoped for reform and purification. In younger life, she is said to have prayed that she might be made a stopper in the mouth of Hell to prevent other souls from entering; through the quaint mediaeval figure one reads the prevailing impulse of her life.

The longer Catherine lived, the darker became the religious prospect. She saw her aims in practical politics realized one by one, only to mock her by spiritual failure. Those whom she best loved disappointed her ideal. She witnessed iniquity in high religious places, violence and corruption enlisted in the defence of truth. As she watched these things, the sense of an inward expiation to be accomplished became overpowering. It summoned her to death, and at the same time offered her a unique consolation.

These letters must now speak for themselves. They were written shortly before her death to Fra Raimondo, who, sadly though he had failed her, remained her most trusted friend. We have impressive accounts from other sources of Catherine's slow *transitus*--of the long weeks during which she was literally dying, and by her own choice, of a broken heart. They corroborate many of the details here given. But of still higher value is this transcript by the woman herself--minutely painstaking, while yet obviously composed under strong excitement--of the experience in the secret places of her soul. The first of these letters is written under stress of emotion so intense that coherence is hardly possible. The mind is baffled in seeking to find human speech which shall even adumbrate reality. What Catherine has to describe is the culmination of her earthly life: the final triumph of faith over despair, the final offering of herself as a sacrificial victim, in obedience, as she believes, to the express Voice of God. The second letter is more calm. The sacrifice has been accepted. She is dying, not indeed by the violence of men, like the martyrs for whose fate she has yearned, but by the agony of her own heart, breaking for the sins of Holy Church. "I in this way," she writes exulting, "as the holy martyrs with blood." And her agony is serene and joyous; her last thoughts are for others; her soul is full of the victory of peace. Outwardly, all was confusion around her; but her own life--the only region in which unity is within our reach--was rounded into a harmonious whole. To read the expression of that life in her letters is to follow one of those tragedies that are the salvation of the world.

TO MASTER RAIMONDO OF CAPUA

... I was breathless with grief from the crucified desire which had been newly conceived in the sight of God. For the light of the mind had mirrored itself in the Eternal Trinity; and in that abyss was seen the dignity of rational being, and the misery into which man falls by fault of mortal sin, and the necessity of Holy Church, which God revealed to His servant's bosom; and how no one can attain to enjoy the beauty of God in the abyss of the Trinity but by means of that sweet Bride; for it befits all to pass by the door of Christ crucified, and this door is not found elsewhere than in Holy Church. She saw that this Bride brought life to men, because she holds in herself such life that there is no one who can kill her; and that she gave fortitude and light, and that there is no one who can weaken her, in her true self, or cast her into darkness. And she saw that her fruit never fails, but increases for ever.

Then said Eternal God: "All this dignity, which your intellect could not compass, is given you men by Me. Consider, therefore, in grief and bitterness, and thou shalt see that people are approaching this Bride only for her outer raiment--that is, for temporal possessions. But thou seest her wholly deserted by those who seek her very essence--that is, the fruit of Blood. He who pays not the price of charity with true humility and the light of most holy faith, would share this, not unto life, but unto death; he would do like the thief, who takes what is not his. For the fruit of Blood is for those who pay the price of love, because she is founded in love, and is Very Love itself. And I will," said Eternal God, "that every one give to her through love, according as I give to My servants to minister in diverse ways, even as they have received. But I grieve that I find none who ministers there. Nay, it seems that every one has abandoned her. But I will be the Mediator once more."

And the pain and fire of her desire increasing, she cried in the sight of God, saying: "What can I do, O unsearchable Fire?" And His benignity replied: "Do thou offer thy life anew. Thou canst refrain from ever giving thyself repose. To this work

I have appointed thee--thee and all who follow thee or are to follow. Take ye then heed never to relax, but always to increase in desires; for I, impelled by love, am taking good heed to aid you with My bodily and spiritual grace. And in order that your minds may not be occupied by anything else, I have made provision, arousing her whom I have appointed to govern you, and I have led her, and put her to this work by mysteries and in new ways; so that she serves My Church with temporal substance, and you with continual humble faithful prayer, and with what activities shall be needed, which shall be appointed to thee and to them by My Goodness, to each according to his rank. Devote, then, thy life and heart and mind wholly to that Bride, for Me, with no regard to thyself. Contemplate Me, and behold the Bridegroom of this Bride, that is the highest Pontiff, and see his holy and good intention--an intention without reserves. And as the Bride is alone, so also is the bridegroom. I permit him to cleanse Holy Church by methods which he applies immoderately, and by fear, with which he inspires his subjects. But another shall come, who shall draw close to her in love, and shall fulfil her. It shall befall this Bride as it befalls the soul; for first fear possesses her, but when she is divested of sins, then love fills her and clothes her with virtue. All this it shall do, with sweet sustaining, sweet and suave, of those who shall nourish them at her breast in truth. But do thou this: Say to My Vicar that he pacify himself to the extent of his power, and grant peace to whosoever will receive it. And to the columns of Holy Church say that if they wish to remedy great disasters they are to do thus: let them unite, and form a cloak to cover the methods of their father that may seem faulty. And let them adopt a well-ordered life, close to those who fear and love Me, and cling together, casting their lower natures aside. If they do thus, I who am Light will give them the light needful to Holy Church. And seeing that there is something which ought to be done among them, let them refer it to My Vicar in true unity, quickly, boldly, and after much reflection. He then will be constrained not to resist their goodwills; for he really has a holy and good intention."

The tongue does not suffice to narrate such mysteries, nor what intellect saw and affection conceived. And the day passing by, full of marvel, the evening came. And I, feeling that the heart was so drawn by the force of love that I could offer no resistance to going to the place of prayer, and feeling that disposition come upon me which was at the time of my death, prostrated me with great compunction because

I had served the Bride of Christ with much ignorance and negligence, and had been cause that others had done the same. And rising, with the impression of what I have said before the eye of my mind, God placed me before Himself--not but that I am always before Him, because He contains everything in Himself--but in a new way, as if memory, intellect, and will had nothing whatever to do with my body. And this Truth was reflected in me with such light that in that abyss were then renewed the mysteries of Holy Church, and all the graces received in my life, past and present, and the day in which my soul was wedded to Him. All which then vanished from me through the increase of the inward fire: and I paid heed only to what should be done, that I should make a sacrifice of myself to God for Holy Church and for the sake of removing ignorance and negligence from those whom God had put into my hands. Then the devils called out havoc upon me, seeking to hinder and slacken with their terrors my free and burning desire. So these beat upon the shell of the body; but desire became the more kindled, crying, "O Eternal God, receive the sacrifice of my life in this mystical body of Holy Church! I have naught to give save what Thou hast given to me. Take then my heart, and may Thy Bride lean her face upon it!" Then Eternal God, turning the eyes of His mercy, removed my heart, and offered it to Holy Church. And He had drawn it to Himself with such force that had He not at once bound it about with His strength--not wishing that the vessel of my body should be broken--my life would have gone. Then the devils cried much more clamorously, as if they had felt an intolerable pain; forcing themselves to leave terror with me, threatening me so to disport them that such an act as this could not be wrought. But because Hell cannot resist the virtue of humility with the light of most holy faith, the spirit became more single, and worked with tools of fire, hearing in the sight of the Divine Majesty words most charming, and promises to give gladness. And because in truth it was thus in so great a mystery, the tongue henceforth can suffice to speak of it no more.

Now I say: Thanks, thanks be to the Highest God Eternal, who has placed us in the battlefield as knights, to fight for His Bride with the shield of holiest faith. The field is left free to us by that virtue and power which routed the devil who possessed the human race; who was routed, not in the strength of humanity, but of Deity. Thus the devil neither is nor shall be routed by the suffering of our bodies, but by strength of the fire of divine, most ardent, and immeasurable love.

TO MASTER RAIMONDO OF
CAPUA OF THE ORDER OF THE PREACHERS

In the Name of Jesus Christ crucified and of sweet Mary:

Dearest and sweetest father in Christ sweet Jesus: I Catherine, servant and slave of the servants of Jesus Christ, write to you in His precious Blood; with the desire to see you a pillar newly established in the garden of Holy Church, like a faithful bridegroom of truth, as you ought to be; and then shall I account my soul as blessed. Therefore I do not wish you to look back for any adversity or persecution, but I wish you to glory in adversity. For by endurance and in no other wise we show our love and constancy, and give glory to God's Name. Now is the time, dearest father, wholly to lose one's self, not to think of one's self an atom: as the glorious work-men did who were ready with such love and desire to give their life, and watered this garden with blood, with humble continual prayer, and with endurance unto death. Beware lest I see you timid; let not your shadow make you afraid; but be a manly fighter, and never desert that yoke of obedience which the highest pontiff has placed on you. Moreover, in the Order do what you see to be to the honour of God; for the great goodness of God demands this of us, and He has appointed us for nothing else.

Behold what necessity we see in Holy Church; for we see her left utterly alone! Thus the Truth showed, as I write you in another letter. And as the Bride has been left solitary, so is her bridegroom. Oh, sweetest father, I will not be silent to you of the great mysteries of God, but I will tell them the most briefly that I can, so far as the frail tongue can express them by telling. And further, I say to you what I want you to do. But receive what I say to you without pain, for I do not know what the Divine Goodness will do with me, whether It will have me remain here, or will call me to Itself.

Father, father and sweetest son, wonderful mysteries has God wrought, from the Day of the Circumcision till now; such that no tongue could suffice to tell them. But let us pass over all that time, and come to Sexagesima Sunday, when occurred, as I am writing you briefly, those mysteries which you shall hear: never have I seemed to bear anything like them. For the pain in my heart was so great, that the tunic which clothed me burst, as much as I could clasp of it; and I circled around in the chapel like a person in spasms. He who had held me had surely taken away my life. Then, Monday coming, in the evening I was constrained to write to Christ on earth and to three cardinals. So I had myself helped, and went into the study. And when I had written to Christ on earth, I had no way of writing more, the pains had so greatly increased in my body. And, waiting a little, the terror of demons began, in such wise that they stunned me entirely; raging against me as if I, worm that I am, had been the means of taking from their hands what they had possessed a long time in Holy Church. So great was the terror, with the bodily pain, that I wanted to fly from the study and go to the chapel--as if the study had been the cause of my pains. So I rose up, and not being able to walk, I leaned on my son Barduccio. But suddenly I was thrown down; and lying there, it seemed to me as if my soul were parted from my body; not in such wise as when it really was parted, for then my soul tasted the good of the Immortals, receiving that Highest Good together with them; but this now seemed like a special case, for I did not seem to be in the body, but I saw my body as if it had been someone else. And my soul, seeing the grief of him who was with me, wished to know if I had any power over the body, to say to him: "Son, do not fear"; and I saw that I could not move the tongue or any member of it, any more than a body quite dead. Then I let the body stay just as it was; and the intellect was fixed on the abyss of the Trinity. Memory was full of recollection of the need of Holy Church and of all the Christian people; and I cried before His Face, and demanded divine help with assurance, offering to Him my desires, and constraining Him by the Blood of the Lamb and the pains that had been borne. And so eager was the demand that it seemed to me sure that He would not deny that petition. Then I asked for all you others, praying Him that He would fulfil in you His will and my desires. Then I asked that He would save me from eternal condemnation. And while I stayed thus for a very long time, so that the Family was mourning me as dead, at this point all the terror of the demons was gone away. Then the Presence of the Humble Lamb came before my soul, saying: "Fear not: for I will fulfil thy desires, and those of My other servants. I will that thou see that I am a good master, who plays the potter, unmaking and remaking vessels as His pleasure is. These My vessels I know how to unmake and remake; and therefore I take the vessel of thy body, and remake it in the garden of Holy Church, in different wise than in past time." And as this Truth held me close, with ways and words most charming, which I pass over, the body began to breathe a little, and to show that the soul was returned to its vessel. Then I was full of wonder. And such pain remained in my heart that I have it there still. All pleasure and all refreshment and all food was then taken away from me. Being carried afterward into a place above, the room appeared full of devils: and they began to wage another battle, the most terrible that I ever had, trying to make me believe and see that I was not she who was in the body, but an impure spirit. I, having invoked the divine help with a sweet tenderness, refusing no labour, yet said: "God, listen for my help! Lord, haste Thee to help me! Thou hast permitted that I be alone in this battle, without the refreshment of the father of my soul, of whom I am deprived for my ingratitude."

Two nights and two days passed in these tempests. It is true that mind and desire received no break, but remained ever fixed on their object; but the body seemed almost to have failed. Afterward, on the Day of the Purification of Mary, I wished to hear Mass. Then all the mysteries were renewed; and God showed the great need that existed, as later appeared; for Rome has all been on the point of revolution, backbiting disgracefully, and with much irreverence. Only that God has poured oil on their hearts, and I think the thing will have a good end. Then God imposed this obedience on me, that during the whole of this holy season of Lent I should offer in sacrifice the desires of all the Family, and have Mass celebrated before Him with this one intention alone--that is, for Holy Church--and that I should myself hear a Mass every morning at dawn--a thing which you know is impossible to me; but in obedience to Him all things have been possible. And this desire has become so much a part of my flesh, that memory retains nothing else, intellect can see nothing else, and will can desire nothing else. Not so much that the soul turns aside from things here below for this reason--but, conversing with the True Citizens, it neither can nor will rejoice in their joy, but in their hunger, which they still feel, and which they felt while pilgrims and wayfarers in this life.

In this way, and many others which I cannot tell, my life is consumed and shed for this sweet Bride: I by this road, and the glorious martyrs with blood. I pray the Divine Goodness soon to let me see the redemption of His people. When it is the hour of terce, I rise from Mass, and you would see a dead woman go to St. Peter's; and I enter anew to labour in the ship of Holy Church. There I stay thus till near the hour of vespers: and from this place I would depart neither day nor night until I see this people at least a little steadily established in peace with their father. This body of mine remains without any food, without even a drop of water: in such sweet physical tortures as I never at any time endured; insomuch that my life hangs by a thread. Now I do not know what the Divine Goodness will do with me: as far as my feelings go, I do not say that I perceive His will in this matter; but as to my physical sensations, it seems to me that this time I am to confirm them with a new martyrdom in the sweetness of my soul--that is, for Holy Church; then, perhaps, He will make me rise again with Him. He will put so an end to my miseries and to my crucified desires. Or He may employ His usual ways to strengthen my body. I have prayed and pray His mercy that His will be fulfilled in me, and that He leave not you or the others orphans. But may He ever guide you in the way of the doctrine of Truth, with true and very perfect light. I am sure that He will do it.

Now I pray and constrain you, father, and son given by that sweet Mother, Mary, that you feel that if God is turning the eye of His mercy upon me, He wills to renew your life; and as dead to all fleshly impulse do you cast yourself into that ship of Holy Church. And be always discreet in your conversations. You will be able to have the actual cell little; but I wish you to have the cell of the heart always, and always carry it with you. For as you know, while we are locked therein enemies can do us no wrong. Then every act you shall do will be guided and ordered of God. Also, I beg you that you ripen your heart with holy and true prudence; and that your life be an example to worldly men by your never conforming to the world's customs. May that generosity toward the poor and that voluntary poverty which you have always practised, be renewed and refreshed in you with true and perfect humility. Do not slacken in these, for any dignity or exaltation that God may give you, but descend more deep into that Valley of Humility, rejoicing in the table of the Cross. There receive the food of souls: embracing the Mother, humble, faithful, and continual prayer, and holy vigil: celebrating every day, unless for some special reason. Flee idle and light talking, and be and show yourself mature in your speech and in every way. Cast from you all tenderness for yourself and all servile fear; for the sweet Church has no need of such folk, but of persons cruel to themselves and compassionate to her. These are the things which I beg you to study to observe. Also I beg you that you and Brother Bartolomeo and Brother Tommaso and the Master should gather together in your hands the book, and any writing of mine that you might find, and do with them what you see will be most to the honour of God: you and Misser Tommaso too--things in which I found some recreation. I beg you also, that so far as shall be possible to you, you be a shepherd and ruler to this Family, as a father, keeping them in the joy of charity and in perfect union; that they be not scattered as sheep without a shepherd. And I think to do more for them and for you after my death than in my life. I shall pray the Eternal Truth that He pour forth upon you others all plenitude of grace and gifts which He may have given to my soul, so that you may be lights placed in a candlestick. I beg you to pray the Eternal Bridegroom that He make me manfully fulfil His obedience, and pardon me the multitude of my iniquities. And I beg you that you pardon me every disobedience, irreverence, and ingratitude which I showed to you or committed against you, and all pain and bitterness which I may have caused you: and the slight zeal which I have had for our salvation. And I ask you for your blessing.

Pray earnestly for me, and have others pray, for the love of Christ crucified. Pardon me, that I have written you words of bitterness. I do not write them, however, to cause you bitterness, but because I am in doubt, and do not know what the Goodness of God will do with me. I wish to have done my duty. And do not feel regret because we are separated one from the other in the body; although you would have been the very greatest consolation to me, greater are my consolation and gladness to see the fruit that you are bearing in Holy Church. And now I beg you to labour yet more zealously, for she never had so great a need: and do you never depart for any persecution without permission from our lord the Pope. Comfort you in Christ sweet Jesus, without any bitterness. I say no more to you. Remain in the holy and sweet grace of God. Sweet Jesus, Jesus Love.

The Codes Of Hammurabi And Moses
W. W. Davies

QTY

The discovery of the Hammurabi Code is one of the greatest achievements of archaeology, and is of paramount interest, not only to the student of the Bible, but also to all those interested in ancient history...

Religion   **ISBN:** *1-59462-338-4*   **Pages:132**
MSRP $12.95

The Theory of Moral Sentiments
Adam Smith

QTY

This work from 1749. contains original theories of conscience amd moral judgment and it is the foundation for systemof morals.

Philosophy **ISBN:** *1-59462-777-0*   **Pages:536**
MSRP $19.95

Jessica's First Prayer
Hesba Stretton

QTY

In a screened and secluded corner of one of the many railway-bridges which span the streets of London there could be seen a few years ago, from five o'clock every morning until half past eight, a tidily set-out coffee-stall, consisting of a trestle and board, upon which stood two large tin cans, with a small fire of charcoal burning under each so as to keep the coffee boiling during the early hours of the morning when the work-people were thronging into the city on their way to their daily toil...

Pages:84

Childrens   **ISBN:** *1-59462-373-2*   *MSRP $9.95*

My Life and Work
Henry Ford

QTY

Henry Ford revolutionized the world with his implementation of mass production for the Model T automobile. Gain valuable business insight into his life and work with his own auto-biography... "We have only started on our development of our country we have not as yet, with all our talk of wonderful progress, done more than scratch the surface. The progress has been wonderful enough but..."

Pages:300

Biographies/   **ISBN:** *1-59462-198-5*   *MSRP $21.95*

The Art of Cross-Examination
Francis Wellman

QTY

I presume it is the experience of every author, after his first book is published upon an important subject, to be almost overwhelmed with a wealth of ideas and illustrations which could readily have been included in his book, and which to his own mind, at least, seem to make a second edition inevitable. Such certainly was the case with me; and when the first edition had reached its sixth impression in five months, I rejoiced to learn that it seemed to my publishers that the book had met with a sufficiently favorable reception to justify a second and considerably enlarged edition. ..

Reference   **ISBN:** *1-59462-647-2*

Pages:412

MSRP $19.95

On the Duty of Civil Disobedience
Henry David Thoreau

QTY

Thoreau wrote his famous essay, On the Duty of Civil Disobedience, as a protest against an unjust but popular war and the immoral but popular institution of slave-owning. He did more than write—he declined to pay his taxes, and was hauled off to gaol in consequence. Who can say how much this refusal of his hastened the end of the war and of slavery ?

Law   **ISBN:** *1-59462-747-9*

Pages:48

MSRP $7.45

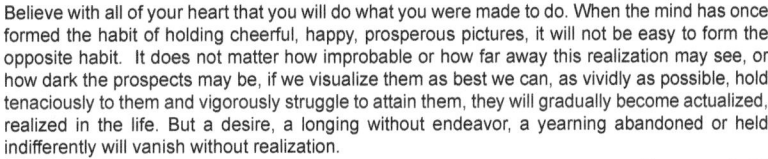

Dream Psychology Psychoanalysis for Beginners
Sigmund Freud

QTY

Sigmund Freud, born Sigismund Schlomo Freud (May 6, 1856 - September 23, 1939), was a Jewish-Austrian neurologist and psychiatrist who co-founded the psychoanalytic school of psychology. Freud is best known for his theories of the unconscious mind, especially involving the mechanism of repression; his redefinition of sexual desire as mobile and directed towards a wide variety of objects; and his therapeutic techniques, especially his understanding of transference in the therapeutic relationship and the presumed value of dreams as sources of insight into unconscious desires.

Psychology   **ISBN:** *1-59462-905-6*

Pages:196

MSRP $15.45

The Miracle of Right Thought
Orison Swett Marden

QTY

Believe with all of your heart that you will do what you were made to do. When the mind has once formed the habit of holding cheerful, happy, prosperous pictures, it will not be easy to form the opposite habit. It does not matter how improbable or how far away this realization may see, or how dark the prospects may be, if we visualize them as best we can, as vividly as possible, hold tenaciously to them and vigorously struggle to attain them, they will gradually become actualized, realized in the life. But a desire, a longing without endeavor, a yearning abandoned or held indifferently will vanish without realization.

Self Help   **ISBN:** *1-59462-644-8*

Pages:360

MSRP $25.45

www.bookjungle.com *email: sales@bookjungle.com fax: 630-214-0564 mail: Book Jungle PO Box 2226 Champaign, IL 61825*

QTY

The Rosicrucian Cosmo-Conception Mystic Christianity by *Max Heindel*   ISBN: *1-59462-188-8*   **$38.95**
The Rosicrucian Cosmo-conception is not dogmatic, neither does it appeal to any other authority than the reason of the student. It is: not controversial, but is: sent forth in the, hope that it may help to clear...   New Age/Religion Pages 646

Abandonment To Divine Providence by *Jean-Pierre de Caussade*   ISBN: *1-59462-228-0*   **$25.95**
"The Rev. Jean Pierre de Caussade was one of the most remarkable spiritual writers of the Society of Jesus in France in the 18th Century. His death took place at Toulouse in 1751. His works have gone through many editions and have been republished...   Inspirational/Religion Pages 400

Mental Chemistry by *Charles Haanel*   ISBN: *1-59462-192-6*   **$23.95**
Mental Chemistry allows the change of material conditions by combining and appropriately utilizing the power of the mind. Much like applied chemistry creates something new and unique out of careful combinations of chemicals the mastery of mental chemistry...   New Age Pages 354

The Letters of Robert Browning and Elizabeth Barret Barrett 1845-1846 vol II   ISBN: *1-59462-193-4*   **$35.95**
by *Robert Browning* and *Elizabeth Barrett*   Biographies Pages 596

Gleanings In Genesis (volume I) by *Arthur W. Pink*   ISBN: *1-59462-130-6*   **$27.45**
Appropriately has Genesis been termed "the seed plot of the Bible" for in it we have, in germ form, almost all of the great doctrines which are afterwards fully developed in the books of Scripture which follow...   Religion/Inspirational Pages 420

The Master Key by *L. W. de Laurence*   ISBN: *1-59462-001-6*   **$30.95**
In no branch of human knowledge has there been a more lively increase of the spirit of research during the past few years than in the study of Psychology, Concentration and Mental Discipline. The requests for authentic lessons in Thought Control, Mental Discipline and...   New Age/Business Pages 422

The Lesser Key Of Solomon Goetia by *L. W. de Laurence*   ISBN: *1-59462-092-X*   **$9.95**
This translation of the first book of the "Lernegton" which is now for the first time made accessible to students of Talismanic Magic was done, after careful collation and edition, from numerous Ancient Manuscripts in Hebrew, Latin, and French...   New Age/Occult Pages 92

Rubaiyat Of Omar Khayyam by *Edward Fitzgerald*   ISBN:*1-59462-332-5*   **$13.95**
Edward Fitzgerald, whom the world has already learned, in spite of his own efforts to remain within the shadow of anonymity, to look upon as one of the rarest poets of the century, was born at Bredfield, in Suffolk, on the 31st of March, 1809. He was the third son of John Purcell...   Music Pages 172

Ancient Law by *Henry Maine*   ISBN: *1-59462-128-4*   **$29.95**
The chief object of the following pages is to indicate some of the earliest ideas of mankind, as they are reflected in Ancient Law, and to point out the relation of those ideas to modern thought.   Religion/History Pages 452

Far-Away Stories by *William J. Locke*   ISBN: *1-59462-129-2*   **$19.45**
"Good wine needs no bush, but a collection of mixed vintages does. And this book is just such a collection. Some of the stories I do not want to remain buried for ever in the museum files of dead magazine-numbers an author's not unpardonable vanity..."   Fiction Pages 272

Life of David Crockett by *David Crockett*   ISBN: *1-59462-250-7*   **$27.45**
"Colonel David Crockett was one of the most remarkable men of the times in which he lived. Born in humble life, but gifted with a strong will, an indomitable courage, and unremitting perseverance...   Biographies/New Age Pages 424

Lip-Reading by *Edward Nitchie*   ISBN: *1-59462-206-X*   **$25.95**
Edward B. Nitchie, founder of the New York School for the Hard of Hearing, now the Nitchie School of Lip-Reading, Inc, wrote "LIP-READING Principles and Practice". The development and perfecting of this meritorious work on lip-reading was an undertaking...   How-to Pages 400

A Handbook of Suggestive Therapeutics, Applied Hypnotism, Psychic Science   ISBN: *1-59462-214-0*   **$24.95**
by *Henry Munro*   Health/New Age/Health/Self-help Pages 376

A Doll's House: and Two Other Plays by *Henrik Ibsen*   ISBN: *1-59462-112-8*   **$19.95**
Henrik Ibsen created this classic when in revolutionary 1848 Rome. Introducing some striking concepts in playwriting for the realist genre, this play has been studied the world over.   Fiction/Classics/Plays 308

The Light of Asia by *sir Edwin Arnold*   ISBN: *1-59462-204-3*   **$13.95**
In this poetic masterpiece, Edwin Arnold describes the life and teachings of Buddha. The man who was to become known as Buddha to the world was born as Prince Gautama of India but he rejected the worldly riches and abandoned the reigns of power when...   Religion/History/Biographies Pages 170

The Complete Works of Guy de Maupassant by *Guy de Maupassant*   ISBN: *1-59462-157-8*   **$16.95**
"For days and days, nights and nights, I had dreamed of that first kiss which was to consecrate our engagement, and I knew not on what spot I should put my lips..."   Fiction/Classics Pages 240

The Art of Cross-Examination by *Francis L. Wellman*   ISBN: *1-59462-309-0*   **$26.95**
Written by a renowned trial lawyer, Wellman imparts his experience and uses case studies to explain how to use psychology to extract desired information through questioning.   How-to/Science/Reference Pages 408

Answered or Unanswered? by *Louisa Vaughan*   ISBN: *1-59462-248-5*   **$10.95**
Miracles of Faith in China   Religion Pages 112

The Edinburgh Lectures on Mental Science (1909) by *Thomas*   ISBN: *1-59462-008-3*   **$11.95**
This book contains the substance of a course of lectures recently given by the writer in the Queen Street Hall, Edinburgh. Its purpose is to indicate the Natural Principles governing the relation between Mental Action and Material Conditions...   New Age/Psychology Pages 148

Ayesha by *H. Rider Haggard*   ISBN: *1-59462-301-5*   **$24.95**
Verily and indeed it is the unexpected that happens! Probably if there was one person upon the earth from whom the Editor of this, and of a certain previous history, did not expect to hear again...   Classics Pages 380

Ayala's Angel by *Anthony Trollope*   ISBN: *1-59462-352-X*   **$29.95**
The two girls were both pretty, but Lucy who was twenty-one who supposed to be simple and comparatively unattractive, whereas Ayala was credited, as her Bombwhat romantic name might show, with poetic charm and a taste for romance. Ayala when her father died was nineteen...   Fiction Pages 484

The American Commonwealth by *James Bryce*   ISBN: *1-59462-286-8*   **$34.45**
An interpretation of American democratic political theory. It examines political mechanics and society from the perspective of Scotsman James Bryce   Politics Pages 572

Stories of the Pilgrims by *Margaret P. Pumphrey*   ISBN: *1-59462-116-0*   **$17.95**
This book explores pilgrims religious oppression in England as well as their escape to Holland and eventual crossing to America on the Mayflower, and their early days in New England...   History Pages 268

www.bookjungle.com *email: sales@bookjungle.com fax: 630-214-0564 mail: Book Jungle PO Box 2226 Champaign, IL 61825*

QTY

The Fasting Cure *by Sinclair Upton*   ISBN: *1-59462-222-1*   **$13.95**
In the Cosmopolitan Magazine for May, 1910, and in the Contemporary Review (London) for April, 1910, I published an article dealing with my experi-
ences in fasting. I have written a great many magazine articles, but never one which attracted so much attention... New Age/Self Help/Health Pages 164

Hebrew Astrology *by Sepharial*   ISBN: *1-59462-308-2*   **$13.45**
In these days of advanced thinking it is a matter of common observation that we have left many of the old landmarks behind and that we are now pressing
forward to greater heights and to a wider horizon than that which represented the mind-content of our progenitors...   Astrology Pages 144

Thought Vibration or The Law of Attraction in the Thought World   ISBN: *1-59462-127-6*   **$12.95**

by William Walker Atkinson   *Psychology/Religion Pages 144*

Optimism *by Helen Keller*   ISBN: *1-59462-108-X*   **$15.95**
Helen Keller was blind, deaf, and mute since 19 months old, yet famously learned how to overcome these handicaps, communicate with the world, and
spread her lectures promoting optimism. An inspiring read for everyone...   Biographies/Inspirational Pages 84

Sara Crewe *by Frances Burnett*   ISBN: *1-59462-360-0*   **$9.45**
In the first place, Miss Minchin lived in London. Her home was a large, dull, tall one, in a large, dull square, where all the houses were alike, and all the
sparrows were alike, and where all the door-knockers made the same heavy sound...   Childrens/Classic Pages 88

The Autobiography of Benjamin Franklin *by Benjamin Franklin*   ISBN: *1-59462-135-7*   **$24.95**
The Autobiography of Benjamin Franklin has probably been more extensively read than any other American historical work, and no other book of its kind
has had such ups and downs of fortune. Franklin lived for many years in England, where he was agent...   Biographies/History Pages 332

Name	
Email	
Telephone	
Address	
City, State ZIP	

☐ **Credit Card**   ☐ **Check / Money Order**

Credit Card Number	
Expiration Date	
Signature	

Please Mail to: Book Jungle
PO Box 2226
Champaign, IL 61825
or Fax to: 630-214-0564

ORDERING INFORMATION

web: *www.bookjungle.com*
email: *sales@bookjungle.com*
fax: *630-214-0564*
mail: *Book Jungle PO Box 2226 Champaign, IL 61825*
or PayPal *to sales@bookjungle.com*

Please contact us for bulk discounts

DIRECT-ORDER TERMS

**20% Discount if You Order
Two or More Books**
Free Domestic Shipping!
Accepted: Master Card, Visa,
Discover, American Express

www.ingramcontent.com/pod-product-compliance
Lightning Source LLC
Chambersburg PA
CBHW080859020726
47502CB00008B/2288